R.A. SALVATORE

FORGOTTEN REALMS

THE PIRATE KING

T R A N S I T I O N S

II

THE PIRATE KING

TRANSITIONS

BOOK II

©2008 Wizards of the Coast, Inc.

Published by Wizards of the Coast, Inc. FORGOTTEN REALMS, WIZARDS OF THE COAST, THE LEGEND OF DRIZZT, and their respective logos are trademarks of Wizards of the Coast, Inc., in the U.S.A. and other countries.

Printed in the U.S.A.

Cover art by Todd Lockwood
First Printing: October 2008

9 8 7 6 5 4 3 2 1

ISBN: 978-0-7869-4964-9
620-21769720-001-EN

Library of Congress Cataloging-in-Publication Data

Salvatore, R. A., 1959-
The pirate king / R.A. Salvatore.
p. cm. -- (Transitions ; bk. 2)
ISBN 978-0-7869-4964-9
I. Title.
PS3569.A462345P57 2008
813'.54--dc22

2008030393

U.S., CANADA,	EUROPEAN HEADQUARTERS
ASIA, PACIFIC, & LATIN AMERICA	Hasbro UK Ltd
Wizards of the Coast, Inc.	Caswell Way
P.O. Box 707	Newport, Gwent NP9 0YH
Renton, WA 98057-0707	GREAT BRITAIN
+1-800-324-6496	Save this address for your records.

Visit our web site at www.wizards.com

FORGOTTEN REALMS

PRELUDE

Suljack, one of the five high captains ruling Luskan and a former commander of one of the most successful pirate crews ever to terrorize the Sword Coast, was not easily intimidated. An extrovert who typically bellowed before he considered his roar, his voice often rang loudest among the ruling council. Even the Arcane Brotherhood, who many knew to be the true power in the city, were hard-pressed to cow him. He ruled Ship Suljack, and commanded a solid collection of merchants and thugs from Suljack Lodge, in the south central section of Luskan. It was not a showy or grand place, certainly nothing to match the strength of High Captain Taerl's four-spired castle, or High Captain Kurth's mighty tower, but it was well-defended and situated comfortably near the residence of Rethnor, Suljack's closest ally among the captains.

Still, Suljack found himself on unsteady ground as he walked into the room in Ten Oaks, the palace of Ship Rethnor. The old man Rethnor wasn't there, and wasn't supposed to be. He spoke through what seemed to be the least intimidating man in the room, the youngest of his three sons.

But Suljack knew that appearances could be deceiving.

Kensidan, a small man, well-dressed in dull gray and black tones, and well-groomed, with his hair cut short in all the appropriate angles and clips, sat with a leg crossed over one knee in a comfortable chair in the center-back of the plain room. He was sometimes called "The Crow," as he always wore a high-collared black cape, and high black shoes that tied tightly halfway up his calf. He walked with an awkward gait, stiff-legged like a bird. Put that together with his long, hooked nose, and any who saw him would immediately understand the nickname, even a year ago, before he'd first donned the high-collared cape. Any minor wizard could easily discern that there was magic in that garment, powerful magic, and such items were often reputed to affect changes on their bearer. As with the renowned girdle of dwarvenkind, which gradually imparted the characteristics of a dwarf to its wearer, so too Kensidan's cloak seemed to be acting upon him. His gait grew a bit more awkward, and his nose a bit longer and more hooked.

His muscles were not taut, and his hands were not calloused. Unlike many of Rethnor's men, Kensidan didn't decorate his dark brown hair. He carried nothing flashy at all on his person. Furthermore, the cushions of the seat made him appear even smaller, but somehow, inexplicably, all of it seemed to work for him.

Kensidan was the center of the room, with everyone leaning in to hear his every soft-spoken word. And whenever he happened to twitch or shift in his seat, those nearest him inevitably jumped and glanced nervously around.

Except, of course, for the dwarf who stood behind and to the right of Kensidan's chair. The dwarf's burly arms were crossed over his barrel chest, their flowing lines of corded muscles broken by the black, beaded braids of his thick beard. His weapons stabbed up diagonally behind him, spiked heads dangling at the end of glassteel chains. No one wanted a piece of that one, not even Suljack. Kensidan's "friend," recently imported muscle from the east, had waged a series of fights along the docks that had left any and all opposing him dead or wishing they were.

"How fares your father?" Suljack asked Kensidan, though he hadn't yet pried his eyes from the dangerous dwarf. He took his seat before and to the side of Kensidan.

"Rethnor is well," Kensidan answered.

"For an old man?" Suljack dared remark, and Kensidan merely nodded.

"There is a rumor that he wishes to retire, or that he already has," Suljack went on.

Kensidan put his elbows on the arms of his chair, finger-locked his hands together, and rested his chin upon them in a pensive pose.

"Will he announce you as his replacement?" Suljack pressed.

The younger man, barely past his mid-twenties, chuckled a bit at that, and Suljack cleared his throat.

"Would that eventuality displease you?" asked the Crow.

"You know me better than that," Suljack protested.

"And what of the other three?"

Suljack paused to consider that for a moment then shrugged. "It's not unexpected. Welcomed? Perhaps, but with a wary eye turned your way. The high captains live well, and don't wish to upset the balance."

"Their ambition falls victim to success, you mean."

Again Suljack shrugged and said lightheartedly, "Isn't enough ever enough?"

"No," Kensidan answered simply, with blunt and brutal honesty, and once again Suljack found himself on shifting sands.

Suljack glanced around at the many attendants then dismissed his own. Kensidan did likewise—except for his dwarf bodyguard. Suljack looked past the seated man sourly.

"Speak freely," Kensidan said.

Suljack nodded toward the dwarf.

"He's deaf," Kensidan explained.

"Can't hear a thing," the dwarf confirmed.

Suljack shook his head. What he meant to say needed saying, he told himself, and so he started, "You are serious about going after the brotherhood?"

Kensidan sat expressionless, emotionless.

"There are more than a hundred wizards who call the Hosttower home," Suljack announced.

No response, not a whit.

"Many of them archmages."

"You presume that they speak and act with a singular mind," said Kensidan finally.

"Arklem Greeth holds them fast."

"No one holds a wizard fast," Kensidan replied. "Theirs is the most selfish and self-serving of professions."

"Some say that Greeth has cheated death itself."

"Death is a patient opponent."

Suljack blew out a frustrated sigh. "He consorts with devils!" he blurted. "Greeth is not to be taken lightly."

"I take no one lightly," Kensidan assured him, a clear edge to his words.

Suljack sighed again and managed to calm himself. "I'm wary of them, is all," he explained more quietly. "Even the people of Luskan know it now, that we five high captains, your father among us, are puppets to the master Arklem Greeth. I've been so long under his thumb I've forgotten the feel of wind breaking over the prow of my own ship. Might be that it's time to take back the wheel."

"Past time. And all we need is for Arklem Greeth to continue to feel secure in his superiority. He weaves too many threads, and only a few need unravel to unwind his tapestry of power."

Suljack shook his head, clearly less than confident.

"*Thrice Lucky* is secured?" Kensidan asked.

"Maimun sailed this morning, yes. Is he to meet with Lord Brambleberry of Waterdeep?"

3

"He knows what he is to do," Kensidan replied.

Suljack scowled, understanding that to mean that Suljack need not know. Secrecy was power, he understood, though he was far too emotional a thug to ever keep a secret for long.

It hit Suljack then, and he looked at Kensidan with even more respect, if that was possible. Secrecy was the weight of the man, the pull that had everyone constantly leaning toward him. Kensidan had many pieces in play, and no one saw more than a few of them.

That was Kensidan's strength. Everyone around him stood on shifting sand, while he was rooted in bedrock.

"So it's Deudermont, you say?" Suljack asked, determined to at least begin weaving the young man's threads into some sensible pattern. He shook his head at the irony of that possibility.

"*Sea Sprite*'s captain is a true hero of the people," Kensidan replied. "Perhaps the only hero for the people of Luskan, who have no one to speak for them in the halls of power."

Suljack smirked at the insult, reminding himself that if it were a barb aimed at him then logic aimed it at Kensidan's own father as well.

"Deudermont is unbending in principle, and therein lies our opportunity," Kensidan explained. "He is no friend of the brotherhood, surely."

"The best war is a proxy war, I suppose," said Suljack.

"No," Kensidan corrected, "the best war is a proxy war when no one knows the true power behind it."

Suljack chuckled at that, and wasn't about to disagree. His laughter remained tempered, however, by the reality that was Kensidan the Crow. His partner, his ally . . . a man he dared not trust.

A man from whom he could not, could never, escape.

* * * * *

"Suljack knows enough, but not too much?" Rethnor asked when Kensidan joined him a short while later.

Kensidan spent a few moments studying his father before nodding his assent. How old Rethnor looked these days, with his pallid skin sagging below his eyes and down his cheeks, leaving great flopping jowls. He had thinned considerably in the last year or so, and his skin, so leathery from years at sea, had little resilience left. He walked stiff-legged and bolt upright, for his back had locked securely in place. And when he talked, he sounded as if he had his mouth stuffed with fabric, his voice muffled and weak.

"Enough to throw himself on my sword," Kensidan replied, "but he will not."

"You trust him?"

Kensidan nodded. "He and I want the same thing. We have no desire to serve under the thumb of Arklem Greeth."

"As I have, you mean," Rethnor retorted, but Kensidan was shaking his head even as the old man spoke the words.

"You put in place everything upon which I now build," he said. "Without your long reach, I wouldn't dare move against Greeth."

"Suljack appreciates this, as well?"

"Like a starving man viewing a feast at a distant table. He wants a seat at that table. Neither of us will feast without the other."

"You're watching him closely, then."

"Yes."

Rethnor gave a wheezing laugh.

"And Suljack is too stupid to betray me in a manner that I couldn't anticipate," Kensidan added, and Rethnor's laugh became a quick scowl.

"Kurth is the one to watch, not Suljack," said Kensidan.

Rethnor considered the words for a few moments, then nodded his agreement. High Captain Kurth, out there on Closeguard Island and so close to the Hosttower, was possibly the strongest of the five high captains, and surely the only one who could stand one-to-one against Ship Rethnor. And Kurth was so very clever, whereas, Rethnor had to admit, his friend Suljack often had to be led to the trough with a carrot.

"Your brother is in Mirabar?" Rethnor asked.

Kensidan nodded. "Fate has been kind to us."

"No," Rethnor corrected. "Arklem Greeth has erred. His Mistresses of the South Tower and North Tower both hold vested interests in his planned infiltration and domination of their homeland, interests that are diametrically opposed. Arklem Greeth is too prideful and cocksure to recognize the insecurity of his position—I doubt he understands Arabeth Raurym's anger."

"She is aboard *Thrice Lucky*, seeking *Sea Sprite*."

"And Lord Brambleberry awaits Deudermont at Waterdeep," Rethnor stated, nodding in approval.

Kensidan the Crow allowed a rare smile to crease his emotionless facade. He quickly suppressed it, though, reminding himself of the dangers of pride. Surely, Kensidan had much to be proud of. He was a juggler with many balls in the air, seamlessly and surely spinning their orbits. He was two steps ahead of Arklem Greeth in the east, and facilitating unwitting allies in the south. His considerable investments—bags of gold—had been well spent.

"The Arcane Brotherhood must fail in the east," Rethnor remarked.

"Maximum pain and exposure," Kensidan agreed.

"And beware Overwizard Shadowmantle," the old high captain warned, referring to the moon elf, Valindra, Mistress of the North Tower. "She will become incensed if Greeth is set back in his plans for dominion over the Silver Marches, a place she loathes."

"And she will blame Overwizard Arabeth Raurym of the South Tower, daughter of Marchion Elastul, for who stands to lose as much as Arabeth by Arklem Greeth's power grab?"

Rethnor started to talk, but he just looked upon his son, flashed a smile of complete confidence, and nodded. The boy understood it, all of it.

He had overlooked nothing.

"The Arcane Brotherhood must fail in the east," he said again, only to savor the words.

"I will not disappoint you," the Crow promised.

PART
1

WEAVING THE TAPESTRY

WEAVING THE TAPESTRY

A million, million changes—uncountable changes!—every day, every heartbeat of every day. That is the nature of things, of the world, with every decision a crossroad, every drop of rain an instrument both of destruction and creation, every animal hunting and every animal eaten changing the present just a bit.

On a larger level, it's hardly and rarely noticeable, but those multitude of pieces that comprise every image are not constants, nor, necessarily, are constant in the way we view them.

My friends and I are not the norm for the folk of Faerûn. We have traveled half the world, for me both under and above. Most people will never see the wider world outside of their town, or even the more distant parts of the cities of their births. Theirs is a small and familiar existence, a place of comfort and routine, parochial in their church, selective in their lifelong friends.

I could not suffer such an existence. Boredom builds like smothering walls, and the tiny changes of everyday existence would never cut large enough windows in those opaque barriers.

Of my companions, I think Regis could most accept such a life, so long as the food was plentiful and not bland and he was given some manner of contact with the goings-on of the wider world outside. I have often wondered how many hours a halfling might lie on the same spot on the shore of the same lake with the same un-baited line tied to his toe.

Has Wulfgar moved back to a similar existence? Has he shrunk his world, recoiling from the harder truths of reality? It's possible for him, with his deep emotional scars, but never would it be possible for Catti-brie to go with him to such a life of steadfast routine. Of that I'm most certain. The wanderlust grips her as it grips me, forcing us along the road—even apart along our separate roads, and confident in the love we share and the eventual reunions.

And Bruenor, as I witness daily, battles the smallness of his existence with growls and grumbles. He is the king of Mithral Hall, with riches untold at his fingertips. His every wish can be granted by a host of subjects loyal to him unto death. He accepts the responsibilities of his lineage, and fits that throne well, but it galls him every day as surely as if he was tied to his kingly seat. He has often found and will often find again excuses to get himself out of the hall on some mission or other, whatever the danger.

He knows, as Catti-brie and I know, that stasis is boredom and boredom is a wee piece of death itself.

For we measure our lives by the changes, by the moments of the unusual. Perhaps that manifests itself in the first glimpse of a new city, or the first breath of air on a tall mountain, a swim in a river cold from the melt or a frenzied battle in the shadows of Kelvin's Cairn. The unusual experiences are those that create the memories, and a tenday of memories is more life than a year of routine. I remember my first sail aboard *Sea Sprite*, for example, as keenly as my first kiss from Catti-brie, and though that journey lasted mere tendays in a life more than three-quarters of the way through a century, the memories of that voyage play out more vividly than some of the years I spent in House Do'Urden, trapped in the routine of a drow boy's repetitive duties.

It's true that many of the wealthier folk I have known, lords of Waterdeep even, will open their purses wide for a journey to a far off place of respite. Even if a particular journey does not go as anticipated for them, with unpleasant weather or unpleasant company, or foul food or even minor illnesses, to a one, the lords would claim the trip worth the effort and the gold. What they valued most for their trouble and treasure was not the actual journey, but the memory of it that remained behind, the memory of it that they will carry to their graves. Life is in the experiencing, to be sure, but it's just as much in the recollection and in the telling!

Contrastingly, I see in Mithral Hall many dwarves, particularly older folk, who revel in the routine, whose every step mirrors those of the day before. Every meal, every hour of work, every chop with the pick or bang with the hammer follows the pattern ingrained throughout the years. There is a game of delusion at work here, I know, though I wouldn't say it aloud. It's an unspoken and internal logic that drives them ever on in the same place. It's even chanted in an old dwarven song:

> For this I did on yesterday
> And not to Moradin's Hall did I fly
> So's to do it again'll keep me well
> And today I sha'not die.

The logic is simple and straightforward, and the trap is easily set, for if I did these things the day before and do these same things today, I can reasonably assume that the result will not change.

And the result is that I will be alive tomorrow to do these things yet again.

Thus do the mundane and the routine become the—false—assurance of continued life, but I have to wonder, even if the premise were true, even if doing the same thing daily would ensure immortality, would a year of such existence not already be the same as the most troubling possibility of death?

From my perspective, this ill-fated logic ensures the opposite of that delusional promise! To live a decade in such a state is to ensure the swiftest path to death, for it is to ensure the swiftest passage of the decade, an unremarkable recollection that will flitter by without a pause, the years of mere existence. For in those hours and heartbeats and passing days, there is no variance, no outstanding memory, no first kiss.

To seek the road and embrace change could well lead to a shorter life in these dangerous times in Faerûn. But in those hours, days, years, whatever the measure, I will have lived a longer life by far than the smith who ever taps the same hammer to the same familiar spot on the same familiar metal.

For life is experience, and longevity is, in the end, measured by memory, and those with a thousand tales to tell have indeed lived longer than any who embrace the mundane.

—Drizzt Do'Urden

CHAPTER

FAIR WINDS AND FOLLOWING SEAS

Sails billowing, timbers creaking, water spraying high from her prow, *Thrice Lucky* leaped across the swells with the grace of a dancer. All the multitude of sounds blended together in a musical chorus, both invigorating and inspiring, and it occurred to young Captain Maimun that if he had hired a band of musicians to rouse his crew, their work would add little to the natural music all around them.

The chase was on, and every man and woman aboard felt it, and heard it.

Maimun stood forward and starboard, holding fast to a guide rope, his brown hair waving in the wind, his black shirt half unbuttoned and flapping refreshingly and noisily, bouncing out enough to show a tar-black scar across the left side of his chest.

"They are close," came a woman's voice from behind him, and Maimun half-turned to regard Overwizard Arabeth Raurym, Mistress of the South Tower.

"Your magic tells you so?"

"Can't you feel it?" the woman answered, and gave a coy toss of her head so that her waist-length red hair caught the wind and flipped back behind her. Her blouse was as open as Maimun's shirt, and the young man couldn't help but look admiringly at the alluring creature.

He thought of the previous night, and the night before that, and before that as well—of the whole enjoyable journey. Arabeth had promised him a wonderful and exciting sail in addition to the rather large sum she'd offered for her passage, and Maimun couldn't honestly say that she'd disappointed him. She was around his age, just past thirty, intelligent, attractive, sometimes brazen, sometimes coy, and just enough of each to keep Maimun and every other man around her off-balance and keenly interested in pursuing her. Arabeth knew her power well, and Maimun knew that she knew it, but still, he couldn't shake himself free of her.

Arabeth stepped up beside him and playfully brushed her fingers through his thick hair. He glanced around quickly, hoping none of the crew had seen, for the action only accentuated that he was quite young to be captaining a ship, and that he looked even younger. His build was slight, wiry yet strong, his features boyish and his eyes a delicate light blue. While his hands were calloused, like those of any honest seaman, his skin had not yet taken on the weathered, leathery look of a man too much under the sparkling sun.

Arabeth dared to run her hand under the open fold of his shirt, her fingers dancing across his smooth skin to the rougher place where skin and tar had melded together, and it occurred to Maimun that he typically kept his shirt open just a bit more for exactly the reason of revealing a hint of that scar, that badge of honor, that reminder to all around that he had spent most of his life with a blade in his hand.

"You are a paradox," Arabeth remarked, and Maimun merely smiled. "Gentle and strong, soft and rough, kind and merciless, an artist and a warrior. With your lute in hand, you sing with the voice of the sirens, and with your sword in hand, you fight with the tenacity of a drow weapons master."

"You find this off-putting?"

Arabeth laughed. "I would drag you to your cabin right now," she replied, "but they are close."

As if on cue—and Maimun was certain Arabeth had used some magic to confirm her prediction before she'd offered it—a crewman from the crow's nest shouted down, "Sails! Sails on the horizon!"

"Two ships," Arabeth said to Maimun.

"Two ships!" the man in the nest called down.

"*Sea Sprite* and *Quelch's Folly*," said Arabeth. "As I told you when we left Luskan."

Maimun could only chuckle helplessly at the manipulative wizard. He reminded himself of the pleasures of the journey, and of the hefty bag of gold awaiting its completion.

He thought, too, in terms bitter and sweet, of *Sea Sprite* and Deudermont, his old ship, his old captain.

* * * * *

"Aye, Captain, that's Argus Retch or I'm the son of a barbarian king and an orc queen," Waillan Micanty said. He winced as he finished, reminding himself of the cultured man he served. He scanned Deudermont head to toe, from his neatly trimmed beard and hair to his tall and spotless black boots. The captain showed more gray in his hair, but still not much for a man of more than fifty years, and that only made him appear more regal and impressive.

"A bottle of the finest wine for Dhomas Sheeringvale, then," Deudermont said in a light tone that put Micanty back at ease. "Against all of my doubts, the information you garnered from him was correct and we've finally got that filthy pirate before us." He clapped Micanty on the back and glanced back over his shoulder and up to *Sea Sprite*'s wizard, who sat on the edge of the poop deck, his skinny legs dangling under his heavy robes. "And soon in range of our catapult," Deudermont added loudly, catching the attention of the mage, Robillard, "if our resident wizard there can get the sails straining."

"Cheat to win," Robillard replied, and with a dramatic flourish he waggled his fingers, the ring that allowed him control over a fickle air elemental sending forth another mighty gust of wind that made *Sea Sprite*'s timbers creak.

"I grow weary of the chase," Deudermont retorted, his way of saying that he was eager to finally confront the beastly pirate he pursued.

"Less so than I," the wizard replied.

Deudermont didn't argue that point, and he knew that the benefit of Robillard's magic filling the sails was mitigated by the strong following winds. In calmer seas, *Sea Sprite* could still rush along, propelled by the wizard and his ring, while their quarry would typically flee at a crawl. The captain clapped Micanty on the shoulder and led him to the side, in view of *Sea Sprite*'s new and greatly improved catapult. Heavily banded in metal strapping, the dwarven weapon could heave a larger payload. The throwing arm and basket strained under the weight of many lengths of chain, laid out for maximum extension by gunners rich in experience.

"How long?" Deudermont asked the sighting officer, who stood beside the catapult, spyglass in hand.

"We could hit her now with a ball of pitch, mighten be, but getting the chains up high enough to shred her sails . . . That'll take another fifty yards closing."

"One yard for every gust," Deudermont said with a sigh of feigned resignation. "We need a stronger wizard."

"You'd be looking for Elminster himself, then," Robillard shot back. "And he'd probably burn your sails in some demented attempt at a colorful flourish. But please, hire him on. I would enjoy a holiday, and would enjoy more the sight of you swimming back to Luskan."

This time Deudermont's sigh was real.

So was Robillard's grin.

Sea Sprite's timbers creaked again, forward-leaning masts driving the prow hard against the dark water.

Soon after, everyone on the deck, even the seemingly-dispassionate wizard, waited with breath held for the barked command, "Tack starboard!"

Sea Sprite bent over in a water-swirling hard turn, bending her masts out of the way for the aft catapult to let fly. And let fly she did, the dwarven siege engine screeching and creaking, hurling several hundred pounds of wrapped metal through the air. The chains burst open to near full length as they soared, and whipped in above the deck of *Quelch's Folly*, slashing her sails.

As the wounded pirate ship slowed, *Sea Sprite* tacked hard back to port. A flurry of activity on the pirate's deck showed her archers preparing for the fight, and *Sea Sprite's* crack crew responded in kind, aligning themselves along the port rail, composite bows in hand.

But it was Robillard who, by design, struck first. In addition to constructing the necessary spells to defend against magical attacks, the wizard used an enchanted censer and brought forth a denizen from the Elemental Plane of Air. It appeared like a waterspout, but with hints of a human form, a roiling of air powerful enough to suck up and hold water within it to better define its dimensions. Loyal and obedient because of the ring Robillard wore, the cloudlike pet all but invisibly floated over the rail of *Sea Sprite* and glided toward *Quelch's Folly*.

Captain Deudermont lifted his hand high and looked to Robillard for guidance. "Alongside her fast and straight," he instructed the helmsman.

"Not to rake?" Waillan Micanty asked, echoing perfectly the sentiments of the helmsman, for normally *Sea Sprite* would cripple her opponent and come in broadside to the pirate's taffrail, giving *Sea Sprite's* archers greater latitude and mobility.

Robillard had convinced Deudermont of a new plan for the ruffians of *Quelch's Folly*, a plan more straightforward and more devastating to a crew deserving of no quarter.

Sea Sprite closed—archers on both decks lifted their bows.

"Hold for me," Deudermont called along his line, his hand still high in the air.

More than one man on *Sea Sprite's* deck rubbed his arm against his sweating face; more than one rolled eager fingers over his drawn bowstring. Deudermont was asking them to cede the initiative, to let the pirates shoot first.

Trained, seasoned, and trusting in their captain, they obliged.

And so Argus's crew let fly . . . right into the suddenly howling winds of Robillard's air elemental.

The creature rose up above the dark water and began to spin with such suddenness and velocity that by the time the arrows of Argus's archers cleared their bows, they were soaring straight into a growing tornado, a water spout. Robillard willed the creature right to the side of *Quelch's Folly,* its winds so strong that they deterred any attempt to reload the bows.

Then, with only a few yards separating *Sea Sprite* from the pirate, the wizard nodded to Deudermont, who counted down from three—precisely the time Robillard needed to simply dismiss his elemental and the winds with it. Argus's crew, mistakenly thinking the wind to be as much a defense as a deterrent to their own attacks, had barely moved for cover when the volley crossed deck to deck.

* * * * *

"They are good," Arabeth remarked to Maimun as the two stared into a scrying bowl she had empowered to give them a close-up view of the distant battle. Following the barrage of arrows, a second catapult shot sent hundreds of small stones raking the deck of *Quelch's Folly.* With brutal efficiency, *Sea Sprite* sidled up to the pirate ship, grapnels and boarding planks flying.

"It will be all but over before we get there," Maimun said.

"Before *you* get there, you mean," Arabeth said with a wink. She cast a quick spell and faded from sight. "Put up your proper pennant, else *Sea Sprite* sinks you beside her."

Maimun laughed at the disembodied voice of the invisible mage and started to respond, but a flash out on the water told him that Arabeth had already created a dimensional portal to rush away.

"Up Luskan's dock flag!" Maimun called to his crew.

Thrice Lucky was in a wonderful position, for she had no outstanding crimes or warrants against her. With a flag of Luskan's wharf above her, stating a clear intent to side with Deudermont, she would be well-received.

And of course Maimun would side with Deudermont against Argus Retch. Though Maimun, too, was considered a "pirate" of sorts, he was nothing akin to the wretched Retch—whose last name had been taken with pride, albeit misspelled. Retch was a murderer, and took great pleasure in torturing and killing even helpless civilians.

Maimun wouldn't abide that, and part of the reason he had agreed to take Arabeth out was to see, at long last, the downfall of the dreadful pirate. He realized he was leaning over the rail. His greatest pleasure would be crossing swords with Retch himself.

But Maimun knew Deudermont too well to believe that the battle would last that long.

"Take up a song," the young captain, who was also a renowned bard, commanded, and his crew did just that, singing rousing praises to *Thrice Lucky*, warning her enemies, "Beware or be swimming!"

Maimun shook his thick brown locks from his face, his light blue eyes—orbs that made him look much younger than his twenty-nine years—squinting as he measured the fast-closing distance.

Deudermont's men were already on the deck.

* * * * *

Robillard found himself quickly bored. He had expected better out of Argus Retch, though he'd wondered for a long time if the man's impressive reputation had been exaggerated by the ruthlessness of his tactics. Robillard, formerly of the Hosttower of the Arcane, had known many such men, rather ordinary in terms of conventional intelligence or prowess, but seeming above that because they were unbounded by morality.

"Sails port and aft!" the man in the crow's nest shouted down. Robillard waved his hand, casting a spell to enhance his vision, his gaze locking on the pennant climbing the new ship's rigging.

"Thrice Lucky," he muttered, noting young Captain Maimun standing midrail. "Go home, boy."

With a disgusted sigh, Robillard dismissed Maimun and his boat and turned his attention to the fight at hand.

He brought his pet air elemental back to him then used his ring to enact a spell of levitation. On his command, the elemental shoved him across the expanse toward *Quelch's Folly*. He visually scoured the deck as he glided in, seeking her wizard. Deudermont and his crack crew weren't to be outdone with swords, he well knew, and so the only potential damage would be wrought by magic.

He floated over the pirate's rail, caught a rope to halt his drift, and calmly reached out to tap a nearby pirate, releasing a shock of electrical magic as he did. That man hopped weirdly once or twice, his long hair dancing crazily, then he fell over, twitching.

Robillard didn't watch it. He glanced from battle to battle, and anywhere it seemed as though a pirate was getting the best of one of Deudermont's men, he flicked his finger in that direction, sending forth a stream of magical missiles that laid the pirate low.

But where was her wizard? And where was Retch?

"Cowering in the hold, no doubt," Robillard muttered to himself.

He released the levitation spell and began calmly striding across the deck.

A pirate rushed at him from the side and slashed his saber hard against the wizard, but of course Robillard had well-prepared his defenses for any such crude attempts. The saber hit his skin and would have done no more against solid rock, a magical barrier blocking it fully.

Then the pirate went up into the air, caught by Robillard's elemental. He flew out over the rail, flailing insanely, to splash into the cold ocean waters.

A favor for an old friend? Came a magical whisper in Robillard's ear, and in a voice he surely recognized.

"Arabeth Raurym?" he mouthed in disbelief, and in sadness, for what might that promising young lass be doing at sea with the likes of Argus Retch?

Robillard sighed again, dropped another pair of pirates with a missile volley, loosed his air elemental on yet another group, and moved to the hatch. He glanced around then "removed" the hatch with a mighty gust of wind. Using his ring again to buoy him, for he didn't want to bother with a ladder, the wizard floated down belowdecks.

* * * * *

What little fight remained in Argus Retch's crew dissipated at the approach of the second ship, for *Thrice Lucky* had declared her allegiance with Deudermont. With expert handling, Maimun's crew brought their vessel up alongside *Quelch's Folly,* opposite *Sea Sprite,* and quickly set their boarding planks.

Maimun led the way, but he didn't get two steps from his own deck before Deudermont himself appeared at the other end of the plank, staring at him with what seemed a mixture of curiosity and disdain.

"Sail past," *Sea Sprite*'s captain said.

"We fly Luskan's banner," Maimun replied.

Deudermont didn't blink.

"Have we come to this, then, my captain?" Maimun asked.

"The choice was yours."

"'The choice,'" Maimun echoed. "Was it to be made only with your approval?" He kept approaching as he spoke, and dared hop down to the deck beside Deudermont. He looked back at his hesitant crew, and waved them forward.

"Come now, my old captain," Maimun said, "there is no reason we cannot share an ocean so large, a coast so long."

"And yet, in such a large ocean, you somehow find your way to my side."

"For old times' sake," Maimun said with a disarming chuckle, and despite himself, Deudermont couldn't suppress his smile.

"Have you killed the wretched Retch?" Maimun asked.

"We will have him soon enough."

"You and I, perhaps, if we're clever," Maimun offered, and when Deudermont looked at him curiously, he added a knowing wink.

Maimun motioned Deudermont to follow and led him toward the captain's quarters, though the door had already been ripped open and the anteroom appeared empty.

"Retch is rumored to always have a means of escape," Maimun explained as they crossed the threshold into the private room, exactly as Arabeth had instructed Maimun to do.

"All pirates do," Deudermont replied. "Where is yours?"

Maimun stopped and regarded Deudermont out of the corner of his eye for a few moments, but otherwise let the jab pass.

"Or are you implying that you have an idea where Retch's escape might be found?" Deudermont asked when his joke flattened.

Maimun led the captain through a secret door and into Retch's private quarters. The room was gaudily adorned with booty from a variety of places and with a variety of designs, rarely complimentary. Glass mixed with metal-work, fancy-edge and block, and a rainbow of colors left onlookers more dizzy than impressed. Of course, anyone who knew Captain Argus Retch, with his red-and-white striped shirt, wide green sash, and bright blue pants, would have thought the room perfectly within the wide parameters of the man's curious sensibilities.

The moment of quiet distraction also brought a revelation to the two—one that Maimun had expected. A conversation from below drifted through a small grate in the corner of the room, and the sound of a cultured woman's voice fully captured Deudermont's attention.

"I care nothing for the likes of Argus Retch," the woman said. "He is an ugly and ill-tempered dog, who should be put down."

"Yet you are here," a man's voice—Robillard's voice—answered.

"Because I fear Arklem Greeth more than I fear *Sea Sprite,* or any of the other pretend pirate hunters sailing the Sword Coast."

"Pretend? Is this not a pirate? Is it not caught?"

"You know *Sea Sprite* is a show," the woman argued. "You are a facade offered by the high captains so the peasants believe they're being protected."

"So the high captains approve of piracy?" asked an obviously doubting Robillard.

The woman laughed. "The Arcane Brotherhood operates the pirate trade, to great profit. Whether the high captains approve or disapprove is not important, because they don't dare oppose Arklem Greeth. Feign not your ignorance of this, Brother Robillard. You served at the Hosttower for years."

"It was a different time."

"Indeed," the woman agreed. "But now is as now is, and now is the time of Arklem Greeth."

"You fear him?"

"I'm terrified of him, and horrified of what he is," the woman answered without the slightest hesitation. "And I pray that someone will rise up and rid the Hosttower of him and his many minions. But I'm not that person. I take pride in my prowess as an overwizard and in my heritage as daughter of the marchion of Mirabar."

"Arabeth Raurym," Deudermont mouthed in recognition.

"But I wouldn't involve my father in this, for he is already entangled with the brotherhood's designs on the Silver Marches. Luskan would be well-served by being rid of Arklem Greeth—even Prisoner's Carnival might then be brought back under lawful and orderly control. But he will outlive my children's children's children—or out-exist them, I mean, since he long ago stopped drawing breath."

"Lich," Robillard said quietly. "It's true, then."

"I am gone," Arabeth answered. "Do you intend to stop me?"

"I would be well within my province to arrest you here and now."

"But will you?"

Robillard sighed, and up above, Deudermont and Maimun heard a quick chant and the sizzle of magical release as Arabeth spirited away.

The implications of her revelations—rumors made true before Deudermont's very ears—hung silently in the air between Deudermont and Maimun.

"I don't serve Arklem Greeth, if that's what you're wondering," Maimun said. "But then, I am no pirate."

"Indeed," replied an obviously unconvinced Deudermont.

"As a soldier is no murderer," said Maimun.

"Soldiers can be murderers," Deudermont deadpanned.

"So can lords and ladies, high captains and archmages, pirates and pirate hunters alike."

"You forgot peasants," said Deudermont. "And chickens. Chickens can kill, I've been told."

Maimun tipped his fingers against his forehead in salute and surrender.

"Retch's escape?" Deudermont asked, and Maimun moved to the back of the cabin. He fumbled about a small set of shelves there, moving trinkets and statues and books alike, until finally he smiled and tugged a hidden lever.

The wall pulled open, revealing an empty shaft.

"An escape boat," Maimun reasoned, and Deudermont started for the door.

"If he knew it was *Sea Sprite* pursuing him, he is long gone," Maimun said, and Deudermont stopped. "Retch is no fool, nor is he loyal enough to follow his ship and crew to the depths. He no doubt recognized that it was *Sea Sprite* chasing him, and relieved himself of his command quietly and quickly. These escape boats are clever things; some submerge for many hours and are possessed of magical propulsion that can return them to a designed point of recall. You can take pride, though, for the escape boats are often referred to as 'Deuderboats.' "

Deudermont's eyes narrowed.

"It's something, at least," Maimun offered.

Deudermont's handsome face soured and he headed through the door.

"You won't catch him," Maimun called after him. The young man—bard, pirate, captain—sighed and chuckled helplessly, knowing full well that Retch was likely already back in Luskan, and knowing the ways of Kensidan, his employer, he wondered if the notorious pirate wasn't already being compensated for sacrificing his ship.

Arabeth had come out there for a reason, to have that conversation with Robillard within earshot of Captain Deudermont. It all started to come together for clever Maimun. Kensidan was soon to be a high captain, and the ambitious warlord was working hard to change the very definition of that title.

Despite his deep resentment, Maimun found himself glancing at the door through which Deudermont had exited. Despite his falling out with his former captain, he felt uneasy about the prospect of this too-noble man being used as a pawn.

And Arabeth Raurym had just seen to that.

* * * * *

"She was a good ship—best I ever had," Argus Retch protested.

"Best of a bad lot, then," Kensidan replied. He sat—he was always sitting, it seemed—before the blustering, gaudy pirate, his dark and somber clothing so in contrast to Argus Retch's display of mismatched colors.

"Salt in your throat, ye damned Crow!" Retch cursed. "And lost me a good crew, too!"

"Most of your crew never left Luskan. You used a band of wharf-rats and a few of your own you wished to be rid of. Captain Retch, don't play me for a fool."

"W-well . . . well," Retch stammered. "Well, good enough, then! But still a crew, and still workin' for me. And I lost *Folly!* Don't you forget that."

"Why would I forget that which I ordered? And why would I forget that for which you were compensated?"

"Compensated?" the pirate blustered.

Kensidan looked at Retch's hip, where the bag of gold hung.

"Gold's all well and fine," Retch said, "but I need a ship, and I'm not for finding one with any ease. Who'd sell to Argus Retch, knowing that Deudermont got his last and is after him?"

"In good time," said Kensidan. "Spend your gold on delicacies. Patience. Patience."

"I'm a man of the sea!"

Kensidan shifted in his seat, planting one elbow on the arm of the chair, forearm up. He pointed his index finger and rested his temple against it, staring at Retch pensively, and with obvious annoyance. "I can put you back to sea this very day."

"Good!"

"I doubt you'll think so."

The deadpan clued Retch in to Kensidan's true meaning. Rumors had been filtering around Luskan that several of Kensidan's enemies had been dropped into the deep waters outside the harbor.

"Well, I can be a bit patient, no doubt."

"No doubt," Kensidan echoed. "And it will be well worth your time, I assure you."

"You'll get me a good ship?"

Kensidan gave a little chuckle. "Would *Sea Sprite* suffice?"

Argus Retch's bloodshot eyes popped open wide and the man seemed to simply freeze in place. He stayed like that for a very long time—so long that Kensidan simply looked past him to several of Rethnor's lieutenants who stood against the walls of the room.

"I'm sure it will," Kensidan said, and the men laughed. To Retch, he added, "Go and play," and he waved the man away.

As Retch exited through one door, Suljack came in through another.

"Do you think that wise?" the high captain asked.

The Crow shrugged and smirked as if it hardly mattered.

"You intend to give him *Sea Sprite?*"

"We're a long way from having *Sea Sprite.*"

"Agreed," said Suljack. "But you just promised . . ."

"Nothing at all," said Kensidan. "I asked if he thought *Sea Sprite* would suffice, nothing more."

"Not to his ears."

Kensidan chuckled as he reached over the side of his seat to retrieve his glass of whiskey, along with a bag of potent leaves and shoots. He downed the drink in one gulp and brought the leaves up below his nose, inhaling deeply of their powerful aroma.

"He'll brag," Suljack warned.

"With Deudermont looking for him? He'll hide."

Suljack's shake of his head revealed his doubts, but Kensidan brought his herbs up beneath his nose again and seemed not to care.

Seemed not to care because he didn't. His plans were flowing exactly as he had predicted.

"Nyphithys is in the east?"

Kensidan merely chuckled.

CHAPTER

DEFYING EXPECTATIONS

The large moonstone hanging around Catti-brie's neck glowed suddenly and fiercely, and she brought a hand up to clench it.

"Devils," said Drizzt Do'Urden. "So Marchion Elastul's emissary wasn't lying."

"Telled ye as much," said the dwarf Torgar Hammerstriker, who had been of Elastul's court only a few short years before. "Elastul's a shooting pain in a dwarf's arse, but he's not so much the liar, and he's wanting the trade. Always the trade."

"Been more than five years since we went through Mirabar on our road that bringed us home," King Bruenor Battlehammer added. "Elastul lost a lot to our passing, and his nobles ain't been happy with him for a long time. He's reachin' out to us."

"And to him," Drizzt added, nodding down in the direction of Obould, master of the newly formed Kingdom of Many-Arrows.

"The world's gone Gutbuster," Bruenor muttered, a phrase referring to his wildest guardsmen and which Bruenor had aptly appropriated as a synonym for "crazy."

"Better world, then," Thibbledorf Pwent, leader of said guardsmen, was quick to respond.

"When we're done with this, ye're going back to Mirabar," Bruenor said to Torgar. Torgar's eyes widened and he blanched at the notion. "As me own emissary. Elastul done good and we're needing to tell him he done good. And not one's better for telling him that than Torgar Hammerstriker."

Torgar seemed less than convinced, to be sure, but he nodded. He had pledged his loyalty to King Bruenor and would follow his king's commands without complaint.

"Business here first, I'm thinking," Bruenor said.

The dwarf king looked at Catti-brie, who had turned to stare off in the direction the gemstone amulet indicated. The westering sun backlit her, reflecting off the red and purple blouse she wore, a shirt that had once been the magical robes of a gnome wizard. Bruenor's adopted daughter was in her late thirties—not old in the counting of a dwarf, but near middle-aged for a human. And though she still had that luminescence, a beauty that radiated from within, luster to her auburn hair and the sparkle of youth in her large blue eyes, Bruenor could see the changes that had come over her.

She had Taulmaril the Heartseeker, her deadly bow, slung over one shoulder, though of late, Drizzt was the one with that bow in hand. Catti-brie had become a wizard, and one with a tutor as fine as any in the land. Alustriel herself, the Lady of Silverymoon and of the famed Seven Sisters, had taken Catti-brie in as a student shortly after the stalemated war between Bruenor's dwarves and King Obould's orcs. Other than the bow, Catti-brie carried only a small dagger, one that seemed hardly used as it sat on her hip. An assortment of wands lined her belt, though, and she wore a pair of powerfully enchanted rings, including one that she claimed could bring the stars themselves down from the sky upon her enemies.

"They're not far," she said in a voice still melodic and filled with wonder.

"They?" asked Drizzt.

"Such a creature would not travel alone—certainly not for a meeting with an orc of Obould's ferocious reputation." Catti-brie reminded him.

"But escorted by other devils, not a more common guard?"

Catti-brie shrugged, tightened her grip on the amulet, and concentrated for a few moments then nodded.

"A bold move," said Drizzt, "even when dealing with an orc. How confident must the Arcane Brotherhood be to allow devils to openly walk the land?"

"Less confident tomorrow than today's all I'm knowing," muttered Bruenor. He moved down to the side of the stony hill that afforded him the best view of Obould's encampment.

"Indeed," Drizzt agreed, throwing a wink at Catti-brie before moving down beside the dwarf. "For never would they have calculated that King Bruenor Battlehammer would rush to the aid of an orc."

"Just shut yer mouth, elf," Bruenor grumbled, and Drizzt and Catti-brie shared a smile.

* * * * *

Regis glanced around nervously. The agreement was for Obould to come out with a small contingent, but it was clear to the halfling that the orc had unilaterally changed that plan. Scores of orc warriors and shamans had been set around the main camp, hiding behind rocks or in crevices, cunningly concealed and prepared for swift egress.

As soon as Elastul's emissaries had delivered the word that the Arcane Brotherhood meant to move on the Silver Marches, and that enlisting Obould would be their first endeavor, the orc king's every maneuver had been aggressive.

Too aggressive? Regis wondered.

Lady Alustriel and Bruenor had reached out to Obould, but so too had Obould begun to reach out to them. In the four years since the treaty of Garumn's Gorge, there hadn't been all that much contact between the various kingdoms, dwarf and orc, and indeed, most of that contact had come in the form of skirmishes along disputed boundaries.

But they had come to join in their first common mission since Bruenor and his friends, Regis among them, had traveled north to help Obould stave off a coup attempt by a vicious tribe of half-ogre orcs.

Or had they? The question nagged at Regis as he continued to glance around. Ostensibly, they had agreed to come together to meet the brotherhood's emissaries with a show of united force, but a disturbing possibility nagged at the halfling. Suppose Obould instead planned to use his overwhelming numbers in support of the fiendish emissary and against Regis and his friends?

"You wouldn't have me risk the lives of King Bruenor and his princess Catti-brie, student of Alustriel, would you?" came Obould's voice from behind, shattering the halfling's train of thought.

Regis sheepishly turned to regard the massive humanoid, dressed in his overlapping black armor with its abundant and imposing spikes, and with that tremendous greatsword strapped across his back.

"I-I know not what you mean," Regis stammered, feeling naked under the knowing gaze of the unusually perceptive orc.

Obould laughed at him and turned away, leaving the halfling less than assured.

Several of the forward sentries began calling then, announcing the arrival of the outsiders. Regis rushed forward and to the side to get a good look, and when he did spy the newcomers a few moments later, his heart leaped into his throat.

A trio of beautiful, barely-dressed women led the way up the path. One stepped proudly in front, flanked left and right by her entourage. Tall, statuesque, with beautiful skin, they seemed almost angelic to Regis, for from behind their strong but delicate shoulders, they each sprouted a pair of shining white feathered wings. Everything about them spoke of otherworldliness, from their natural—or supernatural!—charms, like hair too lustrous and eyes too shining, to their adornments such as the fine swords and delicate rope, all magically glowing in a rainbow of hues, carried on belts twined of shining gold and silver fibers that sparkled with enchantments.

It would have been easy to confuse these women with the goodly celestials, had it not been for their escort. For behind them came a mob of gruesome and beastly warriors, the barbazu. Each carried a saw-toothed glaive, great tips waving in the light as the hunched, green-skinned creatures shuffled behind their leaders. Barbazu were also known as "bearded devils" because of a shock of facial hair that ran ear to ear down under their jawline, beneath a toothy mouth far too wide for their otherwise emaciated-looking faces. Scattered amongst their ranks were their pets, the lemure, oozing, fleshy creatures that had no more definable shape than that of a lump of molten stone, continually rolling, spreading, and contracting to propel themselves forward.

The group, nearly two score by Regis's count, moved steadily up the rock path toward Obould, who had climbed to the top to directly intercept them. Just a dozen paces before him the leading trio motioned for their shock troops to hold and came forward as a group, again with the same one, a most striking and alluring creature with stunning too-red hair, too-red eyes, and too-red lips, taking the point.

"You are Obould, I am sure," the erinyes purred, striding forward to stand right before the imposing orc, and though he was more than half a foot taller than her and twice her weight, she didn't seem diminished before him.

"Nyphithys, I assume," Obould replied.

The she-devil smiled, showing teeth blindingly white and dangerously sharp.

"We're honored to speak with King Obould Many-Arrows," the devil said, her red eyes twinkling coyly. "Your reputation has spread across Faerûn. Your kingdom brings hope to all orcs."

"And hope to the Arcane Brotherhood, it would seem," Obould said, as Nyphithys's gaze drifted over to the side, where Regis remained half-hidden by a large rock. The erinyes grinned again—and Regis felt his knees go weak—before finally, mercifully, looking back to the imposing orc king.

"We make no secret of our wishes to expand our influence," she admitted. "Not to those with whom we wish to ally, at least. To others. . . ." Her voice trailed off as she again looked Regis's way.

"He is a useful infiltrator," Obould remarked. "One whose loyalty is to whoever pays him the most gold. I have much gold."

Nyphithys's accepting nod seemed less than convinced.

"Your army is mighty, by all accounts," said the devil. "Your healers capable. Where you fail is in the Art, which leaves you dangerously vulnerable to the mages that are so prevalent in Silverymoon."

"And this is what the Arcane Brotherhood offers," Obould reasoned.

"We can more than match Alustriel's power."

"And so with you behind me, the Kingdom of Many-Arrows will overrun the Silver Marches."

Regis's knees went weak again at Obould's proclamation. The halfling's thoughts screamed of double-cross, and with his friends so dangerously exposed—and with himself so obviously doomed!

"It would be a beautiful coupling," the erinyes said, and ran her delicate hand across Obould's massive chest.

"A coupling is a temporary arrangement."

"A marriage, then," said Nyphithys.

"Or an enslavement."

The erinyes stepped back and looked at him curiously.

"I would provide you the fodder to absorb the spears and spells of your enemies," Obould explained. "My orcs would become to you as those barbezu."

"You misunderstand."

"Do I, Nyphithys?" Obould said, and it was his turn to offer a toothy grin.

"The brotherhood seeks to enhance trade and cooperation."

"Then why do you approach me under the cloak of secrecy? All the kingdoms of the Silver Marches value trade."

"Surely you don't consider yourself kin and kind with the dwarves of Mithral Hall, or with Alustriel and her delicate creatures. You are a god among orcs. Gruumsh adores you—I know this, as I have spoken with him."

Regis, who was growing confident again at Obould's strong rebuke, winced as surely as did Obould himself when Nyphithys made that particular reference.

"Gruumsh has guided the vision that is Many-Arrows," Obould replied after a moment of collecting himself. "I know his will."

Nyphithys beamed. "My master will be pleased. We will send . . ."

Obould's mocking laughter stopped her, and she looked at him with both curiosity and skepticism.

"War brought us to this, our home," Obould explained, "but peace sustains us."

"Peace with *dwarves?*" the devil asked.

Obould stood firm and didn't bother to reply.

"My master will not be pleased."

"He will exact punishment upon me?"

"Be careful what you wish for, king of orcs," the devil warned. "Your puny kingdom is no match for the magic of the Arcane Brotherhood."

"Who ally with devils and will send forth a horde of barbezu to entangle my armies while their overwizards rain death upon us?" Obould asked, and it was Nyphithys's turn to stand firm.

"While my own allies support my ranks with elven arrows, dwarven war machines, and Lady Alustriel's own knights and wizards," the orc said and drew out his greatsword, willing its massive blade to erupt with fire as it came free of its sheath.

To Nyphithys and her two erinyes companions, none of whom were smiling, he yelled, "Let us see how my orc fodder fares against your barbezu and flesh beasts!"

From all around, orcs leaped out of hiding. Brandishing swords and spears, axes and flails, they howled and rushed forward, and the devils, ever eager for battle, fanned out and met the charge.

"Fool orc," Nyphithys said. She pulled out her own sword, a wicked, straight-edged blade, blood red in color, and took her strange rope from her belt as well, as did her sister erinyes devils. "Our promise to you was of greater power than you will ever know!"

To the sides of the principals, orcs and lesser devils crashed together in a sudden torrent of howls and shrieks.

Obould came forward with frightening speed, his sword driving for the hollow between Nyphithys's breasts. He roared with victory, thinking the kill assured.

But Nyphithys was gone—just gone, magically disappeared, and so were her sisters.

"Fool orc," she called down to him from above, and Obould whirled and looked up to see the three devils some twenty feet off the ground, their feathered wings beating easily, holding them aloft and steady against the wind.

A bearded devil rushed at the seemingly distracted orc king, but Obould swept around at the last moment, his flaming greatsword cutting a devastating arc, and the creature fell away . . . in pieces.

As he turned back to regard Nyphithys, though, a rope slapped down around him. A magical rope, he quickly discerned, as it began to entwine him of its own accord, wrapping with blinding speed and the strength of a giant constrictor snake around his torso and limbs. Before he even began sorting that out, a second rope hit him and began to enwrap him, as each of Nyphithys's fellow erinyes, flanking their alluring leader, caught him in their extended magical grasp.

"Destroy them all!" Nyphithys called down to her horde. "They are only orcs!"

* * * * *

"Only orcs!" a bearded devil echoed, or tried to, for it came out "only or-*glul,*" as a spike blasted through the devil's spine and lungs, exploding out its chest with a spray of blood and gore.

"Yeah, ye keep tellin' yerself that," said Thibbledorf Pwent, who had leaped down from a rocky abutment head first—helmet spike first—upon the unsuspecting creature. Pwent pulled himself to his feet, yanking the flailing, dying devil up over his head as he went. With a powerful jerk and twitch, he sent the creature flying away. "It'll make ye feel better," he said after it then he howled and charged at the next enemy he could find.

"Slow down, ye durned stoneheaded pile o' road apples!" Bruenor, who was more gingerly making his way down the same abutment, called after Pwent, to no avail. "So much for formations," the dwarf king grumbled to Drizzt, who rushed by with a fluid gait, leaping down ledge to ledge as easily as if he were running across flat tundra.

The drow hit the ground running. He darted off to the side and fell into a sidelong roll over a smooth boulder, landing solidly on his feet and with his scimitars already weaving a deadly pattern before him. Oozing lemures bubbled and popped under the slashes of those blades as Drizzt fell fully into his dance. He stopped, and whirled around just in time to double-parry the incoming glaive of a barbezu. Not wanting to fully engage the saw-toothed weapon, Drizzt instead slapped it with a series of shortened strikes, deflecting its thrust out wide.

His magical anklets enhancing his strides, the drow rushed in behind the glaive, Icingdeath and Twinkle, his trusted blades, making short work of the bearded devil.

"I got to get me a fast pony," Bruenor grumbled.

"War pig," one of the other dwarves coming down, another Gutbuster, corrected.

"Whatever's about," Bruenor agreed. "Anything to get me in the fight afore them two steal all the fun."

As if on cue, Pwent roared, "Come on, me boys! There's blood for spillin'!" and all the Gutbusters gave a great cheer and began raining down around Bruenor. They leaped from the stones and crashed down hard, caring not at all, and rolled off as one with all the frenzy of a tornado in an open market.

Bruenor sighed and looked at Torgar, the only other one left beside him at the base of the abutment, who couldn't suppress a chuckle of his own.

"They do it because they love their king," the Mirabarran dwarf remarked.

"They do it because they want to hit things," Bruenor muttered. He glanced over his shoulder, back up the rocks, to Catti-brie, who was crouched low, using a stone to steady her aim.

She looked down at Bruenor and winked then nodded forward, leading the dwarf's gaze to the three flying erinyes.

A dozen orc missiles reached up at Nyphithys and her sisters in the few moments Bruenor regarded them, but not one got close to penetrating the skin of the devils, who had enacted magical shields to prevent just such an attack.

Bruenor looked back to Catti-brie, who winked again and drew back far on her powerfully enchanted bow. She let fly a sizzling, lightning-like arrow that flashed brilliantly, cutting the air.

Nyphithys's magical shield sparked in protest as the missile slashed in, and to the devil's credit, the protection did deflect Catti-brie's arrow—just enough to turn it from the side of Nyphithys's chest to her wings. White feathers flew in a burst as the missile exploded through one wing then the other. The devil, her face a mask of surprise and agony, began to twist in a downward spiral.

"Good shot," Torgar remarked.

"Wasting her time with that stupid wizard stuff. . . ." Bruenor replied.

A cacophony of metallic clangs turned them both to the side, to see Drizzt backing furiously, skipping up to the top of rocks, leaping from one to another, always just ahead of one or another of a multitude of glaives slashing at him.

"Who's wasting time?" the dark elf asked between desperate parries.

Bruenor and Torgar took the not-so-subtle hint, hoisted their weapons, and ran in support.

From on high, another arrow flashed, splitting the air just to the side of Drizzt and splitting the face of the bearded devil standing before him.

Bruenor's old, notched axe took out the devil chasing the drow from the other side, and Torgar rushed past the drow, shield-blocking another glaive aside, and as he passed, Drizzt sprinted in behind him to slash out the surprised devil's throat.

"We kill more than Pwent and his boys do, and I'm buying the ale for a year and a day," Bruenor cried, charging in beside his companions.

"Ten o' them, three of us," Torgar reminded his king as another arrow from Taulmaril blasted a lemure that roiled toward them.

"Four of us," Bruenor corrected with a wink back at Catti-brie, "and I'm thinking I'll make that bet!"

* * * * *

Either unaware or uncaring for the fall of Nyphithys, the other erinyes tightened their pressure and focus on Obould. Their magical ropes had wrapped him tightly and the devils pulled with all their otherworldly might in opposing directions to wrench and tear the orc king and lift him from the ground.

But they weren't the only ones possessed of otherworldly strength.

Obould let the ropes tighten around his waist, and locked his abdominal muscles to prevent them from doing any real damage. He dropped his greatsword to the ground, slapped his hands on the ropes running diagonally from him, and flipped them over and around once to secure his grasp. While almost any other creature would have tried to free itself from the grasp of two devils, Obould welcomed it. As soon as he was satisfied with his grip, his every muscle corded against the tightening rope and the pull of the erinyes, the orc began a series of sudden and brutal downward tugs.

Despite their powerful wings, despite their devilish power, the erinyes couldn't resist the pull of the mighty orc, and each tug reeled them down. Working like a fisherman, Obould's every muscle jerked in synch, and he let go of the ropes at precisely the right moment to grasp them higher up.

Around him the battle raged and Obould knew that he was vulnerable, but rage drove him on. Even as a barbezu approached him, he continued his work against the erinyes.

The barbezu howled, thinking it had found an opening, and leaped forward, but a series of small flashes of silver whipped past Obould's side. The barbezu jerked and gyrated, trying to avoid or deflect the stream of daggers. Obould managed a glance back to see the halfling friend of Bruenor shrugging, almost apologetically, as he loosed the last of his missiles.

That barrage wasn't about to stop a barbezu, of course, but it did deter the devil long enough. Another form, lithe and fast, rushed past Regis and Obould. Drizzt leaped high as he neared the surprised bearded devil, too high for the creature to lift its saw-toothed glaive to intercept. Drizzt managed to stamp down on the flat of its heavy blade as he descended, and he skipped right past the barbezu, launching a knee into its face for good measure as he soared by. That knee was more to slow his progress than to defeat the creature, though it caught the devil off guard. The real attack came from behind, Drizzt spinning around and putting his scimitars to deadly work before the devil could counter with any semblance of a defense.

The wounded barbezu, flailing crazily, looked around for support, but all around it, its comrades were crumbling. The orcs, the Gutbusters, and Bruenor's small group simply overwhelmed them.

Obould saw it, too, and he gave another huge tug, pulling down the erinyes. Barely a dozen feet from the ground, the devils recognized their doom. As one, they unfastened their respective ropes in an attempt to soar away, but before they could even get free of their own entanglement, a barrage of spears, stones, knives, and axes whipped up at them. Then came a devastating missile at the devil fluttering to Obould's left. A pair of dwarves, hands locked between them, made a platform from which jumped one Thibbledorf Pwent. He went up high enough to wrap the devil in a great hug, and the wild dwarf immediately went into his frenzied gyrations, his ridged armor biting deep and hard.

The erinyes screamed in protest, and Pwent punched a spiked gauntlet right through her face.

The two fell like a stone. Pwent expertly twisted to put the devil under him before they landed.

* * * * *

"You know not what you do, drow," Nyphithys said as Drizzt, fresh from his kill of the barbezu, approached. The devil's wings hung bloody and useless behind her, but she stood steadily, and seemed more angry than hurt. She held her sword in her left hand, her enchanted rope, coiled like a whip, in her right.

"I have battled and defeated a marilith and a balor," Drizzt replied, though the erinyes laughed at him. "I do not tremble."

"Even should you beat me, you will be making enemies more dangerous than you could ever imagine!" Nyphithys warned, and it was Drizzt's turn to laugh.

"You don't know my history," he said dryly.

"The Arcane Brotherhood—"

Drizzt cut her short. "Would be a minor House in the city of Menzoberran-zan, where all the families looked long to see the end of me. I do not tremble, Nyphithys of Stygia, who calls Luskan her home."

The devil's eyes flashed.

"Yes, we know your name," Drizzt assured her. "And we know who sent you."

"Arabeth," Nyphithys mouthed with a hiss.

The name meant nothing to Drizzt, though if she had added Arabeth's surname, Raurym, he would have made the connection to Marchion Elastul Raurym, who had indeed tipped them off.

"At least I will see the end of you before I am banished to the Nine Hells," Nyphithys declared, and she raised her right arm, letting free several lengths of rope, and snapped it like a whip at Drizzt.

He moved before she ever came forward, turning sidelong to the snapping rope. He slashed at it with Icingdeath, his right-hand blade, turned fully to strike it higher up with a backhanded uppercut of Twinkle in his left hand, then came around again with Icingdeath, slashing harder.

And around he went again, and again, turning three circles that had the rope out wide, and shortened its length with every powerful slash.

As he came around the fourth time, he met Nyphithys's thrusting sword with a slashing backhand parry.

The devil was ready for it, though, and she easily rolled her blade over the scimitar and thrust again for Drizzt's belly as he continued his turn.

Drizzt was ready for her to be ready for it, though, and Icingdeath came up under the long sword, catching it with its curved back edge. The dark elf completed the upward movement, rotating his arm up and out, throwing Nyphithys's blade far and high to his right.

Before the devil could extract her blade, Drizzt did a three-way movement of perfect coordination, bringing Twinkle snapping up and across to replace its companion blade in keeping the devil's sword out of the way, stepping forward and snapping his right down and ahead, its edge coming in tight against the devil's throat.

He had her helpless.

But she kept smiling.

And she was gone—just gone—vanished from his sight.

Drizzt whirled around and fell into a defensive roll, but relaxed somewhat when he spotted the devil, some thirty feet away on an island of rock a few feet up from his level.

"Fool drow," she scolded. "Fools, all of you. My masters will melt your land to ash and molten stone!"

A movement to the side turned her, to see Obould stalking her way.

"And you are the biggest fool of all," she roared at him. "We promised you power beyond anything you could ever imagine."

The orc took three sudden and furious strides then leaped as only Obould could leap, a greater leap than any orc would even attempt, a leap that seemed more akin to magical flight.

Nyphithys didn't anticipate it. Drizzt didn't, either. And neither did Bruenor or Catti-brie, who was readying an arrow to try to finish off the devil. She quickly deduced that there was no need for it, when Obould cleared the remaining distance and went high enough to land beside Nyphithys. He delivered his answer by transferring all of his momentum into a swing of his powerful greatsword.

Drizzt winced, for he had seen that play before. He thought of Tarathiel, his fallen friend, and pictured the elf in Nyphithys's place as she was shorn in half by the orc's mighty, fiery blade.

The devil fell to the stone, in two pieces.

* * * * *

"By Moradin's own mug," said Thibbledorf Pwent, standing between Bruenor and Regis. "I'm knowin' he's an orc, but I'm likin' this one."

Bruenor smirked at his battlerager escort, but his gaze went right back to Obould, who seemed almost godlike standing up on that stone, his foe, vanquished, at his feet.

Realizing that he had to react, Bruenor stalked the orc's way. "She'd have made a fine prisoner," he reminded Obould.

"She makes a better trophy," the orc king insisted, and he and Bruenor locked their typically angry stares, the two always seeming on the verge of battle.

"Don't ye forget that we came to help ye," said Bruenor.

"Don't you forget that I let you," Obould countered, and they continued to stare.

Over to the side, Drizzt found his way to Catti-brie. "Been four years," the woman lamented, watching the two rival kings and their unending growling at each other. "I wonder if I will live long enough to see them change."

"They're staring, not fighting," Drizzt replied. "You already have."

CHAPTER

T O   D A R E   T O   D R E A M

3

A few years earlier, *Sea Sprite* would have just sent *Quelch's Folly* to the ocean floor and sailed on her way in search of more pirates. And *Sea Sprite* would have found other pirates to destroy before she needed to sail back into port. *Sea Sprite* could catch and destroy and hunt again with near impunity. She was faster, she was stronger, and she was possessed of tremendous advantages over those she hunted in terms of information.

A catch, though, was becoming increasingly rare, though pirates were plentiful.

A troubled Deudermont paced the deck of his beloved pirate hunter, occasionally glancing back at the damaged ship he had put in tow. He needed the assurance. Like an aging gladiator, Deudermont understood that time was fast passing him by, that his enemies had caught up to his tactics. The ship in tow alleviated those fears somewhat, of course, like a swordsman's win in the arena. And it would bring a fine payoff in Waterdeep, he knew.

"For months now I have wondered. . . ." Deudermont remarked to Robillard when he walked near the wizard, seated on his customary throne behind the mainmast, a dozen feet up from the deck. "Now I know."

"Know what, my captain?" Robillard asked with obviously feigned interest.

"Why we don't find them."

"We found one."

"Why we don't more readily find them," the captain retorted to his wizard's unending dry humor.

"Pray tell." As he spoke, Robillard apparently caught on to the intensity of

Deudermont's gaze, and he didn't look away.

"I heard your conversation with Arabeth Raurym," Deudermont said.

Robillard replaced his shock with an amused grin. "Indeed. She is an interesting little creature."

"A pirate who escaped our grasp," Deudermont remarked.

"You would have had me put her in chains?" the wizard asked. "You are aware of her lineage, I presume."

Deudermont didn't blink.

"And her power," Robillard added. "She is an overwizard of the Hosttower of the Arcane. Had I tried to detain her, she would have blown the ship out from under our boarding party, yourself included."

"Isn't that exactly the circumstance for which you were hired?"

Robillard smirked and let the quip pass.

"I don't like that she escaped," Deudermont said. He paused and directed Robillard's gaze to starboard.

The sun dipped below the ocean horizon, turning a distant line of clouds fiery orange, red, and pink. The sun was setting, but at least it was a beautiful sight. Deudermont couldn't dismiss the symbolism of the sunset, given his feelings as he considered the relative inefficiency of *Sea Sprite* of late, those nagging suspicions that his tactics had been successfully countered by the many pirates running wild along the Sword Coast.

He stared at the sunset.

"The Arcane Brotherhood meddles where they should not," he said quietly, as much to himself as to Robillard.

"You would expect differently?" came the wizard's response.

Deudermont managed to tear his eyes from the natural spectacle to regard Robillard.

"They have always been meddlesome," Robillard explained. "Some, at least. There are those—I counted myself among them—who simply wanted to be left alone to our studies and experiments. We viewed the Hosttower as a refuge for the brilliant. Sadly, others wish to use that brilliance for gain or for dominance."

"This Arklem Greeth creature."

"Creature? Yes, a fitting description."

"You left the Hosttower before he arrived?" Deudermont asked.

"I was still among its members as he rose to prominence, sadly."

"Do you count his rise among your reasons for leaving?"

Robillard considered that for a moment then shrugged. "I don't believe Greeth alone was the catalyst for the changes in the tower, he was more a symptom. But perhaps the fatal blow to whatever honor remained at the Hosttower."

"Now he supports the pirates."

"Likely the least of his crimes. He is an indecent creature."

Deudermont rubbed his tired eyes and looked back to the sunset.

* * * * *

Three days later, *Sea Sprite* and *Quelch's Folly*—whose name had been purposely marred beyond recognition—put into Waterdeep Harbor. They were met by eager wharf hands and the harbormaster himself, who also served as auctioneer for the captured pirate ships Deudermont and a very few others brought in.

"Argus Retch's ship," he said to Deudermont when the captain walked down from *Sea Sprite*. "Tell me ye got him in yer hold, and me day'll be brighter."

Deudermont shook his head and looked past the harbormaster, to a young friend of his, Lord Brambleberry of the East Waterdeep nobility. The man moved swiftly, with a boyish spring still in his step. He had passed the age of twenty, but barely, and while Deudermont admired his youth and vigor, and indeed believed that he was looking at a kindred spirit—Brambleberry so reminded him of himself at that age—he sometimes found the young man too eager and anxious to make a name for himself. Such rushed ambition could lead to a premature visit to the Fugue Plane, Deudermont knew.

"Ye killed him, then, did ye?" the harbormaster asked.

"He was not aboard when we boarded," Deudermont explained. "But we've a score of pirate prisoners for your gaolers."

"Bah, but I'd trade the lot of them for Argus Retch's ugly head," the man said and spat. Deudermont nodded quickly and walked by him.

"I heard that your sails had been sighted, and was hoping that you would put in this day," Lord Brambleberry said as the captain neared. He extended his hand, which Deudermont grasped in a firm shake.

"You wish to get in an early bid on Retch's ship?" Deudermont asked.

"I may," the young nobleman replied. He was taller than most men—as tall as Deudermont—with hair the color of wheat in a bright sun and eyes that darted to and fro with inquisitiveness and not wariness, as if there was too much of the world yet to be seen. He had thin and handsome features, again so much like Deudermont, and unblemished skin and clean fingernails bespeaking his noble birthright.

"May?" asked Deudermont. "I had thought you intended to construct a fleet of pirate hunters."

"You know I do," the young lord replied. "Or did. I fear that the pirates have learned to evade such tactics." He glanced at *Quelch's Folly* and added, "Usually."

"A fleet of escort ships, then," said Deudermont.

"A prudent adjustment, Captain," Brambleberry replied, and led Deudermont away to his waiting coach.

They let the unpleasant talk of pirates abate during their ride across the fabulous city of Waterdeep. The city was bustling that fine day, and too noisy for them to speak and be heard without shouting.

A cobblestone drive led up to Brambleberry's estate. The coach rolled under an awning and the attendants were fast to open the door and help the lord and his guest climb out. Inside the palatial dwelling, Brambleberry went first to the wine rack, a fine stock of elven vintages. Deudermont watched him reach to the lower rack and pull forth one bottle, then another, examining the label and brushing away the dust.

Brambleberry was retrieving the finest of his stock, Deudermont realized and smiled in appreciation, and also in recognizing that the Lord Brambleberry must have some important revelations waiting for him if he was reaching so deep into his liquid treasure trove.

They moved up to a comfortable sitting room, where a hearth blazed and fine treats had been set out on a small wooden table set between two plush chairs.

"I have wondered if we should turn to defensive measures, protecting the merchant ships, instead of our aggressive pirate hunts," Brambleberry said almost as soon as Deudermont took his seat.

"It's no duty I would wish."

"There is nothing exciting about it—particularly not for *Sea Sprite,*" Brambleberry agreed. "Since any pirates spying such an escort would simply raise sail and flee long before any engagement. The price of fame," he said, and lifted his glass in toast.

Deudermont tapped the glass and took a sip, and indeed the young lord had provided him with a good vintage.

"And what has been the result of your pondering?" Deudermont asked. "Are you and the other lords convinced of the wisdom of escorts? It does sound like a costly proposition, given the number of merchant ships sailing out of your harbor every day."

"Prohibitive," the lord agreed. "And surely unproductive. The pirates adjust, cleverly and with . . . assistance."

"They have friends," Deudermont agreed.

"Powerful friends," said Lord Brambleberry.

Deudermont started the next toast, and after his sip asked, "Are we to dance around in circles, or are you to tell me what you know or what you suspect?"

Brambleberry's eyes flashed with amusement and he grinned smugly.

"Rumors—perhaps merely rumors," he said. "It's whispered that the pirates have found allies in the greater powers of Luskan."

"The high captains, to a one, once shared their dishonorable profession, to some degree or another," said Deudermont.

"Not them," said the still elusive Brambleberry. "Though it wouldn't surprise me to learn that one or another of the high captains had an interest, perhaps financial, with a pirate or two. Nay, my friend, I speak of a more intimate and powerful arrangement."

"If not the high captains, then. . . ."

"The Hosttower," said Brambleberry.

Deudermont's expression showed his increased interest.

"I know it's surprising, Captain," Brambleberry remarked, "but I have heard whispers, from reliable places, that the Hosttower is indeed involved in the increasing piracy of late—which would explain your more limited successes, and those of every other authority trying to track down and rid the waters of the scum."

Deudermont rubbed his chin, trying to put it all in perspective.

"You don't believe me?" Brambleberry asked.

"Quite the contrary," the captain replied. "Your words only confirm similar information I have recently received."

With a wide smile, Brambleberry reached again for his wineglass, but he paused as he lifted it, and stared at it intently.

"These were quite expensive," he said.

"Their quality is obvious."

"And the wine contained within them is many times more precious." He looked up at Deudermont.

"What would you have me say?" the captain asked. "I'm grateful to share in such luxury as this."

"That is my whole point," Brambleberry said, and Deudermont's face screwed up with confusion.

"Look around you," the Waterdhavian nobleman bade him. "Wealth—unbelievable wealth. All mine by birthright. I know that you have been well-rewarded for your efforts these years, good Captain Deudermont, but if you were to collect all of your earnings combined, I doubt you could afford that single rack of wine from which I pulled our present drink."

Deudermont set his glass down, not quite knowing how to respond, or how Brambleberry wanted him to respond. He easily suppressed his nagging, prideful anger and bade the man to continue.

"You sail out and bring down Argus Retch, through great effort and at great risk," Brambleberry went on. "And you come here with his ship, which I might purchase at a whim, with a snap of my fingers, and at a cost to my fortune that wouldn't be noticed by any but the most nitpicking of coin-counters."

"We all have our places," Deudermont replied, finally catching on to where the man was heading.

"Even if those places are not attained through effort or justice," said Brambleberry. He gave a self-deprecating chuckle. "I feel that I'm living a good life and the life of a good man, Captain. I treat my servants well, and seek to serve the people."

"You are a well-respected lord, and for good reason."

"And you are a hero, in Luskan and in Waterdeep."

"And a villain to many others," the captain said with a grin.

"A villain to villains, perhaps, and to no others. I envy you. And I salute you and look up to you," he added, and lifted his glass in toast, finally. "And I would trade places with you."

"Tell your staff and I will tell my crew," Deudermont said with a laugh.

"I jest with you not at all," Brambleberry replied. "Would that it were so simple. But we know it's not, and I know that to follow in your footsteps will be a journey of deeds, not of birthright. And not of purchases. I would have the people speak of me, one day, as they now speak of Captain Deudermont."

To Deudermont's surprise, Brambleberry threw his wineglass against the hearth, shattering it.

"I have earned none of this, other than by the good fortune of my birth. And so you see, Captain, I'm determined to put this good fortune to work. Yes, I will purchase Argus Retch's ship from you, to make three in my fleet, and I will sail them, crewed by mercenaries, to Luskan—beside you if you'll join me—and deal such a blow to those pirates sailing the Sword Coast as they have never before known. And when we're done, I will turn my fleet loose to the seas, hunting as *Sea Sprite* hunts, until the scourge of piracy is removed from the waters."

Deudermont let the proclamation hang in the air for a long while, trying to wind his thoughts along the many potential paths, most of them seeming quite disastrous.

"If you mean to wage war on the Hosttower, you will be facing a formidable foe—and a foe no doubt supported by the five high captains of Luskan," he finally replied. "Do you mean to start a war between Waterdeep and the City of Sails?"

"No, of course not," said Brambleberry. "We can be quieter than that."

"A small force to unseat Arklem Greeth and his overwizards?" Deudermont asked.

"Not just any small force," Brambleberry promised. "Waterdeep knows no shortage of individuals of considerable personal power."

Deudermont sat there staring as the heartbeats slipped past.

"Consider the possibilities, Captain Deudermont," Brambleberry begged.

"Are you not being too anxious to make your coveted mark, my young friend?"

"Or am I offering you the opportunity to truly finish that which you started so many years ago?" Brambleberry countered. "To deal a blow such as this would ensure that all of your efforts these years were far more than a temporary alleviation of misery for the merchants sailing the Sword Coast."

Captain Deudermont sat back in his chair and lifted his glass before him to drink. He paused, though, seeing the flickering fire in the hearth twisting through the facets of the crystal.

He couldn't deny the sense of challenge, and the hope of true accomplishment.

CHAPTER

FISHING FOR MEMORIES

I t was a prime example of the good that can come through cooperation," Drizzt remarked, and his smirk told Regis that he was making the lofty statement more to irk Bruenor than to make any profound philosophical point.

"Bah, I had to choose between orcs and demons . . ."

"Devils," the halfling corrected and Bruenor glared at him.

"Between orcs and *devils*," the dwarf king conceded. "I picked the ones what smelled better."

"You were bound to do so," Regis dared say, and it was his turn to toss a clever wink Drizzt's way.

"Bah, the Nine Hells I was!"

"Shall I retrieve the Treaty of Garumn's Gorge that we might review the responsibilities of the signatories?" Drizzt asked.

"Yerself winks at him and I put me fist into yer eye, then I toss Rumblebelly down the hallway," Bruenor warned.

"You cannot blame them for being surprised that King Bruenor would go to the aid of an orc," came a voice from the door, and the three turned as one to watch Catti-brie enter the room.

"Don't ye join them," Bruenor warned.

Catti-brie bowed with respect. "Fear not," she said. "I've come for my husband, that he can see me on my way."

"Back to Silverymoon for more lessons with Alustriel?" Regis asked.

"Beyond that," Drizzt answered for her as he walked across to take her arm. "Lady Alustriel has promised Catti-brie a journey that will span half the continent and several planes of existence." He looked at his wife and smiled with obvious envy.

"And how long's that to take?" Bruenor demanded. He had made it no secret to Catti-brie that her prolonged absences from Mithral Hall had created extra work for him, though in truth, the woman and everyone else who had heard the dwarf's grumbling had understood it to be his way of admitting that he sorely missed Catti-brie without actually saying the words.

"She gets to escape another Mithral Hall winter," Regis said. "Have you room for a short but stout companion?"

"Only if she turns you into a toad," Drizzt answered and led Catti-brie away.

* * * * *

Later that same day, Regis walked outside of Mithral Hall to the banks of the River Surbrin. His remark about winter had reminded him that the unfriendly season was not so far away, and indeed, though the day was glorious, the wind swept down from the north, blustery and cold, and the leaves on the many trees across the river were beginning to show the colors of autumn.

Something in the air that day, the wind or the smell of the changing season, reminded Regis of his old home in Icewind Dale. He had more to call his own in Mithral Hall, and security—for where could be safer than inside the dwarven hall?—but the things he'd gained did little to alleviate the halfling's sense of loss for what had been. He had known a good life in Icewind Dale. He'd spent his days fishing for knucklehead trout from the banks of Maer Dualdon. The lake had given him all he needed and more, with water and food—he knew a hundred good recipes for cooking the delicious fish. And few could carve their skulls more wonderfully than Regis. His trinkets, statues, and paperweights had earned him a fine reputation among the local merchants.

Best of all, of course, was the fact that his "work" consisted mostly of lying on the banks of the lake, a fishing line tied to his toe.

With that in mind, Regis spent a long time walking along the riverbank, north of the bridge, in search of the perfect spot. He finally settled on a small patch of grass, somewhat sheltered from the north wind by a rounded gray stone, but one not high enough to shade him at all. He took great care in getting his line out to just the right spot, a quieter pool around the edge of a stony jut in the dark water. He used a heavy weight, but even that wouldn't hold if he put the line into the main flow of the river; the strong currents would wash it far downstream.

He waited a few moments, and confident that his location would hold steady, he removed a shoe, looped the line around his big toe, and dropped his pack to use as a pillow. He had barely settled down and closed his eyes when a noise from the north startled him.

He recognized the source before he even sat up to look beyond the rounded stone.

Orcs.

Several young ones had gathered at the water's edge. They argued noisily—why were orcs always so boisterous?—about fishing lines and fishing nets and where to cast and how to cast.

Regis almost laughed aloud at himself for his bubbling annoyance, for he understood his anger even as he felt it. They were orcs, and so he was angry. They were orcs, and so he was impatient. They were orcs, and so his first reaction had to be negative.

Old feelings died hard.

Regis thought back to another time and another place, recalling when a group of boys and girls had begun a noisy splash fight not far from where he had cast his line in Maer Dualdon. Regis had scolded them that day, but only briefly.

As he thought of it, he couldn't help grin, remembering how he had then spent a wonderful afternoon showing those youngsters how to fish, how to play a hooked knucklehead, and how to skin a catch. Indeed, that long-ago night, the group of youngsters had arrived at Regis's front door, at his invitation, to see some of his carvings and to enjoy a meal of trout prepared only as Regis knew how.

Among so many uneventful days on the banks of Maer Dualdon, that one stood out in Regis's memory.

He considered the noisy orc youngsters again, and laughed as he watched them try to throw a net—and wind up netting one young orc girl instead.

He almost got up, thinking to go and offer lessons as he had on that long ago day in Icewind Dale. But he stopped when he noticed the boundary marker between his spot and the orcs. Where the mountain spilled down to the Surbrin marked the end of Mithral Hall and the beginning of the Kingdom of Many-Arrows, and across that line, Regis could not go.

The orcs noticed him, then, just as he scowled. He lifted a hand to wave, and they did likewise, though more than a little tentatively.

Regis settled back behind the stone, not wanting to upset the group. One day, he thought, he might be able to go up there and show them how to throw a net or cast a line. One day soon, perhaps, given the relative peace of the past four years and the recent cooperative ambush that had destroyed a potential threat to the Silver Marches.

Or maybe he would one day wage war against those very orc youngsters, kill one with his mace or be taken in the gut by another's spear. He could picture Drizzt dancing through that group then and there, his scimitars striking with brilliant precision, leaving the lot of them squirming and bleeding on the rocks.

A shudder coursed the halfling's spine, and he shook away those dark thoughts.

They were building something there, Regis had to believe. Despite Bruenor's stubbornness and Obould's heritage, the uneasy truce had already become an accepted if still uneasy peace, and it was Regis's greatest hope that every day that passed without incident made the prospect of another dwarf-orc war a bit more remote.

A tug on the line had him sitting up, and once he had the line in hand, he scrambled to his feet, working the line expertly. Understanding that he had an audience, he took his time landing the fish, a fine, foot-long ice perch.

When at last he landed it, he held it up to show the young orcs, who applauded and waved enthusiastically.

"One day I will teach you," Regis said, though they were too far away—and upwind and with a noisy river bubbling by—and could not hear. "One day."

Then he paused and listened to his own words and realized that he was musing about orcs. Orcs. He had killed orcs, and with hardly a care. A moment of uncomfortable regret seized the halfling, followed quickly by a sense of complete confusion. He suppressed all of that, but only momentarily, by going back to work on his line, putting it back out in the calmer waters of the pool.

Orcs.

Orcs!

Orcs?

* * * * *

"Bruenor wishes to speak with you?" Catti-brie asked Drizzt when he returned to their suite of rooms late one night, only to be met by Bruenor's page with a quiet request. A tenday had passed since the fight with the devils and the situation had calmed considerably.

"He is trying to sort through the confusion of our recent adventure."

"He wants you to go to Mirabar with Torgar Hammerstriker," Catti-brie reasoned.

"It does seem ridiculous," Drizzt replied, agreeing with Catti-brie's incredulous tone. "In the best of times, and the most secure, Marchion Elastul would not grant me entrance."

"A long way to hike to camp out on the cold ground," Catti-brie quipped.

Drizzt moved up to her, grinning wickedly. "Not so unwelcome an event if I bring along the right bedroll," he said, his hands sliding around the woman's waist as he moved even closer.

Catti-brie laughed and responded to his kiss. "I would enjoy that."

"But you cannot go," Drizzt said, moving back. "You have a grand adventure before you, and one you would not wisely avoid."

"If you ask me to go with you, I will."

Drizzt stepped back, shaking his head. "A fine husband I would be to do so! I have heard hints of some of the wonders Alustriel has planned for you throughout the next few months, I could not deny you that for the sake of my own desires."

"Ah, but don't you understand how alluring it is to know that your desires for me overwhelm that absolute sense of right and wrong that is so deeply engrained into your heart and soul?"

Drizzt fell back at that and stared at Catti-brie, blinking repeatedly. He tried to respond several times, but nothing decipherable came forth.

Catti-brie let her laughter flow. "You are insufferable," she said, and danced across the room from Drizzt. "You spend so much time wondering how you *should* feel that you rarely ever simply *do* feel."

Knowing he was being mocked, Drizzt crossed his arms over his chest and turned his confused stare into a glare.

"I admire your judgment, all the while being frustrated by it," Catti-brie said. "I remember when you went into Biggrin's cave those many years ago, Wulfgar at your side. It was not a wise choice, but you followed your emotions instead of your reason. What has happened to that Drizzt Do'Urden?"

"He has grown older and wiser."

"Wiser? Or more cautious?" she asked with a sly grin.

"Are they not one and the same?"

"In battle, perhaps," Catti-brie replied. "And since that is the only arena in which you have ever been willing to take a chance. . . ."

Drizzt blew a helpless sigh.

"A span of a few heartbeats can make for a greater memory than the sum of a mundane year," Catti-brie continued.

Drizzt nodded his concession. "There are still risks to be had." He started for the door, saying, "I will try to be brief, though I suspect your father will wish to talk this through over and over again." He glanced back as he grabbed the handle and pulled the door open, shaking his head and smiling.

His expression changed when he considered his wife.

She had unfastened the top two buttons of her colorful shirt and stood looking at him with a sly and inviting expression. She gave a little grin and shrug, and chewed her bottom lip teasingly.

"It wouldn't be a wise choice to keep the king waiting," she said in a voice far too innocent.

Drizzt nodded, paused, and slammed and locked the door. "I'm his son by marriage now," he explained, gliding across the room, his sword belt falling to the floor as he went. "The king will forgive me."

"Not if he knew what you were doing to his daughter," Catti-brie said as Drizzt wrapped her in a hug and tumbled down to the bed with her.

* * * * *

"If Marchion Elastul will not grant me entrance, I will walk past his gates and along my road," Drizzt was saying when Catti-brie entered Bruenor's chambers later on that night.

Regis was there as well, along with Torgar Hammerstriker and his Mirabarran companion, Shingles McRuff.

"He's a stubborn one," Shingles agreed with Drizzt after giving a nod to Catti-brie. "But ye've a longer road by far."

"Oh?" Catti-brie asked.

"He's for Icewind Dale," Bruenor explained. "Him and Rumblebelly."

Catti-brie stepped back at the surprising news and looked to Drizzt for an explanation.

"Me own decision," Bruenor said. "We're hearing that Wulfgar's settled back there, so I'm thinking that Drizzt and Rumblebelly might be looking in on him."

Catti-brie considered it for a few moments then nodded her agreement. She and Drizzt had discussed a journey to Icewind Dale to see their old friend. Word had come to Mithral Hall not long after the signing of the Treaty of Garumn's Gorge that Wulfgar was well and back in Icewind Dale, and Catti-brie and Drizzt had immediately begun plotting how they might go to him.

But they had delayed, for Wulfgar's sake. He didn't need to see them together. He had left Mithral Hall to start anew, and it wouldn't be fair for them to remind him of the life he could have had with Catti-brie.

"I will be back in Mithral Hall before your return," Drizzt promised her.

"Maybe," Catti-brie replied, but with an accepting smile.

"Both of our roads are fraught with adventure," Drizzt said.

"And neither of us would have it any other way," Catti-brie agreed. "I expect that's why we're in love."

"Ye're knowing that other people are in the room, I'm guessin'," Bruenor said rather gruffly, and the two looked at the dwarf to see him shaking his head and rolling his eyes.

CHAPTER

With a sigh, Bellany Tundash rolled over to the side, away from her lover. "You ask too many questions, and always at the wrong moments," she complained.

The small man, Morik by name, scrambled over to sit beside her on the edge of the bed. They looked like two cut of the same cloth, petite and dark-haired, only Bellany's eyes shone with a mischievousness and luster that had been lacking from Morik's dark orbs of late. "I take an interest in your life," he explained. "I find the Hosttower of the Arcane . . . fascinating."

"You're looking for a way to rob it, you mean."

Morik laughed, paused and considered the possibility, then shook his head at the absurdity of the thought and remembered why he was there. "I can undo any trap ever made," he boasted. "Except those of trickster wizards. Those traps, I leave alone."

"Well, every door has one," Bellany teased, and she poked Morik hard in the chest. "Ones that would freeze you, ones that would melt you . . ."

"Ah, so if I just open two doors simultaneously. . . ."

"Ones that would jolt you so forcefully you would bite out that feisty tongue!" Bellany was quick to add.

In response, Morik leaned over, nibbled her ear and gave her a little lick, drawing a soft moan.

"Then do tell me all the knowledge that I need to keep it," he whispered.

Bellany laughed and pulled away. "This is not about you at all," she replied. "This is about that smelly dwarf. Everything seems to be about him of late."

Morik rested back on his elbows. "He is insistent," he admitted.

"Then kill him."

Morik's laugh was one of incredulity.

"Then I will kill him—or get one of the overwizards to do it. Valindra . . . Yes, she hates ugly things and hates dwarves most of all. She will kill the little fellow."

Morik's expression grew deadly serious, so much so that Bellany didn't chuckle at her own clever remark and instead quieted and looked back at him in all seriousness.

"The dwarf is not the problem," Morik explained, "though I've heard he's devastating in battle."

"More boast than display, I wager," said Bellany. "Has he even fought anyone since his arrival in Luskan?"

Again Morik stopped her with a serious frown. "I know who it is he serves," he said. "And know that he wouldn't serve them if his exploits and proficiency were anything less than his reputation. I warn you because I care for you. The dwarf and his masters are not to be taken lightly, not to be threatened, and not to be ignored."

"It sounds as if I should indeed inform Valindra," said Bellany.

"If you do, I will be dead in short order. And so will you."

"And so will Valindra, I suppose, if you're correct in your terror-filled assessment. Do you really believe the high captains, any or all together, are of more than a pittance of concern to the Hosttower?"

"This has nothing to do with the high captains," Morik assured her.

"The dwarf has been seen with the son of Rethnor."

Morik shook his head.

"Then who?" she demanded. "Who are these mysterious ringleaders who seek information about the Hosttower? And if they are a threat, then why should I answer any of your questions?"

"Enemies of some within the tower, I would guess," Morik calmly answered. "Though not necessarily enemies of the tower, if you can see the distinction."

"Enemies of mine, perhaps."

"No," Morik answered. "Be glad you have my ear, and I yours." As he said it, Morik leaned in and bit Bellany on the ear softly. "I will warn you if anything is to come of this."

"Enemies of my friends," the woman said, pulling away forcefully, and for the first time, there seemed no playfulness in her tone.

"You have few friends in the Hosttower," Morik reminded her. "That's why you come down here so often."

"Perhaps down here, I simply feel superior."

"To me?" Morik asked with feigned pain. "Am I just an object of lust for you?"

"In your prayers."

Morik nodded and smiled lewdly.

"But you still haven't given me any reason to help you," Bellany replied. "Other than to forestall your own impending death, I mean."

"You wound me with every word."

"It's a talent. Now answer."

"Because the Hosttower does not recruit from outside the Hosttower, other than acolytes," said Morik. "Think about it. You have spent the better part of a decade in the Hosttower, and yet you are very low in the hierarchy."

"Wizards tend to stay for many, many years. We're a patient lot, else we would not be wizards."

"True, and those who come in with some heritage of power behind their name—Dornegal of Baldur's Gate, Raurym of Mirabar—tend to fill all the vacancies that arise higher up the chain of power. But were the Hosttower to suffer many losses all at once. . . ."

Bellany smirked at him, but her sour expression couldn't hide the sparkle of intrigue in her dark eyes.

"Besides, you'll help me because I know the truth of Montague Gale, who didn't die in an accident of alchemy."

Bellany narrowed her eyes. "Perhaps I should have eliminated the only witness," she said, but there was no real threat in her voice. She and Morik competed on many levels—in their lovemaking most of all—but try as either might to deny the truth of their relationship, they both knew they were more than lovers; they were in love.

"And in so doing eliminate the finest lover you've ever known?" Morik asked. "I think not."

Bellany had no immediate answer, but after a pause, she said in all seriousness, "I don't like that dwarf."

"You would like his masters even less, I assure you."

"Who are they?"

"I care too much about you to tell you. Just get what I need and get far out of the way when I tell you to."

After another pause, Bellany nodded.

* * * * *

They called him "the general" because among all the mid-level battle-mages at the Hosttower, Dondom Maealik was considered the finest. His repertoire was dominated by evocations, of course, and he could throw lightning bolts and fireballs more intense than any but the overwizards and the Archmage Arcane Arklem Greeth himself. And Dondom sprinkled in just enough defensive spells—transmutations that could blink him away to safety, an abjuration to make his skin like stone, various protection auras and misdirection dweomers—so that on a battlefield, he always seemed one step ahead of any adversary. Some of his maneuvers were the stuff of growing legend at the Hosttower, like the time he executed a dimensional retreat at the last second to escape a mob of orc warriors, who were left swinging at empty air before Dondom engulfed them in a conflagration that melted them to a one.

This night, though, because of information passed through a pair of petite, dark-haired lovers, Dondom's adversaries knew exactly what spells he had remaining in his daily repertoire, and had already put in place a plethora of countermeasures.

He came out of a tavern that dark night, after having tipped a few too many to end off a day of hard work at the Hosttower—a day when he had exhausted all but a few of his available spells.

The dwarf came out of an alleyway two doors down and fell into cadence with the walking wizard. He made no attempt to cover his heavy footsteps, and Dondom glanced back, though still he tried to hide the fact that he knew he was being followed. The wizard picked up his pace and the dwarf did likewise.

"Idiot," Dondom muttered under his breath, for he knew that it was the same dwarf who'd been heckling him inside the tavern earlier that night. The unpleasant fellow had professed vengeance when he'd been escorted out, but Dondom was surprised—pleasantly so!—to learn that there was more than bluster to the ugly little fellow.

Dondom considered his remaining spells and nodded to himself. As he neared the next alleyway, he broke into a run, propelling himself around the corner where he pulled up fast and traced a line on the ground. He had only a few heartbeats, and his head buzzed from too much liquor, but Dondom knew the incantation well, for most of his research occurred on distant planes.

The line on the ground glowed in the darkness. Both ends of it rolled into the center, then climbed into the air, drawing a column taller than Dondom by well over a foot. That vertical slice of energy cut through the planar continuum, splitting to two and moving out from each other. In between loomed a darkness more profound than the already black shadows.

But the dwarf wouldn't notice, Dondom knew.

The wizard settled his portal into place, and nodded as the glowing lines fast disappeared. Then Dondom ran down the alley, hoping he would hear the dwarf's screams.

* * * * *

Another form came out of the shadows as soon as the wizard had departed. With equal deftness, the lithe creature created a second magical gate, right in front of Dondom's, and dismissed the original as soon as the second was secure.

A dark hand waved on the street, motioning the dwarf to continue.

The dwarf had to take a deep breath. He trusted his boss—well, as much as anyone could trust a creature of that particular . . . persuasion, but traveling to the lower planes didn't come with many assurances, no matter who was doing the assuring.

But he was a good soldier, and besides, what worse could happen to him than all that had already transpired? He picked up his pace and came around the alleyway entrance in full run, yelling so that the clever wizard would know he'd gone through the gate.

* * * * *

"Ruffian," Dondom muttered as he strolled back to review his handiwork—and to dismiss the gate so that the obstinate and ugly dwarf—or one of the foul denizens of the Abyss—didn't somehow figure out how to get back through. The last thing Dondom wanted was to feel the wrath of Arklem Greeth for loosing demons onto the streets of Luskan. Or it was the next to the last thing he wanted, Dondom realized as he walked around and waved his hand to dispel his magic.

The gate didn't close.

The dwarf walked calmly back out onto the street and said, "Hate those places."

"H-how did you . . ." Dondom stuttered.

"Just went in to get me dog," said the dwarf. "Every dwarf's needin' a dog, don't ya know." He shoved his thumb and index finger against his lips and blew a shrill whistle.

Dondom more forcefully willed his gate to close—but it wasn't his gate. "You fool!" he cried at the dwarf. "What have you done?"

The dwarf pointed at his own chest. "Me?"

With a strange shriek, half roar of outrage, half squeal of fear, Dondom launched into spellcasting, determined to blow the vile creature into nothingness.

He stammered, though, as a second creature came forth from the blackness of the gate. It stepped out bent way over, for that was the only way it could fit through the man-sized portal, its horned head leading the way. Even in the dark of night, the bluish hue of its skin was apparent, and when it stood to full height, some twelve feet, Dondom nearly fainted.

"A—a glabrezu," he whispered, his gaze locked on the demon's lower arms—it sported two sets—that ended in large pincers.

"I just call him 'Poochie,' " said the dwarf. "We play a game."

With a howl, Dondom spun around and ran.

"Yeah, that's it!" cried the dwarf. To the demon, he commanded, "Fetch."

A fine sight greeted those revelers exiting the many taverns on Whiskey Row at that moment of the evening. Out of an alleyway came a wizard of the Hosttower, flailing his arms, screaming indecipherably. With his long and voluminous sleeves he looked rather like a frantic, wounded bird.

Behind him came the dwarf's dog, a twelve-foot, bipedal, four-armed, blue-skinned demon, taking one stride for the wizard's three and gaining ground easily.

"Teleport! Teleport!" Dondom shrieked. "Yes I must! Or blink . . . phase in and out . . . find a way."

That last word came out in a long, rolling syllable, covering several octaves, as one of the demon's pincers clamped around his waist and easily lifted him off the ground. He looked like a wounded bird that had gained a bit of altitude, except that he was moving backward, back into the alley.

And into the gate.

"I could've just smacked him in the skull," the dwarf said to his master's friend, a strange one who wasn't really a wizard but could do so many wizardly things.

"You bore me," came the reply he always got from that one.

"Haha!"

The gate blinked out, and the lithe, dark creature moved into the shadows—and probably blinked out, too. The dwarf walked along his merry way, the heads of his glassteel morningstars bouncing at the ends of their chains behind his shoulders.

He found himself smiling more often these days. There might not have been enough bloodletting for his tastes, but life was good.

* * * * *

"He wasn't a bad sort," Morik said to Kensidan. He tried to look the man in the eye as he spoke, but he always had trouble doing that with the Crow.

Morik held a deep-seated, nagging fear that Kensidan was possessed of some magical charming power, that his gaze would set even his most determined adversary whimpering at his feet. That skinny little man with soft arms and knobby knees that he always kept crossed, that shrinking runt who had done nothing noteworthy in his entire life, held such power over all those around him . . . and that was a group, Morik knew, that included several notorious killers. They all served the Crow. Morik didn't understand it, and yet he, too, found himself thoroughly intimidated every time he stood in the room, before that chair, looking down at a knobby knee.

Kensidan was more than the son of Rethnor. He was the brains behind Rethnor's captaincy. Too smart, too clever, too much the *sava* master. Imposing as he seemed when he sat, when he stood up and walked that awkward gait, his cloak collar up high, his black boots laced tightly halfway up his skinny shins, Kensidan appeared even more intimidating. It made no logical sense, but somehow that frailty played off as the exact opposite, an unfathomable and ultimately deadly strength.

Behind the chair, the dwarf stood quietly, picking at his teeth as if all was right in the world. Bellany didn't like the dwarf, which was no surprise to Morik, who wondered if anyone had ever liked that particular dwarf.

"Dondom was a dangerous sort, by your own word," the Crow answered in those quiet, even, too controlled tones that he had long-ago perfected— probably in the cradle, Morik mused. "Too loyal to Arklem Greeth and a dear friend to three of the tower's four overwizards."

"You feared that if Dondom allied with Arklem Greeth then his friends who might otherwise stay out of the way would intervene on behalf of the archmage arcane," Morik reasoned, nodding then finally looking Kensidan in the eye.

To find a disapproving stare.

"You twist and turn into designs of which you have no knowledge, and no capacity to comprehend," Kensidan said. "Do as you are bid, Morik the Rogue, and no more."

"I'm not just some unthinking lackey."

"Truly?"

Morik couldn't match the stare and couldn't hold the line of defiance, either. Even if he somehow summoned the courage to deny the terrible Crow and run free of him, there was the not-so-little matter of those other puppeteers. . . .

"You have no one to blame for your discomfort but yourself," Kensidan remarked, seeming quite amused by it all. "Was it not you who planted the seeds?"

Morik closed his eyes and cursed the day he'd ever met Wulfgar, son of Beornegar.

"And now your garden grows," said Kensidan. "And if the fragrance is not to your liking . . . well, you cannot pull the flowers, for they have thorns. Thorns that make you sleep. Deadly thorns."

Morik's eyes darted to and fro as he scanned the room for an escape route. He didn't like where the conversation was leading; he didn't like the smile that had creased the face of the dangerous dwarf standing behind Kensidan.

"But you need not fear those thorns," Kensidan said, startling the distracted rogue. "All you need to do is continue feeding them."

"And they feast on information," Morik managed to quip.

"Your lady Bellany is a fine chef," Kensidan remarked. "She will enjoy her ascent when the garden is in full bloom."

That put Morik a bit more at ease. He had been commanded to Kensidan's court by one he dared not refuse, but the tasks he had been assigned the last few months had come with promises of great rewards. And it wasn't so difficult a job, either. All he had to do was continue his love affair with Bellany, which was reward enough in itself.

"You need to protect her," he blurted as his thoughts shifted to the woman. "Now, I mean."

"She is not in jeopardy," the Crow replied.

"You've used the information she passed to the detriment of several powerful wizards of the Hosttower."

Kensidan considered that for a moment then smiled again, wickedly. "If you wish to describe being carried through a gate to the Abyss in the clutches of a glabrezu as 'detrimental,' so be it. I might have used a different word."

"Without Bellany—" Morik started to say, but Kensidan finished for him.

"The end result would be a battle far more bloody and far more dangerous for everyone who lives in Luskan. Think not that you are instrumental to my designs, Morik the Rogue. You are a convenience, nothing more, and would do well to keep it that way."

Morik started to reply several times, but found no proper retort, looking all the while, as he was, at the evilly grinning dwarf.

Kensidan waved him away and turned to an aide, striking up a conversation on an entirely different subject. He paused after only a few words, shot Morik a warning glare, and waved him away again.

Back out on the street, walking briskly and cursing under his breath, Morik the Rogue again damned the day he'd met the barbarian from Icewind Dale. All the while, though, he secretly hoped he would soon be blessing that day, for as terrified as he was of his masters, their promises of rewards were neither inconsequential nor hollow. Or so he hoped.

CHAPTER
E X P E D I E N C E

6

"Bruenor is still angry with him," Regis said to Drizzt. Torgar and Shingles had moved out ahead of them to look for familiar trails, for the dwarves believed they were nearing their old home city of Mirabar.

"No."

"He holds grudges for a long, long time."

"And he loves his adopted children," Drizzt reminded the halfling. "Both of them. True, he was angry when first he learned that Wulfgar had left, and at a time when the world seemed dark indeed."

"We all were," said Regis.

Drizzt nodded and didn't disagree, though he knew the halfling was wrong. Wulfgar's departure had saddened him, but hadn't angered him, for he understood it all too well. Carrying the grief of a dead wife, one he had let down terribly by missing all her signs of misery, had bowed his shoulders. Following that, Wulfgar had to watch Catti-brie, the woman he had once dearly loved, wed his best friend. Circumstance had not been kind to Wulfgar, and had wounded him profoundly.

But not mortally, Drizzt knew, and he smiled despite the unpleasant memories. Wulfgar had come to accept the failures of his past and bore nothing but love for the other Companions of the Hall. But he had decided to look forward, to find his place, his wife, his family, among his ancient people.

So when Wulfgar departed for the east, Drizzt harbored no anger, and when word had arrived back in Mithral Hall that following autumn that Wulfgar was back in Icewind Dale, the news lifted Drizzt's heart.

R. A. SALVATORE

He couldn't believe that four years had passed. It seemed like only a day, and yet, when he thought of Wulfgar, it seemed as though he hadn't been beside his friend in a hundred years.

"I hope he is well," Regis stated, and Drizzt nodded.

"I hope he is alive," Regis added, and Drizzt patted his friend on the shoulder.

"Today," Torgar Hammerstriker announced, coming up over a rocky rise. He pointed back behind him and to the left. "Two miles for a bird, four for a dwarf." He paused and grinned. "Five for a fat halfling."

"Who ate too much of last night's rations," Shingles McRuff added, moving up to join his old friend.

"Then let us be quick to the gates," Drizzt remarked, stealing the mirth with his serious tone. "I wish to be long away before the fall of night if Marchion Elastul holds true to his former ways."

The two dwarves exchanged concerned looks, their excitement at returning to their former home tempered by the grim reminder that they had left under less than ideal circumstances those years before. They, along with many of their kin, more than half the dwarves of Mirabar, had deserted Elastul and his city over a dispute concerning King Bruenor. Over the last three years, many more Mirabarran dwarves, *Delzoun* dwarves, had come to Mithral Hall to join them, and not all of the hundreds formerly of Mirabar that called Bruenor their king had agreed with Torgar's decision to trust the emissary and return.

More than one had warned that Elastul would throw Torgar and Shingles in chains.

"He won't make ye walk away," Torgar said with determination. "Elastul's a stubborn one, but he's no fool. He's wanting his eastern trade route back. He never thought that Silverymoon and Sundabar would side with Mithral Hall."

"We shall see," was all Drizzt would concede, and off they went at a swift pace.

They passed through the front gates of Mirabar soon after, hustled in by excited guards both dwarf and human. They were greeted by cheers—even Drizzt, who had been denied entrance just a few short years earlier when King Bruenor had returned to Mithral Hall. Before any of the companions could even digest the pleasant surprise the four found themselves before Elastul himself, a highly unusual circumstance.

"Torgar Hammerstriker, never did I expect to see you again," the old marchion—and indeed, he seemed much, much older than when Torgar had left—said with a tone as warm as the dancing licks of faerie fire.

Torgar, ever mindful of his place, bowed low, as did Shingles. "We come to ye as emissaries of King Bruenor Battlehammer of Mithral Hall, both

62

in appreciation of your warning to us and in reply to yer request for an audience."

"Yes, and I hear that went quite well," said Elastul. "With the emissary of the Arcane Brotherhood, I mean."

"Devil feathers all over the field," Torgar assured him.

"You were there?" asked Elastul, and Torgar nodded. "Holding up the pride of Mirabar, I hope."

"Don't ye go there," the dwarf replied, and Regis sucked in his breath. "Was one day I'd get me to the Nine Hells and back, singing for Mirabar all the while. Me axe's for Bruenor now and Mithral Hall, and ye're knowin' as much and knowin' it's not to change."

For a brief moment, Elastul seemed as if he were about to shout at Torgar, but he suppressed his anger. "Mirabar is not the city you left, my old friend," he said instead, and again Drizzt sensed that the sweetness of his tone was tearing the old marchion apart behind his facade. "We have grown, in understanding if not in size. Witness your dark-skinned friend, here, standing before my very throne."

Torgar snickered. "If ye was any more generous, Moradin himself'd drop down and kiss ye."

Elastul's expression soured at the dwarf's sarcasm, but he worked hard to bring himself back to a neutral posture.

"I'm serious in my offer, Torgar Hammerstriker," he said. "Full amnesty for you and any of the others who went over to Mithral Hall. You may return to your previous status—indeed, I will grant you a commendation and promotion within the ranks of the Shield of Mirabar, because it was your courageous determination that forced me to look beyond my own walls and beyond the limitations of a view too parochial."

Torgar bowed again. "Then thank me and me boys by accepting what is, and what's going to be," he said. "I come for Bruenor, me king and me friend. And all hopes o' Mithral Hall are that we're both for lettin' past . . . unpleasantness, pass. The orcs're tamed well enough and the route's an easy one for yer own trade east and ours back west."

Elastul slumped back in his throne and seemed quite deflated, again on the verge of screaming. He looked at Drizzt instead and said, "Welcome to Mirabar, Drizzt Do'Urden. It's far past time that you enjoyed the splendors of my most remarkable city."

Drizzt bowed and replied, "I have heard of them often, and am honored."

"You have unfettered access, of course," Elastul said. "All of you. And I will prepare a treaty for King Bruenor that you may take and deliver before the blows of the northern winds bury those easy routes under deep snows."

He motioned for them to go and they were more than happy to oblige, with Torgar muttering to Drizzt as they walked out of the audience chamber's door, "He's needing the trade . . . badly."

The city's reaction to Torgar and Shingles proved to be as mixed as the structures of the half above-ground, half below-ground city. For every two smiling dwarves, the former Mirabarrans found the scowl of another obviously harboring feelings of betrayal, and few of the many humans in the upper sections even looked at Torgar, though their eyes surely weighed uncomfortably on the shoulders of a certain dark elf.

"It was all a ruse," Regis remarked after one old woman spat on the winding road as Drizzt passed her by.

"Not all of it," Drizzt answered, though Shingles was nodding and Torgar wore a disgusted look.

"They expected we would come, and practiced for it," Regis argued. "They hustled us right in to see Elastul, not because he was so thrilled at our arrival, but because he wanted to greet us before we knew the extent of Mirabar's grudge."

"He let us in, and most o' me kin'll be glad for it," Torgar said. "The pain's raw. When me and me boys left, we cut open a wound long festerin' in the town."

"Uppity dwarves, huzzah," Shingles deadpanned.

"The wound will heal," said Drizzt. "In time. Elastul has placed a salve on it now by greeting us so warmly." As he finished, he gave a slight bow and salute to a couple of elderly men who glared at him with open contempt. His disarming greeting brought a harrumph of disgust from the pair, and they turned away in a huff.

"The voice of experience," Regis dryly observed.

"I'm no stranger to scorn," Drizzt agreed. "Though my charm wins them over every time."

"Or yer blades cut them low," said Torgar.

Drizzt let it go with a chuckle. He knew already that it would be the last laugh the four would share for some time. The reception in Mirabar, Elastul's promise of hospitality notwithstanding, would fast prove counterproductive to Bruenor's designs.

Very soon after the group descended the great lift to the town's lower reaches, where the dwarves proved no less scornful of Drizzt than had the humans above. The drow had seen enough.

"We've a long road and a short season remaining," Drizzt said to Torgar and Shingles. "Your city is as wondrous as you've oft told me, but I fear that my presence here hinders your desire to bring good will from Mithral Hall."

"Bah, but they'll shut their mouths!" Torgar insisted, and he seemed to be winding himself into a froth. Drizzt put a hand on his shoulder.

"This is for King Bruenor, not for you and not for me," the drow explained. "And my reason is not false. The trail to Icewind Dale fast closes, often before winter proper, and I would see my old and dear friend before the spring melt."

"We're leaving already?" Regis put in. "I've been promised a good meal."

"And so ye're to get one," said Torgar, and he steered them toward the nearest tavern.

But Drizzt grabbed him by the arm and pulled him up short, and Torgar turned to see the drow shaking his head. "There's likely to be a commotion that will do none of us any good."

"Getting dark outside," Torgar argued.

"It has been dark every night since we left Mithral Hall, as expected," the drow replied with a disarming grin. "I don't fear the night. Many call it the time of the drow, and I am, after all. . . ."

"But I'm not, and I'm hungry," Regis argued.

"Our packs are half full!"

"With dry bread and salted meat. Nothing juicy and tender and . . ."

"He'll moan all the way to Icewind Dale," Torgar warned.

"Long road," Shingles added.

Drizzt knew he was defeated, so he followed the dwarves into the common room. It was as expected, with every eye turning on Drizzt the moment he walked through the door. The tavernkeeper gave a great sigh of resignation; word had gone out from Elastul that the drow must be served, Drizzt realized.

He didn't argue, nor did he press the point, allowing Torgar and Shingles to go to the bar to get the food while he and Regis settled at the most remote table. The four spent the whole of their meal suffering the glares of a dozen other patrons. If it bothered Regis at all, he didn't show it, for he never looked up from his plate, other than to scout out the next helping.

It was no leisurely meal, to be sure. The tavernkeeper and his serving lady showed great efficiency in producing the meal and cleaning the empty plates.

That suited Drizzt, and when the last of the bones and crumbs were removed and Regis pulled out his pipe and began tapping it on the table, the drow put his hand atop it, holding it still. He held still, too, the halfling's gaze.

"It's time to go," he said.

"Mirabar won't open her gates at this hour," Torgar protested.

"I'm betting they will," Drizzt replied, "to let a dark elf leave."

Torgar was wise enough to refuse that bet, and as the gates of the city above swung open, Drizzt and Regis said farewell to their two dwarf companions and went out into the night.

"That bothers me more than it bothers you, doesn't it?" Regis asked as the city receded into the darkness behind them.

"Only because it costs you a soft bed and good food."

"No," the halfling said, in all seriousness.

Drizzt shrugged as if it didn't matter, and of course, to him it didn't. He had found similar receptions in so many surface communities, particularly during his first years on the World Above, before his reputation had spread before him. The mood of Mirabar, though the folk harbored resentment against the dwarves and Mithral Hall as well, had been light compared to Drizzt's early days—days when he dared not even approach a city's gates without an expectation of mortal peril.

"I wonder if Ten-Towns is different now," Regis remarked some time later, as they set their camp in a sheltered dell.

"Different?"

"Bigger, perhaps. More people."

Drizzt shook his head, thinking that unlikely. "It's a difficult journey through lands not easily tamed. We will find Luskan a larger place, no doubt, unless plague or war has visited it, but Icewind Dale is a land barely touched by the passage of time. It is now as it has been for centuries, with small communities surviving on the banks of the three lakes and various tribes of Wulfgar's people following the caribou, as they have beyond memory."

"Unless war or a plague has left them empty."

Drizzt shook his head again. "If any or all of the ten towns of Icewind Dale were destroyed, they would be rebuilt in short order and the cycle of life and death there is returned to balance."

"You sound certain."

That brought a smile to the drow's face. There was indeed something comforting about the perpetuity of a land like Icewind Dale, some solace and a sense of belonging in a place where traditions reached back through the generations, where the rhythms of nature ruled supreme, where the seasons were the only timepiece that really mattered.

"The world is grounded in places like Icewind Dale," Drizzt said, as much to himself as to Regis. "And all the tumult of Luskan and Waterdeep, prey to the petty whims of transient, short-lived rulers, cannot take root there. Icewind Dale serves no ruler, unless it be Toril herself, and Toril is a patient mistress." He looked at Regis and grinned to lighten the mood. "Perhaps a thousand years from now, a halfling fishing the banks of Maer Dualdon will happen upon a piece of ancient scrimshaw, and will see the mark of Regis upon it."

"Keep talking, friend," Regis replied, "and Bruenor and your wife will wonder, years hence, why we didn't return."

CHAPTER

W e go with the rising sun and the morning tide," Lord Brambleberry said to the gathering in the great room of his estate, "to deal a blow to the pirates as never before!"

The guests, lords and ladies all, lifted their crystal goblets high in response, but only after a moment of whispering and shrugging, for Brambleberry's invitation had mentioned nothing about any grand adventure. Those shrugs fast turned to nods as the news settled in, however, for rumors had been growing around "impatient Lord Brambleberry" for many months. He had made no secret of his desire to transform good fortune into great deed.

Up to that point, though, his blather had been considered the typical boasting of almost any young lord of Waterdeep, a game to impress the ladies, to create stature where before had been only finery. Many in the room carried reputations as worthy heroes, after all, though some of them had never set foot outside of Waterdeep, except traveling in luxury and surrounded by an army of private guards. Some other lords with actual battlefield credentials to their names had gained such notoriety over the bodies of hired warriors, only arriving on the scene of a victory after the fact for the heroic pose to be captured on a painter's canvas.

There were real heroes in the room, to be sure. Morus Brokengulf the Younger, paladin of great renown and well-earned reputation, had just returned to Waterdeep to inherit his family's vast holdings. He stood talking to Rhiist Majarra, considered the greatest bard of the city, perhaps of the entire Sword Coast, though he'd barely passed his twentieth year. Across the way from them, the ranger Aluar Zendos, "who could track a shadow at midnight," and the famous Captain Rulathon tapped glasses of fine wine and commiserated of great adventures and heroic deeds. These men, usually the least boastful of the crowd, knew the difference between the posers and the doers, and often relished in such gossip, and up to that moment they had been evenly split on which camp the striking young Lord Brambleberry would ultimately inhabit.

It was hard not to take him seriously at that moment, however, for standing beside the young Brambleberry was Captain Deudermont of *Sea Sprite*, well known in Waterdeep and very highly considered among the nobility. If Brambleberry sailed with Deudermont, his adventure would be no ruse. Those true heroes in the room offered solemn nods of approval to each other, but quietly, for they didn't want to spoil the excited and humorously inane conversations erupting all across the hall, squealed in the corners under cover of the rousing symphony or whispered on the dance floor.

Roaming the floor, Deudermont and Robillard took it all in; the wizard even cast an enchantment of clairaudience so that they could better spy on the amusing exchanges.

"He's not satisfied with wealth and wine," one lady of court whispered. She stood in the corner near a table full of tallglasses, which she not-so-gracefully imbibed one after another.

"He'll add the word 'hero' to his title or they'll put him in the cold ground for trying," said her friend, with hair bound up in a woven mound that climbed more than a foot above her head.

"To get such fine skin dirty at the feet of an ogre. . . ." another decried.

"Or bloody at the end of a pirate's sword," yet another lamented. "So much the pity."

They all stopped chattering at once, all eyes going to Brambleberry, who swept across their field of view on the dance floor, gracefully twirling a pretty young thing. That brought a collective sigh from the four, and the first remarked, "One would expect the older and wiser lords to temper this one. So much a waste!"

"So much to lose."

"The young fool."

"If he is in need of physical adventure. . . ." the last said, ending in a lewd smile, and the others burst out in ridiculous tittering.

* * * * *

The wizard waved his hand to dismiss the clairaudience dweomer, having heard more than enough.

"Their attitude makes it difficult to take the young lord's desires seriously," Robillard remarked to Deudermont.

"Or easier to believe that our young friend needs more than this emptiness to sustain him," the captain answered. "Obviously he needs no further laurels to be invited to any of their beds. Which is a blessing, I say, for there is nothing more dangerous than a young man trying to hero himself into a lady's arms."

Robillard narrowed his eyes as he turned to his companion. "Spoken like a young man I knew in Luskan, so many years ago, when the world was calmer and my life held a steady cadence."

"Steady and boring," Deudermont replied without hesitation. "You remember that young man well because of the joy he has brought to you, stubborn though you have been through it all."

"Or perhaps I just felt pity for the fool."

With a helpless chuckle, Deudermont lifted his tallglass, and Robillard tapped it with his own.

* * * * *

Without fanfare, the four ships glided out of Waterdeep Harbor to the wider waters of the Sea of Swords the next morning. No trumpets heralded their departure, no crowds gathered on the docks to bid them farewell, and even the Chaplain Blessing for favorable winds and gentle swells was kept quiet, held aboard each ship instead of the common prayer on the wharves with sailors and dockhands alike.

From the deck of *Sea Sprite,* Robillard and Deudermont regarded the skill and discipline, or lack thereof, of Brambleberry's three ships as they tried to form a tight squadron. At one point, all three nearly collided. The quick recovery left Brambleberry's flagship, formerly *Quelch's Folly,* and since lettered with the additional *"—Justice,"* with tangled rigging. Brambleberry had wanted to rename the ship entirely, but Deudermont had dissuaded him. Such practices were considered bad luck, after all.

"Keep us well back," Deudermont ordered his helmsman. "And to port. Always in the deeper water."

"Afraid that we might have to dodge their wreckage?" Robillard quipped.

"They are warriors, not seamen," Deudermont replied.

"If they fight as well as they sail, they'll be corpses," Robillard said and looked out to sea, leaning on the rail. He added, "Probably will be anyway," under his breath, but loudly enough so that Deudermont heard.

"This adventure troubles you," said Deudermont. "More than usual, I mean. Do you fear Arklem Greeth and your former associates so much?"

Robillard shrugged and let the question hang in the air for a few heartbeats before replying, "Perhaps I fear the absence of Arklem Greeth."

"How so? We know now what we have suspected for some time. Surely the people of the Sword Coast will be better off without such treachery."

"Things are not always as simple as they seem."

"I ask again, how so?"

Robillard merely shrugged.

"Or is it that you hold some affinity for your former peer?"

Robillard turned to look at the captain and said, "He is a beast . . . a lich, an abomination."

"But you fear his power."

"He is not a foe to be taken lightly, nor are his minions," the wizard replied. "But I'm assured that our young Lord Brambleberry there has assembled a capable and potent force, and, well, you have me beside you, after all."

"Then what? What do you mean when you say that you fear the *absence* of Greeth? What do you know, my friend?"

"I know that Arklem Greeth is the absolute ruler of Luskan. He has established his boundaries."

"Yes, and extended them to pirates running wild along the Sword Coast."

"Not so wild," said Robillard. "And need I remind you that the five high captains who appear to rule Luskan once skirted similar boundaries?"

"Shall we explain to the next shipwrecked and miserable victims we happen across, good and decent folk who just watched family and friends murdered, that the pirates who scuttled them were operating within acceptable boundaries?" asked Deudermont. "Are we to tolerate such injustice and malevolence out of some fear of an unknown future?"

"Things are not always as simple as they seem," Robillard said again. "The Hosttower of the Arcane, the Arcane Brotherhood itself, might not be the most just and deserving rulers of Luskan, but we have seen the result of their rule: Peace in the city, if not in the seas beyond. Are you so confident that without them, Luskan can steer better course?"

"Yes," Deudermont declared. "Yes, indeed."

"I would expect such surety from Brambleberry."

"I have lived my life trying to do right," said Deudermont. "And it's not for fear of any god or goddess, nor of the law and its enforcers. I follow that course because I believe that doing good will bring about good results."

"The wide world is not so easily controlled."

"Indeed, but do you not agree that the better angels of man will win out? The world moves forward to better times, times of peace and justice. It's the nature of humanity."

"But it's not a straight road."

"I grant you that," said Deudermont. "And the twists and turns, the steps backward to strife, are ever facilitated by creatures like Arklem Greeth, by those who hold power but should not. They drive us to darkness when men do nothing, when bravery and honor is in short supply. They are a suffocating pall on the land, and only when brave men lift that pall can the better angels of men stride forward."

"It's a good theory, a goodly philosophy," said Robillard.

"Brave men must act of their heart!" Deudermont declared.

"And of their reason," Robillard warned. "Strides on ice are wisely tempered."

"The bold man reaches the mountaintop!"

Robillard thought, but didn't say, *or falls to his death.*

"You will fight beside me, beside Lord Brambleberry, against your former brother wizards?"

"Against those who don't willingly come over to us, yes," Robillard answered. "My oath of loyalty is to you, and to *Sea Sprite*. I have spent too many years saving you from your own foolishness to let you die so ingloriously now."

Deudermont clapped his dearest friend on the shoulder and moved to the rail beside him, leading Robillard's gaze back out to the open sea. "I do fear that you may be right," he conceded. "When we defeat Arklem Greeth and end the pirate scourge, the unintended consequences might include the retirement of *Sea Sprite*. We'll have nothing left to hunt, after all."

"You know the world better than that. There were pirates before Arklem Greeth, there are pirates in the time of Greeth, and there will be pirates when his name is lost to the ashes of history. Better angels, you say, and on the whole, I believe—or at least I pray—that you are correct. But it's never the whole that troubles us, is it? It's but a tiny piece of humanity who sail the Sword Coast as pirates."

"A tiny piece magnified by the powers of the Hosttower."

"You may well be right," said Robillard. "And you may well be wrong, and that, my friend, is my fear."

Deudermont held fast to the rail and kept his gaze to the horizon, unblinking though the sun had broken through and reflected brilliantly off the rolling waters. It was a good man's place to act for the cause of justice. It was a brave man's place to battle those who would oppress and do harm to helpless innocents. It was a leader's place to act in concert with his principles and trust enough in those principles to believe that they would lead him and those who followed him to a better place.

Those were the things Deudermont believed, and he recited them in his mind as he stared at the brilliant reflections on the waters he loved so dearly. He had lived his life, had shaped his own code of conduct, through his faith in the dictums of a good and brave leader, and they had served him well as he in turn had served so well the people of Luskan, Waterdeep, and Baldur's Gate.

Robillard knew the Hosttower and the ways of the Arcane Brotherhood, and so Deudermont would indeed defer to him on the specifics of their present enemy.

But Captain Deudermont would not shy from the duty he saw before him, not with the opportunity of having eager Lord Brambleberry and his considerable resources sailing beside him.

He had to believe that he was right.

CHAPTER

8

"Perhaps I'm just getting older and harder to impress," Regis said to Drizzt as they walked across a wide fields of grass. "She's not so great a city, not near the beauty of Mithral Hall—and surely not Silverymoon—but I'm glad they let you in through the gates, at least. Folk are stubborn, but it gives me hope that they can learn."

"I was no more impressed by Mirabar than you were," Drizzt replied, tossing a sidelong glance at his halfling friend. "I had long heard of her wonders, but I agree they're lacking beside Mithral Hall. Or maybe it's just that I like the folk who live in Mithral Hall better."

"It's a warmer place," Regis decided. "From the king on down. But still, you must be glad of your acceptance in Mirabar."

Drizzt shrugged as though it didn't matter, and of course, it didn't. Not to him, anyway; he could not deny his hope that Marchion Elastul would truly make peace with Mithral Hall and his lost dwarves. That development could only bode well for the North, particularly with an orc kingdom settled on Mithral Hall's northern border.

"I'm more glad that Bruenor found the courage to go to Obould's aid for a cause of common good," the drow remarked. "We've seen a great change in the world."

"Or a temporary reprieve."

Again Drizzt shrugged, but the gesture was accompanied by a look of helpless resignation. "Every day Obould holds the peace is a day of greater security than we could have expected. When his hordes rushed down from the mountains, I believed we would know nothing but war for years on end. When they surrounded Mithral Hall, I feared we would be driven from the place forever more. Even in the first months of stalemate, I, like everyone else, expected that it would surely descend into war and misery."

"I still expect it."

Drizzt's smile showed that he didn't necessarily disagree. "We stay vigilant for good reason. But every passing day makes that future just a bit less certain. And that's a good thing."

"Or is every passing day nothing more than another day Obould prepares to finish his conquest?" Regis asked.

Drizzt draped his arm over the halfling's shoulders.

"Am I too cynical for fearing such?" Regis asked.

"If you are, then so am I, and so is Bruenor—and Alustriel, who has spies working all through the Kingdom of Many-Arrows. Our experience with the orcs is long and bitter, full of treachery and war. To think that all we've known to be true is not necessarily an absolute is unsettling and almost incomprehensible, and so to walk the road of acceptance and peace often takes more courage than the way of the warrior."

"It always is more complicated than it seems, isn't it?" Regis asked with a wry grin. "Like you, for example."

"Or like a halfling friend of mine who fishes with one foot and flees with the other, fights with a mace in his right hand and pickpockets an unsuspecting fool with his left, and all the while manages to keep his belly full."

"I have a reputation to uphold," Regis answered, and handed Drizzt back the purse he'd just lifted from the drow's belt.

"Very good," Drizzt congratulated. "You almost had it off my belt before I felt your hand." As he took the purse, he handed Regis back the unicorn-headed mace he'd deftly slid from the halfling's belt as the rogue was lifting his purse.

Regis shrugged innocently. "If we steal one-for-one, I will end up with the more valuable items of magic."

Drizzt looked across the halfling and out to the north, leading Regis's gaze to a huge black panther moving their way. Drizzt had summoned Guenhwyvar from her Astral home that afternoon and let her go to run a perimeter around them. He hadn't brought the panther forth much of late, not needing her in the halls of King Bruenor and not wanting to spark some tragic incident with any of the orcs in Obould's kingdom, who might react to such a sight as Guenhwyvar with a volley of spears and arrows.

"It's good to be on the road again," Regis declared as Guenhwyvar loped up beside him, opposite Drizzt. He ruffled the fur on the back of the great cat's neck and Guenhwyvar tilted her head and her eyes narrowed to contented slits of approval.

"And you are complicated, as I said," Drizzt remarked, viewing this rarely seen side of his comfort-loving friend.

"I believe I was the one to say that," Regis corrected. "You just applied it to me. And it's not that I'm a complicated sort. It's just that I ever keep my enemies confused."

"And your friends."

"I use you for practice," said the halfling, and as he gave a rather vigorous rub of Guenhwyvar's neck, the panther let out a low growl of approval that resonated across the dales and widened the eyes of every deer within range.

The fields of tall grass and wild flowers gave way to cultivated land as the sun neared the horizon before them. In the waning twilight, with farmhouses and barns dotting both sides, the path had become a road. The companions spotted a familiar hill in the distance, one sporting the zigzagging silhouette of a house magnificent and curious, with many towers tall and thin, and many more short and squat. Lights burned in every window.

"Ah, but what mysteries might the Harpells have in store for us this visit?" Drizzt asked.

"Mysteries for themselves as well, no doubt," said Regis. "If they haven't all killed each other by accident by now."

As lighthearted as the quip was meant to be, it held an undeniable ring of truth for them both. They'd known the eccentric family of wizards for many years, and never had visited, or been visited by, any of the clan, particularly one Harkle Harpell, without witnessing some strange occurrence. But the Harpells were good friends of Mithral Hall. They had come to the call of Bruenor when the drow of Menzoberranzan assaulted his kingdom, and had fought valiantly among the dwarven ranks. Their magic lacked predictability, to be sure, but there was no shortage of power behind it.

"We should go straight to the Ivy Mansion," Drizzt said as darkness closed in on the small town of Longsaddle. Even as he finished speaking, almost in response, it seemed, a shout of anger erupted in the stillness, followed by an answering bellow and a cry of pain. Without hesitation, the drow and halfling turned and headed that way, Guenhwyvar trotting beside them. Drizzt's hands stayed near his sheathed scimitars, but he didn't draw them.

Another shout, words too distant to be decipherable, followed by a cheer, followed by a cacophony of shouted protests . . .

Drizzt sprinted out ahead of Regis. He scrambled down a long embankment, picking a careful route over fallen branches and between the tightly-packed trees. He broke out of the copse and skidded to a stop, surprised.

"What is it?" Regis asked, stumbling down past him, and the halfling would have gone headlong into a small pond had Drizzt not caught him by the shoulder and held him back.

"I don't remember this pond," Drizzt said, and glanced back in the general direction of the Ivy Mansion to try to get his bearings. "I don't believe it was here the last time I came through, though it was only a couple of years back."

"A couple of years is an eternity where the Harpells are concerned," Regis reminded him. "Had we come here and found a deep hole where the town had once stood, would you have been surprised? Truly?"

Drizzt was only half listening. He moved to a clear, flat space and noted the dark outline of a forested island and the light of a larger fire showing through breaks in the thick foliage.

Another ruckus of arguing sounded from the island.

Cheers came from the right bank, the protests from the left, both groups hidden from Drizzt's view by thick foliage, with only a few campfire lights twinkling through the leaves.

"What?" the perplexed Regis asked, a simple question that accurately reflected Drizzt's confusion as well. The halfling poked Drizzt's arm and pointed back to the left, to the outline of a boat dock with several craft bobbing nearby.

"Be gone, Guenhwyvar," Drizzt commanded his panther companion. "But be ready to return to me."

The cat began to pace in a tight circle, moving faster and faster, and dissipating into a thick gray smoke as she returned to her extraplanar home. Drizzt replaced her small onyx likeness in his belt pouch and rushed to join Regis at the dock. The halfling already had a small rowboat unmoored and was readying the oars.

"A spell gone awry?" Regis asked as yet another yell of pain sounded from the island.

Drizzt didn't answer, but for some reason, didn't think that to be the case. He motioned Regis aside and took up the oars himself, pulling strongly.

Then they heard more than bickering and screams. Whimpers filled in the gaps between the arguing, along with feral snarls that prompted Regis to ask, "Wolves?"

It was not a large lake and Regis soon spotted a dock at the island. Drizzt worked to keep the boat in line with it. They glided in unnoticed and scrambled onto the wharf. A path wound up from it between trees, rocks, and thick brush, which rustled almost constantly from some small animals rushing to and fro. Drizzt caught sight of a fluffy white rabbit hopping away.

He dismissed the animal with a shake of his head and pressed onward, and once over a short rise, he and Regis finally saw the source of the commotion.

And neither understood a bit of it.

A man, stripped to the waist, stood in a cage constructed of vertical posts wrapped with horizontal ropes. Three men dressed in blue robes sat behind him and to the left, with three in red robes similarly seated, only behind and to the right. Directly before the caged man stood a beast, half man and half wolf, he seemed, with a canine snout but eyes distinctly human. He jumped about, appearing on the very edge of control, snarling, growling, and chomping his fangs right in front of the wide eyes of the terrified prisoner.

"Bidderdoo?" Drizzt asked.

"Has to be," said Regis, and he stepped forward—or tried to, for Drizzt held him back.

"No guards," the drow warned. "The area is likely magically warded."

The werewolf roared in the poor prisoner's face, and the man recoiled and pleaded pathetically.

"You *did!*" the werewolf growled.

"He had to!" shouted one of the blue-robed men.

"Murderer!" argued one wearing red robes.

Bidderdoo whirled and howled, ending the conversation abruptly. The Harpell werewolf spun back to the prisoner and began chanting and waving his arms.

The man cried out in alarm and protest.

"What . . . ?" Regis asked, but Drizzt had no answer.

The prisoner's babbling began to twist into indecipherable grunts and groans, pain interspersed with protest. His body began to shake and quiver, his bones crackling.

"Bidderdoo!" Drizzt yelled, and all eyes save those of the squirming, tortured man and the concentrating Harpell wizard, snapped the drow's way.

"Dark elf!" yelled one of the blue-robed onlookers, and all of them fell back, one right off his seat to land unceremoniously on the ground.

"Drow! Drow!" they yelled.

Drizzt hardly heard them, his lavender eyes popping open wide as he watched the prisoner crumble before him, limbs transforming, fur sprouting.

"No stew will ever be the same," Regis muttered helplessly, for no man remained in the wood and rope prison.

The rabbit, white and fluffy, yipped and yammered, as if trying to form words that would not come. Then it leaped away, easily passing through the wide ropes as it scurried for the safety of the underbrush.

Spell completed, the werewolf snarled and howled as it spun on the intruders.

But the creature quickly calmed, and in a voice too cultured for such a hairy and wild mein said, "Drizzt Do'Urden! Well met!"

"I want to go home," Regis mumbled at Drizzt's side.

* * * * *

A warm fire burned in the hearth, and there was no denying the comfort of the overstuffed chair and divan set before it, but Drizzt didn't recline or even sit, and felt little of the room's warmth.

They had been ushered into the Ivy Mansion, accompanied by the almost continual flash of lightning bolts, searing the darkness with hot white light on either side of the pond below. Shouts of protest dissipated under the magical explosions, and the howl of a lone wolf—a lone *were*wolf—silenced them even more completely.

The people of Longsaddle had come to understand the dire implications of that howl, apparently.

For some time, Drizzt and Regis paced or sat in the room, with only an occasional visit by a maid asking if they wanted more to eat or drink, to which Regis always eagerly nodded.

"That seemed very un-Harpell-like," he mentioned to Drizzt between bites. "I knew Bidderdoo was a fierce one—he killed Uthegental of House Barrison Del'Armgo, after all—but that was simply tor—"

"Justice," interrupted a voice from the door, and the pair turned to see Bidderdoo Harpell enter from the hallway. He no longer looked the werewolf, but rather like a man who had seen much of life—too much, perhaps. He stood in a lanky pose that made him look taller than his six-foot frame, and his hair, all gray, stood out wildly in every conceivable direction, giving the impression that it had not been combed or even finger-brushed in a long, long time. Strangely, though, he was meticulously clean-shaven.

Regis seemed to have no answer as he looked at Drizzt.

"Harsher justice than we would expect to find at the hands of the goodly Harpells," Drizzt explained for him.

"The prisoner meant to start a war," Bidderdoo explained. "I prevented it."

Drizzt and Regis exchanged expressions full of doubt.

"Fanaticism requires extreme measures," the Harpell werewolf—a curse of his own doing due to a badly botched polymorph experiment—explained.

"This is not the Longsaddle I have known," said Drizzt.

"It changed quickly," Bidderdoo was fast to agree.

"Longsaddle, or the Harpells?" Regis asked, crossing his arms over his chest and tapping his foot impatiently.

The answer, "Both," came from the hallway, and even the outraged halfling couldn't hold his dour posture and expression at the sound of the familiar voice. "One after the other, of course," Harkle Harpell explained, bounding in through the door.

The lanky wizard was dressed all in robes, three shades of blue, ruffled and wrinkled, with sleeves so long they covered his hands. He wore a white beret topped by a blue button that matched the darkest hue of his robes, as did his dyed beard, which had grown—with magical assistance, no doubt—to outrageous proportions. One long braid ran down from Harkle's chin to his belt, flanked by two short, thick scruffs of wiry hair hanging below each jowl. The hair on his head had gone gray, but his eyes held the same luster and eagerness the friends had seen flash so many times in years gone by—usually right before some Harkle-precipitated disaster had befallen them all.

"The town changed first," Regis remarked.

"Of course!" said Harpell. "You don't think we enjoy this, do you?" He bounded over to Drizzt and took the drow's hand in a great shake—or started to before wrapping Drizzt in a powerful embrace that nearly lifted him off the ground.

"It's grand to see you, my old pirate-hunting companion!" Harkle boomed.

"Bidderdoo seemed to enjoy his work," Regis said, cutting Harkle's turn toward him short.

"You come to pass judgment after so short a time?" Bidderdoo replied.

"I know what I saw," said the halfling, not backing down an inch.

"What you saw without context, you mean," said Bidderdoo.

Regis glared at him then turned his judgment upon Harkle.

"You understand, of course," Harkle said to Drizzt, seeking support. But he found little in the drow's rigid expression.

Harkle rolled his eyes and sighed then nearly fell over as one of his orbs kept on rolling, over and over, in its socket. After a few moments, the discombobulated wizard slapped himself hard on the side of the head, and the eye steadied into place.

"My orbs have never been the same since I went to look in on Bruenor," he quipped with an exaggerated wink, referring, of course, to the time he'd accidentally teleported just his eyes to Mithral Hall to roll around on Bruenor's audience chamber floor.

"Indeed," said Regis, "and Bruenor bids you to never do so in such a manner ever again."

Harkle looked at him curiously for a few moments then burst out laughing. Apparently thinking the tension gone, the wizard moved to wrap Regis in a tight hug.

The halfling stopped him with an upraised hand. "We make peace with orcs while the Harpells torture humans."

"Justice, not torture," Harkle corrected. "Torture? Hardly that!"

"I know what I saw," said the halfling, "And I saw it with both of my eyes in my head and neither of them rolling around in circles."

"There are a lot of rabbits on that small island," Drizzt added.

"And do you know what you would have seen if we hadn't dealt harshly with men like that priest Ganibo?"

"Priest?" both Drizzt and Regis said together.

"Aren't they all and aren't they always?" Bidderdoo answered with obvious disgust.

"More than our share of them, to be sure," Harkle agreed. "We're a tolerant bunch here in Longsaddle, as you know."

"As we *knew,*" said Regis, and it was Bidderdoo who rolled his eyes, though having never botched a teleportation like his bumbling cousin, his eyes didn't keep rolling.

"Our acceptance of . . . strangeness . . ." Harkle started.

"Embrace of strangeness, you mean," said Drizzt.

"What?" the wizard asked, and looked curiously at Bidderdoo before catching on and giving a burst of laughter. "Indeed, yes!" he said. "We who so play in the extremes of Mystra's Weave are not so fast to judge others. Which invited trouble to Longsaddle."

"You are aware of the disposition of Malarites in general, yes?" Bidderdoo clarified.

"Malarites?" Drizzt asked.

"The worshipers of Malar?" asked the more surface-worldly Regis.

"A battle of gods?" Drizzt asked.

"Worse," said Harkle. "A battle of followers."

Drizzt and Regis looked at him curiously.

"Different sects of the same god," Harkle explained. "Same god with different edicts, depending on which side you ask—and oh, but they'll kill you if you disagree with their narrow interpretations of their beast god's will! And how these Malarites always disagree, with each other and with everyone else. One group built a chapel on the eastern bank of Pavlel. The other on the western bank."

"Pavlel? The lake?"

"We named it after him," said Harkle.

"In memoriam, no doubt," Regis said.

"Well, we don't really know," Harkle replied. "Since he and the mountain flew off together."

"Of course," said the halfling who knew he shouldn't be surprised.

"The blue-robed and red-robed onlookers at the . . . punishment," said Drizzt.

"Priests of Malar all," Bidderdoo replied. "One side witnessing justice, the other accepting consequences. It's important that we make a display of such punishment to deter future acts."

"He burned down a house," Harkle explained. "With a family inside."

"And so he was punished," Bidderdoo added.

"By being polymorphed into a rabbit?" asked Regis.

"At least they can't hurt anyone in that state," said Bidderdoo.

"Except for that one," Harkle corrected. "The one with the big teeth, who could jump so high!"

"Ah, him," Bidderdoo agreed. "That rabbit was smokepowder! It seemed as if he was possessed of the edge of a vorpal weapon, that one, giving nasty bites!" He turned to Drizzt. "Can I borrow your cat?"

"No," the drow replied.

Regis growled with frustration. "You turned him into a rabbit!" he shouted, as if there could be no suitable reply.

Bidderdoo shook his head solemnly. "He remains happy and with bountiful leaves, brush, and flowers on the island."

"Happy? Is he man or rabbit? Where is his mind?"

"Somewhere in between, at this point, I would expect," Bidderdoo admitted.

"That's ghastly!" Regis protested.

"Time's passage will align his thoughts with his new body."

"To live as a rabbit," said Regis.

Bidderdoo and Harkle exchanged concerned, and guilty, glances.

"You killed him!" Regis shouted.

"He is very much alive!" Harkle protested.

"How can you say that?"

Drizzt put a hand on the halfling's shoulder, and when he looked up to meet the drow's gaze, Drizzt shook his head slowly, backing him down.

"Would that we could simply obliterate them all, that Longsaddle would know her days of old," Bidderdoo mumbled and left the room.

"The task that has befallen us is not a pleasant one," Harkle said. "But you don't understand . . ."

Drizzt motioned for him to stop, needing no further elaboration, for indeed, the drow did understand the untenable situation that had descended upon his friends, the Harpells. A foul taste filled his throat and he wanted to scream in protest of it all, but he didn't. Truly there was nothing to say, and nothing left for him to see in Longsaddle.

He informed Harkle, "We're traveling down the road to Luskan and from there to Icewind Dale."

"Ah, Luskan!" said Harkle. "I was to apprentice there once, long ago, but for some reason, they wouldn't let me into the famed Hosttower. A pity." He sighed profoundly and shook his head, but brightened immediately, as Harkle always did. "I can get you there in an instant," he said, snapping his fingers in such dramatic fashion, waving his hand with such zest, that he knocked over a lamp.

Or would have, except that Drizzt, his speed enhanced by magical anklets, darted forward in a blur, caught the lamp, and righted it.

"We prefer to walk," the drow said. "It's not so far and the weather is clear and kind. It's not the destination that matters most, after all, but the journey."

"True, I suppose," Harkle muttered, seeming disappointed for just a moment before again brightening. "But then, we could not have dragged *Sea Sprite* across the miles to Carradoon, could we?"

"Fog of fate?" Regis asked Drizzt, recalling the tale of how Drizzt and Catti-brie wound up in a landlocked lake with Captain Deudermont and his oceangoing pirate hunter. Harkle Harpell had created a new enchantment, which, as expected, had gone terribly awry, transporting the ship and all aboard her to a landlocked lake in the Snowflake Mountains.

"I have a new one!" Harkle squealed. Regis blanched and fell back, and Drizzt waved his hands to shut down the wizard before he could fully launch into spellcasting.

"We will walk," the drow said again. He looked down at Regis and added, "At once," which brought a curious expression from the halfling.

They were out of Longsaddle soon after, hustling down the road to the west, and despite Drizzt's determined stride, Regis kept pausing and glancing left and right, as if expecting the drow to turn.

"What is it?" Drizzt finally asked him.

"Are we really leaving?"

"That was our plan."

"I thought you meant to come out of town then circle back in to better view the situation."

Drizzt gave a helpless little chuckle. "To what end?"

"We could go to the island."

"And rescue rabbits?" came the drow's sarcastic reply. "Do not underestimate Harpell magic—their silliness belies the strength of their enchantments. For all the folly of Fog of Fate, not many wizards in the world could have so warped Mystra's Weave to teleport an entire ship and crew. We go and collect the rabbits, but then what? Seek audience of Elminster, who perhaps alone might undue the dweomer?"

Regis stammered, logically cornered.

"And to what end?" Drizzt asked. "Should we, new to the scene, interject ourselves in the Longsaddle's justice?" Regis started to argue, but Drizzt cut him short. "What might Bruenor do to one who burned a family inside a house?" the drow asked. "Do you think his justice would be less harsh than the polymorph? I think it might come at the end of a many-notched axe!"

"This is different," Regis said, shaking his head in obvious frustration. Clearly the sight of a man violently transformed into a rabbit had unnerved the halfling profoundly. "You cannot . . . that's not what the Harpells . . . Longsaddle shouldn't . . ." Regis stammered, looking for a focus for his frustration.

"It's not what I expected, and no, I'm not pleased by it."

"But you will accept it?"

"It's not my choice to make."

"The people of Longsaddle call out to you," Regis said.

The drow stopped walking and moved to a boulder resting on the side of the trail, where he sat down, gazing back the way they'd come.

"These situations are more complicated than they appear," he said. "You grew up among the pashas of Calimport, with their personal armies and thuggish ways."

"Of course, but that doesn't mean I accept the same thing from the Harpells."

Drizzt shook his head. "That's not my point. In their respective neighborhoods, how were the pashas viewed?"

"As heroes," Regis said.

"Why?"

Regis leaned back against a stone, a perplexed look on his face.

"In the lawless streets of Calimport, why were thugs like Pasha Pook seen as heroes?"

"Because without them, it would have been worse," Regis said, and caught on.

"The Harpells have no answer to the fanaticism of the battling priests, and so they respond with a heavy hand."

"You agree with that?"

"It's not my place to agree or disagree," said Drizzt. "The Harpells are the lid on a boiling cauldron. I don't know if their choice of justice is the correct one, but I suspect from what we were told that without that lid, Longsaddle would know strife beyond anything you or I can imagine. Sects of opposing gods battling for supremacy can be terrifying indeed, but when the fight is between two interpretations of the same god, the misery can reach new proportions. I saw this intimately in my youth, my friend. You cannot imagine the fury of opposing matron mothers, each convinced that she, and not her enemy, spoke the will of Lolth!

"You would have me descend upon Longsaddle and use my influence, even my blades, to somehow alter the situation. But what would that, even if I could accomplish anything, which I strongly doubt, loose upon the common folk of Longsaddle?"

"Better to let Bidderdoo continue his brutality?" Regis asked.

"Better to let the people with a stake in the outcome determine their own fate," Drizzt answered. "We've not the standing or the forces to better the situation in Longsaddle."

"We don't even know what that situation really is."

Drizzt took a deep, steadying breath, and said, "I know enough to recognize that if the problems in Longsaddle are not as profound as I—as we—fear, then the Harpells will find their way out of it. And if it is as dangerous then there's nothing we can do to help. However we intervene, one or even both sides will see us as meddling. Better that we go on our way. I think we are both unnerved by the unusual nature of the Harpells' justice, but I have to say that there is a temperate manner to it."

"Drizzt!"

"It is not a permanent punishment, for Bidderdoo can undo that which he has enacted," the drow explained. "He is neutering the warring offenders by rendering them harmless—unless, of course, he is turning the other side into carrots."

"That's not funny."

"I know," Drizzt admitted with an upraised hand and a smirk. "But who are we to intervene, and haven't the Harpells earned our trust?"

"You trust in what you saw?"

"I trust that if the situation alters and calls for a recanting of the justice delivered, the Harpells will undo the transformations and return the no-doubt shaken and hopefully repentant men to their respective places. Easier that than the dwarves of Mithral Hall sewing a head back on a criminal there."

Regis sighed and seemed to let it all go. "Can we stop back here on our return to Mithral Hall?"

"Do you want to?"

"I don't know," Regis answered honestly, and he too looked back toward the distant town, profound disappointment on his normally cheery face. "It's like Obould Many-Arrows," Regis mumbled.

Drizzt looked at him curiously.

"Everything is like Obould lately," the halfling went on. "Always the best of a bad choice."

"I will be certain to relay your feelings to Bruenor."

Regis stared blankly for just a moment then a grin widened and widened until it was followed by a belly-laugh, both heartfelt and sadly resigned.

"Come along," Drizzt bade him. "Let us go and see if we can save the rest of the world."

And so the two friends lightened their steps and headed down the western trail, oblivious to the prophecy embedded in Drizzt Do'Urden's joke.

CHAPTER

9

Pymian Loodran burst out the tavern door, arms flailing with terror. He fell as he turned, tearing the skin on one knee, but he hardly slowed. Scrambling, rolling, and finally getting back to his feet, he sprinted down the way. Behind him, out of the tavern, came a pair of men dressed in the familiar robes of the Hosttower of the Arcane, white with broad red trim, talking as if nothing was amiss.

"You don't believe he's fool enough to enter his own house," one said.

"You accepted the bet," the other reminded.

"He will flee for the gate and the wider road beyond," the first insisted, but even as he finished the other pointed down the road to a three-story building. The terrified man ascended an outside stairway on all fours, grabbing and pulling at the steps.

The first wizard, defeated, handed over the wand. "May I open the door, at least?" he asked.

"I would be an unappreciative victor to deny you at least some enjoyment," his friend replied.

They made their way without rushing, even though the stairway moved back along an alleyway and away from the main road, so the hunted man had passed out of sight.

"He resides on the second floor?" the first wizard asked.

"Does it matter?" said the second, to which the first nodded and smiled.

As they reached the alleyway, they came in sight of the second story door. The first wizard pulled out a tiny metal rod and began to mutter the first words of a spell.

"High Captain Kurth's man," his companion interrupted. He motioned with his chin across to the other side of the street where a large-framed thug had exited a building and taken a particular interest in the two wizards.

"Very fortunate," the first replied. "It's always good to give a reminder to the high captains." And he went right back to his spellcasting.

A few heartbeats later, a sizzling lightning bolt rent the air between the wizard and the door, blasting the flimsy wooden portal from its hinges and sending splinters flying into the flat.

The second wizard, already deep in chanting to activate the wand, took careful aim and sent a small globe of orange fire leaping up to the opening. It disappeared into the flat and a blood-curdling, delicious scream told both wizards that the fool knew it for what it was.

A fireball.

A moment later, one that no doubt seemed like an eternity to the fugitive in the flat—and his wife and children, too, judging from the chorus of screams coming forth from the building—the spell burst to life. Flames roared out the open door, and out every window and every unsealed crack in the wall as well. Though not a concussive blast, the magical fire did its work hungrily, biting at the dry wood of the old building, engulfing the entire second floor and roaring upward to quickly engulf the third.

As the wizards admired their handiwork, a young boy appeared on the third story balcony, his back and hair burning. Out of his mind with pain and terror, he leaped without hesitation, thumping down with bone-cracking force against the alleyway cobblestones.

He lay moaning, broken, and probably dying.

"A pity," said the first wizard.

"It's the fault of Pymian Loodran," the second replied, referring to the fugitive who had had the audacity to steal the purse of a lower-ranking acolyte from the Hosttower. The young mage had indulged too liberally of potent drink, making him easy prey, and the rogue Loodran had apparently been unable to resist.

Normally, Loodran's offense would have gotten him arrested and dragged to Prisoner's Carnival, where he likely would have survived, though probably without all of his fingers. But Arklem Greeth had decided that it was time for a show of force in the streets. The peasants were becoming a bit more bold of late, and worse, the high captains seemed to be thinking of themselves as the true rulers of the city.

The two wizards turned back to regard Kurth's scout, but he had already melted into the shadows, no doubt to run screaming to his master.

Arklem Greeth would be pleased.

"This work invigorates and wearies me at the same time," the second said to the first, handing him back his wand. "I do love putting all of my practice into true action." He glanced down the alley, where the boy lay unmoving, though still quietly groaning. "But . . ."

"Take heart, brother," the other said, leading him away. "The greater purpose is served and Luskan is at peace."

The fire burned through the night, engulfing three other structures before the area residents finally contained it. In the morning, they dug out eleven bodies, including that of Pymian Loodran, who had been so proud the day before when he had brought a chicken and fresh fruit home to his hungry family. A real chicken! A real meal, their first that was not just moldy bread and old vegetables in more than a year.

The first real meal his young daughter had ever known.

And the last.

* * * * *

"If I wanted to speak with Rethnor's brat, I'd've come here looking for him!" said Duragoe, a ranking captain in the Ship of High Captain Baram. He finished his rant and moved as if to strike the Ship Rethnor soldier who had tried to divert him to Kensidan's audience chamber, but held the slap when he noted the dreaded Crow himself entering the small antechamber with a look on his face that showed he'd heard every word.

"My father has passed the daily business onto my shoulders," Kensidan said calmly. In the other room, out of sight of Duragoe, High Captain Suljack quietly snickered. "If you wish to speak with Ship Rethnor, your discussion is with me."

"Me orders from High Captain Baram are to speak with Rethnor hisself. Ye'd deny a high captain a direct audience with another of his ilk, would ye?"

"But you are not a high captain."

"I'm his appointed speaker."

"As am I, to my father."

That seemed to fluster the brutish Duragoe a bit, but he shook his head vigorously—so much so that Kensidan almost expected to see bugs flying out of his ears—and brought one of his huge hands up to rub his ruddy face. "And yerself'll take me words to Rethnor, so he's getting it second-hand . . ." he tried to argue.

"Third-hand, if your words are Baram's words relayed to you."

"Bah yerself," Duragoe fumed. "I'm to say them exactly as Baram told me to say them!"

"Then say them."

"But I'm not for liking that ye're to then take them to yer father that we might get something done!"

"If anything is to be done due to your request, good Duragoe, the action will be at my command, not my father's."

"Are ye calling yerself a high captain, then?"

"I have done no such thing," Kensidan was wise to reply. "I handle my father's daily business, which includes speaking to the likes of you. If you wish to deliver High Captain Baram's concerns, then please do so, and now. I have much else to do this day."

Duragoe looked around and rubbed his grizzled and ruddy face again. "In there," he demanded, pointing to the room behind the young Kensidan.

Kensidan held up a hand to keep the man at bay and walked back just inside the audience chamber's door. "Be gone. We have private matters to discuss," he called, ostensibly to the guards within, but also to give Suljack the time he needed to move to the next room, from which he could eavesdrop on the whole conversation.

He motioned for Duragoe to follow him into the audience chamber and took his seat on the unremarkable, but tallest, chair in the room.

"Ye smell the smoke?" Duragoe asked.

A thin smile creased Kensidan's face, purposely tipping his hand that he was pleased to see that another of the high captains had taken note of the devastation the two Hosttower enforcers had rained upon a section of Luskan the previous night.

"Not a funny thing!" Duragoe growled.

"High Captain Baram told you to say that?" Kensidan asked.

Duragoe's eyes widened and his nostrils flared as if he was on the verge of catastrophe. "My captain lost a valuable merchant in that blaze," Duragoe insisted.

"And what would you ask Rethnor to do about that?"

"We're looking to find out which high captain the crook who brought the fires of justice down was working for," Duragoe explained. "Pymian Loodran's his name."

"I'm certain that I have never heard that name before," said Kensidan.

"And yer father's to say the same?" a skeptical Duragoe asked.

"Yes," came the even response. "And why would you care? Pymian Loodran is dead, correct?"

"And how would ye be knowing that if ye don't know the name?" the suspicious Duragoe asked.

"Because I was told that a pair of wizards burned down a house into which had fled a man who had angered the Hosttower of the Arcane," came the reply. "I assume the target of their devastation didn't escape, though I care not whether he did or not. Is it recompense you seek from the high captain who employed this Loodran fool, if indeed any high captain did so?"

"We're looking to find out what happened."

"That you can file a grievance at the Council of Five, and no doubt attach a weight of gold to repair your mercantile losses?"

"Only be fair. . . ." Duragoe said.

" 'Fair' would be for you to take up your grievance with the Hosttower of the Arcane and Arklem Greeth," said Kensidan. The Crow smiled again as the tough Duragoe shrank at the mere mention of the mighty archmage arcane.

"The events of last night, the manner and extent of the punishment exacted, were decided by Arklem Greeth or his enforcers," Kensidan reasoned. He sat back comfortably and crossed his thin legs at the knee, and even though Duragoe remained standing, he seemed diminished by the casual, dismissive posture of the acting high captain. "Whatever this fool—what did you name him? Loodran?—did to exact the ire of the Hosttower is another matter all together. Perhaps Arklem Greeth has a case to present against one of the high captains, should it be discovered that this fool indeed was in the employ of one, though I doubt that to be the case. Still, from the perspective of High Captain Baram, the perpetrator of his loss was none other than Arklem Greeth."

"We don't see it that way," Duragoe said with amusing vigor—amusing only because it reinforced the man's abject terror at the thought of bringing his bluster to the feet of the archmage arcane.

Kensidan shrugged. "You have no claim with Ship Rethnor," he said. "I know not of this fool, Loodran, nor does my father."

"Ye haven't even asked him," Duragoe said with a growl and an accusatory point of his thick finger.

Kensidan brought his hands up before his face, tapped his fingertips a couple of times, then folded the hands together, staring all the while at Duragoe, and without the slightest hint of a blink.

Duragoe shrank back even more, as if he had realized for the first time that he might be in enemy territory, and that he might be wise to take greater care before throwing forth his accusations. He glanced left and right nervously, sweat showing at his temples, and his breathing became noticeably faster.

"Go and tell High Captain Baram that he has no business with Ship Rethnor regarding this matter," Kensidan explained. "We know nothing of it beyond the whispers filtering through the streets. That is my last word on the subject."

Duragoe started to respond, but Kensidan cut him short with a sharp and loud, "Ever."

The thug straightened and tried to regain a bit of his dignity. He looked around again, left and right, to see Ship Rethnor soldiers entering the room, having heard Kensidan's declaration that their discussion was at its end.

"And pray do tell High Captain Baram that if he wishes to discuss any matters with Ship Rethnor in the future, then Kensidan will be pleased to host him," Kensidan said.

Before the flustered Duragoe could respond, the Crow turned to a pair of guards and motioned them to escort the visitor away.

As soon as Duragoe had exited the room, High Captain Suljack came back in through a side door. "Good fortune to us that Arklem Greeth overplayed his hand, and that this man, Loodran, happened to intersect with one of Baram's merchants," he said. "Baram's not an easy one to bring to our side. A favorable coincidence with favorable timing."

"Only a fool would leave necessary good fortune to coincidence at a critical time," Kensidan not-so-cryptically replied.

Behind him, the tough dwarf with the morningstars giggled, drawing a concerned look from High Captain Suljack, who had long ago realized that the son of Rethnor was many steps ahead of his every move.

"*Sea Sprite* will put in today at high tide," Kensidan said, trying not to grin as Suljack tried hard not to look surprised, "along with Lord Brambleberry of Waterdeep and his fleet."

"Int'resting times," High Captain Suljack managed to sputter.

* * * * *

"We could have gone straight to Icewind Dale," Regis remarked as he and Drizzt passed through the heavily guarded gate of Luskan. The halfling looked back over his shoulder as he spoke, eyeing the guards with contempt. Their greeting at the gate had not been warm, but condescending and full of suspicion regarding Regis's dark-skinned companion.

Drizzt didn't look back, and if he was bothered at all by the icy reception, he didn't show it.

"I never would have believed that my friend Regis would choose a hard trail over a comfortable bed in a city full of indulgences," the drow said.

"I'm weary from the comments, always the comments," Regis said. "And the looks of derision. How can you ignore it? How many times do you have to prove your worth and value?"

"Why should the ignorance of a pair of guards in a city that is not my home concern me at all?" Drizzt replied. "Had they not allowed us through, as with Mirabar when we ventured through there with Bruenor on our way to Mithral Hall, then their actions affect me and my friends, and so yes, that is a concern. But we're past the gate, after all. Their stares at my back don't invade my body, and wouldn't even if I were not wearing this fine mithral shirt."

"But you have been nothing other than a friend and ally to Luskan!" Regis protested. "You sailed with *Sea Sprite* for years, to their benefit. And that was not so long ago."

"I knew neither of the sentries."

"But they had to know you—your reputation at least."

"If they believed I was who I said I was."

Regis shook his head in frustration.

"I don't have to prove my worth and value to any but those I love," Drizzt said to him, dropping his arm across the halfling's shoulders. "And that I do by being who I am, with confidence that those I love appreciate the good and accept the bad. Does anything else really matter? Do the looks of guards I don't know and who don't know me truly affect the pleasures, the triumphs, and the failings of my life?"

"I just get angry . . ."

Drizzt pulled him close and laughed, appreciating the support. "If I ever get such a scornful look from you, Bruenor, or Catti-brie, then I will fret," the drow said.

"Or from Wulfgar," Regis remarked, and indeed that did put a bit of weight into Drizzt's stride, for he didn't truly know what to expect when he glanced upon his barbarian friend again.

"Come," he said, veering down the first side street. "Let us enjoy the comforts of the Cutlass and prepare for the road beyond."

"Drizzt Do'Urden! Huzzah!" a man on the opposite side of the road cheered, recognizing the drow who had served so well with the hero Captain Deudermont. Drizzt returned his wave and smile.

"And does that affect you more than the scornful looks from the guards?" Regis slyly asked.

Drizzt considered his answer for a few heartbeats, recognizing the trap of inconsistency and hypocrisy Regis had lain before him. If nothing really mattered other than the opinions of his friends, then such logic and insistence would need to include the positive receptions as well as the negative.

"Only because I allow it to," the drow answered.

"Because of vanity?"

Drizzt shrugged and laughed. "Indeed."

Soon after, they went into the Cutlass, a rather unremarkable tavern serving the docks of Luskan, particularly the returning or visiting merchant crews. So close to the harbor, it was not hard to understand the moniker given to Luskan: the City of Sails. Many tall ships were tied beside her long wharves, and many more sat at anchor out in the deeper waters—so many, it seemed to Drizzt, that the whole of the city could just up and sail away.

"I have never had the wanderlust for ocean voyages," Regis said, and when Drizzt tore his eyes from the spectacle of the harbor, he found the halfling staring up at him knowingly.

Drizzt merely smiled in reply and led his friend into the tavern.

More than one mug lifted to toast the pair, particularly Drizzt, who had a long history there. Still, most of the many patrons of the bustling place gave no more than a casual glance at the unusual pair, for few in the Cutlass were not considered unusual elsewhere.

"Drizzt Do'Urden, in the black flesh," the portly proprietor said as the drow came up to the bar. "What brings you back to Luskan after these long years?" He extended a hand, which Drizzt grasped and shook warmly.

"Well met, Arumn Gardpeck," he replied. "Perhaps I have returned merely to see if you continued to ply your trade—I take comfort that some things ever remain the same."

"What else would an old fool like me do?" Arumn replied. "Have you sailed in with Deudermont, then?"

"Deudermont? Is *Sea Sprite* in port?"

"Aye, and with a trio of ships of a Waterdhavian lord beside her," Arumn replied.

"And spoiling for a fight," said one of the patrons, a thin and weasely little man leaning heavily on the bar, as if needing its support.

"You remember Josi Puddles," Arumn said as Drizzt turned to regard the speaker.

"Yes," Drizzt politely replied, though he wasn't so sure he did remember. To Josi, he added, "If Captain Deudermont is indeed seeking a battle, then why has he come ashore?"

"Not a fight with pirates this time," Josi replied, despite Arumn shaking his head for the man to shut up, and nodding his chin in the direction of various patrons who seemed to be listening a bit too intently. "Deudermont is looking for a bigger prize!" Josi ended with a laugh, until he finally noticed Arumn's scowl, whereupon he shrugged innocently.

"There's talk of a fight coming in Luskan," Arumn explained quietly, leaning in close so that only Drizzt and Regis—and Josi, who similarly leaned in—could hear. "Deudermont sailed in with an army, and there's talk that he's come here with purpose."

"His army's not one for fighting on the open seas," Josi said more loudly, drawing a hush from Arumn.

The two quieted as Drizzt and Regis exchanged glances, neither knowing what to make of the news.

"We're going north, straightaway," Regis reminded Drizzt, and though the drow nodded, albeit half-heartedly, the halfling suddenly wasn't so sure of his claim.

"Deudermont will be glad to see you," Arumn said. "Thrilled, I'd bet."

"And if he sees you, you will stay and fight beside him," Regis said with obvious resignation. "I'd bet."

Drizzt chuckled but held quiet.

He and Regis left the Cutlass early the next morning, supposedly for Icewind Dale, but on a route that took them down by Luskan's docks, where *Sea Sprite* sat in her customary, honorary berth.

Drizzt met with Captain Deudermont and the brash young Lord Brambleberry before noon.

And the two companions from Mithral Hall didn't leave the City of Sails that day.

PART
2

MORAL GROUNDING

MORAL GROUNDING

I put Regis at ease as we walked out of Longsaddle. I kept my demeanor calm and assuring, my stride solid and my posture forward-leaning. Yet inside, my stomach churned and my heart surely ached. What I saw in the once-peaceful village shook me profoundly. I had known the Harpells for years, or thought so, and I was pained to see that they were walking a path that could well lead them to a level of authoritarian brutishness that would have made the magistrates at Luskan's wretched Prisoner's Carnival proud.

I cannot pretend to judge the immediacy and criticality of their situation, but I can certainly lament the potential outcome I so clearly recognized.

I wonder, then, where is the line between utilitarian necessity and morality? Where does one cross that line, and more importantly, when, if ever, is the greater good not served by the smaller victories of, or concessions to, basic standards of morality?

This world in which I walk often makes such distinctions based on racial lines. Given my dark elf heritage, I certainly know and understand that. Moral boundaries are comfortably relaxed in the concept of "the other." Cut down an orc or a drow with impunity, indeed, but not so a dwarf, a human, an elf?

What will such moral surety do in light of King Obould should he consider his unexpected course? What did such moral surety do in light of myself? Is Obould, am I, an anomaly, the exception to a hard and fast rule, or a glimpse of wider potential?

I know not.

Words and blades, I kept in check in Longsaddle. This was not my fight, since I had not the time, the standing, or the power to see it through to any logical conclusion. Nor could I and Regis have done much to alter the events at hand. For all their foolishness, the Harpells are a family of powerful magic-users. They didn't ask the permission or the opinion from a dark elf and halfling walking a road far from home.

Is it pragmatism, therefore, to justify my lack of action, and my subsequent assurances to Regis, who was so openly troubled by what we had witnessed?

I can lie to him—or at least, conceal my true unease—but I cannot do so to myself. What I saw in Longsaddle wounded me profoundly; it broke my heart as much as it shocked my sensibilities.

It also reminded me that I am one small person in a very large world. I hold in reserve my hope and faith in the general weal of the family Harpell. This is a good and generous family, grounded in morality if not in common sense. I cannot consider myself so wrong in trusting in them. But still . . .

Almost in answer to that emotional turmoil, I now find a situation not so different waiting for me in Luskan, but one from a distinctly opposing perspective. If Captain Deudermont and this young Waterdhavian lord are to be believed, then the authorities in Luskan have gone over to a dangerous place. Deudermont intends to lead something not quite a revolution, since the Hosttower of the Arcane is not the recognized leadership of the city.

Is Luskan now what Longsaddle will become as the Harpells consolidate their power with clever polymorphs and caged bunnies? Are the Harpells susceptible to the same temptations and hunger for greater power that has apparently infected the hierarchy of the Hosttower? Is this a case of better natures prevailing?

My fear is that in any ruling council where the only check against persecuting power is the better nature of the ruling principles is doomed to eventual, disastrous failure. And so I ride with Deudermont as he begins his correction of that abuse.

Here, too, I find myself conflicted. It is not a lament for Longsaddle that drives me on in Luskan; I accept the call because of the man who calls. But my words to Regis were more than empty comforts. The Harpells were behaving with brutality, it seemed, but I hold no doubt that the absence of suffocating justice would precipitate a level of wild and uncontrollable violence between the feuding clerics.

If that is true, then what will happen in Luskan without the power behind the throne? It is well understood that the Arcane Brotherhood keeps under its control the five high captains, whose individual desires and goals are often conflicting. These high captains were all men of violence and personal power before their ascent. They are a confederation whose individual domains have never been subservient to the betterment of the whole of Luskan's populace.

Captain Deudermont will wage his battle against the Hosttower. I fear that defeating Arklem Greeth will be the easier task than replacing the control exerted by the archmage arcane.

I will be there beside Deudermont, one small person in a very large world. And as we take actions that will no doubt hold important implications for so many people, I can only hope that Deudermont and I, and those who walk with us, will create good results from good desires.

If so, should I reverse my steps and return to Longsaddle?

—Drizzt Do'Urden

CHAPTER

Brilliant thought, this battling against wizards!" Regis said, ending in a shriek as he dived aside and behind a water trough. A lightning bolt blasted out the distant building's open front door, digging a small trench across the ground just to the side of where Regis had been.

"They are annoying," Drizzt said, accentuating his point by popping up from behind a barrel and letting fly three arrows in rapid succession from Taulmaril. All three, magically sizzling like lightning bolts of their own, disappeared into the darkness of the house and popped loudly against some unseen surface within.

"We should move," Regis remarked. "He—or they—know where we are."

Drizzt shook his head, but dived low and cried out as a second bolt of lightning came forth. It hit the barrel in front of him, blasting it to kindling and sending out a thick spray of foamy beer.

Regis started to cry out for his friend, but stopped when he discovered that Drizzt, moving with speed enhanced by magical anklets, was already crouching beside him.

"You may be right," the drow conceded.

"Call Guenhwyvar, at the least!" Regis said, but Drizzt was shaking his head through every word.

Guenhwyvar had fought beside them throughout the night, and the Astral panther had limitations on the time she could spend on the Prime Material Plane. Exceeding those limitations rendered Guenhwyvar a feeble and pained companion.

Regis glanced back down the road the other way, at a column of black smoke that rose into the late afternoon sky. "Where is Deudermont?" he lamented.

"Fighting at the Harbor Cross bridge, as we knew he would be."

"Some should have pushed through to our aid!"

"We're forward scouts," Drizzt reminded. "It was not our place to engage."

"Forward scouts in a battle that came too swiftly," Regis remarked.

Only the day before, Drizzt and Regis sat in Deudermont's cabin on *Sea Sprite*, none of them sure there would even be a fight. But apparently, over the course of the afternoon, the captain had communicated with one or more of the high captains, and had received a reply to his and Lord Brambleberry's offer. They'd received an answer from the Hosttower, as well. In fact, had not the ever-vigilant Robillard intercepted that reply with a diffusion of magical energies, seaman Waillan Micanty would have been turned into a frog.

And so it was on, suddenly and brutally, and the Luskan Guard, their loyalties split between the five high captains, had made no overt moves to hinder Deudermont's circuitous march.

They had gone north first, past the ruins of ancient Illusk and the grand open market of Luskan to the banks of the Mirar River. To cross out onto the second island, Cutlass by name, and assault the Hosttower directly would have been a foolish move, for the Arcane Brotherhood had established safehouses and satellite fortresses all over the city. Deudermont meant to shrink Arklem Greeth's perimeter of influence, but every step was proving difficult indeed.

"Let us hope we can extract ourselves from this unwanted delay," Drizzt remarked.

Regis turned his cherubic but frowning face up at Drizzt, recognizing from the drow's tone that his words were a not so subtle reminder of why they had been spotted by the wizard in the house in the first place.

"I was thirsty," Regis muttered under his breath, eliciting a grin from Drizzt and a sidelong glance at the shattered beer barrel that had so lured the halfling scout into the open.

"Wars will do that to you," Drizzt replied, ending in another yelp and shoving Regis down beside him as a third lightning bolt shot forth, skimming in across the top of the trough and taking out one of the higher boards in the process. Even as the ground shook beneath them from the retort, water began to drain out onto them.

Regis rolled one away, Drizzt the other, the drow coming up to one knee. "Drink up," he said, putting his bow to use again, first through the open door, then shattering a glass window and another on the second floor for good measure. He kept drawing and letting fly, his magical quiver forever replenishing his supply of enchanted missiles.

A different sort of missile came forth from the house, though, a trio of small pulses of magical light, spinning over each other, bending and turning and sweeping unerringly for Drizzt.

One split off at the last moment as the retreating drow tried futilely to dodge. It veered right into Regis's chest, singeing his vest and sending a jolt of energy through him.

Drizzt took his two hits with a grimace and a growl, and turned around to send an arrow at the window from which the missiles had flown. As he let fly, he envisioned his path to the house, looking for barriers against the persistent magical barrage. He sent another magical arrow flying. It hit the doorjamb and exploded with a shower of magical sparks.

Using that as cover, the drow sprinted at an angle to the right side of the street, heading behind a group of barrels.

He thought he would make it, expecting to dive past another lightning stroke, as he lowered his head and sprinted full out. He felt foolish for so over-balancing, though, as he saw a pea of flame gracefully arc out of the second floor window.

"Drizzt!" Regis cried, seeing it too.

And the halfling's friend was gone, just gone, when the fireball exploded all around the barrels and the front of the building backing them.

* * * * *

Sea Sprite tacked hard against the current at the mouth of the Mirar River. Occasional lightning bolts reached out at her from the northern bank, where a group of Hosttower wizards fought desperately to hold back Brambleberry's forces at the northern, longer span of Harbor Cross, the westernmost bridge across the Mirar.

"We would need to lose a score of men to each wizard downed, you claimed, if we were to have any chance," Deudermont remarked to Robillard, who stood beside him at the rail. "But it would seem that Lord Brambleberry has chosen his soldiers well."

Robillard let the sarcasm slip past as he, too, tried to get a better summation of the situation unfolding before them. Parts of the bridge were aflame, but the fires seemed to be gaining no real traction. One of Brambleberry's wizards had brought up an elemental from the Plane of Water, a creature that knew no fear of such fires.

One of the enemy wizards had responded with an elemental summoning of his own, a great creature of the earth, a collection of rock, mud, and grassy turf that seemed no more than a hillside come to life, sprouting arms of connected stone and dirt with boulder hands. It splashed into the river to do battle, its magical consistency strong enough to keep the waters from washing its binding dirt away, and both sides of the battle seemed intent on the other's elemental proxy—or proxies as more wizards brought forth their own otherworldly servants.

A trumpet sounded on the southern end of Harbor Cross, from Blood Island, and out from Brambleberry's position came a host of riders, all in shining armor, banners flying, spear tips glistening in the morning sun.

"Idiots," Robillard muttered with a shake of his head as they charged out onto the wide bridge.

"Harder to port!" Deudermont shouted to his crew, recognizing, as had Robillard, that Brambleberry's men needed support. *Sea Sprite* groaned under the strain as she listed farther, the river waters pounding into her broadside, threatening to drive her against one of the huge rocks that dotted the banks of the Mirar. She couldn't hold her position, of course, but she didn't need to. Her crack catapult team had a ball of fiery pitch away almost immediately, cutting through the wind.

A barrage of lightning bolts, capped by a fireball, slammed the bridge, and the riders disappeared in a cloud of smoke, flame, and blinding flashes.

When they re-emerged, a bit fewer in number, battered and seeming much less eager and much less proud, they were heading back the way they'd come.

Any sense of victory the Hosttower wizards might have felt, though, was short-lived, as *Sea Sprite's* shot thundered into the side of one of the structures they used for cover, one of several compounds that had been identified as secret safehouses for the Arcane Brotherhood. The wooden building went up in flames, and wizards scrambled for safety.

Brambleberry's men charged across the bridge once more.

"Fight the current!" Deudermont implored his crew as his ship groaned back the other way, barely holding her angle.

A second ball of pitch went flying, and though it fell short, it splattered up against the barricades used by the enemy, creating more smoke, more screaming, and more confusion.

Deudermont's knuckles whitened as he grasped the rail, cursing at the less-than-favorable winds and tide. If he could just get *Sea Sprite's* archers in range, they could quickly turn the tide of the fight.

The captain winced and Robillard gave an amused but helpless chuckle, as the leading edge of Brambleberry's assault hit a stream of evocation magic. Missiles of glowing energy, lightning bolts, and a pair of fireballs burst upon them, sending men writhing and flailing to the ground, or leaping from the bridge, which shook under the continuing thunder of the earth elemental's pounding.

"Just take her near to the wharf and debark!" the captain cried, and to Robillard, he added, "Bring it up."

"You wanted to hold our surprise," the wizard replied.

"We cannot lose this battle," Deudermont said. "Not like this. Brambleberry stands in sight of the Luskan garrison, and they are watching intently, knowing not where to join in. And the young lord has the Hosttower behind him and soon to awaken to the fighting."

"He has two secured bridges and the roads around the ruins of Illusk," Robillard reminded the captain. "And a busy marketplace as buffer."

"The Hosttower wizards need not cross to the mainland. They can strike at him from the northern edge of Closeguard."

"They're not on Closeguard," Robillard argued. "High Captain Kurth's men block the bridges, east and west."

"We don't know that Kurth's men would even try to slow the wizards," Deudermont stubbornly replied. "He has not professed his loyalty."

The wizard shrugged, gave another of his all-too-common sighs, and faced the northern bank. He began chanting and waving his arms. Recognizing that the Hosttower kept several safehouses in the northern district, Robillard and some of Brambleberry's men had set up a wharf just below the waves, but far enough out into the river for *Sea Sprite* to get up beside it safely. As Robillard ignited the magical dweomers he had set on the bridge, the front poles of the makeshift dock rose up out of the dark waters, guiding the helmsman.

Still, *Sea Sprite* wouldn't have been able to tack enough to make headway and come alongside, but again, Robillard provided the answer. He snapped his fingers, propelling himself through a dimensional gate back to his customary spot on the raised deck behind the mainsail. He reached into his ring, first to bring up gusts of wind to help fill the sails then to communicate with his own elemental from the Plane of Water. *Sea Sprite* lurched and bucked, the river slamming in protest against her starboard side. The elemental set itself against the port side and braced with its otherworldly strength.

The catapult crew let fly a third missile, and a fourth right behind.

On the bridge, Brambleberry's forces pushed hard against the magic barrage and the leading edge managed to get across just as *Sea Sprite* slid in behind the secret, submerged wharf, a hundred yards downriver. Planks went out beside the securing ropes, and the crew wasted no time in scrambling to the rail.

Robillard closed his eyes, trusting fully in his detection spell, and sensed for the magic target. Still with his eyes closed, the wizard loosed a searing line of lightning into the water just before the wharf's guide poles. His shot proved precise, severing the locking chain of the wharf. Buoyed by a line of empty barrels, free of its shackles, the wharf lifted up and broke the water with a great splash and surge. The crew poured down.

"Now we have them," Deudermont cried.

He had barely finished speaking, though, when a great crash sounded upriver, as a span of the century-old Harbor Cross Bridge collapsed into the Mirar.

"Back to stations!" Deudermont yelled to those crewmen still aboard. The captain, though, ran to the nearest plank and scrambled over the rail, not willing to desert his crewmen who had already left the ship. "Port! Port!" he cried for his ship to flee.

"By the giggling demons," Robillard cursed, and as soon as Deudermont hit the wharf running, the wizard commanded his elemental to let go the ship and slide under it to catch the drifting flotsam. Then he helped free *Sea Sprite* by pulling a wand and shooting a line of lightning at the heavy rope tying her off forward, severing it cleanly.

Before the crew aft could even begin to free that second heavy rope, *Sea Sprite* swung around violently to the left, and a pair of unfortunate crewmen flipped over the rail to splash into the cold Mirar.

Sputtering curses, the wizard blinked himself to the taffrail and blasted the second rope apart.

The first pieces of the shattered bridge expanse swept down at them. Robillard's elemental deflected the bulk, but a few got through, chasing *Sea Sprite* as she glided away toward the harbor.

Robillard ordered his elemental to rush up and push her along. He breathed a sigh of relief as he saw his friend Deudermont get off the makeshift dock, right before a large piece of the fallen bridge slammed against it, shattering its planking and destroying its integrity, as it, too, became another piece of wreckage. Barrels and dock planks joined the sweep of debris.

Robillard had to stay with the ship, at least long enough for his summoned monster to assist *Sea Sprite* safely out of the river mouth and into quieter waters. He never took his eyes off of Deudermont, though, thinking that his dearest friend was surely doomed, trapped as he was on the northern bank with only a fraction of Brambleberry's forces in support, and a host of angry wizards against them.

* * * * *

Drizzt saw it coming, a little burning ball of flame, enticing as a candlelight, gentle and benign.

He knew better, though, and knew, too, that he couldn't hope to get out of its explosive range. So he threw his shoulders back violently and kicked his feet

108

out in front of him, and didn't even try to break his fall as he slammed down on his back. He even resisted the urge to throw his arms out wide to somehow mitigate the fall, instead curling them over his face, hands grasping his cloak to wrap it around him.

Even covered as he was with the wet clothing and cloak, the darkness flew away when the fireball exploded, and hot flames bit at Drizzt, igniting a thousand tiny fires in his body. It lasted only an instant, mercifully, and winked out as immediately as it had materialized. Drizzt knew he couldn't hesitate—the wizard could strike at him again within the span of a few heartbeats, or if another wizard was inside the house, a second fireball might already be on its way.

He rolled sidelong away from his enemy to put out the little fires burning on his cloak and clothing, and even left the cloak smoldering on the ground when he leaped back to his feet. Again Drizzt ran full out, leaning forward in complete commitment to his goal, a tight strand of birch trees. He dived in headlong, rolling to a sitting position and curling up, expecting another blast.

Nothing happened.

Gradually, Drizzt uncoiled and looked back Regis's way, to see the halfling still crouched in the muddied ground behind the damaged water trough.

Regis's little hands flashed the rough letters of the drow silent alphabet, approximating the question, *Is he gone?*

His arsenal is depleted, perhaps, Drizzt's fingers replied.

Regis shook his head—he didn't understand.

Drizzt signaled again, more slowly, but the halfling still couldn't make sense of the too-intricate movements.

"He may be out of spells," the drow called quietly, and Regis nodded enthusiastically—until a rumble from inside the distant house turned them both that way.

Trailing a line of fire that charred the floorboards, it came through the open door, a great beast comprised entirely of flame: orange, red, yellow, and white when it swirled more tightly. It seemed vaguely bipedal, but had no real form, as the flames would commit to nothing but moving forward, and with purpose.

When it cleared the door, leaving smoking wood at every point of the jamb, it grew to its full, gigantic proportions, towering over the distant companions, mocking them with its intensity and its size.

A fiery monstrosity from the Elemental Plane of Fire.

Drizzt sucked in his breath and lifted Taulmaril, not even thinking to go to his more trusted scimitars. He couldn't fight the creature in close; of all the four primary elemental beasts, fire was the type any melee warrior was least capable of battling. Its flames burned with skin-curling intensity, and the strike of a scimitar, though it could hurt the beast, would heat the weapon as well.

Drizzt drew back and let fly, and the arrow disappeared into the swirl of flames.

The fire elemental swung around toward him and roared, the sound of a thousand trees crackling, then spat forth a line of flames that immediately set the birch stand aflame.

"How do we fight it?" Regis cried, and yelped as the elemental scorched the trough he hid behind, filling the air with thick steam.

Drizzt didn't have an answer. He shot off another arrow, and again had no way of knowing if it scored any damage on the creature or not.

Then, on instinct, the drow angled his bow to the side and let fly a third, right past the elemental to slam into, and punch through, the wall of the structure housing the wizard.

A cry from inside told him that he had startled the mage, and the sudden and angry turn of the fire elemental, back toward the house, confirmed what the drow had hoped.

He fired off a continual stream, then, a volley placed all around the wooden structure, blasting hole after hole and without discernable pattern. He judged his effect by the motions of the elemental, gliding one stride toward him, then one back at the wizard. For controlling such a beast was no easy feat, and one that required absolute concentration. And if that control was lost, Drizzt knew, the summoned creature would almost always take out its rage upon the summoner.

More arrows flashed into the house but to less effect; Drizzt needed to actually score a hit on the mage to turn the elemental fully.

But he didn't, and he soon recognized that the creature was inevitably edging his way. The wizard had adjusted.

Drizzt kept up the barrage anyway, and began moving away as he fired, confident that he could turn and outdistance the creature, or at least get to the water's edge, where the Mirar would protect him from the elemental's fury. He turned and glanced to the water trough, thinking to tell Regis to run.

But the halfling was already gone.

The wizard was protected from the arrows, Drizzt realized as the elemental bore down on him with renewed enthusiasm. The drow fired off a pair of shots into it for good measure then turned and sprinted back the way he'd come, around the edge of the building hit by the same fireball that had nearly melted him, which was burning furiously.

"Clever wizard," he heard himself muttering as he almost ran headlong into a giant web that stretched from building to building in the alleyway. He spun to see the elemental blocking the exit, its flames licking the structures to either side.

"Have at it, then," Drizzt said to the beast and drew his scimitars.

He couldn't really speak to a creature from an elemental plane, of course, but it seemed to Drizzt as if the monster heard him, for as he finished, the elemental rushed forward, its fiery arms sweeping ferociously.

Drizzt ducked the first swing then leaped out to his right just ahead of the second, running up the wall—and feeling that its integrity was diminished by the fires roaring within—and spinning into a back somersault. He came down in a spin, scimitars slashing across, backhand leading forehand, and both sent puffs of flame into the air as they slashed against the life-force that held those flames together into a physical, solid creature.

That second weapon, Icingdeath, sent a surge of hope through Drizzt, for its properties were not only affording him some substantial protection from flames, as it had done against the wizard's fireball, but the frostbrand scimitar took a particular pleasure in inflicting cold pain upon creatures with affinity to fire. The fire elemental shook off Twinkle's backhand hit, as it had all but ignored the shots from Taulmaril, but when Icingdeath connected, the creature seemed to burn less bright. The elemental whirled away and seemed to shrink in on itself, spinning around tightly.

Its flames burned brighter, white hot, and the creature came out enraged and huge once more.

Drizzt met its charge with a furious flurry of whirling blades. He shortened Twinkle's every stroke, using that blade to fend off the elemental's barrage of punches. He followed every strike with Icingdeath, knowing that he was hurting the elemental.

But not killing it.

Not anytime soon at least, and despite the protection of Icingdeath, Drizzt felt the heat of the magnificent, deadly beast. More than that, the power of the elemental's swings could fell an ogre even without the fiery accompaniment.

The elemental stomped its foot and a circular gout of flames rushed out from the point of impact, sweeping past Drizzt and making him hop in surprise.

The creature came forward and let fly a sweeping right hook, and Drizzt fell low, barely escaping the hit, which smashed hard into the burning building, crushing through the wooden wall.

From that hole came a blast of fire, and as it retracted, Drizzt leaped for the broken wood. He planted his foot on the bottom rim of the opening and came up flat against the wall, but only for the brief second it took him to swing his momentum and leap away into a backward somersault and turn, and as he came around, climbing higher across the alleyway, he somehow managed to sheathe his blades and catch on to the rim of the opposite building's roof. He ignored the stun of the impact as he crashed against the structure and scrambled, lifting his legs just above another heavy, fiery slug.

As fast as he went, though, the elemental was faster. It didn't climb the wall in any conventional sense, but just fell against it and swirled up over itself, rising as flames would climb a dry tree. Even as Drizzt stood tall on the roof, so did the elemental, and that building, too, was fully involved.

The elemental shot a line of flames at Drizzt, who dived aside, but still got hit—and though Icingdeath helped him avoid the brunt of the burn, he surely felt that sting!

Worse, the roof was burning behind him, and the elemental sent out another line, and another, all designed, Drizzt recognized, to seal off his avenues of escape.

The elemental hadn't done that in the alley, the drow realized as he drew out his scimitars yet again. The creature was smart enough to recognize a web, and knew that such an assault would have freed its intended prey. This creature was not dumb.

"Wonderful," Drizzt muttered.

* * * * *

"To the bridge!" Deudermont ordered, running from the collapsing wharf to the collection of rocks and crates, stone walls and trees his crewmen were using as cover. "We have to turn the wizards from Brambleberry's men."

"We be fifteen strong!' one man shouted back at him. "Or fifteen *weak,* I'm saying!"

"Two fireballs from extinction," said another, a fierce woman from Baldur's Gate who, for the last two years, had led almost every boarding charge.

Deudermont didn't disagree with their assessments, but he knew, too, that there was no other choice before them. With the collapse of the bridge, the Hosttower wizards had gained the upper hand, but despite the odds, Brambleberry's leading ranks had nowhere to retreat. "If we flee or if we wait, they die," the captain explained, and when he charged northeast along the river's northern bank, not one of the fifteen sailors hesitated before following.

Their charge turned into a series of stops and starts as the wizards took note of them and began loosing terrible blasts of magic their way. Even with the volume of natural and manmade cover available to them, it occurred to Deudermont that his entire force might be wiped out before they ever got near the bridge.

And worse, Brambleberry's force could not make progress, as every attempt to break out from the solid structures at the edge of the bridge was met with fire and ice, electricity and summoned monsters. The earth elemental was finally brought down by the coordinated efforts of many soldiers and friendly wizards, but another beast, demonic in nature, rushed out from the enemy wizards' position to take its place before any of Brambleberry's men had even begun to cheer the earth beast's fall.

Deudermont looked downriver, hoping to witness the return of *Sea Sprite*, but she was far into the harbor by then. He looked forlornly to the southeast, to Blood Island, where Brambleberry and the bulk of his forces remained, and was not encouraged to see that the young lord had only then begun to swing his forces back to the bridge that would bring them to the south-bank mainland and Luskan's market, where they could march up the riverbank and cross along the bridge farther to the east.

This would be a stinging defeat, the captain reasoned, with many men lost and few of the Hosttower's resources captured or destroyed.

Even as he began to rethink his assault, considering that perhaps he and his men should hunker down and wait for Brambleberry, a shout to the north distracted him.

The mob rushing to enter the fray, men and dwarves with an assortment of weapons, terrified him. The northwestern section of Luskan was known as the Shield, the district housing merchants' storehouses and assembling grounds for visiting caravans from Luskan's most important trading partner, the city of Mirabar. And the marchion of Mirabar was known to have blood connections among the Hosttower's highest ranks.

But the rumors of a rift between Mirabar and the Arcane Brotherhood were apparently true. Deudermont saw that as soon as it became obvious that the new force entering the fray was no ally of the Hosttower wizards. They swept toward the wizards' position, leading with a volley of sling bullets, spears, and arrows that brought howls of protest from the wizards and a chorus of cheers from Brambleberry's trapped warriors.

"Onward!" the captain cried. "They are ours!"

Indeed they were, at least those poor lesser mages who didn't possess the magical ability to fly or teleport from the field. Enemies closed in on them from three sides, and the wizards fleeing east, the only open route, could not hope to get past the next bridge before Brambleberry swept across and cut them off.

* * * * *

The fire elemental reared up to its full height, towering over the drow, who used the moment to rush ahead and sting it with Icingdeath before running back the other way as the great arms flashed in powerful swipes.

Thinking pursuit imminent, Drizzt cut to the side and dived headlong into a roll, turning halfway into the circuit in case he had to continue right over the edge of the building.

The elemental, though, didn't pursue. Instead it roared off the other way, burning a line over the front edge of the building, then down into the street where it left a scarred trail back to the house from which it had emerged.

* * * * *

"It's a pretty gem," the wizard agreed, staring stupidly at the little ruby pendant the halfling had spinning at the end of a chain. On every rotation, the gem caught the light, bending it and transforming it into the wizard's fondest desires.

Regis giggled and gave it another spin, deftly moving it back from the wizard's grabbing hand. "Pretty, yes," he said.

His smile disappeared, and so did the gem, scooped up into his hand in the blink of an astonished wizard's eye.

"What are you doing?" the mage asked, seeming sober once more. "Where did it . . . ?" His eyes widened with horror, and he started to say, "What have you done?" as he spun back toward the door just in time to see his angry elemental rushing into the house.

"Stay warm," Regis said, and he fell backward out of the same window through which he'd entered, hitting the alleyway in a roll and running along with all speed.

Fire puffed out every window in the house, and between the wooden planks as well. Regis came back into the street. Drizzt, smoke wafting from his shoulders and hair, emerged from the front door of the house behind the battered water trough.

They met in the middle of the road, both turning back to the house that served as battleground between the wizard and his pet. Booms of magical thunder accompanied the crackle of burning beams. The roar of flames, given voice by the elemental, howled alongside the screams of the terrified wizard. The outer wall froze over suddenly, hit by some magical, frosty blast, only to melt and steam almost immediately as the fire elemental's handiwork won the contest.

It went on for a few moments before the house began to fall apart. The wizard staggered out the front door, his robes aflame, his hair burned away, his skin beginning to curl.

The elemental, defeated, didn't come out behind him, but the man could hardly call it a victory as he toppled face down in the road. Regis and Drizzt ran to him, patting out the flames and rolling him over.

"He won't live for long without a priest," the halfling said.

"Then we must find him one," Drizzt replied, and looked back to the south-west, where Deudermont and Brambleberry assaulted the bridge. Smoke rose along with dozens of screams, the ring of metal, and the booming of magic.

Regis blew a long sigh as he answered, "I think most of the priests are going to be busy for a while."

CHAPTER

The building resembled a tree, its arms lifting up like graceful branches, tapering to elegant points. Because of the five prominent spires, one for each compass point and a large central pillar, the structure also brought to mind a gigantic hand.

In the centermost spire of the famous Hosttower of the Arcane, Arklem Greeth looked out upon the city. He was a robust creature, rotund and with a thick and full gray beard and a bald head that gave him the appearance of a jolly old uncle. When he laughed, if he wanted to, it came from a great belly that shook and jiggled with phony but hearty glee. When he smiled, if he pretended to, great dimples appeared and his whole face brightened.

Of course Arklem Greeth had an enchantment at his disposal that made his skin look positively flushed with life, the epitome of health and vigor. He was the Archmage Arcane of Luskan, and it wouldn't do to have people put off by his appearance, since he was, after all, a skeletal, undead thing, a lich who had cheated death. Magical illusions and perfumes hid the more unpleasant aspects of his decaying corporeal form well enough.

Fires burned in the north—he knew them to be the largest collection of his safehouses. Several of his wizards were likely dead or captured.

The lich gave a cackling laugh—not his jolly one, but one of wicked and perverse enjoyment—wondering if he might soon find them in the netherworld and bring them back to his side, even more powerful than they had been in life.

Beneath that laughter, though, Arklem Greeth seethed. The Luskar guards had allowed it to happen. They had turned their backs on law and order for the sake of the upstart Captain Deudermont and that miserable Waterdhavian brat, Brambleberry. The Arcane Brotherhood would have to repay the Brambleberry family, to be sure. Every one of them would die, Arklem Greeth decided, from the oldest to the infants.

A sharp knock on his door broke through the lich's contemplation.

"Enter," he called, never looking back. The door magically swung open.

In rushed the young wizard Tollenus the Spike. He nearly tripped and fell on his face as he crossed the threshold, he was so excited and out of sorts.

"Archmage, they have attacked us," he gasped.

"Yes, I am watching the smoke rise," said an unimpressed Greeth. "How many are dead?"

"Seven, at least, and more than two-score of our servants," the Spike answered. "I know not of Pallindra or Honorus—perhaps they managed to escape as did I."

"By teleporting."

"Yes, Archmage."

"Escape? Or flee?" Greeth asked, turning slowly to stare at the flustered young man. "You left without knowing the disposition of your superior, Pallindra?"

"Th-there was nothing . . ." the Spike stuttered. "All was—was lost . . ."

"Lost? To a few warriors and half a ship's crew?"

"Lost to the Mirabarrans!" the Spike cried. "We thought victory ours, but the Mirabarrans . . ."

"Do tell."

"They swept upon us like a great wave, m-men and dwarves alike," the Spike stammered. "We had little power remaining to us in the way of destructive magic, and the hearty dwarves could not be slowed."

He kept rambling with the details of their last stand, but Greeth tuned him out. He thought of Nyphithys, his darling erinyes, lost to him in the east. He had tried to summon her, and when that had failed, had brought from the lower planes one of her associates, who had told him of the betrayal of King Obould of the orcs and the interference of that wretched Bruenor Battlehammer and his friends.

Arklem Greeth had long wondered how such an ambush had been so carefully planned. He had feared that he had completely underestimated that Obould creature, or the strength of the truce between Many-Arrows and Mithral Hall. He wondered if it hadn't been a bit more than that strange alliance, though.

And now the Shield of Mirabar in Luskan had surprisingly joined into a fight that the Luskar guards had avoided.

A curious thought crossed Arklem Greeth's mind.

That thought had a name: Arabeth Raurym.

* * * * *

"They will be compensated," Lord Brambleberry assured the angry guard captain, who had followed the Waterdhavian lord all the way from Blood Island to the Upstream Span, the northern and westernmost of Luskan's three Mirar bridges. "Houses can be rebuilt."

"And children can be re-birthed?" the man snapped back.

"There will be unfortunate circumstances," said Brambleberry. "It's the way of battle. And how many were killed by my forces and how many by the Host-tower's wizards with their wild displays of magic?"

"None would have died if you hadn't started the fight!"

"My good captain, some things are worth dying for."

"Shouldn't that be the choice of him what's dying?"

Lord Brambleberry smirked at the man, but really had no response. He wasn't pleased at the losses incurred around the Harbor Cross Bridge. A fire had broken out just north of their perimeter and several homes had been reduced to smoldering ruin. Innocent Luskar had died.

The guard captain's forward-leaning posture weakened when Captain Deudermont walked over to stand beside Lord Brambleberry.

"Is there a problem?" the legend of Luskan asked.

"N-no, Mr. Deudermont," the guard stammered, for he was clearly intimidated. "Well, yes, sir."

"It pains you to see smoke over your city," Deudermont replied. "It tears at my heart as well, but the worm must be cut from the apple. Be glad that the Hosttower is on a separate island."

"Yes, Mr. Deudermont." The guard captain gave one more curt look at Lord Brambleberry then briskly turned and marched away to join his men and their rescue work at the site of the battle.

"His resistance was less strident than I'd anticipated," Brambleberry said to Deudermont. "Your reputation here makes this much easier."

"The fight has only just begun," the captain reminded him.

"Once we have them driven into the Hosttower, it will go quickly," Brambleberry said.

"They're wizards. They won't be held back by lines of men. We'll be looking over our shoulders for the entirety of the war."

"Then make it a short one," the eager Waterdhavian lord said. "Before my neck stiffens."

He offered a wink and a bow and hurried away, nearly bumping into Robillard, who was coming Deudermont's way.

"Pallindra is among the dead, and that is no small loss for the Hosttower, and an even greater one for Arklem Greeth, personally, for she was known to be fiercely loyal to him," Robillard reported. "And our scout of questionable heritage . . ."

"His name is Drizzt," Deudermont said.

"Yes, that one," the wizard replied. "He defeated a wizard by name of Huantar Seashark, paramount among the Hosttower at summoning elementals and demons—even elder elementals and demon lords."

"Paramount? Even better than Robillard?" Deudermont said to lighten the wizard's typically dour mood.

"Be not a fool," Robillard replied, drawing a wide smile from Deudermont, who took note that Robillard hadn't actually answered the question. "Huantar's prowess would have served Arklem Greeth well when our flames tickle at his towers."

"Then it's a day of great victory," Deudermont reasoned.

"It's the day we awakened the beast. Nothing more."

"Indeed," Deudermont replied, though in a tone that showed neither agreement nor concession, but rather more of a detached amusement as the captain looked past Robillard and nodded.

Robillard turned to see Drizzt and Regis coming down the road, the drow with a tattered cloak over one arm.

"You found a fine battle, I'm told," Deudermont called to them as they neared.

"Those two words rarely go together," said the drow.

"I like him more all the time," Robillard said so that only Deudermont could hear, and the captain snorted.

"Come, let us four retire to a warm hearth and warmer brandy, that we might exchange tales," said Deudermont.

"And cake," Regis said. "Never forget the cake."

* * * * *

"Cause or effect?" Arklem Greeth asked quietly as he padded down the hallway leading to the chambers of the Overwizard of the South Spire.

Beside him Valindra Shadowmantle, Overwizard of the North Tower, widely considered to be next in line to succeed Arklem Greeth—which of course was a rather useless tribute, since the lich planned to live forever—gave a derisive snort. She was a tiny thing, much shorter than Greeth and with a lithe moon elf frame that was many times more diminutive than the archmage arcane's burly and bloated animated vessel.

"No, truly," Arklem Greeth went on. "Did the Mirabarrans join in the battle against Pallindra and our safehouse because of the rumors that we had threatened to intervene with the stability of the Silver Marches? Or was their interference part of a wider revolt against the Arcane Brotherhood? Cause or effect?"

"The latter," Valindra replied with a flip of her long and lustrous black hair, so clear in contrast to eyes that seemed as if they had stolen all the blue from the waters of the Sword Coast. "The Mirabarrans would have joined in the fight against us whether Nyphithys had gone to Obould or not. This betrayal has Arabeth's stench all over it."

"Of course you would say that of your rival."

"Do you disagree?" the forceful elf said without the slightest hesitation, and Arklem Greeth gave a wheezing chuckle. It wasn't often that anyone had the courage to speak to him so bluntly—in fact, beyond Valindra's occasional outbursts, he couldn't remember the last person who had done so. Someone he had subsequently murdered, no doubt.

"You would then imply that Overwizard Raurym sent word ahead of the meeting between Nyphithys and King Obould," reasoned the lich. "Following your logic, I mean."

"Her treachery is not so surprising, to me at least."

"And yet you too have your roots in the Silver Marches," Greeth said with a wry grin. "In the Moonwood, I believe, and among the elves who wouldn't be pleased to see the Arcane Brotherhood bolster King Obould."

"All the more reason for you to know that I did not betray you," said Valindra. "I have made no secret of my feelings for my People. And it was I who first suggested to you that the Arcane Brotherhood would do well to stake a claim in the bountiful North."

"Perhaps only so that you could foil me later and weaken my position," said Greeth. "And that after you had gained my favor with your prodding for the spread of our influence. Clever of you to insinuate yourself as my heir apparent before leading me to a great chasm, yes?"

Valindra stopped abruptly and Arklem Greeth had to turn and look back to look at her. She stood with one arm on her hip, the other hanging at her side, and her expression absent any hint of amusement.

The lich laughed all the louder. "You are offended that I credit you with such potential for deviousness? Why, if half of what I said were true, you would be a credit to the twisted dealings of the dark elves themselves! It was a compliment, girl."

"Half was true," Valindra replied. "Except that I wouldn't be so clever to desire anything good to befall the Silver Marches or the worthless fools of the Moonwood. Were I to love my homeland, I might take your words as a compliment, though I insist I would have come up with something a bit less transparent than the plot you lay at my feet. But I take no pleasure in the loss of Nyphithys and the setback for the Arcane Brotherhood."

Arklem Greeth stopped smiling at the sheer bitterness and venom in the elf woman's words. He nodded somberly. "Arabeth Raurym, then," he said. "The cause for this troubling and costly effect."

"Her heart has ever remained in Mirabar," said Valindra, and under her breath, she added, "The little wretch."

Arklem Greeth smiled again when he heard that, having already turned back for the door to the South Tower. He recited a quiet incantation and waved a thick hand at the door. The locks clicked and humming sounds of various pitches emanated from all around the portal. At last, the heavy bar behind the door fell away with a clang and the portal swung open toward Arklem Greeth and Valindra, revealing a darkened room beyond.

The archmage arcane stared into the black emptiness for a few moments before turning back to regard the elf as she walked up beside him.

"Where are the guards?" the Overwizard of the South Tower asked.

Arklem Greeth lifted a fist up before his face and summoned around it a globe of purple, flickering flames. With that faerie fire "torch" thrust before him, he strode into the south tower.

The pair went up room by room, the stubborn and confident lich ignoring Valindra's continual complaints that they should go and find an escort of capable battle-mages. The archmage arcane whispered an incantation into every torch on the walls, so that soon after he and Valindra had made their way out of the room, the enchanted torches would burst into flame behind them.

They found themselves outside the door to Arabeth's private quarters not long after, and there the lich paused to consider all they had seen, or had not seen.

"Did you notice an absence of anything?" he asked his companion.

"People," Valindra dryly replied.

Arklem Greeth smirked at her, not appreciating the levity. "Scrolls," he explained. "And rods, staves, and wands—and any other magical implements. Not a spellbook to be found. . . ."

"What might it mean?" Valindra asked, seeming more curious.

"That the chamber beyond this door is equally deserted," said Greeth. "That our guesses about Arabeth ring true, and that she knew that we knew."

He ended with a grimace and spun back at Arabeth's door, waving his hand forcefully its way as he completed another spell, one that sent the reinforced, many-locked door flinging wide.

Revealing nothing but darkness behind.

With a growl, Valindra started past Greeth, heading into the room, but the archmage arcane held out his arm and with supernatural power held the elf back. She started to protest, but Arklem Greeth held up the index finger of his free hand over pursed lips, and again added the power of supernatural dominance, hushing the woman as surely as he had physically gagged her.

He looked back into the darkness, as did Valindra, only it wasn't as pitch black as before. In the distance to the left, a soft light glowed and a tiny voice lessened the emptiness.

Arklem Greeth strode in, Valindra on his heel. He cast a spell of detection and moved slowly, scanning for glyphs and other deadly wards. He couldn't help but pick up his pace, though, as he came to understand the light source as a crystal ball set on a small table, and came to recognize the voice as that of Arabeth Raurym.

The lich walked up to the table and stared into the face of his missing overwizard.

"What is she doing out of . . . ?" Valindra started to ask as she, too, came to recognize Arabeth, but Arklem Greeth waved his hand and snarled in her direction. Her words caught in her throat so fully that she fell back, choking.

"Well met, Arabeth," he said to the crystal ball. "You didn't inform me that you and your associate wizards would be leaving the Hosttower."

"I didn't know that your permission was required for an overwizard to leave the tower," Arabeth replied.

"You knew enough to leave an active scrying ball in place to greet any visitors," Greeth replied. "And who but I would deign to enter your chambers without permission?"

"Perhaps that permission has been given to others."

Arklem Greeth paused and considered the sly comment, the veiled threat that Arabeth had co-conspirators within the Hosttower.

"There is an army assembled against you," Arabeth went on.

"Against us, you mean."

The woman in the crystal ball paused and didn't blink. "Captain Deudermont leads them, and that is no small thing."

"I tremble at the thought," Arklem Greeth replied.

"He is a hero of Luskan, known to all," Arabeth warned. "The high captains will not oppose him."

"Good, then they won't get in my way," said Arklem Greeth. "So pray tell me, daughter of Mirabar, in this time of trial for the Hosttower, why is one of my overwizards unavailable to me?"

"The world changes around us," Arabeth said, and Arklem Greeth took note that she seemed a bit shaken, that as the reality of her choice opened wide before her, as expected as that eventuality had to be, doubts nibbled at her arrogant surety. "Deudermont has arrived with a Waterdhavian lord, and an army trained specifically in tactics for battling wizards."

"You know much of them."

"I made it a priority to learn."

"And you have not once addressed me by my title, Overwizard Raurym. Not once have you spoken to me as the archmage arcane. What am I to garner from your lack of protocol and respect, to say nothing of your conspicuous absence in this, our time of trial?"

The woman's face grew stern.

"Traitor," said Valindra, who had at last rediscovered her magically muted voice. "She has betrayed us!"

Arklem Greeth turned a condescending look over the perceptive elf.

"Tell me then, daughter of Mirabar," the archmage arcane said, seeming amused, "have you fled the city? Or do you intend to side with Captain Deudermont?"

As he finished, he closed his eyes and sent more than his thoughts or voice into the crystal ball. He sent a piece of his life essence, his very being, the undead and eternal power that had held Arklem Greeth from passing into the netherworld.

"I choose self-preservation, whatever course that—" She stopped and winced, then coughed and shook her head. It seemed as if she would simply topple over. The fit passed, though, and she steadied herself and looked back at her former master.

The crystal ball went black.

"She will run, the coward," said Valindra. "But never far enough. . . ."

Arklem Greeth grabbed her and tugged her along, hustling her out of the room. "Wraithform, at once!" he instructed, and he cast the enchantment upon himself, his body flattening to a two-dimensional form. He slipped through a crack in the wall then through the floor, rushing swiftly and in a nearly straight line back to the main section of the Hosttower with the similarly flattened Valindra close behind.

And not a moment too soon, both learned as they slipped out of a crease in the tower's main audience chamber just as the south tower was wracked by a massive, fiery explosion.

"The witch!" Valindra growled.

"Impressive witch," Greeth said.

All around them, other wizards began scrambling, shouting out warnings of fire in the south tower.

"Summon your watery friends," Arklem Greeth said to them all, calmly, almost amused, as if he truly enjoyed the spectacle. "Perhaps I have at last found a worthy challenge in this Deudermont creature, and in the allies he has inspired," he said to Valindra, who stood with her jaw hanging open in disbelief.

"Arabeth Raurym is still in the city," he told her. "In the northern section, with the Shield of Mirabar. I looked through her eyes, albeit briefly," he explained as she started to ask the obvious question. "I saw her heart, too. She means to fight against us, and has gathered an impressive number of our lesser acolytes to join her. I'm wounded by their lack of loyalty, truly."

"Archmage Arcane, I fear you don't understand," Valindra said. "This Captain Deudermont is not to be taken—"

"Don't tell me how I should take him!" Arklem Greeth shouted in her face, his dead eyes going wide and flashing with inner fires that came straight from the Nine Hells.

"I will take him roasted and basted before this is through, or I will devour him raw! The choice is mine, and mine alone. Now go and oversee the fighting in the south tower. You bore me with your fretting. We have been issued a challenge, Valindra Shadowmantle. Are you not up to fighting it?"

"I am, Archmage Arcane!" the moon elf cried. "I only feared—"

"You feared I didn't understand the seriousness of this conflict."

"Yes," Valindra said, or started to say, before she gasped as an unseen magical hand grabbed at her throat and lifted her to her tip-toes then right off the ground.

"You are an overwizard of the Hosttower of the Arcane," Arklem Greeth said. "And yet, I could snap your neck with a thought. Consider your power, Valindra, and lose not your confidence that it's considerable."

The woman squirmed, but could not begin to break free.

"And while you are remembering who you are, while you consider your power and your present predicament, let that remind you of who I am." He finished with a snort and Valindra went flying away, stumbling and nearly falling over.

With a last look at the grumbling archmage arcane, Valindra ran for the south tower.

Arklem Greeth didn't watch her go. He had other things on his mind.

CHAPTER

M y bilge rats are grumbling!" High Captain Baram protested, referring to the peasants who lived in the section of the city that was his domain, the northeastern quadrant of Luskan south of the Mirar. "I can't have fires taking down their hovels, now can I? Your war's not a cheap thing!"

"My war?" old Rethnor replied, leaning back in his chair. Kensidan sat beside him, his chair pushed back from the table, as was the protocol, and with his thin legs crossed as always.

"Word's out that you provoked Deudermont from the start," Baram insisted. He was the heaviest of the five high captains by far, and the tallest, though in their sailing days, he was the lightest of the bunch, a twig of a man, thinner even than the fretful Taerl, who very much resembled a weasel.

A bit of grumbling ensued around the table, but it ended when the most imposing of the five interjected, "I heard it, too."

All eyes turned to regard High Captain Kurth, a dark man, second oldest of the five high captains, who seemed always cloaked in shadow. That was due in part to his grizzled beard, which seemed perpetually locked in two days' growth, but more of that shadowy cloak was a result of the man's demeanor. He alone among the five lived out on the river, on Closeguard Island, the gateway to Cutlass Island, which housed the Hosttower of the Arcane. With such a strategic position in the current conflict, many believed that Kurth held the upper hand.

From his posture, it seemed to Kensidan that Kurth agreed with that assessment.

Never a boisterous or happy man, Kurth seemed all the more grim, and understandably so. His domain, though relatively unscathed so far, seemed most in peril.

"Rumors!" Suljack insisted, pounding his fist on the table, a display that brought a knowing smile to Kensidan's face. The perceptive son of Rethnor realized then where Baram and Kurth had heard the rumor. Suljack was not the most discreet of men, nor the most intelligent.

"These rumors are no doubt due to my father's—" Kensidan began, but such an outcry came at him as to stop him short.

"Ye're not for talking here, Crow!" Baram cried.

"Ye come and ye sit quiet, and be glad that we're letting ye do that!" Taerl, the third of the five, agreed, his large head bobbing stupidly at the end of his long, skinny neck—a neck possessed of the largest Adam's apple Kensidan had ever seen. Standing beside Taerl, Suljack wore an expression of absolute horror and rubbed his face nervously.

"Have you lost your voice, Rethnor?" High Captain Kurth added. "I've been told that you've turned your Ship over to the boy, all but formally. If you're wishing him to speak for you here, then mayhaps it's time for you to abdicate."

Rethnor's laugh was full of phlegm, a clear reminder of the man's failing health, and it did more to heighten the tension than to alleviate it. "My son speaks for Ship Rethnor, because his words come from me," he said, seemingly with great difficulty. "If he utters a word that I don't like, I will say so."

"High captains alone may speak at our gathering," Baram insisted. "Am I to bring all my brats and have them blabber at all of Taerl's brats? Or maybe our street captains, or might that Kurth could bring a few of his island whores. . . ."

Kensidan and Rethnor exchanged looks, the son nodding for his father to take the lead.

"No," Rethnor said to the others, "I have not yet surrendered my Ship to Kensidan, though the day be fast approaching." He began to cough and hock and continued for a long while—long enough for more than one of the others to roll their eyes at the not-so-subtle reminder that they might have been able to listen to a young, strong voice instead of all that ridiculous wheezing.

"It's not my war," Rethnor said at last. "I did nothing *to* Deudermont or *for* him. The archmage arcane has brought this on himself. In his supreme confidence, he has overreached—his work with the pirates has become too great an annoyance for the lords of Waterdeep. Solid information tells that he has made no friend of Mirabar, either. It's all perfectly reasonable, a pattern that has played out time and again through history, all across Faerûn."

A long pause ensued, where the old man seemed to be working hard to catch his breath. After another coughing session, he continued, "What is more amazing are the faces of my fellow high captains."

"It's a startling turn-around!" Baram protested. "The south spire of the Hosttower is burning. There is smoke rising from the northern section of the city. Powerful wizards lay dead in our streets."

"Good. A cleansing leaves opportunity, a truth not reflected in these long and frightened faces."

Rethnor's remark left three of the others, including Suljack, staring wide-eyed. Kurth, though, just folded his hands on his lap and stared hard at old Rethnor, ever his most formidable opponent. Even back in their sailing days, the two had often tangled, and none of that had changed when they traded their waterborne ships for their respective "Ships" of state.

"My bilge rats—" Baram protested.

"Will grump and complain, and in the end accept what is offered to them," said Rethnor. "They have no other choice."

"They could rise up."

"And you would slaughter them until the survivors sat back down," said Rethnor. "View this as an opportunity, my friends. Too long have we sat on our hands while Arklem Greeth reaps and rapes the wealth of Luskan. He pays us well, indeed, but our gains are a mere pittance beside his own."

"Better the archmage arcane, who knows and lives for Luskan . . ." Baram started, but stopped as a few others began to chuckle at his curious choice of words.

"He knows Luskan," Baram corrected, joining in the mirth with a grin of his own. "Better him than some Waterdhavian lord."

"This Brambleberry idiot has no designs on Luskan," said Rethnor. "He is a young lord, borne to riches, who fancies himself a hero, and nothing more. I doubt he will survive his folly, and even should he, he will take his thousand bows and seek ten thousand more cheers in Waterdeep."

"Which is leaving us with Deudermont," said Taerl. "He fancies nothing, and already has a greater reputation than Brambleberry'd ever imagine."

"True, but not to our loss," Rethnor explained. "Should Deudermont prevail, the people of Luskan would all but worship him."

"Some already do that," said Baram.

"Many do, if the numbers o' his swelling ranks are to be told," Taerl corrected. "I'd not've thought folks would dare follow anyone against the likes o' Arklem Greeth, but they are."

"And at no cost to us," said Rethnor.

"You would want Deudermont as ruler above us five, then?" asked Baram.

Rethnor shrugged. "Do you really think him as formidable as Arklem Greeth?"

"He has the numbers—*growing* numbers—and so he might prove to be," Taerl replied.

"In this fight, perhaps, but Arklem Greeth has the resources to see where Deudermont cannot see, and to kill quickly where Deudermont would need to send an army," said Rethnor, again after a long pause. It was obvious that the man was nearing the limit of his stamina. "For our purposes, we wouldn't be worse off with Deudermont at the head of Luskan, even openly, as Arklem Greeth is secretly."

He ended with a fit of coughing as the other high captains exchanged curious glances, some seeming intrigued, others obviously simmering.

Kensidan stood up and moved to his father. "The meeting is ended," he announced, and he called a Ship Rethnor guard over to thump his ailing father on the back in the hopes that they could extract some of that choking phlegm.

"We haven't even answered the question we came to discuss," Baram protested. "What are we to do with the city guard? They're getting eager, and they don't rightly know which side to join. They sat in their barracks on Blood Island and let Deudermont march through, and the northern span of the Harbor Cross fell into the water!"

"We do nothing with them," Kensidan replied, and Taerl shot him an angry look then turned to Kurth for support. Kurth, though, just sat there, hands folded, expression hidden behind his dark cloud.

"My father will not allow those guards who heed Ship Rethnor's call, at least, to act," the Crow explained. "Let Deudermont and Arklem Greeth have their fight, and we will join in as it decisively turns."

"For the winner, of course," Taerl reasoned in sarcastic tones.

"It's not our fight, but that does not mean that it cannot be our spoils," Suljack said. He looked at Kensidan, seeming quite proud of his contribution.

"The archmage arcane will turn the whole of the guard against Deudermont," Kurth warned.

"And against us for not doing just that!" Taerl added.

"Then . . . why . . . hasn't he?" Rethnor shouted between gasps and coughs.

"Because they won't listen to him," Suljack added at Kensidan's silent prompting. "They won't fight against Deudermont."

"Just what Luskan needs," Kurth replied with a heavy sigh. "A hero."

* * * * *

"Unexpected allies from every front," Deudermont announced to Robillard, Drizzt, and Regis. Lord Brambleberry had just left them, heading for a meeting with Arabeth Raurym and the Mirabarran dwarves and humans who had unexpectedly thrown in with Brambleberry and Deudermont in their fight against Arklem Greeth. "The first battles have been waged in the Hosttower and we have not even crossed to Closeguard Isle yet."

"It's going better than we might have hoped," Drizzt agreed, "but these are wizards, my friend, and never to be underestimated."

"Arklem Greeth has a trick or ten ready for us, I don't doubt," said Deudermont. "But with an overwizard and her minions now on our side, we can better anticipate and so better defeat such tricks. Unless, of course, this Arabeth Raurym is the first of those very deceptions. . . ."

He said it in jest, but his glance at Robillard showed anything but levity.

"She isn't," the wizard assured him. "Her betrayal of the Hosttower is genuine, and not unexpected. It was she, I'm sure—and so is Arklem Greeth—who betrayed the Arcane Brotherhood's advances into the Silver Marches. No, her survival depends upon Arklem Greeth losing, and losing everything."

"She has put everything on the line for our cause."

"Or for her own," Robillard replied.

"So be it," said Deudermont. "In any case, her defection brings us needed strength to ensure the destruction of the Hosttower's perverse leader."

"And then what?" Regis asked.

Deudermont stared hard at Regis and replied, "What do you mean? You cannot support the rule of Arklem Greeth, who is not even alive. His very existence is a perversion!"

Regis nodded. "All true, I expect," he replied. "I only wonder . . ." He looked to Drizzt for support, but then just shook his head, not believing himself qualified to get into such a debate with Captain Deudermont.

Deudermont smiled at him then moved to pour wine into four tallglasses, handing them around.

"Follow your heart and do what is good and just, and the world will be aright," Deudermont said, and lifted his glass in toast.

The others joined in, though the tapping of glasses was not enthusiastic.

"Enough time has passed," Deudermont said after a sip. He referred to Lord Brambleberry's bidding that he should go and join Brambleberry with Arabeth and the Mirabarrans. His intentional delay in going was a calculated stutter in bringing in the leadership, to keep the balance of power on Brambleberry's side. He and Deudermont were more impressive introduced separately than together.

Drizzt motioned to Regis to go with the captain. "The Mirabarrans will not yet understand my new relationship with their marchion," Drizzt said. "Go and represent Bruenor's interests at this meeting."

"I don't know Bruenor's interests," Regis quipped.

Drizzt tossed a wink at Deudermont. "He trusts the good captain," the drow said.

"Trusting the good captain's heart and trusting his judgment might be two entirely different matters, wouldn't you agree?" Robillard said to Drizzt when the other two had gone. He dumped his remaining wine into the hearth and moved to a different bottle, a stronger liquor, to refill his glass, and to fill another one for Drizzt, who gingerly accepted it.

"You don't trust his judgment?" the drow asked.

"I fear his enthusiasm."

"You loathe Arklem Greeth."

"More so because I know him," Robillard agreed. "But I know Luskan, too, and recognize that she is not a town predisposed to peace and law."

"What will we have when the smothering mantle of the Hosttower is removed?" asked Drizzt.

"Five high captains of questionable demeanor—men Captain Deudermont would have gladly killed at sea had he caught them in their swaggering days of piracy. Perhaps they have settled into reasonable and capable leaders, but . . ."

"Perhaps not," Drizzt offered, and Robillard lifted his glass in solemn agreement.

"I know the devil who rules Luskan, and the limits of his demands and depravations. I know his thievery, his piracy, his murder. I know the sad injustice of Prisoner's Carnival, and how Greeth cynically uses it to keep the peasants terrified even as they're entertained. What I don't know is what devil will come after Greeth."

"So believe in Captain Deudermont's premise," the drow offered. "Do what is good and just, and trust that the world will be aright."

"I like the open seas," Robillard replied. "Out there, I find clear demarcations of right and wrong. There is no real twilight out there, and no dawn light filtered by mountains and trees. There is light and there is darkness."

"To simplicity," Drizzt said with another tip of his glass.

Robillard looked out the window to the late afternoon skyline. Smoke rose from several locations, adding to the gloom.

"So much gray out there," the wizard remarked. "So many shades of gray. . . ."

* * * * *

"I didn't think you would have the courage to come here," High Captain Kurth said when Kensidan, seeming so much the Crow, walked unescorted into his private parlor. "You could disappear. . . ."

"And how would that benefit you?"

"Perhaps I just don't like you."

Kensidan laughed. "But you like what I have allowed to take place."

"What you have allowed? You speak for Ship Rethnor now?"

"My father accepts my advice."

"I should kill you for simply admitting that. It's not your prerogative to so alter the course of my life, whatever promise of better things you might expect."

"This need not affect you," Kensidan said.

Kurth snorted. "To get to the Hosttower, Brambleberry's forces will have to cross Closeguard. By allowing that, I'm taking sides. You and the others can hide and wait, but you—or your father—have forced a choice upon me that threatens my security. I don't like your presumption."

"Don't allow them passage," Kensidan replied. "Closeguard is your domain. If you tell Deudermont and Brambleberry that they cannot pass, then they will have to sail to the Hosttower's courtyard."

"And if they win?"

"You have my assurance—the assurance of Ship Rethnor—that we will speak on your behalf with Captain Deudermont should he ascend to lead Luskan. There will be no residual acrimony toward Ship Kurth for your reasonable decision."

"In other words, you expect me to be in your debt."

"No . . ."

"Do not play me for a fool, young man," said Kurth. "I was indenturing would-be leaders before your mother spread her legs. I know the price of your loyalty."

"You misjudge me, and my Ship," said Kensidan. "When Arklem Greeth is no more, the high captains will find a new division of spoils. There is only one among that group, outside of Ship Rethnor, who is truly formidable, and who will be able seize the right opportunity."

"Flattery . . ." Kurth said with a derisive snort.

"Truth, and you know it."

"I know that you said 'outside of Ship Rethnor' and not 'other than Rethnor,' " Kurth remarked. "It's official then, though secret, that Kensidan captains that Ship."

Kensidan shook his head. "My father is a great man."

"Was," Kurth corrected. "Oh, take no offense at a statement you know to be true," he added when Kensidan bristled, like a Crow ruffling the feathers of its black wings. "Rethnor recognizes it, as well. He is wise to know when it's time to pass along the reins of power. Whether or not he chose wisely is another matter entirely."

"Flattery . . ." Kensidan said, mocking Kurth's earlier tone.

Kurth cracked a smile at that.

"How long has Suljack suckled at your teat, boy?" Kurth asked. "You should coach him to stop looking at you for approval whenever he makes a suggestion or statement favorable to your position."

"He sees the potential."

"He is an idiot, and you know him to be just that."

Kensidan didn't bother replying to the obvious. "Captain Deudermont and Lord Brambleberry chart their own course," he said. "Ship Rethnor neither encourages nor dissuades them, but seeks only to find profit in the wake."

"I don't believe you."

Kensidan shrugged.

"Will Arklem Greeth believe you if he proves victorious?"

"Will Captain Deudermont understand your refusal to allow passage across Closeguard if he wins the fight?"

"Should we just draw sides now and be done with it?"

"No," Kensidan answered with a tone of finality that stopped Kurth cold. "No, none of us are served in this fight. In the aftermath, likely, but not in the fight. If you throw in with Greeth against Deudermont, and with the implication that you would then use a successful Arklem Greeth against Ship Rethnor, then I . . . then my father would need to throw in with Deudermont to prevent such an outcome. Suljack will follow our lead. Baram and Taerl would find themselves isolated if they followed yours, you being out here on Closeguard, don't you think? Neither of them would stand against Brambleberry and Deudermont for a few days, and how much help would the wretch Arklem Greeth send them, after all?"

Kurth laughed. "You have it all charted, it seems."

"I see the potential for gain. I hedge against the potential for loss. My father raised no fool."

"Yet you are here, alone."

"And my father didn't send me out this day without an understanding of High Captain Kurth, a man he respects above all others in Luskan."

"More flattery."

"Deserved, I'm told. Was I misinformed?"

"Go home, young fool," Kurth said with a wave of his hand, and Kensidan was more than happy to oblige.

You heard that? Kensidan asked the voice in his head as soon as he had exited the high captain's palace, making his way with all speed to the bridge, where his men waited.

Of course.

The assault on the Hosttower will be much more difficult by sea.

High Captain Kurth will allow passage, the voice assured him.

CHAPTER

13

Help me! They want to kill me!" the man cried.

He ran to the base of the stone tower, where he began pounding on the ironbound wooden door. Though he wore no robes, the nondescript fellow was known to be a wizard.

"Out of spells and tricks, then?" one of the sentries called down. Beside the sentry, his companion chuckled then elbowed him and nodded for him to look out across the square to the approaching warrior.

"Wouldn't want to be this one," the second sentry said.

The first looked down at the desperate wizard. "Threw a few bolts at that one, did you? I'm thinking I'd rather punch my fist through a wasp nest."

"Let me in, you fools!" the wizard yelled up. "He'll kill me."

"We're not doubting that."

"He is a drow!" the wizard yelled. "Can you not see that? You would side with a dark elf against one of your own race?"

"Aye, a drow by the name of Drizzt Do'Urden," the second sentry shouted back. "And he's working for Captain Deudermont. You wouldn't expect us to go against the master of *Sea Sprite,* would you?"

The wizard started to protest, but stopped as reality settled in. The guards weren't going to help him. He rolled his back to the door so he could face the approaching drow. Drizzt came across the square, weapons in hand, his expression emotionless.

"Well met, Drizzt Do'Urden," one of the sentries called down as the drow stopped a few steps from the whimpering wizard. "If you're thinking to kill him, then let us turn away so that we can't bear witness against you." The other sentry laughed.

"You are caught, fairly and fully," Drizzt said to the frantic man. "Do you accept that?"

"You have no right!"

"I have my blades, you have no spells remaining. Need I ask you again?"

Perhaps it was the deathly calm of Drizzt's tone, or the laughter of the amused sentries, but the wizard found a moment of strength then, and straightened against the door, squaring his shoulders to his adversary. "I am an overwizard of the Hosttower of . . ."

"I know who you are, Blaskar Lauthlon," Drizzt replied. "And I witnessed your work. There are dead men back there, by your hand."

"They attacked my position! My companions are dead . . ."

"You were offered quarter."

"I was bade to surrender, and to one who has no authority."

"Few in Luskan would agree with that, I fear."

"Few in Luskan would suffer a drow to live!"

Drizzt chuckled at that. "And yet, here I am."

"Be gone from this place at once!" Blaskar yelled. "Or feel the sting of Arklem Greeth!"

"I ask only one more time," said Drizzt. "Do you yield?"

Blaskar straightened his shoulders again. He knew his fate, should he surrender.

He spat at Drizzt's feet—feet that moved too quickly to be caught by the spittle, slipping back a step then rushing forward with blinding speed. Blaskar shrieked as the drow's blades came up and closed on him. Above, the guards also cried out in surprise, though their yelps seemed more full of glee than fear.

Drizzt's scimitars hummed in a cross, then a second, one blade stabbing left past Blaskar's head to prod the door, the other cutting the air just above the man's brown hair. The flurry went on for many moments, scimitars spinning, Drizzt spinning, blades slashing at every conceivable angle.

Blaskar yelled a couple of times. He tried to cover up, but really had no way to avoid any of the drow's stunningly swift, sure movements. When the barrage ended, the wizard stood in a slight crouch, arms tight against him and afraid to move, as if expecting that pieces of his extremities would simply fall away.

But he hadn't been touched.

"What?" he said, before realizing that the show had been merely to put Drizzt into just the right position.

The drow, much closer to Blaskar than when the flurry began, punched out, and the pommel of Icingdeath smashed hard into the overwizard's face, slamming him up against the door.

He held his balance for just a moment, shooting an accusatory look and pointing a finger at Drizzt before crumbling to the ground.

"Bet that hurt," said one of the sentries from above.

Drizzt looked up to see that four men, not two, stared down at him, admiring his handiwork.

"I thought you'd cut him to bits," said one, and the others laughed.

"Captain Deudermont will arrive here soon," Drizzt replied. "I expect you will open the door for him."

The sentries all nodded. "Only four of us here," one mentioned, and Drizzt looked at him curiously.

"Most aren't at their posts," another explained. "They're watching over their families as the battles draw near."

"We got no orders to join in for either side," said the third.

"Nor to stay out," the last added.

"Captain Deudermont fights for justice, for all of Luskan," Drizzt said to them. "But I understand that your choice, should you make it, will be based on pragmatism."

"Meaning?" asked the first.

"Meaning that you have no desire to be on the side that loses," Drizzt said with a grin.

"Can't argue that."

"And I cannot blame you for it," said the drow. "But Deudermont will prevail, don't doubt. Too long has the Hosttower cast a dark shadow over Luskan. It was meant to be a shining addition to the beauty of the city, but under the control of the lich Greeth, it has become a tombstone. Join with us, and we'll take the fight to Greeth's door—and through it."

"Do it fast, then," said one of the men, and he motioned out toward the wider city, where fires burned and smoke clouded nearly every street, "before there's nothing left to win."

* * * * *

A woman ran screaming out onto the square, flames biting at her hair and clothing. She tried to drop and roll, but merely dropped and squirmed as the fire consumed her.

More screams emanated from the house she'd run from, and flashes of lightning left thundering reports. An upper story window shattered and a man came flying out, waving his arms wildly all the way to the hard ground. He pulled himself up, or tried to, but fell over, grasping at a torn knee and a broken leg.

A wizard appeared at the window from which the man had fallen, and pointed a slender wand down at him, sneering with wicked glee.

A hail of arrows arched above the square from rooftops across the way, and the wizard staggered back into the room, killed by the unexpected barrage.

The battle raged with missiles magical and mundane. A group of warriors charged across the square at the house, only to be driven back by a devastating volley of magical flame and lightning.

A second magical volley rose up just south of the house, aimed at it, and despite all the wards of the Hosttower wizards trapped inside, a corner of the building roared in flames.

From a large palace some distance to the northwest, High Captains Taerl and Suljack watched it all with growing fascination.

"It's the same tale each time," Suljack remarked.

"No less than twenty o' Deudermont's followers dead," Taerl replied, to which Suljack merely shrugged.

"Deudermont will replace archers and swordsmen far more readily than Arklem Greeth will find wizards to throw fireballs at them," Suljack said. "This is to end the same way all of them have, with Deudermont's men drawing out every ounce of magical energy from Greeth's wizards then rushing over them.

"And look out in the harbor," he went on, pointing to the masts of four ships anchored in the waterway between Fang and Harbor Arm Islands, and between Fang Island and Cutlass Island, which housed the Hosttower. "Word is that Kurth's shut the Sea Tower down, so it can't oppose *Sea Sprite,* or anyone else that tries to put in on southern Cutlass. Deudermont's already got Greeth blocked east, west, and north, and south'll be closed within a short stretch. Arklem Greeth's not long for the world, or not long for Luskan, at least."

"Bah, but ye're not remembering the power o' that one!" Taerl protested. "He's the archmage arcane!"

"Not for long."

"When those boys get close to the Hosttower, you'll see how long," Taerl argued. "Kurth won't let them cross Closeguard, and going at Arklem Greeth by sea alone will fill the harbor with bodies, whether Sea Tower's to oppose them or not. More likely, Greeth's wanting Sea Tower empty so that Deudermont and his boys'll foolishly walk onto Cutlass Island and he can sink their ships behind them."

"Nothing foolish about Captain Deudermont," Suljack reminded his companions, something every living man who ever sailed the Sword Coast knew all too well. "And nothing weak about that dog Robillard who walks beside him. If this was just Brambleberry, I'd be thinking you're right, friend."

A loud cheer went up across the way, and Suljack and Taerl looked across to see Deudermont riding down one of the side streets, the crowd swelling behind him. Both high captains turned to the wizards' safehouse, knowing the fight would be over all too soon.

"He's to win, I tell you," said Suljack. "We should all just throw in with him now and ride the wind that's filling Deudermont's sails."

The stubborn Taerl snorted and turned away, but Suljack grabbed him and turned him right back, pointing to a group of men flanking Deudermont. They wore the garb of city guards, and seemed as enthusiastic as the men Brambleberry had brought along from Waterdeep—more so, even.

"Your boys," Suljack said with a grin.

"Their choice, not me own," the high captain protested.

"But you didn't stop them," Suljack replied. "Some of Baram's boys are down there, too."

Taerl didn't respond to Suljack's knowing grin. The fight for Luskan was going exactly as Kensidan had predicted, to Arklem Greeth's ultimate dismay, no doubt.

* * * * *

"Fires in the east, fires in the north," Valindra said to Arklem Greeth, the two of them looking out from the Hosttower to the same scene as Taerl and Suljack, though from an entirely different direction and an entirely different perspective.

"Anyone of worth to us will have the spells needed to get back to the Hosttower," Greeth replied.

"Only those skilled in such schools," said Valindra. "Unlike Blaskar—we have not heard from him."

"My mistake in appointing him overwizard," said Greeth. "As it was my mistake in ever trusting that Raurym creature. I will see her dead before this is ended, don't you doubt that."

"I don't, but I wonder to what end."

Arklem Greeth turned on her fiercely, but Valindra Shadowmantle didn't back down.

"They press us," she said.

"They will not cross Closeguard and we can fend them off from the rocky shores of Cutlass," Greeth replied. "Station our best invokers and our most clever illusionists to every possible landing point, and guard their positions with every magical fortification you can assemble. Robillard and whatever other wizards Deudermont holds at his disposal are not to be taken lightly, but as they are aboard ship and we're on solid ground, the advantage is ours."

"For how long?"

"For as long as need be!" Arklem Greeth yelled, his undead eyes glowing with inner fires. He calmed quickly, though, and nodded, conceding, "You are correct, of course. Deudermont and Brambleberry will be relentless and patient as long as Luskan accepts them. Perhaps it's time we turn that game back on them."

"You will speak with the high captains?"

Arklem Greeth scoffed before she ever finished the question. "With Kurth, perhaps, or perhaps not. Are you so certain those foolish pirates are not in fact behind this peasant uprising?"

"Deudermont learned of our complicity in the piracy along the Sword Coast, I'm told."

"And suddenly found a willing ally in Brambleberry, and a willing traitor in Arabeth Raurym? Convenience is often a matter of careful planning, and as soon as I'm finished with the idiot Deudermont, I intend to have a long discussion with each of the high captains. One I doubt any of them will enjoy."

"And until then?"

"Allow that to be my concern," Arklem Greeth told her. "You see to the defense of Cutlass Island. But first pry Overwizard Rimardo from his library in the east tower and bid him go and learn what has happened to Blaskar. And remind our muscular friend that if he is too busy shaking hands, he'll have one less arm available for casting spells."

"Are you sure I shouldn't go find Blaskar while Rimardo prepares the defenses?"

"If Rimardo is too stupid or distracted to do his work correctly, I would rather have the consequences befall him when I'm not standing right behind him," said the lich. He grinned wickedly, taking Valindra's measure with his undressing stare. "Besides, you only wish to go that you might find an opportunity to unearth our dear Arabeth. Nothing would please you more than destroying that one, yes?"

"Guilty as charged, Archmage."

Arklem Greeth lifted a cold hand to cup Valindra's narrow elf chin. "If I were only alive," he said wistfully. "Or perhaps, if you were only dead."

Valindra swallowed hard at that one, and fell back a step, out of Greeth's deathly cold grasp. The archmage arcane cackled his wheezing laugh.

"It's time to punish them," he said. "Arabeth Raurym most of all."

* * * * *

Late that night, Arklem Greeth, a gaseous and insubstantial cloud, slipped out of the Hosttower of the Arcane. He drifted across Closeguard Island and resisted the urge to go into Kurth Tower and disturb the high captain's sleep.

Instead, he went right past the structure and across the bridge to the mainland, to Luskan proper. Just off the bridge, he turned left, north, and entered an overgrown region of brambles, creepers, broken towers, and general disrepair: Illusk, the only remaining ruins of an ancient city. It wasn't more than a couple of acres—at least above ground. There was much more below, including damp old tunnels reaching out to Closeguard Island, and to Cutlass Island beyond that. The place smelled of rotting vegetation, for Illusk also served as a dump for waste from the open market just to the north.

Illusk was entirely unpleasant to the sensibilities of the average man. To the lich, however, there was something special there. It was the place where Arklem Greeth had at last managed the transformation from living man to undead lich. In that ancient place with its ancient graves, the boundary between life and death was a less tangible barrier. It was a place of ghosts and ghouls, and the people of Luskan knew that well. Among the Hosttower's greatest accomplishments, the first real mark the wizards had put upon Luskan during its founding so long ago, was an enchantment of great power that kept the living dead in their place, in Illusk. That was a favor that had, of course, elicited great favor among the people of the City of Sails for the founders of the Hosttower of the Arcane.

Arklem Greeth had studied that dweomer in depth before his transformation, and though he too was an undead thing, the power of the dweomer could not touch him.

He came back to corporeal form in the center of the ruins, and sensed immediately that he was being watched by a hungry ghoul, but the realization only humored him. Few undead creatures would dare approach a lich of his power, and fewer still could refuse to approach him if he so beckoned.

Still grinning wickedly, Arklem Greeth moved to the northwestern tip of the ruins, on the banks of the Mirar. He unfastened a large belt pouch and carefully pulled it open, revealing powdered bone.

Arklem Greeth walked along the bank to the south, chanting softly and sprinkling the bone dust as he went. He took greater care when he came around to the southern edge of the ruins, making certain he wasn't being watched. It took him some time, and a second belt pouch full of bone dust, to pace the entirety of the cordoned area—to set the countering magic in place.

The ghouls and ghosts were free. Greeth knew it, but they didn't.

He went to a mausoleum near the center of the ruins, the very structure in which he'd completed his transformation so long ago. The door was heavily bolted and locked, but the lich rattled off a spell that transformed him once more into a gaseous cloud and he slipped through a seam in the door. He turned corporeal immediately upon entering, wanting to feel the hard, wet stones of the ancient grave beneath his feet.

He padded down the stairs, his undead eyes having no trouble navigating through the pitch dark. On the landing below, he found the second portal, a heavy stone trapdoor. He reached his arm out toward it, enacted a spell of tele-kinesis, and reached farther with magical fingers, easily lifting the block aside.

Down he went, into the dank tunnel, and there he sent out his magical call, gathered the ghouls and ghosts, and told them of their freedom.

And there, when the monsters had gone, Arklem Greeth placed one of his most prized items, an orb of exceptional power, an artifact he had created to reach into the netherworld and bring forth the residual life energies of long dead individuals.

Cities of men had been situated on that location for centuries, and before the cities, tribes of barbarians had settled there. Each settlement had been built upon the bones of the previous—the bones of the buildings, and the bones of the inhabitants.

Called by the orb of Arklem Greeth, the latter part of the foundation of Luskan began to stir, to awaken, to rise.

CHAPTER

Drizzt? Drizzt?" a nervous Regis asked. With his eyes fixated on the door of the house across the lane, he reached back to tug at his friend's sleeve. "Drizzt?" he asked again, flailing his hand around. He finally caught on to the truth and turned around to see that his friend was gone.

Across the lane, the woman screamed again, and the tone of her shriek, bloodcurdling and full of primal horror, told Regis exactly what was happening there. The halfling summoned his courage and took up his little mace in one hand, his ruby pendant in the other. As he forced himself across the lane, calling softly for Drizzt with every step, he reminded himself of the nature of his enemy and let the useless pendant drop back to the end of its chain.

The screaming was replaced by gasping and whimpering and the shuffling of furniture as Regis neared the house. He saw the woman rush by a window to the right of the door, her arm whipping out behind her—likely upending a chair to slow her pursuer.

Regis darted to that window and saw that her impromptu missile had some effect, tripping up a wretched ghoul.

Regis fought hard trying to breathe at the sight of the hideous thing. It had once been a man, but was hardly recognizable now, with its emaciated appearance, skin stretched tight over bone, lips rotted away to reveal fangs clotted with strips of freshly devoured flesh. The ghoul grabbed the chair in both hands, nails as long as fingers scraping at the wood, and brought it up to its mouth. Snarling and grumbling with rage, needing to bite something, it seemed, the ghoul tore into the chair before flinging it aside.

The woman screamed again.

The ghoul charged, but so intent was it on the woman that it never noticed the small form crouched on the window pane.

As the ghoul rushed past, Regis leaped out. Both hands clutching his mace, he used his flight and all his strength to whip the weapon across the back of the passing ghoul's head. Bone crackled and withered skin tore free. The ghoul stumbled and fell off to the side, crashing down amidst more chairs.

Regis, too, landed hard, overbalanced from his heavy swing. He caught himself quickly, though, and set with a wide stance facing the fallen ghoul, praying that he had hit it hard enough to keep it down.

No such luck—the ghoul pulled itself back up and turned its lipless grin at the halfling.

"Come on, then, and be done with it," Regis heard himself say, and as if in response, the ghoul leaped at him.

The halfling batted aside its flailing arms, knowing that the poison and filth, the essence of undeath in those clawlike fingernails could render a man or halfling immobile. Back and forth he whipped his mace, slapping against the ghoul's arms, defeating the weight of every attack.

But he still got scratched, and felt his knees wobble against the vile poison. And while his swings were stinging the ghoul, perhaps, he wasn't really hurting it.

Desperation drove Regis to new tactics and he dived in between the ghoul's wide swings, repeatedly bashing his mace about the undead monster's face and chest.

He felt the tearing of his shoulders, arms and back, felt the weakness of paralyzation creeping through him like the cold of death. But he stubbornly resisted the urge to fall down, and kept swinging, kept pounding.

Then his strength was gone and he crumbled to the floor.

The ghoul fell in front of him, its head a mass of blasted pulp.

The woman was holding Regis then, though he couldn't feel her touch. He heard her grateful thanks then her renewed scream of terror as she leaped past him and ran for the door.

Regis couldn't turn to follow her movements. He stared helplessly forward, then saw only their legs—four legs, two ghouls. He tried to find comfort in the knowledge that his paralysis likely meant that he wouldn't feel the wretched things eating him.

* * * * *

"Out to the streets!" Deudermont yelled, running along a lane, his forces behind him, and Robillard beside him. "Come out, one and all! There is safety in unity!"

The people of Luskan heard that call and ran to it, though some houses echoed only with screams. Deudermont directed his soldiers into those houses, to battle ghouls and rescue victims.

"Arklem Greeth freed them from Illusk," Robillard said. He'd been grumbling since sunset, since the onslaught of undead. "He seeks to punish the Luskar for allowing us, his enemies, to take the streets."

"He will only turn the whole of the town against him," Deudermont growled.

"I doubt the monster cares," said Robillard. He stopped and turned, and Deudermont paused to regard him then followed his gaze to a balcony across the way. A group of children hustled into view then disappeared into a different door. Behind them came a pair of hungry ghouls, drooling and slavering.

A bolt of lightning reached out from Robillard, forking into two streaks as it neared the balcony, each fork blasting a monster.

The smoking husks, the former ghouls, fell dead on the balcony as the blackened wood behind them smoldered.

Deudermont was glad to have Robillard on his side.

"I will kill that lich," Robillard muttered.

The captain didn't doubt him.

* * * * *

Drizzt ran along the street, searching for his companion. He'd charged into a building, following the screams, but Regis had not followed.

The streets were dangerous. Too dangerous.

Drizzt nodded to Guenhwyvar, who padded along the rooftops, shadowing his movements. "Find him, Guen," he bade, and the panther growled and sprang away.

Across the way, a woman burst out of a house, staggering, bleeding, terrified. Drizzt instinctively charged for her, expecting pursuit.

When none came, when he realized the proximity of that house to where he'd left Regis, a sickly feeling churned in the dark elf's gut.

He didn't pause to question the woman, guessing that she wouldn't have been able to answer with any coherence anyway. He didn't pause at all. He sprinted flat out for the door, then veered when he noticed an open window—no ghoul would have paused to open a window, and the air was too cold for any to have simply been left wide.

Drizzt knew as he leaped to the sill what he would find inside, and only prayed that he wasn't too late.

He crashed atop a ghoul bent over a small form. A second ghoul slashed at him as he and the other went tumbling aside, scoring a tear on Drizzt's forearm. He ached from that, but his elf constitution rendered him impervious to the debilitating touch of such a creature, and he gave it no thought as he hit the floor in a roll. He slammed the wall, willingly, using the barrier to redirect his momentum and allow him to squirm back to his feet as the ghoul bore down hard.

Twinkle and Icingdeath went to fast work before him, much as Regis had parried with his little mace. But those blades, in those hands, proved far more effective. The ghoul's arms were deflected then they were slashed to pieces before they went falling to the floor.

Out of the corner of his eye, Drizzt saw Regis, poor Regis, lying in blood, and the image enraged him like none before. He drove into the standing ghoul, blades stabbing, poking into the emaciated creature with wet, sickly sounds. Drizzt hit it a dozen times, thrusting his blades with such force that they burst right through the creature's back.

He retracted as the ghoul fell against a wall. Likely, it was already dead, but that didn't slow the outraged drow. He brought his blades back and sent them into complimentary spins and began slashing at the ghoul instead of stabbing it. Skin ripped in great lines, showing gray bones and dried-up entrails.

He kept beating the creature even when he heard its companion approach from behind.

That ghoul leaped upon him, claws slashing for Drizzt's face.

They never got close, for even as the ghoul leaped atop him, the drow ducked low and the creature flipped right over him to slam against its destroyed friend.

Drizzt held his swing as a dark form flew in through the window, the great panther slamming the animated corpse, driving the ghoul to the floor under a barrage of slashing claws and tearing fangs.

Drizzt ran to Regis, dropping his blades and skidding down to his knees. He cradled Regis's head and stared into his wide-open eyes, hoping to see a flash of life left there. Yet another ghoul charged at him, but Guenhwyvar leaped over him as he crouched with Regis and hit the thing squarely, blasting it back into the other room.

"Get me out of here," Regis, seeming so near to death, whispered breathlessly.

* * * * *

In Luskan, they came to call the next two tendays the Nights of Endless Screams. No matter how many ghouls and other undead monsters Deudermont and his charges destroyed, more appeared as the sun set the next evening.

Terror fast turned to rage for the folk of Luskan, and that rage had a definite focus.

Deudermont's work moved all the faster, despite the nocturnal terrors, and almost every able bodied man and woman of Luskan marched with him as he flushed the Hosttower's wizards out of their safehouses, and soon there were thirty ships, not four, anchored in a line facing Cutlass Island.

"Arklem Greeth stepped too far," Regis said to Drizzt one morning. From his bed where he was slowly and painfully recovering, the halfling could see the harbor and the ships, and from beneath his window he could hear the shouts of outrage against the Hosttower. "He thought to cow them, but he only angered them."

"There is a moment when a man thinks he's going to die when he's terrified," Drizzt replied. "Then there is a moment when a man is sure he's going to die when he's outraged. That moment, upon the Luskar right now, is the time of greatest courage and the time when enemies should quiver in fear."

"Do you think Arklem Greeth is quivering?"

Drizzt, staring out at the distant Hosttower and its ruined and charred southern arm, thought for a moment then shook his head. "He is a wizard, and wizards don't scare easily. Nor do they always see the obvious, for their thoughts are elsewhere, on matters less corporeal."

"Remind me to repeat that notion to Catti-brie," said Regis.

Drizzt turned a sharp stare at him. "There are still hungry ghouls to feed," he reminded, and Regis snickered all the louder, but held his belly in pain from the laughter.

Drizzt turned back to the Hosttower. "And Arklem Greeth is a lich," he added, "immortal, and unconcerned with momentary triumphs or defeats. Win or lose, he assumes he will fight for Luskan again when Captain Deudermont and his ilk are dust in the ground."

"He won't win," said Regis. "Not this time."

"No," Drizzt agreed.

"But he'll flee."

Drizzt shrugged as if it didn't matter, and in many ways, it didn't.

"Robillard says he'll kill the lich," said Regis.

"Then let us pray for Robillard's success."

* * * * *

"What?" Deudermont asked Drizzt when he noticed the drow looking at him curiously from across the breakfast table. Diagonal to both, Robillard, whose mouth was full of food, chuckled and brought a napkin over his lips.

Drizzt shrugged, but didn't hide his smile.

"What do you . . . what do both of you know that I don't?" the captain demanded.

"I know we spent the night fighting ghouls," Robillard said through his food. "But you know that, too."

"Then what?" asked Deudermont.

"Your mood," Drizzt replied. "You're full of morning sunshine."

"Our struggles go well," Deudermont replied, as if that should have been obvious. "Thousands have rallied behind us."

"There is a reason for that," said Robillard.

"And that's why you're in such a fine mood—the reason, not the reinforcements," said Drizzt.

Deudermont looked at them both in complete puzzlement.

"Arklem Greeth has erased the shades of gray—or has colored them more darkly, to be precise," said Drizzt. "Any doubts you harbored regarding this action in Luskan have been cast away because of the lich's actions at Illusk. As Arklem Greeth stripped the magical boundary that held the monsters at bay, so too did he peel away the heavy pall of doubt from Captain Deudermont's shoulders."

Deudermont turned his stare upon Robillard, but the wizard's expression only supported Drizzt's words.

The good captain slid his chair back from the table and stared out across the battered city. Several fires still burned in parts of Luskan, their smoke feeding the perpetual gloom. Wide, flat carts moved along the streets, their drivers solemnly clanging bells as a call for the removal of bodies. Those carts, some moving below Deudermont's window, carried the bodies of many dead.

"I knew Lord Brambleberry's plan would exact a heavy price from the city, yes," the captain admitted. "I see it—I smell it!—every day, as do you. And you speak truly. It has weighed heavily upon me." He kept looking out as he spoke, and the others followed his gaze across the dark roads and buildings.

"This is much harder than sailing a ship," Deudermont said, and Drizzt glanced at Robillard and smiled knowingly, for he knew that Deudermont was going down the same philosophical path as had the wizard those tendays ago when the revolt against the Hosttower had first begun. "When you're hunting pirates, you know your actions are for the greater good. There's little debate to be had beyond the argument of sink them and let them drown out there in the emptiness, or return them to Luskan or Waterdeep for trial. There are no hidden designs behind the actions of pirates—none that would change my actions toward them, at least. Whether they serve the greed of a master or of their own black hearts, my fight with them remains grounded in absolute morality."

"To the joys of political expediency," Robillard said, lifting a mug of breakfast tea in toast. "Here, I mean, in an arena far more complicated and full of half-truths and hidden designs."

"I watch Prisoner's Carnival with utter revulsion," said Deudermont. "More than once I fought the urge to charge the stage and cut down the torturing magistrate, and all the while I knew that he acted under the command of the lawmakers of Luskan. High Captain Taerl and I once nearly came to blows over that whole grotesque scene."

"He argued that the viciousness was necessary to maintain order, of course," said Robillard.

"And not without conviction," Deudermont replied.

"He was wrong," said Drizzt, and both turned to him with surprise.

"I had thought you skeptical of our mission here," said Deudermont.

"You know that I am," Drizzt replied. "But that doesn't mean I disagree that some things, at least, needed to change. But that is not my place to decide in all of this, as you and many others are far more familiar with the nature and character of Luskan than I. My blade is for Captain Deudermont, but my fears remain."

"As do mine," said Robillard. "There are hatreds here, and designs, plots, and rivalries that run deeper than a distaste for Arklem Greeth's callous ways."

Deudermont held up his hand for Robillard to stop, and shifted his open palm toward Drizzt when the drow started to cut in.

"I'm not without consternation," he said, "but I will not surrender my faith that right action makes right result. I cannot surrender that faith, else who am I, and what has my life been worth?"

"A rather simple and unfair reduction," the always-sarcastic wizard replied.

"Unfair?"

"To you," Drizzt answered for Robillard. "You and I have not walked so different a road, though we started from vastly different places. Meddlers, both, we be, and always with the hope that our meddling will leave in our wake a more beautiful tapestry than that we first encountered." Drizzt heard the irony in his own words as he spoke them, a painful reminder that he had chosen not to meddle in Longsaddle, where his meddling might have been needed.

"Me with pirates and you with monsters, eh?" the captain said with a grin, and it was his turn to lift a cup of tea in toast. "Easier to kill pirates, and easier still to kill orcs, I suppose."

Given the recent events in the North, Drizzt nearly snorted his tea out of his nose at that, and it took him a long moment to catch his breath and clear his throat. He held up his hand to deflect the curious looks coming at him from both his companions, not wanting to muddy the conversation even more with tales of the improbable treaty between Kings Bruenor and Obould, dwarf and orc. The drow's expectations of absolutism had been thoroughly flattened of late, and so he was both heartened by and fearful of his friend's unwavering faith.

"Beware the unintended consequences," Robillard said.

But Captain Deudermont looked back out over the city and shrugged that away. A bell clanged below the window, followed by a call for the dead. The course had been set. The captain's gaze drifted to Cutlass Island and the tree-like structure of the Hosttower, the masts of so many ships behind it across the harbor and the river.

The threat of the ghouls had diminished. Robillard's wizard friends were on the verge of recreating the seal around Illusk, and most of the creatures had been utterly destroyed.

It was time to take the fight to the source, and that, Deudermont feared, would exact the greatest cost of all.

CHAPTER
FROM THE SHADOWS

The ground shaking beneath his bed awakened High Captain Kurth one dismal morning. As soon as he got his bearings and realized he wasn't dreaming, the former pirate acted with the reflexes of a warrior, rolling off the side of his bed to his feet while in the same movement grabbing his sword belt from the bed pole and slapping it around his waist.

"You will not need that," came a quiet, melodic voice from the shadows across the large, circular room, the second highest chamber in Kurth Tower. As his dreams faded and the moment of alarm passed, Kurth recognized the voice as one that had visited him unbidden twice before in that very room.

The high captain gnashed his teeth and considered spinning and throwing one of the many daggers set in his sword belt.

This is no enemy, he reminded himself, though without much conviction, for he wasn't certain who the mysterious visitor really was.

"The western window," the voice said. "It has begun."

Kurth moved to that window and pulled open the heavy drapes, flooding the room with the dawn's light. He looked in the direction from which the voice had sounded, hoping to catch a glimpse of its source from the shadows, but that edge of his chamber defied the morning light and remained as dark as a moonless midnight—magic, Kurth was certain, and potent magic, indeed. The tower had been sealed against magical intrusion by Arklem Greeth himself. And yet, there was the visitor—again!

Kurth turned back to the west, to the slowly brightening ocean.

A dozen boulders and balls of pitch drew fiery lines in the air, flying fast for the Hosttower, or for various parts of the rocky shore of Cutlass Island.

"See?" asked the voice. "It is as I have assured you."

"Rethnor's son is a fool."

"A fool who will prevail," the voice replied.

It was hard to argue that possibility, given the line of ships throwing their missiles at Cutlass Island. Their work was meticulous. They threw in unison and with concentrated aim. He counted fifteen ships firing, though there might have been a couple more hidden from view. In addition, another group of wide, low boats ferried along the line then back to Whitesails Harbor to get more ammunition.

Whitesails Harbor!

The reality hit Kurth hard. Whitesails served as the harbor for Luskan's navy, a flotilla under the auspices, supposedly, of the five high captains as directed by the Hosttower. The ships at Whitesails were the pretty front to the ugly piracy behind Luskan's riches. Deudermont knew those pirates, and they knew him, and many of them hated him and had lost friends to *Sea Sprite*'s exploits on the open seas.

Despite that, the nagging thought—reinforced as more and more masts lined up beside *Sea Sprite* and Brambleberry's warships—was that the Luskar sailors might well desert. As improbable as it seemed, he couldn't deny what he saw with his own eyes. Luskan's fleet, and the men and women of Whitesails, were directly involved in supporting the bombardment of the Hosttower of the Arcane. The men and women of Luskan's fleet were in open revolt against Arklem Greeth.

"The fool with his undead," Kurth muttered.

Arklem Greeth had pushed too hard, too wickedly. He had crossed a line and had driven the whole of the city against him. The high captain kept his gaze to the northwest, to Whitesails Harbor, and though he couldn't make out much from that distance, he clearly saw the banner of Mirabar among many on the quayside. He imagined Mirabarran dwarves and men working hard to load the courier ships with rocks and pitch.

Full of anxiety, Kurth turned angrily at the hidden visitor. "What do you demand of me?"

"Demand?" came the reassuring reply, in a tone that seemed truly surprised by the accusation. "Nothing! I . . . we, are not here to demand, but to advise. We watch the wave of change and measure the strength of the rocks against which that wave will break. Nothing more."

Kurth scoffed at the obvious understatement. "So, what do you see? And do you truly understand the strength of those rocks to which you so poetically refer? Do you grasp the power of Arklem Greeth?"

"We have known greater foes, and greater allies. Captain Deudermont has an army of ten thousand to march against the Hosttower."

"And what do you see in that?" Kurth demanded.

"Opportunity."

"For that wretch Deudermont."

A chuckle came from the darkness. "Captain Deudermont has no understanding of the forces he will unwittingly unleash. He knows good and evil, but nothing more, but we—and you—see shades of gray. Captain Deudermont will scale to unstable heights in short order. His absolutes will rally the masses of Luskan, then will send them into revolt."

Kurth shrugged, unconvinced, and fearful of the reputation and power of Captain Deudermont. He suspected that those mysterious outside forces, that hidden character who had visited him twice before, never threateningly, but never comfortably, were sorely underestimating the good captain and the loyalty of those who would follow him.

"I see the rule of law, heavy and cumbersome," he said.

"We see the opposite," said the voice. "We see five men of Luskan who will collect the spoils set free when the Hosttower falls. We see only two of those five who are wise enough to separate the copper from the gold."

Kurth paused and considered that for a while. "A speech you give to Taerl, Suljack, and Baram, too, no doubt," he replied at length.

"Nay. We have visited none of them, and come to you only because the son of Rethnor, and Rethnor himself, insist that you are the most worthy."

"I'm flattered, truly," Kurth said dryly. He did well to hide his smile and his suspicion, for whenever his "guest" so singled him out as one of importance, it occurred to him that his guest might indeed be a spy from the Hosttower, even Arklem Greeth himself, come to test the loyalty of the high captains in difficult times. It was Arklem Greeth, after all, who had strengthened the magical defenses of Kurth Tower and Closeguard Island a decade before. What wizard would be powerful enough to circumvent defenses set in place by the archmage arcane, but the archmage arcane himself? What wizard in Luskan could claim the power of Arklem Greeth? None who were not in the Hosttower, as far as Kurth knew, would even be close, other than that Robillard beast who sailed with Deudermont, and if his guest was Robillard, that raised the banner of duplicity even higher.

"You will be flattered," the voice responded, "when you come to understand the sincerity behind the claim. Rethnor and Kensidan will show outward respect to all of their peers—"

"It's Rethnor's Ship alone, unless and until he formally cedes it to Kensidan," Kurth insisted. "Quit referring to that annoying Crow as one whose word is of any import."

"Spare us both your quaint customs, for they are a ridiculous assertion to me, and a dangerous delusion for you. Kensidan's hand is in every twist of that which you see before you: the Mirabarrans, the Waterdhavians, Deudermont himself, and the defection of a quarter of Arklem Greeth's forces."

"You openly admit that to me?" Kurth replied, the implication being that he could wage war on Ship Rethnor for such a reality.

"You needed to hear it to know it?"

Kurth narrowed his eyes as he stared into the darkness. The rest of the room had brightened considerably, but still no daylight touched that far corner—or ever would unless his guest willed it to be so.

"Arklem Greeth's rule is doomed, this day," the voice said. "Five men will profit most from his fall, and two of those five are wise enough and strong enough to recognize it. Is one of those two too stubborn and set in his ways to grasp the chest of jewels?"

"You ask me for a declaration of loyalty," Kurth replied. "You ask me to disavow my allegiance to Arklem Greeth."

"I ask nothing of you. I help to explain to you that which is occurring outside your window, and show you paths I think wise. You walk those paths or you do not of your own volition."

"Kensidan sent you here," Kurth accused.

A telling pause ensued before the voice answered, "He didn't, directly. It's his respect for you that guided us here, for we see the possible futures of Luskan and would prefer that the high captains, above all, above Deudermont and above Arklem Greeth, prevailed."

Just as Kurth started to respond, the door to his room burst open and his most trusted guards rushed in.

"The Hosttower is under bombardment!" one cried.

"A vast army gathers at our eastern bridge, demanding passage!" said the other.

Kurth glanced to the shadows—to where the shadows had been, for they were gone, completely.

So was his guest, whoever that guest might have been.

* * * * *

Arabeth and Robillard walked along *Sea Sprite*'s rail before the line of archers, waggling their fingers and casting devious, countering enchantments on the piles of arrows at each bowman's feet.

The ship lurched as her aft catapult let fly a large ball of pitch. It streaked through the air, unerringly for the Hosttower's westernmost limb, where it hit and splattered, launching lines of fire that lit up bushes and already scorched grass at the base of the mighty structure.

But the tower itself had repelled the strike with no apparent ill effects.

"The archmage arcane defends it well," Arabeth remarked.

"Each hit takes from his defenses, and from him," Robillard replied. He bent low and touched another pile of arrows. Their silvery tips glowed for just a moment before going dim again. "Even the smallest of swords will wear through the strongest warrior's shield if they tap it enough."

Arabeth looked to the Hosttower and laughed aloud, and Robillard followed her gaze. The ground all around the five-limbed structure was thick with boulders, ballista bolts, and smoldering pitch. *Sea Sprite* and her companion vessels had been launching non-stop against Cutlass Island throughout the morning, and at Robillard's direction, all of their firepower had been directed at the Hosttower itself.

"Do you think they will respond?" Arabeth asked.

"You know Greeth as well as I do," Robillard answered. He finished with the last batch of arrows, waited for Arabeth to do likewise, then led her back to his usual perch behind the mainsail. "He will grow annoyed and will order his defenders along the shore to lash out."

"Then we will make them pay."

"Only if we're quick enough," Robillard replied.

"Every one of them will be guarded by spells to counter a dozen arrows," said the woman of Mirabar.

"Then every one will be hit by thirteen," came Robillard's dry reply.

Sea Sprite shuddered again as a rock flew out, along with ten others from the line, all soaring in at the Hosttower with such precision and timing that a pair collided before they reached their mark and skipped harmlessly away. The others shook the ground around the place, or smacked against the Hosttower's sides, to be repelled by its defensive magic.

Robillard looked to the north where one of Brambleberry's boats eased a bit closer against the strong currents of the Mirar.

"Sails!" Robillard cried, and *Sea Sprite*'s crew flipped the lines, unfurling fast.

From the rocks of the northwestern tip of Cutlass Island, a pair of lightning bolts reached out at Brambleberry's ship, scorching her side, tearing one of her sails. With the strong and favorable current, though, the ship was able to immediately reverse direction.

Even as *Sea Sprite* leaned and splashed to life, Robillard and Arabeth filled her sails with sudden and powerful winds. They didn't even take the time to pull up the anchor, but just cut the line, and *Sea Sprite* turned straight in, bucking the currents with such jolting force that all aboard had to grab on and hold tight.

Arklem Greeth's wizards focused on Brambleberry's boat for far too long, as Robillard had hoped, and by the time the Hosttower contingent noticed the sudden charge of *Sea Sprite*, she was close enough so that those on her deck could see the small forms scrambling across the rocks and ducking for whatever cover they could find.

From a more southern vantage on Cutlass Island, a lightning bolt streaked out at *Sea Sprite*, but she was too well warded to be slowed by the single strike. Her front ballista swiveled and threw a heavy spear at the point from which that attack had emanated, and as *Sea Sprite* began her broadside turn, her prow bending to straight north in a run up the coast, the crack catapult crew on her aft deck had another ball of pitch flying away. It splattered among the rocks and several men and women scrambled up from the burning ground, one engulfed in flame, all screaming.

And those weren't even the primary targets, which were to starboard, trying to hide as a bank of archers the length of *Sea Sprite*'s main deck and three deep lifted and bent their bows.

Three separate volleys went in, enchanted arrows all, skipping off the stones or striking against the defensive magic shields Greeth's minions had raised.

But as Robillard had predicted, more arrows found their way than could be defeated by the enchantments, and another Hosttower wizard fell dead on the stones.

Lightning bolts and arrows reached out at *Sea Sprite* from the rocky coastline. Boulders and balls of pitch flew out from the ship line in response, followed by a devastating barrage of arrows as *Sea Sprite* veered due west and sped away with the fast current.

Robillard nodded his approval.

"One dead, perhaps, or perhaps two," said Arabeth. "It's difficult work."

"Another one Arklem Greeth cannot afford to lose," Robillard replied.

"Our tricks will catch fewer and fewer. Arklem Greeth will teach his forces to adapt."

"Then we will not let him keep up with our evolving tricks," Robillard said, and nodded his chin toward the line of ships, all of whom were pulling up anchor. One by one, they began to glide to the south.

"Sea Tower," Robillard explained, referring to the strong guard tower on southern Cutlass Island. "It would cost Arklem Greeth too much energy to have it as fortified as the Hosttower, so we'll bombard it to rubble, and destroy every other defensible position along the southern coast of the island."

"There are few places to land even a small boat in those rocky waters,"

Arabeth replied. "Sea Tower was built so that defenders could assault any ships attempting to enter the southern mouth of the Mirar, and not as a defense for Cutlass Island."

Robillard's deadpan expression quieted her, for of course he knew all of that. "We're tightening the noose," he explained. "I expect that those inside the Host-tower are growing more uncomfortable by the hour."

"We nibble at the edges when we must bite out the heart of the place," Arabeth protested.

"Patience," said Robillard. "Our final fight with the lich will be brutal—no one doubts that. Hundreds will likely die, but hundreds more will surely perish if we attack before we prepare the battlefield. The people of Luskan are on our side. We own the streets. We have Harbor Arm and Fang Island fully under our control. Whitesails Harbor sides with us. Captain's Court is ours, and Illusk has been rendered quiescent once again. The Mirar bridges are ours."

"Those that remain," said Arabeth, to which Robillard chuckled.

"Arklem Greeth hasn't a safehouse left in the city, or if he does, his minions there are huddled in a dark basement, trembling—rightfully so!—in fear. And when we have bombed Sea Tower to rubble, and have chased off or killed all of his minions he placed in the southern reaches of Cutlass, Arklem Greeth will need to look south, on his own shores, as well. Unrelenting bombardment, unrelenting pressure, and keep clear in your mind that if we lose ten men—nay, fifty!—for every Arcane Brotherhood wizard we slay, Captain Deudermont will claim victory in a rout."

Arabeth Raurym considered the older and wiser wizard's words for some time before nodding her agreement. Above all else, she wanted the archmage arcane dead, for she knew with certainty that if he wasn't killed, he would find a way to kill her—a horrible, painful way, no doubt.

She looked south as *Sea Sprite* came around Fang Island, to see that the other ships were already lining up to begin the bombardment of Sea Tower.

Sea Sprite's bell rang and the men tacked accordingly to slow her as a trio of ammunition barges from Whitesails Harbor turned around the horn of Harbor Arm Island and crossed in front of her. Arabeth looked over to regard Robillard and could almost hear the calculations playing out behind his eyes. He had orchestrated every piece of the day's action—the bombardment, the trap and attack, and the turn south, complete with supply lines—to the most minute detail.

She understood how Deudermont had gained such a glorious reputation hunting the ever-elusive pirates of the Sword Coast. He had surrounded himself with the finest crew she had ever seen, and standing beside him was the wizard Robillard, so calculating and so very, very deadly.

A shiver ran along Arabeth's spine, but it was one of hope and reassurance as she reminded herself that Robillard and *Sea Sprite* were on her side.

* * * * *

From his eastern balcony, High Captain Kurth and his two closest advisors, one the captain of his guard and the other a high-ranking commander in Luskan's garrison, watched the gathering of thousands at the small bridge that linked Closeguard Island to the city. Deudermont was there, judging from the banners, and Brambleberry as well, though their ships were active in the continuing, unrelenting bombardment of Cutlass Island to the west.

For a moment, Kurth envisioned the whole of the invading army enveloped in the flames of a gigantic Arklem Greeth fireball, and it was not an unpleasant mental image—briefly, at least, until he considered the practical ramifications of having a third of Luskan's populace lying dead and charred in the streets.

"A third of the populace. . . ." he said aloud.

"Aye, and most o' me soldiers in the bunch," said Nehwerg, who had once commanded the garrison at Sea Tower, which was even then crumbling under a constant rain of boulders.

"They could have ten times that number and not get across, unless we let them," insisted Master Shanty, Kurth Tower's captain of the guard.

The high captain chuckled at the ridiculous, empty boast. He could make Deudermont and the others pay dearly for trying to cross to Closeguard—he could even drop the bridge, which his engineers had long ago rigged for just such an eventuality—but to what gain and to what end?

"There's yer bird," Nehwerg grumbled, and pointed down at a black spec flapping past the crowd and climbing higher in the eastern sky. "The man's got no dignity, I tell ya."

Kurth chuckled again and reminded himself that Nehwerg served a valuable purpose for him, and that the man's inanity was a blessing and not a curse. It wouldn't do to have such a personal liaison to the Luskar garrison who could think his way through too many layers of intrigue, after all.

The black bird, the Crow, closed rapidly on Kurth's position, finally alighting on the balcony railing. It hopped down, and flipped its wings over as it did, enacting the transformation back to a human form.

"You said you would be alone," Kensidan said, eyeing the two soldiers hard.

"Of course my closest advisors are well aware of this particular aspect of your magical cloak, son of Rethnor," Kurth replied. "Would you expect that I wouldn't have told them?"

Kensidan didn't reply, other than to let his gaze linger a bit longer on the two before turning it to Kurth, who motioned for them all to enter his private room.

"I'm surprised you would ask to see me at this tense time," Kurth said, moving to the bar and pouring a bit of brandy for himself and Kensidan. When Nehwerg made a move toward the drink, Kurth turned him back with a narrow-eyed glare.

"It was not Arklem Greeth," said Kensidan, "nor one of his lackeys. You need know that."

Kurth looked at him curiously.

"Your shadowy visitor," Kensidan explained. "It was not Greeth, not an ally of Greeth in any way, and not a mage of the Arcane Brotherhood."

"Bah, but who's he talking about?" demanded Nehwerg, and Master Shanty stepped up beside his high captain. Kurth impatiently waved them both back.

"How do you . . . ?" Kurth started to ask, but stopped short and just smirked at the surprising, dangerous upstart.

"No wizard outside of Arklem Greeth's inner circle could penetrate the magical defenses he has set in place in Kurth Tower," Kensidan said as if reading Kurth's mind.

Kurth tried hard to not look impressed, and just held his smirk, inviting the Crow to continue.

"Because it was no wizard," Kensidan said. "There is another type of magic involved."

"Priests are no match for the web of Arklem Greeth," Kurth replied. "Do you think him foolish enough to forget the schools of those divinely inspired?"

"And no priest," said Kensidan.

"You're running out of magic-users."

Kensidan tapped the side of his head and Kurth's smirk turned back into an unintentional, intrigued expression.

"A mind mage?" he asked quietly, a Luskar slang for those rare and reputably powerful practitioners of the concentration art known as psionics. "A monk?"

"I had such a visitor months ago, when first I started seeing the possibilities of Captain Deudermont's future," Kensidan explained, taking the glass from Kurth and settling into a chair in front of the room's generous hearth, which had only been lit a few minutes earlier and wasn't yet throwing substantial heat.

Kurth took the seat across from Rethnor's son and motioned for Nehwerg and Master Shanty to stand a step behind him.

"So the machinations of this rebellion, the inspiration even, came from outside Luskan?" Kurth asked.

Kensidan shook his head. "This is a natural progression, a response to the overreaching of Arklem Greeth both on the high seas, where Deudermont roams, and in the east, in the Silver Marches."

"Which all came together in this 'coincidental' conglomeration of opponents lining up against the Hosttower?" Kurth asked, doubt dripping from every sarcastic word.

"I don't believe in coincidence," Kensidan replied.

"And yet, here we are. Do you admit that Kensidan's hand, that Ship Rethnor's hands, are in this?"

"Up to our elbows . . . our shoulders, perhaps," Kensidan said with a laugh, and lifted his glass in toast. "I didn't create this opportunity, but neither would I let it pass."

"You, or your father?"

"He is my advisor—you know as much."

"A startling admission, and a dangerous one," said Kurth.

"How so? Have you heard the rumble on the island to your west? Have you seen the gathering at the gates of Closeguard Bridge?"

Kurth considered that for a moment, and it was his turn to tip his glass to his companion.

"So Arklem Greeth has frayed the many strings, and Kensidan of Ship Rethnor has worked to weave them into something to his own benefit," said Kurth.

Kensidan nodded.

"And these others? Our shadowy visitors?"

Kensidan rubbed his long and thin fingers over his chin. "Consider the dwarf," he said.

Kurth stared at him curiously for a few moments, recalling the rumors from the east regarding the Silver Marches. "King Bruenor? The dwarf King of Mithral Hall works for the fall of Luskan?"

"No, not Bruenor. Of course it's not Bruenor, who, by all reports, has troubles enough to keep him busy in the east, thank the gods."

"But it's Bruenor's strange friend who rides with Deudermont," said Kurth.

"Not Bruenor," Kensidan replied. "He has no place or part in any of this, and how the dark elf happened back to Deudermont's side I neither know nor care."

"Then what dwarves? The Ironspur Clan from the mountains?"

"Not dwarves," Kensidan corrected. "Dwarf. You know of my recent acquisition . . . the bodyguard?"

Kurth nodded, finally catching on. "The creature with the unusual morningstars, yes. How could I not know? The one whose ill-fashioned rhymes grate on the nerves of every sailor in town. He has brawled in every tavern in

Luskan over the last few months, mostly over his own wretched poetry, and from what my scouts tell me, he's a far better fighter than he is a poet. Ship Rethnor strengthened her position on the street greatly with that one. But he is tied to all of this?" Kurth waved his arm out toward the western window, where the sound of the bombardment had increased yet again.

Kensidan nodded his chin at Master Shanty and Nehwerg, staring all the while into Kurth's dark eyes.

"They are trusted," Kurth assured him.

"Not by me."

"You have come to my Ship."

"To advise and to offer, and not under duress, and nor under duress shall I stay."

Kurth paused and seemed to be taking it all in, glancing from his guest to his guards. It was obvious to Kensidan that the man was intrigued, though, and so it came as no surprise when he turned at last to the two guards and ordered them out of the room. They protested, but Kurth would hear none of it and waved them away.

"The dwarf was a gift to me from these visitors, who take great interest in establishing strong trading ties with Luskan. They are here for commerce, not conquest—that is my hope at least. And my belief, for were they openly revealed, we would be facing greater lords of Waterdeep than Brambleberry, do not doubt, and King Bruenor, Marchion Elastul of Mirabar, and Lady Alustriel of Silverymoon wouldn't be far behind with their own armies."

Kurth felt a bit more perplexed and defensive, and a lot less intrigued.

"These events were not their doing, but they watch closely, and advise me and my father, as they have visited you," said Kensidan, hoping that naming Rethnor almost as an afterthought had slipped past the perceptive Kurth. The man's arched eyebrow showed that it had not, however, and Kensidan silently berated himself and promised that he would do better in the future. Ship Rethnor wasn't yet officially his. Not officially.

"So you hear voices in the shadows, and these bring you confidence," Kurth said. He held up his hand as Kensidan tried to interrupt and continued, "Then we're back at the initial square of the board, are we not? How do you know your friends in the shadows aren't agents of Arklem Greeth? Perhaps the cunning lich has decided it's time to test the loyalties of his high captains. Are you too young to see the dangerous possibilities? And wouldn't that make you the biggest fool of all?"

Kensidan held up his open palm and finally managed to silence the man. He slowly reached under his strange black cloak and produced a small glass item, a bottle, and within it stood the tiny figure of a tiny man.

No, not a figure, Kurth realized. His eyes widened as the poor soul trapped within shifted about.

Kensidan motioned to the hearth. "May I?"

Kurth responded with a puzzled expression, which Kensidan took as permission. He flung the bottle into the hearth, where it smashed against the back bricks.

The tiny man enlarged, bouncing around the low-burning logs before catching his bearings and his balance enough to roll back out, taking ash and one burning log with him.

"By the Nine Hells!" the man protested, batting at his smoldering gray cloak. Blood dripped from several wounds on his hands and face and he reached up and pulled a small shard of glass out of his cheek. "Don't ever do that to me again!" he cried, still flustered and waving his arms. It seemed then as if he had at last caught his bearings, and only then he realized where he was and who was seated before him. The blood drained from his face.

"Are you settled?" Kensidan asked.

The thoroughly flustered little man toed the log beside him and brushed it back into the fireplace, but didn't otherwise respond.

"High Captain Kurth, I give you Morik," Kensidan explained. "Morik the Rogue, to those who know him enough to care. His lady is a mage in the Hosttower—perhaps that is why he's found a place in all this."

Morik looked anxiously from man to man, dipping many short bows.

Kensidan drew Kurth's gaze with his own. "Our visitors are not agents of Arklem Greeth," he said, before turning to the pathetic little man and motioning for him to begin. "Tell my friend your story, Morik the Rogue," Kensidan bade him. "Tell him of your visitors those years ago. Tell him of the dark friends of Wulfgar of Icewind Dale."

* * * * *

"I told ye they wouldn't get across without a row," Baram insisted to his fellow high captains, Taerl and Suljack. The three stood atop the southwest tower of High Captain Taerl's fortress, looking directly west to the bridge to Kurth's Closeguard Island and the great open square south of Illusk where Deudermont and Lord Brambleberry had gathered their mighty army.

"They will," Suljack replied. "Kensi—Rethnor said they will, and so they will."

"That Crow boy is trouble," said Baram. "He'll bring down Rethnor's great Ship before the old man passes on."

"The gates will open," Suljack replied, but very quietly. "Kurth can't refuse. Not this many, not with almost all of Luskan knocking."

"Hard to be denyin' that number," Taerl said. "Most o' the city's walking with Deudermont."

"Kurth won't go against Arklem Greeth—he's more sense than that," Baram replied. "Deudermont's fools'll be swimming or sailing if they want to get to the Hosttower."

Even as Baram spoke, some of High Captain Kurth's sentries rushed up to the bridge and began throwing the locks. To Baram's utter shock, and to Taerl's as well, despite his words, the gates of the Kurth Tower compound pulled open and Kurth's guards stepped back, offering passage.

"A trick!" Baram protested, leaping to his feet. "She's got to be a trick! Arklem Greeth's bidding them on that he can destroy them."

"He'll have to kill half the city, then," Suljack said.

Deudermont's banner led the way across the small bridge with more than five thousand in his wake. Out in the harbor beyond Cutlass Island, sails appeared and anchors climbed from the water. The fleet began to creep in, boulders and pitch leading the way.

The noose tightened.

CHAPTER

Valindra Shadowmantle's green eyes opened wide as she noted the approaching mob. She turned to rush to Arklem Greeth's chambers, but found the lich standing behind her, wearing a wicked grin.

"They come," Valindra gasped. "All of them."

Arklem Greeth shrugged as if he was hardly concerned. Gripped by her fear, the archmage's casual reaction served only to anger Valindra.

"You have underestimated our enemies at every turn!" she screamed, and several lesser wizards nearby sucked in their breath and turned away, pretending not to have heard.

Arklem Greeth laughed at her.

"You find this amusing?" she replied.

"I find it . . . predictable," Greeth answered. "Sadly so, but alas, the cards were played long ago. A Waterdhavian lord and the hero of the Sword Coast, the hero of Luskan, aligned against us. People are so fickle and easy to sway; it's no wonder that they rally to the empty platitudes of an idiot like Captain Deudermont."

"Because you raised the undead against them," Valindra accused.

The lich laughed again. "Our options were limited from the beginning. The high captains, cowards all, did little to hold back the mounting tide of invasion. I feared we could never depend upon those fools, those thieves, but again alas, you accept what you have and make the best of it."

Valindra stared at her master, wondering if he'd lost his mind. "The whole of the city is rallied against us," she cried. "Thousands! They gather on Closeguard, and will fight their way across."

"We have good wizards guarding our bridge."

"And they have powerful spellcasters among their ranks, as well," said Valindra. "If Deudermont wanted, he could send the least of his warriors against us, and our wizards would expend their energies long before he ran out of fodder."

"It will be amusing to watch," Arklem Greeth said, grinning all the wider.

"You have gone mad," Valindra stated, and beyond Arklem Greeth several lesser wizards shuffled nervously as they went about their assigned tasks, or at least, feigned going about them.

"Valindra, my friend," Greeth said, and he took her by the arm and walked her deeper into the structure of the Hosttower, away from the disquieting sights in the east. "If you play this correctly, you will find great entertainment, a fine practice experience, and little loss," the archmage arcane explained when they were alone. "Deudermont wants my head, not yours."

"The traitor Arabeth is with him, and she is no ally of mine."

The lich waved the notion away. "A minor inconvenience and nothing more. Let them lay the blame fully upon Arklem Greeth—I welcome the prestige of such notoriety."

"You seem to care little about anything at the moment, Archmage," the overwizard replied. "The Hosttower itself is in dire peril."

"It will fall to utter ruin," Arklem Greeth predicted with continuing calm.

Valindra held out her hands and stuttered repeatedly, unable to fashion a response.

"All things fall, and all things can be rebuilt from the rubble," the lich explained. "Surely they're not going to destroy me—or you, if you're sufficiently cunning. I'm nimble enough to survive the likes of Deudermont, and will take great enjoyment in watching the 'reconstruction' of Luskan when he proclaims his victory."

"Why did we ever allow it to come to such a state as this?"

Arklem Greeth shrugged. "Mistakes," he admitted. "My own, as well. I struck out for the Silver Marches at precisely the worst time, it would seem, though by coincidence and bad luck, or more devious coordination on the part of my enemies, I cannot know. Mirabar turned against us, as have even the orcs and their fledgling king. Deudermont and Brambleberry on their own would prove to be formidable opponents, I don't doubt, but with such an alignment of enemies mounting against us, it would do us ill to remain in Luskan. Here we are immobile, an easy target."

"How can you say such things?"

"Because they are true. Aha! I know not all of the conspirators behind this uprising, but surely there are traitors among the ranks of those I thought allies."

"The high captains."

Arklem Greeth shrugged again. "Our enemies are vast, it would seem—even more so than the few thousand who flock to Deudermont's side. They are merely fodder, as you said, while the real power behind this usurpation lays hidden and in wait. We could fight them hard and stubbornly, I expect, but in the end, that would prove to be the more dangerous course for those of us who really matter."

"We are to just run away?"

"Oh no!" Greeth assured her. "Not *just* run away. Nay, my friend, we're going to inflict such pain upon the people of Luskan this day that they will long remember it, and while they may call my abdication a victory, that notion will prove short lived when winter blows in mercilessly on the many households missing a father or mother. And their victory will not claim the most coveted prize, rest assured, for I have long anticipated this eventuality, and long prepared."

Valindra relaxed a bit at that assurance.

"Their victory will reveal the conspirators," said Greeth, "and I will find my way back. You put too much value in this one place, Valindra, this Hosttower of the Arcane. Have I not taught you that the Arcane Brotherhood is much greater than what you see in Luskan?"

"Yes, my master," the elf wizard replied.

"So take heart!" said Arklem Greeth. He cupped her chin in his cold, dead fingers and made her look up into his soulless eyes. "Enjoy the day—ah the excitement! I surely will! Use your wiles, use your magic, use your cunning to survive and escape . . . or to surrender."

"Surrender?" she echoed. "I don't understand."

"Surrender in a manner that exonerates you enough so that they don't execute you, of course." Arklem Greeth laughed. "Blame me—oh, please do! Find your way out of this, or trust in me to come and retrieve you. I surely will. And from the ashes we two will find enjoyment and opportunity, I promise. And more excitement than we have known in decades!"

Valindra stared at him for a few moments then nodded.

"Now be gone from this multi-limbed target," said Greeth. "Get to the coast and our wizards set in defense, and take your shots as you find them. Make them hurt, Valindra, all of them, and hold faith in your heart and in your magnificent mind that this is a temporary setback, one intended to lead to ultimate and enduring victory."

"When?"

The simple question rocked Arklem Greeth back on his heels a bit, for Valindra's tone had made it clear that she understood that her timetable and that of a lich might not be one and the same.

"Go," he bade her, and nodded toward the door. "Make them hurt."

Half-dazed with confusion, Valindra Shadowmantle, Overwizard of the North Tower, in many eyes the second ranking wizard of the great Hosttower of the Arcane of Luskan, ambled toward the door of the mighty structure, fully believing that when she left it, she would never again enter. It was all too over-whelming, these dramatic and dangerous changes.

* * * * *

They crossed the bridge from Closeguard to Cutlass in full charge, banners flying, swords banging against shields, voices raised in hearty cheers.

On the other side of the bridge loomed the eastern wall of the Hosttower's courtyard, ground unblemished by the naval bombardment, and atop that wall, two score wizards crouched and waited, accompanied by a hundred apprentices armed with bows and spears.

They unleashed their fury as one, with the leading edge of Brambleberry's forces barely a dozen running strides from the wall. Men and ladders went up in flames, or flew away under the jolt of lightning bolts. Spears and arrows banged against shields and armor, or found a seam and sent an enemy writhing and screaming to the ground.

But Lord Brambleberry had brought wizards of his own, mages who had enacted wards on shield and man alike, who had brought forth watery elemen-tals to quickly defeat the fireballs' flames. Men and women died or fell to grave wounds, to be sure, but not nearly to the devastating effect the Hosttower's front line of defense had hoped, and needed.

Volleys of arrows skipped in off the battlements, and concentrations of light-ning blasts shook the wall, chipping and cracking the stone. The front row of Brambleberry's forces parted and through the gap ran a concentration of strong men wielding heavy hammers and picks. Lightning blasts led them to specific points on the wall, where they went to work, smashing away, further weakening the integrity of the structure.

"Pressure the top!" Lord Brambleberry yelled, and his archers and wizards let fly a steady stream of devastation, keeping the Hosttower defenders low.

"What ho!" one hammer team commander cried, and his group fell back as some of the Waterdhavian wizards heard the beckon and sent a trio of powerful blasts at the indicated spot. The first rebounded off the broken stone and sent the commander himself flying to the ground. The second bolt, though, broke through, sending stone chips flying into the courtyard, and the third blew out the section's support, dropping blocks and creating an opening through which a man could easily pass.

"What ho!" another team leader called from another spot, and a different trio of wizards was ready to finish the work of the sledges.

At the same time, far to the left and right, ladders went up against the walls. Initial resistance from the defenders fast gave way to calls for retreat.

The Hosttower's first line of defense had killed Brambleberry's men a dozen to one or more, but the swarm of Luskar, following Brambleberry and Deudermont, enraged by the ghouls sent by Arklem Greeth, and excited by the smell of blood and battle, rolled through.

* * * * *

As soon as the charge across the bridge had begun, the warships, too, went into swift action. Knowing that the Hosttower's focus had to be on the eastern wall, half a dozen vessels weighed anchor and filled their sails, crashing in against the current. They let fly long and far, over the western wall and courtyard to the Hosttower itself, or even beyond it to the eastern courtyard. Crewed by a bare minimum of sailors and gunners, they knew their role as one of diversion and pressure, to keep the defenders outside of the Hosttower confused and frightened, and perhaps even to score a lucky throw and kill a few in the process.

To the south of them, another half a dozen ships led by *Sea Sprite* sailed for the battered surrounds of Sea Tower, leading their assault with pitch and arrows, littering the rocky shore with destruction in case any of the Hosttower's wizards lay in wait there.

More than one such defender showed himself, either lashing out with a lightning bolt, or trying to flee back to the north.

Robillard and Arabeth welcomed such moments, and though both hoped to hold their greatest energies for the confrontation with Arklem Greeth and the main tower, neither could resist the temptation to reply to magic with greater evocations of their own.

"Hold and lower!" ordered Robillard, who remained in command of *Sea Sprite* while Deudermont rode at Brambleberry's side.

The ship dropped her sails and the anchor splashed into the dark waters as other crewmen ran to the smaller boats she carried and put them over the side. Taking their cues from *Sea Sprite*, the other five ships acted in concert.

"Sails south!" the man in the crow's nest shouted down to Robillard.

Eyes wide, the wizard ran aft and grabbed the rail hard, leaning out to get a better view of the leading craft, then of another two ships sailing hard their way.

"*Thrice Lucky*," Arabeth said, coming up beside the wizard. "That's Maimun's ship."

"And what side does he choose?" Robillard wondered. He murmured through a quick spell and tapped thumb and forefinger against his temples, imbuing his eyes with the sight of an eagle.

It was indeed Maimun leading the way, the man standing forward at the prow of *Thrice Lucky*, his crew readying boats behind him. More tellingly, the ship's catapult was neither armed nor manned, and no archers stood ready.

"The boy chose well," Robillard said. "He sails with us."

"How can you know?" Arabeth asked. "How can you be certain enough to continue the landing?"

"Because I know Maimun."

"His heart?"

"His purse," Robillard clarified. "He knows the force arrayed against Arklem Greeth and understands that the Hosttower cannot win this day. A fool he would be to stand back and let the city move on without his help, and Maimun is many things, but a fool is not among them."

"Three ships," Arabeth warned, looking at the trio expertly navigating the familiar waters under full sail, and closing with great speed. "As our crews disembark, they could do profound damage. We should hold three at full strength to meet them if they attack."

Robillard shook his head. "Maimun chose well," he said. "He is a vulture seeking to pick the bones of the dead, and he understands which bones will be meatier this day."

He turned and strode back amidships, waving and calling for his crew to continue. He enacted another spell as he neared the gangplank and gingerly hopped down onto the water—onto and not into, for he didn't sink beneath the waves.

Arabeth copied his movements and stood beside him on the rolling sea. Side by side, they walked swiftly toward the rocky shore, small boats overcrowded with warriors bobbing all around them.

Two of the newcomers dropped sail near the fleet and *Sea Sprite*, their crews similarly manning the smaller boats. But one, *Thrice Lucky*, sailed past, weaving in through the narrow, rocky channel.

"The young pirate knows his craft," Valindra marveled.

"He learned from Deudermont himself," said Robillard. "A pity that's all he learned."

* * * * *

The wall had fallen in short order, but Lord Brambleberry's forces quickly came to realize that the defenders of the Hosttower had fallen back by design.

The wall defense had been set only so the tower's wizards could have time to prepare.

As the fierce folk of Luskan crashed into the courtyard, the full fury of the Hosttower of the Arcane fell upon them. Such a barrage of fire, lightning, magical bolts, and conical blasts of frost so intense they froze a man's blood solid fell over them that of the first several hundred who crossed the wall, nine of ten died within a few heartbeats.

Among those survivors, though, were Deudermont and Brambleberry, protected from the intense barrage by powerful Waterdhavian wizards. Because the pennants of their leaders still stood, the rest of the army continued its charge undeterred. The second volley didn't match the first in intensity or duration, and the warriors pushed on.

Undead rose from the ground before them, ghouls, skeletons, and rotting corpses given a grim semblance of life. And from the tower came golems and gargoyles, magical animations sent to turn back the tide.

The folk of Luskan didn't turn in fear, didn't run in horror, with the undead monsters only bitterly reminding them of why they'd joined the fight in the first place. And while Lord Brambleberry was there astride a large roan stallion, a spectacular figure of strength, two others inspired them even more.

First was Deudermont, sitting tall on a blue-eyed paint mare. Though he was no great rider, his mere presence brought hope to the heart of every commoner in the city.

And there was the other, the friend of Deudermont. As the explosions lessened and the Hosttower's melee force came out to meet the charge, so it became the time of Drizzt.

With quickness that mocked allies and foes alike, with anger solidly grounded in the image of his halfling friend lying injured on a bed, the drow burst through the leading ranks and met the enemy monsters head on. He whirled and twirled, leaped and spun through a line of ghouls and skeletons, leaving piles of torn flesh and shattered bones in his wake.

A gargoyle leaped off a balcony from above, swooping down at him, leathery wings wide, clawed hands and feet raking wildly.

The drow dived into a roll, somehow maneuvered out to the side when the gargoyle angled its wings to intercept, and came back to his feet with such force that he sprang high into the air, his blades working in short and devastating strokes. So completely did he overwhelm the creature that it actually hit the ground before he did, already dead.

"Huzzah for Drizzt Do'Urden!" cried a voice above all the cheering, a voice that Drizzt surely knew, and he took heart that Arumn Gardpeck, proprietor of the Cutlass, was among the ranks.

Magical anklets enhancing his speed, Drizzt sprinted for the central tower of the great structure in short, angled bursts, and often with long, diving rolls. He held only one scimitar then, his other hand clutching an onyx figurine. "I need you," he called to Guenhwyvar, and the weary panther, home on the Astral Plane, heard.

Lightning and fire rained down around Drizzt as he continued his desperate run, but every blast came a little farther behind him.

* * * * *

"He moves as if time itself has slowed around him," Lord Brambleberry remarked to Deudermont when they, like everyone else on the field, took note of the dark elf's spectacular charge.

"It has and it does," Deudermont replied, wearing a perfectly smug expression. Lord Brambleberry hadn't taken well to hearing that a drow was joining his ranks, but Deudermont hoped Drizzt's exploits would earn him some inroads into the previously unwelcoming city of Waterdeep.

He'd be making quite an impression on the minions of Arklem Greeth in short order, as well, by Deudermont's calculations.

If he hadn't already.

Even more importantly, Drizzt's charge had emboldened his comrades, and the line moved inexorably for the tower, accepting the blasts and assaults from wizards, smashing the reaching arms of skeletons and ghouls, shooting gargoyles from the air with so many arrows they darkened the sky.

"Many will die," Brambleberry said, "but the day is ours."

Watching the progress of the insurgent army, Deudermont couldn't really disagree, but he knew, too, that they were battling mighty wizards, and any proclamations of victory were surely premature.

* * * * *

Drizzt came around the side of the main structure, skidding to a fast stop, his face a mask of horror, for he found himself wide open to a balcony on which stood a trio of wizards, all frantically waving their arms in the midst of some powerful spellcasting.

Drizzt couldn't turn, couldn't dodge, and had no apparent or plausible defense.

* * * * *

Resistance at the Sea Tower proved almost nonexistent, and the force of Robillard, Arabeth, and the sailors quickly secured the southern end of Cutlass Island. To the north, fireballs and lightning bolts boomed, cheers rose in combination with agonized screams, and horns blew.

Valindra Shadowmantle watched it all from concealment in a cubby formed of Sea Tower's fallen blocks.

"Come on, then, lich," she whispered, for though the magical display seemed impressive, it was nothing of the sort that could result in the explosive ending Arklem Greeth had promised her.

Which made her doubt his other promise to her, that all would be put aright in short order.

Valindra was no novice to the ways and depths of the Art. Her lightning bolts didn't drop men shaking to the ground, but sent their souls to the Fugue Plane and their bodies to the ground in smoldering heaps.

She looked to the beach, where the sailors were putting up their boats and preparing to march north to join the battle.

Valindra knew she could kill many of them, then and there, and when she noted the wretched Arabeth Raurym among their ranks, her desire to do so multiplied many times over, though the sight of the mighty Robillard beside the wretched Mirabarran witch tempered that somewhat.

But she held her spells in check and looked to the north, where the sound of battle—and the horns of Brambleberry and the Luskar insurgents—grew ever stronger.

Would Arklem Greeth be able to save her if she struck against Arabeth and Robillard? Would he even try?

Her doubts holding her back, Valindra stared and pictured Arabeth lying dead on the ground—no, not dead, but writhing in the agony of a slow, burning, mortal wound.

"You surprise me," said a voice behind her, and the overwizard froze in place, eyes going wide. Her thoughts whirled as she tried to discern the speaker, for she knew that she had heard that voice before.

"Your judgment, I mean," the speaker added, and Valindra recognized him then, and spun around to face the pirate Maimun—or more specifically, to face the tip of his extended blade.

"You have thrown in with . . . them?" Valindra asked incredulously. "With *Deudermont?*"

Maimun shrugged. "Seemed better than the alternative."

"You should have stayed at sea."

"Ah, yes, to then sail in and claim allegiance with whichever side won the day. That is the way you would play it, isn't it?"

The moon elf mage narrowed her eyes.

"You reserve your magic when so many targets present themselves," Maimun added.

"Prudence is not a fault."

"Perhaps not," said the grinning young pirate captain. "But 'tis better to join in the fight with the apparent winner than to claim allegiance when the deed is done. People, even celebratory victors, resent hangers-on, you know."

"Have you ever been anything but?"

"By the seas, a vicious retort!" Maimun replied with a laugh. "Vicious . . . and desperate."

Valindra moved to brush the blade away from her face, but Maimun deftly flipped it past her waving hand and poked her on the tip of her nose.

"Vicious, but ridiculous," the pirate added. "There were times when I found that trait endearing in you. Now it's simply annoying."

"Because it reeks of truth."

"Ah, but dear, beautiful, wicked Valindra, I can hardly be called an opportunist now. I have an overwizard in my grasp to prove my worth. A prisoner I suspect a certain Lady Raurym will greatly covet."

Valindra's gaze threw daggers at the slender man. "You claim me as a prisoner?" she asked, her voice low and threatening.

Maimun shrugged. "So it would seem."

Valindra's face softened, a smile appearing. "Maimun, foolish child, for all your steel and all your bluster, I know you won't kill me." She stepped aside and reached for the blade.

And it jumped back from her hand and came forward with sudden brutality, stabbing her hard in the chest, drawing a gasp and a whimper of pain. Maimun pulled the stroke up short, but his words cut deeper.

"Mithral, not steel," he corrected. "Mithral through your pretty little breast before the next beat of your pretty little heart."

"You have . . . chosen," Valindra warned.

"And chosen well, my prisoner."

* * * * *

Guenhwyvar leaped past Drizzt to shield him from the slings and arrows of enemies, from blasts magical and mundane. Lightning bolts reached down from the balcony as Guenhwyvar soared up toward it, and though they stung her, they didn't deter her.

On the scarred field below, Drizzt stumbled forward and regained his balance and looked on with admiration and deep love for his most trusted friend who had, yet again, saved him.

Saved him and vanquished his enemies all at once, the drow noted with a wince, as flailing arms and horrified expressions appeared to him every so often from around the ball of black fury.

He had no time to dwell on the scene, though, for more undead creatures approached him, and more gargoyles swooped down from above.

And lightning roared and his allies died in their charge behind him. But they kept coming, outraged at the lich and his ghoulish emissaries. A hundred died, two hundred died, five hundred died, but the wave rolled for the beach and wouldn't be deterred.

In the middle of it all rode Deudermont and Brambleberry, urging their charges on, seeking battle side by side wherever it could be found.

Drizzt spotted their banners, and whenever he found a moment's reprieve, he glanced back at them, knowing they would eventually lead him to the most coveted prize of all, to the lich whose defeat would end the carnage.

It was to Drizzt's complete surprise, then, that Arklem Greeth did indeed come upon the field to face his foes, but not straightaway to Deudermont and Brambleberry, but straightaway to Drizzt Do'Urden.

He appeared as no more than a thin black line at first, which widened and flattened to a two-dimensional image of the archmage arcane then filled out to become Arklem Greeth in person.

"They are always full of surprises," the archmage said, considering the drow from about five strides away. Grinning wickedly, he lifted his hands and waggled his fingers.

Drizzt sprinted at him with blinding speed, intent on taking him down before he could complete the spell. He dived at the powerful wizard, scimitars leading, and driving right through the image of the lich.

It was just an image—an image masking a magical gate through which tumbled the surprised dark elf. He tried to stop, skidding along the ground, and when it was obvious that he was caught, on pure instinct and a combination of desperate hope and the responsibility of friendship, he tore free his belt pouch and threw it back behind him.

Then he was tumbling in the darkness, a wretched, sulfuric smell thickening around him, great dark shapes moving through the smoky shadows of a vast, dark field of sharp-edged rocks and steaming lines of blood red lava.

Gehenna . . . or the Nine Hells . . . or the Abyss . . . or Tarterus. . . . He didn't know, but it was one of the lower planes, one of the homes of the devils and demons and other wicked creatures, a place in which he could not long survive.

He didn't even have his bearings or his feet back under him when a black beast, dark as the shadows, leaped upon him from behind.

* * * * *

"Pathetic," Arklem Greeth said, shaking his head, almost disappointed that the champion of the lords who had come against him had been so easily dispatched.

Staying close to the central tower, the archmage arcane moved along and spotted the banners of his principle enemies, the invading Lord Brambleberry, so far from home, and the fool Deudermont, who had turned the city against him.

He studied the field for a short while, mentally measuring the distance with supernatural precision. The tumult all around him, the screaming, dying, and explosions, seemed distant and unremarkable. A spear flew his way and struck solidly, except that his magical protections simply flattened its metal tip and dropped it harmlessly to the ground before it got near to his undead flesh.

He didn't even wince. His focus remained on his principle enemies.

Arklem Greeth rubbed his hands together eagerly, preparing his spells.

In a flash he was gone, and when he stepped through the other side of the dimensional portal in the midst of a fighting throng, he tapped his thumbs together before him and brought forth a fan of fire, driving away friend and foe alike. Then he thrust his hands out wide to his sides and from each came a mighty forked lightning bolt, angled down to thump into the ground with such force that men and zombies, dwarves and ghouls went bouncing wildly away, leaving Arklem Greeth alone in his own little field of calm.

Everyone noticed him—how could they not?—for his display of power and fury was so far beyond anything that had been brought to the field thus far, by either Brambleberry or the Hosttower.

Barely controlling their mounts at that point, both Brambleberry and Deudermont turned to regard their foe.

"Kill him!" Brambleberry cried, and even as the words left his mouth, so too came the next of Arklem Greeth's magical barrages.

All around the two leaders, the ground churned and broke apart, soil spraying, rocks flying, roots tearing. Down they tumbled side by side, their horses twisting and breaking around them. Brambleberry's landed atop him with a sickening cracking of bones, and though he was luckier to fall aside from his thrashing and terrified horse, Deudermont still found himself at the bottom of a ten-foot hole, thick with mud and water.

Up above, Arklem Greeth wasn't finished. He ignored the sudden reversal his assault on Brambleberry, and particularly upon beloved Deudermont, had wrought in the army around them, their fear quickly turning to outrage aimed at Greeth alone. Like the one point of calm in a world gone mad, Arklem Greeth followed his earth-shaking spell with an earthquake that had all around him stumbling and falling. The line of the tremor was aimed perfectly for the loose mounds at the sides of the chasm he had created. He meant to bury the Waterdhavian lord and the good captain alive.

All around them realized it, though, and came at Greeth with fury, a roiling throng of outrage closing in on him from every side, throwing spears and rocks—even swords—anything to distract or wound that being of ultimate evil.

"Fools, all," the archmage arcane muttered under his breath.

With one last burst of power that broke apart one side of the deep hole, Greeth fell back into his wraithform, flattening to two dimensions. He narrowed to a black line and slipped down into the ground, running swiftly through narrow cracks until he stood again in his own chamber in the Hosttower of the Arcane.

Exhaustion followed him there, for the lich had not utilized such a sudden and potent barrage of magic in many, many years. He heard the continuing roar outside his window and didn't need to go there to understand that any gains he'd made would prove temporary.

Dropping the leaders had not turned the mob, but had only incensed it further.

There were simply too many. Too many fools . . . too much fodder.

"Fools all," he said again, and he thought of Valindra out along the southern rocks of Cutlass Island. He hoped she was dead already.

With a heavy sigh that crackled across the collection of hardened mucus in Arklem Greeth's unbreathing lungs, the lich went to his private stash of potent drinks—drinks he had created himself, fashioned mostly of blood and living things. Drinks that, like the lich himself, transcended death. He took a long, deep sip of one potent mixture.

He thought of his decades at the Hosttower, a place he had so long called home. He knew that was over, for the time being at least, but he could wait.

And he could make it hurt.

The chamber would come with him—he had fashioned it with magic for just such a sudden and violent transportation, for he had known from the moment he'd achieved lichdom that the day would surely befall him when he'd have to abandon his tower home. But he, and the part he most coveted, would be saved.

The rest would be lost.

Arklem Greeth moved through a small trapdoor, down a ladder to a tiny secret room where he kept one of his most prized possessions: a staff of incredible power. With that staff, a younger, living Arklem Greeth had waged great battles, his fireballs and lightning bolts greater in number and intensity. With that staff, full of its own power to taste of Mystra's Weave, he had escaped certain doom many times on those occasions when his own magical reservoir had been drained.

He rubbed a hand over its burnished wood, considering it as he would an old friend.

It was set in a strange contraption of Greeth's design. The staff itself was laid across a pyramid-shaped stone, the very center of the six-foot long staff right at the narrow tip of the great block. Hanging from chains at either end of the staff were two large metal bowls, and up above those bowls, over the staff and on stout stands of thick iron, sat two tanks of dense silver liquid.

With another sigh, Greeth reached up and pulled a central cord, one that uncorked plugs from the mercury-filled reservoirs, and dropped out chutes directly over the corresponding bowls.

The heavy fluid metal began to flow, slowly and teasingly dripping into the bowls, like the sands of an hourglass counting down the end of the world.

Such staves as that, so full of magical energy, could not be broken without a cataclysmic release.

Arklem Greeth went back to his secure but mobile chamber with confidence that the explosion would send him exactly where he wanted to go.

* * * * *

They were winning the field, but the Luskar and their Waterdhavian allies didn't feel victorious, not with their leaders Brambleberry and Deudermont buried! They set a defensive perimeter around the churned area, and many fell over the loose dirt, digging with sword and dagger, or bare hands. A torn fingernail elicited no more than a grimace among the determined, frantic group. One man inadvertently drove his dagger through his own hand, but merely growled as he went back to tearing at the ground for his beloved Captain Deudermont.

Fury rained upon the field: fire and lightning, monsters undead and magically created. The Luskar matched that fury; they were fighting for their very lives, for their families. There could be no retreat, no withdrawal, and to a man and woman they knew it.

So they fought, and fired their arrows at the wizards on the balconies, and though they died ten-to-one, perhaps more, it seemed that their advance could not be halted.

But then it was, with the snap of a magical staff.

* * * * *

Someone tugged hard at his arm, and Deudermont gasped his first breath in far too long a time as another hand scraped the dirt away from his face.

Through bleary eyes, he saw his rescuers, a woman brushing his face, a strong man yanking at his one extended arm, and with such force that Deudermont feared he would pull his shoulder right out of its socket.

His thoughts went to Brambleberry, who had fallen beside him, and he took heart to see so many clawing at the ground, so much commotion to rescue the Waterdhavian lord. Though he was still fully immersed in the soil, other than that one extended arm, Deudermont somehow managed to nod, and even smile at the woman cleaning off his face.

Then she was gone—a wave of multicolored energy rolled out like a ripple on a pond, crossing over Deudermont with the sound of a cyclone.

The sleeve burned from his extended arm, his face flushed with stinging warmth. It seemed to go on for many, many heartbeats, then came the sound of crashing, like trees falling. Deudermont felt the ground rumble three or four times—too close together for him to accurately take a count.

His arm fell limp to the ground. As he regained his sensibilities, Deudermont saw the boots of the man who had been tugging at his arm. The captain couldn't turn his head enough to follow up the legs, but he knew the man was dead.

He knew that the field was dead.

Too still.

And too quiet, so suddenly, as if all the world had ended.

* * * * *

Robillard kept his forces tight and organized as they made their way north along Cutlass Island. He was fairly certain that they'd meet no resistance until they got within the Hosttower's compound, but he wanted the first response from his force to be coordinated and devastating. He assured those around him that they would clear every window, every balcony, every doorway on the North Spire with their first barrage.

Behind Robillard came Valindra, her arms tightly bound behind her back, flanked by Maimun and Arabeth.

"The archmage arcane falls this day," Robillard remarked quietly, so that only those close to him could hear.

"Arklem Greeth is more than ready for you," Valindra retorted.

Arabeth reacted with a suddenness that shocked the others, spinning a left hook into the face of their moon elf captive. Valindra's head jolted back and came forward, blood showing below her thin, pretty nose.

"You will pay for—" Valindra warned, or started to, until Arabeth hit her again, just as viciously.

Robillard and Maimun looked to each other incredulously, but then both just grinned at Arabeth's initiative. They could clearly see the years of enmity between the two overwizards, and separately reasoned that the taller and more classically beautiful Valindra had often been a thorn in Arabeth's side.

Each man made a mental note to not anger the Lady Raurym.

Valindra seemed to get the message as well, for she said no more.

Robillard led them up a tumble of boulders to get a view over the wall. The fighting was thick and vicious all around the five-spired tower. The ship's wizard quickly formulated an approach to best come onto the field, and was about to relay it to his charges when the staff broke.

The world seemed to fall apart.

Maimun saved Robillard that day, the young pirate reacting with amazing agility to pull the older wizard down behind the rocks beside him. Similarly, Arabeth rescued Valindra, albeit inadvertently, for as she, too, dived back, she brushed the captive enough to send her tumbling down as well.

The wave of energy rolled over them. Rocks went flying and several of Robillard's force fell hard, more than one mortally wounded. They were on the outer edge of the blast and so it passed quickly. Robillard, Maimun, and Arabeth all scrambled to their feet quickly enough to peer over and witness the fall of the Hosttower itself. The largest, central pillar, Greeth's own, was gone, as if it had either been blown to dust or had simply vanished—and it truth, it was a bit of both. The four armlike spires, the once graceful limbs, tumbled down, crashing in burning heaps and billowing clouds of angry gray dust.

The warriors on the field, man and monster alike, had fallen in neat rows, like cut timber, and though groans and cries told Robillard and the others that some had survived, none of the three believed for a heartbeat that number to be large.

"By the gods, Greeth, what have you done?" Robillard asked into the empty and suddenly still morning air.

Arabeth gave a sudden cry of dismay and fell back, and neither Maimun nor Robillard considered her quickly enough to stop her as she leaped down at the face-down and battered Valindra and drove a dagger deep into the captured wizard's back.

"No!" Robillard cried at her when he realized her action. "We need . . ." He stopped and grimaced as Arabeth retracted the blade and struck again, and again, and Valindra's screams became muffled with blood.

Maimun finally got to Arabeth and pulled her back; Robillard called for a priest.

He waved back the first of the clerics that came forward, though, knowing that it was too late, and that others would need his healing prayers.

"What have you done?" Robillard asked Arabeth, who sobbed, but looked at the devastated field, not at her gruesome handiwork.

"It was better than she deserved," Arabeth replied.

Glancing over his shoulder at the utter devastation of the Hosttower of the Arcane, and the men and women who had gone against it, Robillard found it hard to disagree.

CHAPTER

C O N S E Q U E N C E

17

The irony of pulling a battered, but very much alive Deudermont from the ground was not lost on Maimun, who considered how many others—they were all around him on the devastated field—would soon be put *into* the ground, and because of the decisions of that very same captain.

"Don't kick a man who's lying flat, I've been told," Maimun muttered, and Robillard and Arabeth turned to regard him, as well as the half-conscious Deudermont. "But you're an idiot, good captain."

"Watch your tongue, young one," Robillard warned.

"Better to remain silent than speak the truth and offend the powerful, yes Robillard?" Maimun replied with a sour and knowing grin.

"Remind me why *Sea Sprite* didn't sink *Thrice Lucky* on the many occasions we've seen you at sea," the wizard threatened. "I seem to forget."

"My charm, no doubt."

"Enough, you two," Arabeth scolded, her voice trembling with every syllable. "Look around you! Is this travesty all about *you?* About your petty rivalry? About placing blame?"

"How can it not be about who's to blame?" Maimun started to argue, but Arabeth cut him short with a vicious scowl.

"It's about those scattered on this field, nothing more," she said, her voice even. "Alive and dead . . . in the Hosttower and without."

Maimun swallowed hard and glanced at Robillard, who seemed equally out of venom, and indeed, Arabeth's argument was difficult to counter given the carnage around them. They finished extracting Deudermont at the same time

185

that another rescue team called out that they had located Lord Brambleberry.

The ground covering him had saved him from the explosion, but had smothered him in the process. The young Waterdhavian lord, so full of ambition and vision, and the desire to earn his way, was dead.

There would be no cheering that day, and even if there had been, it would have been drowned out by the cries of anguish and agony.

Work went on through the night and into the next day, separating dead from wounded, tending to those who could be helped. Guided by Robillard, assault teams went into each of the four fallen spires of the destroyed Hosttower, and more than a few of Arklem Greeth's minions were pulled from the rubble, all surrendering without a struggle, no fight left in them—not after seeing the unbridled evil of the man they'd once called the archmage arcane.

The cost had been horrific—more than a third of the population of the once-teeming city of Luskan was dead.

But the war was over.

* * * * *

Captain Deudermont shook his head solemnly.

"What does that mean?" Regis yelled at him. "You can't just say he's *gone!*"

"Many are just gone, my friend," Deudermont explained. "The blast that took the Hosttower released all manner of magical power, destructive and altering. Men were burned and blasted, others transformed, and others, many others, banished from this world. Some were utterly destroyed, I'm told, their very souls disintegrated into nothingness."

"And what happened to Drizzt?" Regis demanded.

"We cannot know. He is not to be found. Like so many. I'm sorry. I feel this loss as keenly as—"

"Shut up!" Regis yelled at him. "You don't know anything! Robillard tried to warn you—many did! You don't know anything! You chose this fight and look at what it has gotten you, what it has gotten us all!"

"Enough!" Robillard growled at the halfling, and he moved threateningly at Regis.

Deudermont held him back, though, understanding that Regis's tirade was wrought of utter grief. How could it not be? Why should it not be? The loss of Drizzt Do'Urden was no small thing, after all, particularly not to the halfling that had spent the better part of the last decades by the dark elf's side.

"We could not know the desperation of Arklem Greeth, or that he was capable of such wanton devastation," Deudermont said, his voice quiet and humble. "But the fact that he was capable of it, and willing to do it, only proves that he had to be removed, by whatever means the people of Luskan could muster. He would have rained his devastation upon them sooner or later, and in more malicious forms, no doubt. Whether freeing the undead from the magical bindings of Illusk or using his wizards to slowly bleed the city into submission, he was no man worthy of being the leader of this city."

"You act as if this city is worthy of having a leader," Regis said.

"They stood arm in arm to win," Deudermont scolded, growing excited—so much so that the priest attending him grabbed him by the shoulders to remind him that he had to stay calm. "Every family in Luskan feels grief as keen as your own. Doubt that not at all. The price of their freedom has been high indeed."

"Their freedom, their fight," the halfling spat.

"Drizzt marched with me willingly," Deudermont reminded Regis. That was the last of it, though, as the priest forcibly guided the captain out of the room.

"You throw guilt on the shoulders of a man already bent low by its great weight," Robillard said.

"He made his choices."

"As did you, as did I, and as did Drizzt. I understand your pain—Drizzt Do'Urden was my friend, as well—but does your anger at Captain Deudermont do anything to alleviate it?"

Regis started to answer, started to protest, but stopped and fell back on his bed. What was the point?

Of anything?

He thought of Mithral Hall and felt that it was past time for him to go home.

* * * * *

He couldn't even make out their physical shapes, as they seemed no more than extensions of the endless shadows that surrounded him. Nor could he distinguish the many natural weapons that each of the demonic creatures seemed to possess, and so all of his fighting was purely on instinct, purely on reaction.

There was no victory to be found. He would stay alive only as long as his reactions and reflexes remained fast enough to fend off the gathering cloud of monsters, only as long as his arms held the strength to keep his scimitars high enough to block a serpentine head from tearing out his throat, or a clublike fist from bashing in the side of his skull.

He needed a reprieve, but there was none. He needed to escape, but knew that was just as unlikely.

So he fought, blades and growls denying his own mortality. Drizzt fought and ran, and fought some more and ran some more, always seeking a place of refuge.

And finding only more battle.

A large black shape rose before him, six arms coming at him in an overwhelming barrage, and with overwhelming strength. Knowing better than to try to stand against it, Drizzt dived to the ground to the side, thinking to roll to his feet and rush around to attack the creature from another angle.

But it had prepared for him, and when he hit the ground, he found his momentum stolen by a thick puddle of sticky mucus.

The creature rushed over to him, rising to its full height, twice that of a tall man. It lifted all six of its thunderous arms out wide and high, and bellowed in anticipation of victory.

Drizzt wriggled an arm free and stabbed it hard in the leg, but that would hardly slow the beast.

When Guenhwyvar crashed into the side of its lupine head, though, all thoughts of finishing off the drow fled, as both panther and demon flew away.

Drizzt wasted no time in extracting himself from the muck, muttering thanks to Guenhwyvar all the while. How lifted his spirits had been when he'd realized the identity of his first encounter in that hellish place, when he'd realized that Guenhwyvar had followed him through Arklem Greeth's gate. Together they had defeated every foe thus far, and as Drizzt closed in on the fallen behemoth, scimitars swinging, another demon found its premature victory cries muffled by its own blood.

Drizzt paused to crouch beside Guenhwyvar, though he knew they had to move along, and quickly.

He had been so pleased to see her, so hopeful that his rescue was at hand by his dearest of companions, but he had come to regret that Guenhwyvar had come through, for she was as trapped as he, and surely as doomed.

* * * * *

"Well, now, there's a good one," Queaser said to Skerrit through a mouth half-full of twisted yellow teeth. "I'll get us a good bit for this, I'd be guessin'."

"What'd ye find then, ye dirty cow?" Skerrit replied with an equally wretched grin, and one made worse since he was between bites of some rancid meat he had found in the pocket of a dead soldier.

Queaser motioned for Skerrit to come closer—the field was full of looting thugs, after all—and showed him an onyx figurine beautifully crafted into the likeness of a great black cat.

"Heh, but we should be thanking Deudermont for bringing so much opportunity our way, I'm thinking," said a very pleased Skerrit. "Three-hands'll give us a purse o' gold for that one."

Queaser laughed and stuffed the figurine into a pouch under his dirty and ragged vest, instead of the large, bulging sack where he and Skerrit had placed the more mundane booty.

"Let's get away," Queaser reasoned. "If they're to catch us with the coin and the belts, that's our loss, but I'm not for wanting this treasure tucked into the pocket of a Luskar guard."

"Get her sold," Skerrit agreed. "There'll be more to find on the field tomorrow night, and the night after that, and after that again."

The two wretches shuffled across the dark field. Somewhere in the darkness, a wounded woman, not yet found by the rescue teams, moaned pitifully, but they ignored the plea and went on their profitable way.

CHAPTER

ASCENSION AND SALVATION

18

Y ou are recovering well," Robillard said to Deudermont the next morning, a brilliantly sunny one, quite rare in Luskan that time of year. In response, the captain held up his injured arm, clenched his hand, and nodded. "Or would be, if we could quiet the din," Robillard added. He moved to the room's large window, which overlooked a wide square, and pulled aside a corner of the heavy curtain.

Out in the square, a great cheer arose.

Robillard shook his head and sighed then turned back to see Deudermont sitting up on the edge of his bed.

"My waistcoat, if you would," Deudermont said.

"You should not . . ." Robillard replied, but without much conviction, for he knew the captain would never heed his warning. The resigned wizard went from the window to the dresser and retrieved his friend's clothes.

Deudermont followed him, albeit shakily.

"You're sure you're ready for this?" the wizard asked, helping with the sleeves of a puffy white shirt.

"How many days has it been?"

"Only three."

"Do we know the count of the dead? Has Drizzt been found?"

"Two thousand, at least," Robillard answered. "Perhaps half again that number." Deudermont winced from more than pain as Robillard slid the waistcoat along his injured arm. "And no, I fear that Arklem Greeth's treachery marked the end of our drow friend," Robillard added. "We haven't found as much as a dark-skinned finger. He was right near the tower when it exploded, I'm told."

"Quick and without pain, then," said Deudermont. "That's something we all hope for." He nodded and shuffled to the window.

"I expect Drizzt hoped for it to come several centuries from now," Robillard had to jab as he followed.

Propelled as much by anger as determination, Deudermont grabbed the heavy curtain and pulled it wide. Still using only his uninjured arm, he tugged the window open and stepped into clear view of the throng gathered in the square.

Below him on the street, the people of Luskan, so battered and bereaved, so weary of battle, oppression, thieves, murderers, and all the rest, cheered wildly. More than one of the gathering fainted, overcome by emotion.

"Deudermont is alive!" someone cried.

"Huzzah for Deudermont!" another cheered.

"A third of them dead and they cheer for me," Deudermont said over his shoulder, his expression grim.

"It shows how much they hated Arklem Greeth, I expect," Robillard replied. "But look past the square, past the hopeful faces, and you will see that we haven't much time."

Deudermont did just that, and took in the ruin of Cutlass Island. Even Closeguard had not escaped the weight of the blast, with many of the houses on the western side of the island flattened and still smoldering. Beyond Closeguard, in the harbor, a quartet of masts protruded from the dark waves. Four ships had been damaged, and two fully lost.

All across the city signs of devastation remained, the fallen bridge, the burned buildings, the heavy pall of smoke.

"Hopeful faces," Deudermont remarked of the crowd. "Not satisfied, not victorious, just hopeful."

"Hope is the back of hate's coin," Robillard warned and the captain nodded, knowing all too well that it was past time for him to get out of his bed and get to work.

He waved to the crowd and moved back into his room, followed by the frenzied cheers of desperate folk.

* * * * *

"It's worth a thousand gold if it's worth a plug copper," Queaser argued, shaking the figurine in front of the unimpressed expression of Rodrick Fenn, the most famous pawnbroker in Luskan. Languishing beside the many others who dealt with the minor rogues and pirates of the city, Rodrick had only recently come into prominence, mostly because of the vast array of exotic goods he'd somehow managed to wrangle. A large bounty had been offered for information regarding Rodrick's new source.

"I'll give ye three gold, and ye'll be glad to get it," Rodrick said.

Queaser and Skerrit exchanged sour looks, both shaking their heads.

"You should pay him to take it from you," said another in the store, who seemed an unassuming enough patron. In fact, he had been invited by Rodrick for just such a transaction, since Skerrit had tipped off Rodrick the night before regarding the onyx figurine.

"What d'ye know of it?" Skerrit demanded.

"I know that it was Drizzt Do'Urden's," Morik the Rogue replied. "I know that you hold a drow item, and one the dark elves will want returned. I wouldn't wish to be the person caught with it, to be sure."

Queaser and Skerrit looked at each other again, then Queaser scoffed and waved a hand dismissively at the rogue.

"Think, you fools," said Morik. "Consider who—what—ran beside Drizzt into that last battle." Morik gave a little laugh. "You've managed to place yourself between legions of drow and Captain Deudermont . . . oh, and King Bruenor of Mithral Hall, as well, who will no doubt seek that figurine out. Congratulations are in order." He ended his sarcastic stream with a mocking laugh, and made his way toward the door.

"Twenty pieces of gold, and be glad for it," Rodrick said. "And I'll be turning it over to Deudermont, don't you doubt, and hoping he'll repay me—and if I'm in a good mood, I might tell him that the two of you came to me so that I could give it back to him."

Queaser looked as if he was trying to say something, but no words came out.

"Or I'll just go to Deudermont and make his search a bit easier, and you'll be glad that I sent him and that I had no way to tell any dark elves instead."

"Ye're bluffing," Skerrit insisted.

"Call it, then," Rodrick said with a wry grin.

Skerrit turned to Queaser, but the suddenly pale man was already handing the figurine over.

The two left quickly, passing Morik, who was outside leaning against the wall beside the door.

"You chose well," the rogue assured them.

Skerrit got in his face. "Shut yer mouth, and if ye're ever for telling anyone other than what Rodrick's telling them, then know we're to find ye first and do ye under."

Morik shrugged, an exaggerated movement that perfectly covered the slide of his hand. He went back into Rodrick's shop as the two hustled away.

"I'll be wanting my gold back," Rodrick greeted him, but the smiling Morik was already tossing the pouch the pawnbroker's way. Morik walked over to the counter and Rodrick handed him the statue.

"Worth more than a thousand," Rodrick muttered as Morik took it.

"If it keeps the bosses happy, it's worth our very lives," the rogue replied, and he tipped his hat and departed.

* * * * *

"Governor," Baram spat with disgust. "They're wanting him to be governor, and he's to take the call, by all accounts."

"And well he should," Kensidan replied.

"And this don't bother ye?" Baram asked. "Ye said we'd be finding power when Greeth was gone, and now Greeth's gone and all I'm finding are widows and brats needing food. I'll be emptying half of me coffers to keep the folk of Ship Baram in line."

"Consider it the best investment of your life," High Captain Kurth answered before Kensidan could. "No Ship lost more than my own."

"I lost most of me guards," Taerl put in. "Ye lost a hundred common folk and a score of houses, but I lost fighters. How many of yers marched alongside Deudermont?"

His bluster couldn't hold, though, as Kurth fixed him with a perfectly vicious glare.

"Deudermont's ascension was predictable and desirable," Kensidan said to them all to get the meeting of the five back on track. "We survived the war. Our Ships remain intact, though battered, as Luskan herself is battered. That will mend, and this time, we will not have the smothering strength of the Hosttower holding us in check at every turn. Be at ease, my friends, for this has gone splendidly. True, we could not fully anticipate the devastation Greeth wrought, and true, we have many more dead than we expected, but the war was mercifully short and favorably concluded. We could not ask for a better stooge than Captain Deudermont to serve as the new puppet governor of Luskan."

"Don't underestimate him," Kurth warned. "He is a hero to the people, even to those fighters who serve in our ranks."

"Then we must make sure that the next few tendays shine a different light upon him," said Kensidan. As he finished, he looked at his closest ally, Suljack, and saw the man frowning and shaking his head. Kensidan wasn't quite sure what that might mean, for in truth, Suljack had lost the most soldiers in the battle, with nearly all of his Ship marching beside Deudermont and a good many of them killed at the Hosttower.

* * * * *

"Well enough to get out of bed, I would say," a voice accosted Regis. He lay in his bed, half asleep, feeling perfectly miserable both emotionally and physically. He could deal with his wounds a lot easier than with the loss of Drizzt. How was he going to go back to Mithral Hall and face Bruenor? And Catti-brie!

"I feel better," he lied.

"Then do sit up, little one," the voice replied, and that gave Regis pause, for he didn't recognize the speaker and saw no one when he looked around the room.

He sat up quickly then, and immediately focused on a darkened corner of the room.

Magically darkened, he knew.

"Who are you?" he asked.

"An old friend."

Regis shook his head.

"Fare well on your journey. . . ." the voice said and the last notes of the sentence faded away to nothingness, taking the magical darkness with it.

Leaving a revelation that had Regis gawking with surprise and trepidation.

* * * * *

He knew that he was nearing the end, and that there was no way out. Guenhwyvar, too, would perish, and Drizzt could only pray that her death on that alien plane, removed from the figurine, wouldn't be permanent, that she would, as she had on the Prime Material Plane, simply revert to her Astral home.

The drow cursed himself for leaving the statuette behind.

And he fought, not for himself, for he knew that he was doomed, but for Guenhwyvar, his beloved friend. Perhaps she would find her way home through sheer exhaustion, as long as he could keep her alive long enough.

He didn't know how many hours, days, had passed. He had found bitter nourishment in giant mushrooms and in the flesh of some of the strange beasts that had come against him, but both had left him sickly and weak.

He knew he was nearing the end, but the fighting was not.

He faced a six-armed monstrosity, every lumbering swing from its thick arms heavy enough to decapitate him. Drizzt was too quick for those swipes, of course, and had he been less weary, his foe would have been an easy kill. But the drow could hardly hold his scimitars aloft, and his focus kept slipping. Several times, he managed to duck away just in time to avoid a heavy punch.

"Come on, Guen," he whispered under his breath, having set the fiendish beast up for a sidelong strike from the panther's position on a rocky outcropping to the right. Drizzt heard a growl, and grinned, expecting Guenhwyvar to fly in for the kill.

But Drizzt got hit, and hard, instead, a flying tackle that flung him away from the beast and left him rolling in a tangle with another powerful creature.

He didn't understand—it was all he could do to hold onto his scimitars, let alone try to bring them to bear.

But then the muddy ground beneath him became more solid, and a stinging light blinded him, and though his eyes could not adjust to see anything, he realized from another familiar growl that it was Guenhwyvar who had tackled him.

He heard a friendly voice, a welcomed voice, a cry of glee.

He got hit with another flying tackle almost as soon as he'd extricated himself from the jumble with Guen.

"How?" he asked Regis.

"I don't know and I don't care!" the halfling responded, hugging Drizzt all the tighter.

* * * * *

"Kurth is right," High Captain Rethnor warned his son. "Underestimate Captain Deudermont . . . *Governor* Deudermont, at our peril. He is a man of actions, not words. You were never at sea, and so you don't understand the horror that filled men's eyes when the sails of *Sea Sprite* were spotted."

"I have heard the talés, but this is not the sea," Kensidan replied.

"You have it all figured out," Rethnor said, his mocking tone unmistakable.

"I remain agile in my ability to adapt to whatever comes our way."

"But for now?"

"For now, I allow Kurth to run rampant on Closeguard and Cutlass, and even in the market area. He and I will dominate the streets easily enough, with Suljack playing my fool."

"Deudermont may disband Prisoner's Carnival, but he will raise a strong militia to enforce the laws."

"His laws," Kensidan replied, "not Luskan's."

"They are one and the same now."

"No, not yet, and not ever if we properly pressure the streets," said Kensidan. "Turmoil is Deudermont's enemy, and lack of order will eventually turn the people against him. If he pushes too hard, he will find all of Luskan against him, as Arklem Greeth realized."

"It's a fight you want?" Rethnor said after a contemplative pause.

"It's a fight I insist upon," his conniving son answered. "For now, Deudermont makes a fine target for the anger of others, while Ship Kurth and Ship Rethnor rule the streets. When the breaking point is reached, a second war will erupt in Luskan, and when it's done . . ."

"A free port," said Rethnor. "A sanctuary for . . . merchant ships."

"With ready trade in exotic goods that will find their way to the homes of Waterdhavian lords and to the shops of Baldur's Gate," said Kensidan. "That alone will keep Waterdeep from organizing an invasion of the new Luskan, for the self-serving bastard nobles will not threaten their own playthings. We'll have our port, our city, and all pretense of law and subservience to the lords of Waterdeep be damned."

"Lofty goals," said Rethnor.

"My father, I only seek to make you proud," Kensidan said with such obvious sarcasm that old Rethnor could only laugh, and heartily.

* * * * *

"I'm not easy with this disembodied voice arriving in the darkness," Deudermont said. "But pleased I am, beyond anything, to see you alive and well."

"Well is a relative term," the drow replied. "But I'm recovering—though if you ever happen to travel to the plane of my imprisonment, take care to avoid the mushrooms."

Deudermont and Robillard laughed at that, as did Regis, who was standing at Drizzt's side, both of them carrying their packs for the road.

"I have acquaintances on Luskan's streets," Drizzt reasoned. "Some not even of my knowing, but friends of a friend."

"Wulfgar," said Deudermont. "Perhaps it was that Morik character he ran beside—though he's not supposed to be in Luskan, on pain of death."

Drizzt shrugged. "Whatever good fortune brought Guenhwyvar's statue to Regis, it's good fortune I will accept."

"True enough," said the captain. "And now you are bound for Icewind Dale. Are you sure that you cannot stay the winter, for I've much to do, and your help would serve me well."

"If we hurry, we can beat the snows to Ten-Towns," said Drizzt.

"And you will return to Luskan in the spring?"

"We would be sorry friends indeed if we didn't," Regis answered.

"We will return," Drizzt promised.

With handshakes and bows, the pair left *Sea Sprite,* which served as the governor's palace until the devastation in the city could be sorted out and a new location, formerly the Red Dragon Inn on the northern bank of the Mirar, could be properly secured and readied.

The enormity of the rebuilding task ahead of Luskan was not lost on Drizzt and Regis as they walked through the city's streets. Much of the place had been gutted by flames and so many had died, leaving one empty structure after another. Many of the larger homes and taverns had been confiscated by order of Governor Deudermont and set up as hospitals for the many, many wounded, or as often as not as morgues to hold the bodies until they could be properly identified and buried.

"The Luskar will do little through the winter, other than to try to find food and warmth," Regis remarked as they passed a group of haggard women huddled in a doorway.

"It will be a long road," Drizzt agreed.

"Was it worth the cost?" the halfling asked.

"We can't yet know."

"A lot of folk would disagree with you on that," Regis remarked, nodding in the direction of the new graveyard north of the city.

"Arklem Greeth was intolerable," Drizzt reminded his friend. "If the city can withstand the next few months, a year perhaps, with the rebuilding in the summer, then Deudermont will do well by them, do not doubt. He will call in every favor from every Waterdhavian lord, and goods and supplies will flow fast to Luskan."

"Will it be enough, though?" Regis asked. "With so many of the healthy adults dead, how many of their families will even stay?"

Drizzt shrugged helplessly.

"Perhaps we should stay and help through the winter," said Regis, but Drizzt was shaking his head.

"Not everyone in Luskan accepts me, Deudermont's friend or not," the drow replied. "We didn't instigate their fight, but we helped the correct side win it. Now we must trust them to do what's right—there's little we can do here now. Besides, I want to see Wulfgar again, and Icewind Dale. Its been too long since I've looked upon my first true home."

"But Luskan . . ." Regis started.

Drizzt interrupted with an upraised hand.

"Was it really worth it?" Regis pressed anyway.

"I have no answers, nor do you."

They passed out of the city's northern gate then, to the halfhearted cheers of the few guardsmen along the wall and towers.

"Maybe we could get them all to march to Longsaddle next," Regis remarked, and Drizzt laughed, almost as helplessly as he had shrugged.

PART 3

HARMONY

HARMONY

I am often struck by the parallel courses I find in the wide world. My life's road has led me to many places, back and forth from Mithral Hall to the Sword Coast, to Icewind Dale and the Snowflake Mountains, to Calimport and to the Underdark. I have come to know the truth of the old saying that the only constant is change, but what strikes me most profoundly is the similarity of direction in that change, a concordance of mood, from place to place, in towns and among people who have no, or at least only cursory, knowledge of each other.

I find unrest and I find hope. I find contentment and I find anger. And always, it seems, I'm met with the same general set of emotions among the people from place to place. I understand there is a rationality to it all, for even peoples remote from each other will share common influences: a difficult winter, a war in one land that affects commerce in another, whispers of a spreading plague, the rise of a new king whose message resonates among the populace and brings hope and joy even to those far removed from his growing legend. But still, I often feel as though there is another realm of the senses. As a cold winter might spread through Icewind Dale and Luskan, and all the way to the Silver Marches, so too, it seems, does mood spiderweb the paths and roads of the Realms. It's almost as if there is a second layer of weather, an emotional wave that rolls and roils its way across Faerûn.

There is trepidation and hopeful change in Mithral Hall and the rest of the Silver Marches, a collective holding of breath where the coin of true peace and all-out war spins on its edge, and not dwarf nor elf nor human nor orc knows on which side it will land. There is a powerful emotional battle waging between the status quo and the desire to embrace great and promising change.

And so I found this same unsettling dynamic in Longsaddle, where the Harpells are engaged in a similar state of near disaster with the rival factions of their community. They hold the coin fast, locked in spells to conserve what is, but the stress and strain are obvious to all who view.

And so I found this same dynamic in Luskan, where the potential change is no less profound than the possible—and none too popular—acceptance of an orc kingdom as a viable partner in the league of nations that comprise the Silver Marches.

A wave of unrest and edginess has gripped the land, from Mithral Hall to the Sword Coast—palpably so. It's as if the people and races of the world have all at once declared the unacceptability of their current lot in life, as if the sentient beings have finished their collective exhale and are now taking in a new breath.

I head to Icewind Dale, a land of tradition that extends beyond the people who live there, a land of constants and of constant pressure. A land not unaccustomed to war, a land that knows death intimately. If the same breath that brought Obould from his hole, that brought out ancient hatreds among the priests of Longsaddle, that led to the rise of Deudermont and the fall of Arklem Greeth, has filled the unending winds of Icewind Dale, then I truly fear what I may find there, in a place where the smoke of a gutted homestead is almost as common as the smoke of a campfire, and where the howl of the wolf is no less threatening than the war cry of a barbarian, or the battle call of an orc, or the roar of a white dragon. Under the constant struggle to simply survive, Icewind Dale is on edge even in those times when the world is in a place of peace and contentment. What might I find there now, when my road has passed through lands of strife and battle?

I wonder sometimes if there is a god, or gods, who play with the emotions of the collective of sentient beings as an artist colors a canvas. Might there be supernatural beings watching and taking amusement at our toils and tribulations? Do these gods wave giant wands of envy or greed or contentment or love over us all, that they can then watch at their pleasure, perhaps even gamble on the outcome?

Or do they, too, battle amongst themselves, reflections of our own failures, and their victories and failures similarly extend to us, their insignificant minions?

Or am I simply taking the easier route of reasoning, and ascribing what I cannot know to some irrationally defined being or beings for the sake of my own comfort? This trail, I fear, may be no more than warm porridge on a wintry morning.

Whatever it is, the weather or the rise of a great foe, folk demanding to partake of advancements in comfort or the sweep of a plague, or some unseen and nefarious god or gods at play, or whether, perhaps, the collective I view is no more than an extension of my own inner turmoil or contentment, a projection of Drizzt upon the people he views . . . whatever it may be, this collective emotion seems to me a palpable thing, a real and true motion of shared breath.

—Drizzt Do'Urden

CHAPTER

THE WIND IN THEIR EARS

19

It happened imperceptibly, a delicate transition that touched the memories and souls of the companions as profoundly as it reverberated in their physical senses. For as the endless and mournful wind of Icewind Dale filled their ears, as the smell of the tundra filled their noses, as the cold northern air tickled their skin, and as the sheet of wintry white dazzled their eyes, so too did the aura of the place, the primal savagery, the pristine beauty, fill their thoughts, so too did the edge of catastrophe awaken their conflicting fears.

That was the true power of the dale, exemplified by the wind, always the wind, the constant reminder of the paradox of existence, that one was always alone and never alone, that communion ended at senses' edge and yet that the same communion never truly ended.

They walked side-by-side, without speaking, but not in silence. They were joined by the wind of Icewind Dale, in the same place and same time, and whatever thoughts they each entertained separately could not fully escape the bond of awareness forced by Icewind Dale itself upon all who ventured there.

They crossed out of the pass through the Spine of the World and onto the wider tundra one bright and shining morning, and found that the snows were not yet too deep, and the wind not yet too cold. In a few days, if the weather held, they would arrive in Ten-Towns, the ten settlements around the three deep lakes to the north. There, Regis had once found sanctuary from the relentless pursuit of Pasha Pook, a former employer, from whom he had stolen the magical ruby pendant he still wore. There, the beleaguered and weary Drizzt Do'Urden had at last found a place to call home, and the friends he continued to hold most dear.

For the next few days, they held wistfulness in their eyes and fullness in their hearts. Around their small campfire each night they spoke of times past, of fishing Maer Dualdon, the largest of the lakes; of nights on Kelvin's Cairn, the lone mountain above the caves where Bruenor's clan had lived in exile, where the stars seemed so close that one could grasp them; and questions of immortality seemed crystalline clear. For one could not stand on Bruenor's Climb on Kelvin's Cairn, amidst the stars on a cold and crisp Icewind Dale night and not feel a profound connection to eternity.

The trail, known simply as "the caravan route," ran almost directly northeast to Bryn Shander, the largest of the ten settlements, the accepted seat of power for the region and the common marketplace. Bryn Shander was favorably located within the meager protection of a series of rolling hillocks and nearly equidistant to the three lakes, Maer Dualdon to the northwest, Redwaters to the southeast and Lac Dinneshere, the easternmost of the lakes. Along the same line as the caravan route, just half a day's walk northeast of Bryn Shander, loomed the dormant volcano Kelvin's Cairn, and before it, the valley and tunnels that once, and for more than a century, had housed Clan Battlehammer.

Nearly ten thousand hearty souls lived in those ten settlements, all but those in Bryn Shander on the banks of one of the three lakes.

The approach of a dark elf and a halfling elicited excitement and alarm in the young guards manning Bryn Shander's main gate. To see anyone coming up the caravan route at such a late date was a surprise, but to have one of those approaching be an elf with skin as black as midnight . . . !

The gates closed fast and hard, and Drizzt laughed aloud—loud enough to be heard, though he and Regis were still many yards away.

"I told you to keep your hood up," Regis scolded.

"Better they see me for what I am before we're in range of a longbow."

Regis took a step away from the drow, and Drizzt laughed again, and so did the halfling.

"Halt and be recognized!" a guard shouted at them in a voice too shaky to truly be threatening.

"Recognize me, then, and be done with this foolishness," Drizzt called back, and he stopped in the middle of the road barely twenty strides from the wooden stockade wall. "How many years must one live among the folk of Ten-Towns before the lapse of a few short years so erases the memory of men?"

A long pause ensued before a different guard called out, "What is your name?"

"Drizzt Do'Urden, you fool!" Regis yelled back. "And I am Regis of Lonelywood, who serves King Bruenor in Mithral Hall."

"Can it be?" yet another voice cried out.

The gates swung open as quickly and as forcefully as they had closed.

"Apparently their memories are not as short as you feared," Regis remarked.

"It's good to be home," the drow replied.

* * * * *

The snow-covered trees muffled the wind's mournful song as Regis silently padded through them down to the banks of the partially frozen lake a few days later. Maer Dualdon spread out wide before him, gray ice, black ice, and blue water. One boat bobbed at the town of Lonelywood's longest wharf, not yet caught fast by the winter. From dozens of small houses nestled in the woods, single lines of smoke wafted into the morning air.

Regis was at peace.

He moved to the water's edge, where a small patch remained unfrozen, and dropped a tiny chunk of ice into the lake, then watched as the ripples rolled out from the impact, washing little bits of water onto the surrounding ice. His mind took him through those ripples and into the past. He thought of fishing—this had been his favorite spot. He told himself it would be a good thing to come back one summer and again set his bobber in the waters of Maer Dualdon.

Hardly thinking of the action, he reached into a small sack he had tied to his belt and produced a palm-sized piece of white bone, the famous skull that gave the trout of Icewind Dale their name. From his other hip pouch, he produced his carving knife, and never looking down at the bone, his eyes gazing across the empty lake, he went to work. Shavings fell as the halfling worked to free that which he knew to be in the bone, for that was the true secret of scrimshaw. His art wasn't to carve the bone into some definable shape, but to free the shape that was already in there, waiting for skilled and delicate fingers to show it to the world.

Regis looked down and smiled as he came to understand the image he was freeing, one so fitting for him at that moment of reflection on what had once been, of good times spent among good friends in a land so beautiful and so deadly all at once.

He lost track of time as he stood there reminiscing and sculpting, and soaking in the beauty and the refreshing chill. Half in a daze, half in the past, Regis nearly jumped out of his furry boots when he glanced down again and saw the head of a gigantic cat beside his hip.

209

His little squeak became a call of, "Guenhwyvar!" as the startled halfling tried to catch his breath.

"She likes it here, too," Drizzt said from the trees behind him, and he turned to watch his drow friend's approach.

"You could have called out a warning," Regis said, and he noted that in his startled jump, he'd nicked his thumb with the sharp knife. He brought it up to suck on the wound, and was greatly relieved to learn that his scrimshaw had not been damaged.

"I did," Drizzt replied. "Twice. You've the wind in your ears."

"It's not so breezy here."

"Then the winds of time," said Drizzt.

Regis smiled and nodded. "It's hard to come here and not want to stay."

"It's a more difficult place than Mithral Hall," said Drizzt.

"But a more simple one," Regis answered, and it was Drizzt's turn to smile and nod. "You met with the spokesmen of Bryn Shander?"

Drizzt shook his head. "There was no need," he explained. "Proprietor Faelfaril knew well of Wulfgar's journey through Ten-Towns four years ago. I learned everything we need from the innkeeper."

"And it saved you the trouble of the fanfare you knew would accompany your return."

"As you avoided it by jumping a wagon north to Lonelywood," Drizzt retorted.

"I wanted to see it again. It was my home, after all, and for many, many years. Did fat old Faelfaril mention any subsequent visits by Wulfgar?"

Drizzt shook his head. "Our friend came through, praise Tempus, but very briefly before going straightaway out to the tundra, to rejoin his people. The folk of Bryn Shander heard one other mention of him, just one, a short time after that, but nothing definitive and nothing that Faelfaril remembers well."

"Then he is out there," Regis said, nodding to the northeast, the open lands where the barbarians roamed. "I'd wager he's the king of them all by now."

Drizzt's expression showed he didn't agree. "Where he went, where he is, is not known in Bryn Shander, and perhaps Wulfgar has become chieftain of the Tribe of the Elk, his people. But the tribes are no longer united, and have not been for years. They have only occasional and very minor dealings with the folk of Ten-Towns at all, and Faelfaril assured me that were it not for the occasional campfires seen in the distance, the folk of Ten-Towns wouldn't even know that they were constantly surrounded by wandering barbarians."

Regis furrowed his brow in consternation.

"But neither do they fear the tribes, as they once did," Drizzt said. "They coexist, and there is relative peace, and that is no small legacy of our friend Wulfgar."

"Do you think he's still out there?"

"I know he is."

"And we're going to find him," said Regis.

"Poor friends we would be if we didn't."

"It's getting cold," the halfling warned.

"Not as cold as the ice cave of a white dragon."

Regis rubbed Guenhwyvar's strong neck and chuckled helplessly. "You'll get me there, too, before this is all done," he said, "or I'm an unbearded gnome."

"Unbearded?" Drizzt asked and Regis shrugged.

"Works for Bruenor the other way," he said.

"A furry-footed gnome, then," Drizzt offered.

"A hungry halfling," Regis corrected. "If we're going out there, we'll need ample supplies. Buy some saddlebags for your cat, or bend your back, elf."

Laughing, Drizzt walked over and draped his arm around Regis's sturdy shoulders, and started turning the halfling to leave. Regis resisted, though, and instead forced Drizzt to pause and take a good long look at Maer Dualdon.

He heard the drow sigh deeply, and knew he'd been taken by the same nostalgic trance, by memories of the years they had known in the simple, beautiful, and deadly splendors of Icewind Dale.

"What are you carving?" Drizzt asked after a long while.

"We'll both know when it reveals itself," Regis answered, and Drizzt accepted that inescapable truth with a nod.

They went out that very afternoon, packs heavy with food and extra clothing. They made the base of Kelvin's Cairn as twilight descended, and found shelter in a shallow cave, one that Drizzt knew very well.

"I'm going up tonight," Drizzt informed Regis over supper.

"To Bruenor's Climb?"

"To where it was before the collapse, yes. I will stoke the fire well before I go, I promise, and leave Guenhwyvar beside you until I return."

"Let it burn low, and keep or release the cat as she needs," Regis answered. "I'm going with you."

Surprised, but pleasantly so, Drizzt nodded. He kept Guenhwyvar by his side as he and Regis made a silent ascent to the top of Kelvin's Cairn. It was a difficult climb, with few trails, and those along icy rocks, but less than an hour later, the companions stepped out from behind one overhang to find that they had reached the peak. The tundra spread wide before them, and stars twinkled all around them.

The three of them stood there in communion with Icewind Dale, in harmony with the cycles of life and death, in contemplation of eternity and a oneness of being with all the great universe, for a long time. They took great comfort in feeling so much a part of something larger than themselves.

And somewhere in the north, a campfire flared to life, seeming like another star.

They each wondered silently if Wulfgar might be sitting beside it, rubbing the cold from his strong hands.

A wolf howled from somewhere unseen, and another answered, then still more took up the nighttime song of Icewind Dale.

Guenhwyvar growled softly, not angered, excited, or uneasy, but simply to speak to the heavens and the wind.

Drizzt crouched beside her and looked across her back to meet Regis's stare. Each knew well what the other was thinking and feeling and remembering, and there was no need at all for words, so none were spoken.

It was a night that they, all three, would remember for the rest of their lives.

CHAPTER

"This was not my intent," Captain Deudermont told the gathered Luskar, his strong voice reaching out through the driving rain. "My life was the sea, and perhaps will be again, but for now I accept your call to serve as governor of Luskan."

The cheering overwhelmed the drumbeat of raindrops.

"Marvelous," Robillard muttered from the back of the stage—the stage built for Prisoner's Carnival, the brutal face of Luskar justice.

"I have sailed to many lands and seen many ways," Deudermont went on and many in the crowd demanded quiet of their peers, for they wanted to savor the man's every word. "I have known Waterdeep and Baldur's Gate, Memnon and faraway Calimport, and every port in between. I have seen far better leaders than Arklem Greeth—" the mere mention of the name brought a long hiss from the thousands gathered—"but never have I witnessed a people stronger in courage and character than those I see before me now," the governor went on, and the cheering erupted anew.

"Would that they would shut up that we might be done with this, and out of the miserable rain," Robillard grumbled.

"Today I make my first decree," the governor declared, "that this stage, that this abomination known as Prisoner's Carnival, is now and forever ended!"

The response—some wild cheering, many curious stares, and more than a few sour expressions—reminded Deudermont of the enormity of the task before him. The carnival was among the most barbaric circuses Deudermont had ever witnessed, where men and women, some guilty, some probably not, were

213

publicly tortured, humiliated, even gruesomely murdered. In Luskan, many called it entertainment.

"I will work with the high captains, who will leave our long-ago battles out to sea, I'm sure," Deudermont moved along. "Together we will forge from Luskan a shining example of what can be, when the greater and common good is the goal, and the voices of the least are heard as strongly as those of the nobility."

More cheering made Deudermont pause yet again.

"He is an optimistic sort," muttered Robillard.

"And why not?" asked Suljack, who sat beside him, the lone high captain who had accepted the invitation to sit on the dais behind Deudermont, and had only committed to do so at the insistence of Kensidan. Being out there, listening to Deudermont, and to the cheers coming back at the dais from the throng of Luskar, had Suljack sitting taller and leaning this way and that with some enthusiasm.

Robillard ignored him and leaned forward. "Captain," he called, getting Deudermont's attention. "Would you have half your subjects fall ill from the wet and cold?"

Deudermont smiled at the not-so-subtle hint.

"Go to your homes, now, and take heart," Deudermont bade the crowd. "Be warm, and be filled with hope. The day has turned, and though Talos the Storm Lord has not yet heard, the skies are brighter in Luskan!"

That brought the loudest cheering of all.

* * * * *

"Three times he put me to the bottom," Baram growled, watching with Taerl from a balcony across the way. "Three times that dog Deudermont and his fancy *Sea Sprite*, curse her name, dropped me ship out from under me, and one of them times, 'e got me landed in Prisoner's Carnival." He pulled up his sleeve, showing a series of burn scars where he'd been prodded with a hot poker. "Cost me more to bribe me way out than it cost for a new ship."

"Deudermont's a dog, to be sure," Taerl agreed. He smiled as he finished, nudged his partner, and pointed down to the back of the square, where most of the city's magistrates huddled under an awning. "Not a one o' them's happy at the call for the end o' their fun."

Baram snorted as he considered the grim expressions on the faces of the torturers. They reveled in their duties; they called Prisoner's Carnival a necessary evil for the administration of justice. But Baram, who had sat in the cells of the limestone holding caves, who had been paraded across that stage, who had paid two of them handsomely to get his reduced sentence—he should have

214

been drawn and quartered for the pirate he was—knew they had all profited from bribes, as well.

"I'm thinking that the rain's fitting for the day's events," Baram remarked. "Lots o' storm clouds in Luskan's coming days."

"Ye'd not be thinking that looking at the fool Suljack, sitting there all a'titter at the dog Deudermont's every word," Taerl said, and Baram issued a low growl.

"He's looking for a way to up himself on Deudermont's sleeve," Taerl went on. "He knows he's the least among us, and now's thinking himself to be the cleverest."

"Too clever by half," Baram said, and there was no missing the threatening tone in his voice.

"Chaos," Taerl agreed. "Kensidan wanted chaos, and claimed we five would be better for it, eh? So let's us be better, I say."

* * * * *

As gently as a father lifting an injured daughter, the lich scooped the weathered body of Valindra Shadowmantle into his arms. He cradled her close, that dark and rainy evening, the same day Deudermont had made his "I am your god" speech to the idiot peasants of Luskan.

He didn't use the bridge to cross from blasted Cutlass Island to Closeguard, but simply walked into the water. He didn't need air, nor did Valindra, after all. He moved into an underwater cave beneath the rim of Closeguard then to the sewer system that took him to the mainland, under his new home: Illusk, where he placed Valindra gently in a curtained bed of soft satin and velvet.

When he poured an elixir down her throat a short while later, the woman coughed out the rain, blood, and seawater. Groggily, she sat up and found that her breathing was hard to come by. She forced the air in and out of her lungs, taking in the many unfamiliar and curious smells as she did. She finally settled and glanced through a crack in the canopy.

"The Hosttower . . ." she rasped, straining with every word. "We survived. I thought the witch had killed . . ."

"The Hosttower is gone," Arklem Greeth told her.

Valindra looked at him curiously then struggled to the edge of the bed and parted the canopy, glancing around in confusion at what looked like the archmage arcane's bedchamber in the Hosttower. She ended by turning her puzzled expression to the lich.

"Boom," he said with a grin. "It's gone, destroyed wholly and utterly, and many of Luskan with it, curse their rotting corpses."

"But this is your room."

"Which was never actually *in* the Hosttower, of course," Arklem Greeth sort of explained.

"I entered it a thousand times!"

"Extradimensional travel . . . there is magic in the world, you know."

Valindra smirked at his sarcasm.

"I expected it would come to this one day," Arklem Greeth explained with a chuckle. "In fact, I hoped for it." He looked up at Valindra's stunned expression and laughed all the louder before adding, "People are so fickle. It comes from living so short and miserable a life."

"So then where are we?"

"Under Illusk, our new home."

Valindra shook her head at every word. "This is no place for me. Find me another assignment within the Arcane Brotherhood."

It was Arklem Greeth's turn to shake his head. "This is your place, as surely as it is my own."

"Illusk?" the moon elf asked with obvious consternation and dismay.

"You haven't yet noted that you're not drawing breath, except to give sound to your voice," said the lich, and Valindra looked at him curiously. Then she looked down at her own pale and unmoving breast, then back to him with alarm.

"What have you done?" she barely managed to whisper.

"Not I, but Arabeth," Arklem Greeth replied. "Her dagger was well-placed. You died before the Hosttower exploded."

"But you resurrected . . ."

Greeth was still shaking his head. "I am no wretched priest who grovels before a fool god."

"Then what?" Valindra asked, but she knew. . . .

He had expected the terrorized reaction that followed, of course, for few people welcome lichdom in so sudden—and unbidden—a manner.

He returned her horror with a smile, knowing that Valindra Shadowmantle, his beloved, would get past the shock and recognize the blessing.

* * * * *

"Events move quickly," Tanally, one of Luskan's most prestigious guards, warned Deudermont. The governor had invited Tanally and many other prominent guards and citizens to meet with him in his quarters, and had bade them to speak honestly and forthrightly.

The governor was certainly getting what he'd asked for, to the continual groaning of Robillard, who sat at the window at the back of the spacious room.

"As well they must," Deudermont replied. "Winter will be fast upon us, and many are without homes. I will not have my people—*our* people—starving and freezing in the streets."

"Of course not," Tanally agreed. "I didn't mean to suggest—"

"He means other events," said Magistrate Jerem Boll, formerly a leading adjudicator of the defunct Prisoner's Carnival.

"People will think to loot and scavenge," Tanally clarified.

Deudermont nodded. "They will. They will scavenge for food, so that they won't starve and die. And for that, what? Would you have me serve them up to Prisoner's Carnival for the delight of other starving people?"

"You risk the breakdown of order," Magistrate Jerem Boll warned.

"Prisoner's Carnival epitomized the lack of order!" Deudermont shot back, raising his voice for the first time in the long and often contentious discussion. "Don't sneer at my observation. I witnessed Luskan's meting out of justice for much of my adult life, and know of more than a few who met a grisly and undeserved fate at the hands of the magistrates."

"And yet, under that blanket, the city thrived," said Jerem Boll.

"Thrived? Who is it that thrived, Magistrate? Those with enough coin to buy their way free of your 'carnival'? Those with enough influence that the magistrates dare not touch them, however heinous their affronts?"

"You should take care how you refer to those people," Jerem Boll replied, his voice going low. "You speak of the core of Luskan's power, of the men who allowed their folk to join in your impetuous march to tear down the most glorious structure that this city—nay, the most glorious structure that any city in the north has ever known!"

"A glorious structure ruled by a lich who loosed undead monsters randomly about the streets," Deudermont reminded him. "Would there have been a seat at Prisoner's Carnival for Arklem Greeth, I wonder? Other than a position of oversight, I mean."

Jerem Boll narrowed his gaze, but didn't respond, and on that sour note, the meeting was adjourned.

"What?" Deudermont asked of the surly-faced Robillard when they were alone. "You don't agree?"

"When have I ever?"

"True enough," Deudermont admitted. "Luskan must start anew, and quickly. Forgiveness is the order of the day—it has to be! I will issue a blanket pardon to everyone not directly affiliated with the Arcane Brotherhood who fought against us on the side of the Hosttower. Confusion and fear, not malice, drove their resistance. And even for those who threw in their lot with the brotherhood, we will adjudicate with an even hand."

Robillard chuckled.

"I doubt many knew the truth of Arklem Greeth, and probably, and justifiably, saw Lord Brambleberry and me as invaders."

"In a sense," said the wizard.

Deudermont shook his head at the dry and unending sarcasm, and wondered again why he kept Robillard at his side for all those years. He knew the answer, of course, and it came more from exactly that willingness to disagree than the wizard's formidable skill in the Art.

"The life of the typical Luskar was no more than a prison sentence," Deudermont said, "awaiting the formality of Prisoner's Carnival, or joining in with one of the many street gangs. . . ."

"Gangs, or Ships?"

Deudermont nodded. He knew the wizard was right, and that the thuggery of Luskan had emanated from six distinct locations. One was down now, with Arklem Greeth blown away, but the other five, the Ships of the high captains, remained.

"And though they fought with you, or not against you at least, are you to doubt that some—Baram comes to mind—haven't quite forgiven you for past . . . meetings?"

"If he decides to act upon that old score, let us hope that he's as poor a fighter on land as he was at sea," said Deudermont, and even Robillard cracked a smile at that.

"Do you even understand the level of risk you're taking here—and in the name of the folk you claim to serve?" Robillard asked after a short pause. "These Luskar have known only iron rule for decades. Under the fist of Arklem Greeth and the high captains, their little wars remained little wars, their crimes both petty and murderous were rewarded with harsh retribution, either by a blade in the alley or, yes, by Prisoner's Carnival. The sword was always drawn, ready to slash anyone who got too far out of the boundaries of acceptable behavior— even if that behavior was never acceptable to you. Now you retract that sword and—"

"And show them a better way," Deudermont insisted. "We have seen commoners leading better lives across the wide world, in Waterdeep and even in the wilder cities to the south. Are there any so ill-structured as the Luskan of Arklem Greeth?"

"Waterdeep has its own iron fists, Captain," Robillard reminded him. "The power of the lords, both secret and open, backed by the Blackstaff, is so overwhelming as to afford them nearly complete control of day to day life in the City of Splendors. You cannot compare cities south of here to Luskan. This place has only commerce. Its entire existence settles on its ability to attract merchants, including unsavory types, from Ten-Towns in Icewind Dale to the dwarves of Ironspur to Mirabar and the Silver Marches to the ships that put into her harbors and yes, to Waterdeep as well. Luskan is not a town of noble families, but of rogues. She is not a town of farmers, but of pirates. Do I truly need to explain these truths to you?"

"You speak of *old* Luskan," the stubborn Deudermont replied. "These rogues and pirates have taken homes, have taken wives and husbands, have brought forth children. The transition began long before Brambleberry and I sailed north from Waterdeep. That is why the people so readily joined in against the drawn sword, as you put it. Their days in the darkness are ended."

"Only one high captain accepted the invitation to sit with you for your acceptance speech, and he, Suljack, is considered the least among them."

"The least, or the wisest?"

Robillard laughed. "Wisdom is not something Suljack has oft been accused of, I'm sure."

"If he sees the future of Luskan united, then it's a mantle he will wear more often," Deudermont insisted.

"So says the governor."

"So he does." Deudermont insisted. "Have you no faith in the spirit of humanity?"

Robillard scoffed loudly at that. "I've sailed the same seas you have, Captain. I saw the same murderers and pirates. I've seen the nature of men, indeed. The spirit of *humanity?*"

"I believe in it. Optimism, good man! Shake off your surliness and take heart and take hope. Optimism trumps pessimism, and—"

"And reality slaughters one and justifies the other. Problems are not often simply matters of perception."

"True enough," Deudermont conceded, "but we can shape that reality if we're clever enough and strong enough."

"And optimistic enough," Robillard said dryly.

"Indeed," the captain, the governor, beamed against that unending sarcasm.

"The spirit of humanity and brotherhood," came another dry remark.

"Indeed!"

And wise Robillard rolled his eyes.

CHAPTER

The rocks provided only meager shelter from the relentlessly howling wind. North of Kelvin's Cairn, out on the open tundra, Drizzt and Regis appreciated having found any shelter at all. Somehow the drow managed to get a fire started, though the flames engaged in so fierce a battle with the wind that they seemed to have little heat left over for the companions.

Regis sat uncomplaining, working his little knife fast over a piece of knucklehead bone.

"A cold night indeed," Drizzt remarked.

Regis looked up to see his friend staring at him curiously, as if expecting that Regis would launch into a series of complaints, as, he had to admit, had often been his nature. For some reason even he didn't understand—perhaps it was the feeling of homecoming, or maybe the hope that he would soon see Wulfgar again—Regis wasn't miserable in the wind and certainly didn't feel like grumbling.

"It's the north sea wind come calling," the halfling said absently, still focused on his scrimshaw. "And it's here for the season, of course." He looked up at the sky and confirmed his observation. Far fewer stars shone, and the black shapes of clouds moved swiftly from the northwest.

"Then even if we find Wulfgar's tribe in the morning as we had hoped, we'll not likely get out of Icewind Dale in time to beat the first deep snows," said Drizzt. "We're stuck here for the duration of the winter."

Regis shrugged, strangely unbothered by the thought, and went on with his carving.

A few moments later, Drizzt chuckled, drawing the halfling's eyes up to see the drow staring at him.

"What?"

"You feel it, too," said Drizzt.

Regis paused in his carving and let the drow's words sink in. "A lot of years, a lot of memories."

"And most of them grand."

"And even the bad ones, like Akar Kessell and the Crystal Shard, worth retelling," Regis agreed. "So when we're all gone, even Bruenor dead of old age, will you return to Icewind Dale?"

The question had Drizzt blinking and leaning back from the fire, his expression caught somewhere between confusion and alarm. "It's not something I prefer to think about," he replied.

"I'm asking you to do that very thing."

Drizzt shrugged and seemed lost, seemed almost as if he were drowning. "With all the battles ahead of us, what makes you believe I'll outlive you all?"

"It's the way of things, or could well be . . . elf."

"And if I'm cut down in battle, and the rest with me, would *you* return to Icewind Dale?"

"Bruenor would likely bind me to Mithral Hall to serve the next king, or to serve as steward until a king might be found."

"You'll not escape that easily, my little friend."

"But I asked first."

"But I demand of you an answer before I offer my own."

Drizzt started to settle in stubbornly, crossing his arms over his chest, and Regis blurted out, "Yes!" before he could assume his defiant posture.

"Yes," the halfling said again. "I would return if I had no duties elsewhere. I cannot think of a better place in all the world to live."

"You don't much sound like the Regis who used to button up tight against the winter's chill and complain at the turn of the first leaf of Lonelywood."

"My complaining was . . ."

"Extortion," Drizzt finished. "A way to ensure that Regis's hearth was never short of logs, for those around you could not suffer your whining."

Regis considered the playful insult for a moment, then shrugged in acceptance, not about to disagree. "And the complaints were borne of fear," he explained. "I couldn't believe this was my home—I couldn't appreciate that this was my home. I came here fleeing Pasha Pook and Artemis Entreri, and had no idea I would remain here for so long. In my mind, Icewind Dale was a waypoint and nothing more, a place to set that devilish assassin off my trail."

He gave a little laugh and shake of his head as he looked back down at the small statue taking shape in his hand. "Somewhere along the way, I came to know Icewind Dale as my home," he said, his voice growing somber. "I don't think I understood that until I came back here just now."

"It might be you're just weary of the battles and tribulations of Mithral Hall," said Drizzt, "with Obould so close and Bruenor in constant worry."

"Perhaps," Regis conceded, but he didn't seem convinced. He looked back up at Drizzt and offered a sincere smile. "Whatever the reason, I'm glad we're here, we two together."

"On a cold winter's night."

"So be it."

Drizzt looked at Regis with friendship and admiration, amazed at how much the halfling had grown over the last few years, ever since he had taken a spear in battle several years before. That wound, that near-death experience, had brought a palpable change over Drizzt's halfling friend. Before that fight on the river, far to the south, Regis had always shied from trouble, and had been very good at fleeing, but from that point on, when he'd recognized, admitted, and was horrified to see that he had become a dangerous burden to his heroic friends, the halfling had faced, met, and conquered every challenge put before him.

"I think it'll snow tonight," Regis said, looking up at the lowering and thickening clouds.

"So be it," Drizzt replied with an infectious grin.

* * * * *

Surprisingly, the wind let up before dawn, and though Regis's prediction of snow proved accurate, it was not a driving and unpleasant storm. Thick flakes drifted down from above, lazily pirouetting, dodging and darting on their way to the whitened ground.

The companions had barely started on their way when they saw again the smoke of campfires, and as they neared the camp, still before midday, Drizzt recognized the standards and knew that they had indeed found the Tribe of the Elk, Wulfgar's people.

"Just the Elk?" Regis remarked, and cast a concerned look up at Drizzt at the apparent confirmation of what they had been told in Bryn Shander. When they'd left for Mithral Hall, the barbarians of Icewind Dale had been united, all tribes in one. That seemed not to be the case anymore, both from the small size of the encampment and from the fact of that one, and only one, distinguished banner.

They approached slowly, side by side, hands up, palms out in an unthreatening manner.

Smiles and nods came back at them from the men sitting watch on the perimeter; they were recognized still in that place, and accepted as friends. The vigilant sentries didn't leave their positions to go over and greet them, but did wave, and motion them through.

And somehow signaled ahead to the people in the camp, Drizzt and Regis realized from the movements of the main area. It was set in the shelter of a shallow dell, so there was no way they had been spotted from within the collection of tents before they'd crested the surrounding hillock, and yet the camp was all astir, with people rushing about excitedly. A large figure, a huge man with corded muscles and wisdom in his seasoned eyes, stood in the center of all the commotion, flanked by warriors and priests.

He wore the headdress of leadership, elf-horned and decorated, and he was well-known to Drizzt and Regis.

But to their surprise, it was not Wulfgar.

"You stopped the wind, Drizzt Do'Urden," Berkthgar the Bold said in his strong voice. "Your legend is without end."

Drizzt accepted the compliment with a polite bow. "You are well, Berkthgar, and that gladdens my heart," the drow said.

"The seasons have been difficult," the barbarian admitted. "Winter has been the strongest, and the filthy goblins and giants ever-present. We have suffered many losses, but my people have fared best among the tribes."

Both Regis and Drizzt stiffened at that admission, particularly of the losses, and particularly in light of the fact that it was not Wulfgar standing before them, and that he was nowhere to be seen.

"We survive and we go on," Berkthgar added. "That is our heritage and our way."

Drizzt nodded solemnly. He wanted to ask the pressing question, but he held his tongue and let the barbarian continue.

"How fares Bruenor and Mithral Hall?" Berkthgar asked. "I pray to the spirits that you didn't come to tell me that this foul orc king has won the day."

"Nay, not tha—" Drizzt started to say, but he bit it off and looked at Berkthgar with curiosity. "How do you know of King Obould and his minions?"

"Wulfgar, son of Beornegar, returned to us with many tales to share."

"Then where is he?" Regis blurted, unable to contain himself. "Out hunting?"

"None are out hunting."

"Then where?" the halfling demanded, and such a voice came out of his diminutive form as to startle Berkthgar and all the others, even Drizzt.

"Wulfgar came to us four winters ago, and for three winters, he remained among the people," Berkthgar replied. "He hunted with the Tribe of the Elk, as he always should have. He shared in our food and our drink. He danced and sang with the people who were once his own, but no more."

"He tried to take your crown, but you wouldn't let him!" Regis said, trying futilely to keep any level of accusation out of his voice. He knew he'd failed miserably at that, however, when Drizzt elbowed him in the shoulder.

"Wulfgar never challenged me," Berkthgar replied. "He had no place to challenge my leadership, and no right."

"He was once your leader."

"Once."

The simple answer set the halfling back on his heels.

"Wulfgar forgot the ways of Icewind Dale, the ways of our people," Berkthgar said, addressing Drizzt directly and not even glancing down at the upset halfling. "Icewind Dale is unforgiving. Wulfgar, son of Beornegar, didn't need to be told that. He offered no challenge."

Drizzt nodded his understanding and acceptance.

"He left us in the first draw of light and dark," the barbarian explained.

"The spring equinox," Drizzt explained to Regis. "When day and night are equal."

He turned to Berkthgar and asked directly, "Was it demanded of him that he leave?"

The chieftain shook his head. "Too long are the tales of Wulfgar. Great sorrow, it is, for us to know that he is of us no more."

"He thought he was coming home," said Regis.

"This was not his home."

"Then where is he?" the halfling demanded, and Berkthgar shook his head solemnly, having no answer.

"He didn't go back to Ten-Towns," Regis said, growing more animated as he became more alarmed. "He didn't go back to Luskan. He couldn't have without stopping through Ten—"

"The Son of Beornegar is dead," Berkthgar interrupted. "We're not pleased that it came to this, but Icewind Dale wins over us all. Wulfgar forgot who he was, and forgot where he came from. Icewind Dale does not forgive. He left us in the first draw of light and dark, and we found signs of him for many tendays. But they are gone, and he is gone."

"Are you certain?" Drizzt asked, trying to keep the tremor out of his pained voice.

Berkthgar slowly blinked. "Our words with the people of the three lakes are few," he explained. "But when sign of Wulfgar faded from the tundra of Icewind Dale, we asked of him among them. The little one is right. Wulfgar did not go back to Ten-Towns."

"Our mourning is passed," came a voice from behind Berkthgar and the barbarian leader turned to regard the man who had disregarded custom by speaking out. A nod from Berkthgar showed forgiveness for that, and when they saw the speaker, Drizzt and Regis understood the sympathy, for Kierstaad, grown into a strong man, had ever been a devout champion of the son of Beornegar. No doubt for Kierstaad, the loss of Wulfgar was akin to the loss of his father. None of that pain showed in his voice or his stance, however. He had proclaimed the mourning of Wulfgar passed, and so it simply was.

"You don't know that he's dead," Regis protested, and both Berkthgar and Kierstaad, and many others, scowled at him. Drizzt hushed him with a little tap on the shoulder.

"You know the comforts of a hearth and a bed of down," Berkthgar said to Regis. "We know Icewind Dale. Icewind Dale does not forgive."

Regis started to protest again, but Drizzt held him back, understanding well that resignation and acceptance was the way of the barbarians. They accepted death without remorse because death was all too near, always. Not a man or woman there had not known the specter of death—of a lover, a parent, a child, or a friend.

And so the drow tried to show the same stoicism when he and Regis took their leave of the Tribe of the Elk soon after, walking the same path that had brought them so far out from Ten-Towns. The facade couldn't hold, though, and the drow couldn't hide his wince of pain. He didn't know where to turn, where to look, who to ask. Wulfgar was gone, lost to him, and the taste proved bitter indeed. Black wings of guilt fluttered around him as he walked, images of the look on Wulfgar's face when first he'd learned that Catti-brie was lost to him, betrothed to the drow he called his best friend. It had been no one's fault, not Drizzt's nor Catti-brie's, nor Wulfgar's, for Wulfgar had been lost to them for years, trapped in the Abyss by the balor Errtu. In that time, Drizzt and Catti-brie had fallen in love, or had at last admitted the love they had known for years, but had muted because of their obvious differences.

When Wulfgar had returned from the dead, there was nothing they could do, though Catti-brie had surely tried.

And so it was circumstance that had driven Wulfgar from the Companions of the Hall. Blameless circumstance, Drizzt tried hard to tell himself as he and Regis walked without speaking through the continuing gentle snowfall. He wasn't about to convince himself, but it hardly mattered anyway. All that mattered was that Wulfgar was lost to him forever, that his beloved friend was no more and his world had diminished.

Beside him, the muffling aspect of the snow and breeze did little to hide Regis's sniffles.

CHAPTER

A h, but ye're a thief!" the man accused, poking his finger into the chest of the one who he believed had just pocketed the wares.

"Speak on yer own!" the other shouted back. "The merchant here's pointin' to *yer* vest and not me own."

"And he's wrong, because yerself took it!"

"Says a fool!"

The first man retracted his finger, balled up his fist, and let fly a heavy punch for the second's face.

The other was more than ready, though, dropping low beneath the awkward swing and coming up fast and hard to hit his opponent in the gut.

And not with just a fist.

The man staggered back, clutching at his spilling entrails. "Ah, but he sticked me!" he cried.

The knife-wielder came up straight and grinned, then stabbed his opponent again then a third time for good measure. Though screams erupted all across the open market of Luskan, with guards scrambling every which way, the attacker very calmly stepped over and wiped his blade on the shirt of the bent-over man.

"Fall down and die then, like a good fellow," he said to his victim. "One less idiot walking the streets with the name of Captain Suljack on his sputtering lips."

"Murderer!" a woman screamed at the knifeman as his victim fell to the street at his feet.

"Bah! But th' other one struck first!" a man in the crowd shouted.

"Nay, but just a fist!" another one of Suljack's men protested, and the shouting man replied by punching him in the face.

As if on cue, and indeed it was—though only those working for Baram and Taerl understood that cue—the market exploded into violent chaos. Fights broke out at every kiosk and wagon. Women screamed and children ran to better vantage points, so they could watch the fun.

From every corner, the city guards swooped in to restore order. Some shouted orders, but others countermanded those with opposing commands, and the fighting only widened. One furious guard captain ran into the midst of an opposing group, whose leader had just negated his call for a group of ruffians to stand down.

"And who are you with, then?" the leader of that group demanded of the guard captain.

"With Luskan, ye fool," he retorted.

"Bah, there ain't no Luskan," the thug retorted. "Luskan's dead—there's just the Five Ships."

"What nonsense escapes your flapping lips?" the guard captain demanded, but the man didn't relent.

"Ye're a Suljack man, ain't ye?" he accused. The guard captain, who was indeed affiliated with Ship Suljack, stared at him incredulously.

The man slugged him in the chest, and before he could respond, two others pulled back his arms so that the thug could continue the beating uninterrupted.

The melee went on for a long while, until a sharp boom of thunder, a resounding and reverberating blast of explosive magic, drew everyone's attention to the eastern edge of the market. There stood Governor Deudermont, with Robillard, who had thrown the lightning signal, right beside him. All the crew of *Sea Sprite* and the remainder of Lord Brambleberry's men stood shoulder to shoulder behind them.

"We've no time for this!" the governor shouted. "We stand together against the winter, or we fall!"

A rock flew at Deudermont's head, but Robillard caught it with a spell that gracefully and harmlessly moved it aside.

The fighting broke out anew.

From a balcony at Taerl's castle, Baram and Taerl watched it all with great amusement.

"He wants to be the ruler, does he?" Baram spat over the rail as he leaned on it and stared intently out at the hated Deudermont. "A wish he's to come to regret."

"Note the guards," Taerl added. "As soon as the fighting started, they moved to groups of their own Ship. Their loyalty's not to Deudermont or Luskan, but to a high captain."

"It's our town," Baram insisted. "And I've had enough of Governor Deudermont already."

Taerl nodded his agreement and watched the continuing fracas, one that he and Baram had incited with well-paid, well-fed, and well-liquored proxies. "Chaos," he whispered, smiling all the wider.

* * * * *

"Oh, it's you," Suljack said as the tough dwarf moved through his door and into his private chambers. "What news from Ship Rethnor?"

"A great fight in the market," the dwarf replied.

Suljack sighed and wearily rubbed a hand over his face. "Fools," he said. "They'll not give Deudermont a chance—the man will do great things for Luskan, and for our trade."

The dwarf shrugged as though he hardly cared.

"Now's not the time for us to be fighting among ourselves," Suljack remarked, and paced the room, still rubbing at his face. He stopped and turned on the dwarf. "It's just as Kensidan predicted. We been battered but we'll come out all the better."

"Some will. Some won't."

Suljack looked at Kensidan's bodyguard curiously at that remark. "Why are you here?" he asked.

"That fight in the market weren't random," said the dwarf. "Ye're to be finding more than a few o' yer boys hurtin'—might be a few dead, too."

"*My* boys?"

"Slow on the upkeep, eh?" asked the dwarf.

Again Suljack stared at him with a thoroughly puzzled expression and asked, "Why are you here?"

"To keep ye alive."

The question set the high captain back on his heels. "I'm a high captain of Luskan!" he protested. "I have a guard of my—"

"And ye're needin' more help than meself'll bring ye if ye're still thinking the fight in the market to be a random brawl."

"Are you saying that my men were targeted?"

"Said it twice, if ye was smart enough to hear."

"And Kensidan sent you here to protect me?"

The dwarf threw him an exaggerated wink.

"Preposterous!" Suljack yelled.

"Ye're welcome," said the dwarf, and he plopped down in a seat facing the room's only door and stared at it without blinking.

* * * * *

"They found three bodies this morning," Robillard reported to Deudermont at the next sunrise. They sat in the front guest hall of the Red Dragon Inn, which had come to serve as the official Governor's Palace. The room boasted wide, strong windows, reinforced with intricate iron work, which looked out to the south, to the River Mirar and the main section of Luskan across it. "Only three today, so I suppose that's a good thing. Unless, of course, the Mirar swept ten times that number out into the bay."

"Your sarcasm knows no end."

"It's an easy thing to criticize," Robillard replied.

"Because what I try to do here is a difficult thing."

"Or a foolish thing, and one that will end badly."

Deudermont got up from the breakfast table and walked across the room. "I'll not argue this same point with you every morning!"

"And still, every morning will be just like this—or worse," Robillard replied. He moved to the window and looked out into the distance of Luskan's market. "Do you think the merchants will come out today? Or will they just cancel the next tenday's work and pack up their wagons for Waterdeep?"

"They've still much to sell."

"Or to have pilfered in the next fight, which should be in a few hours, I would guess."

"The guards will be thick about the market this day."

"Whose? Baram's? Suljack's?"

"Luskan's!"

"Of course, foolish of me to think otherwise," said Robillard.

"You cannot deny that High Captain Suljack sat on the dais," Deudermont reminded. "Or that his men shouldered up to us when the market fighting died away."

"Because his men were getting clobbered," Robillard replied with a chuckle. "Which might be due to his sitting on that dais. Have you thought of that?"

Deudermont sighed and waved his hand at the cynical wizard. "Have *Sea Sprite*'s crew visible in the market as well," he instructed. "Order them to stay close to each other, but to be a very obvious presence. The show of force will help."

"And Brambleberry's men?"

"For tomorrow," Deudermont replied.

"They may be gone by then," Robillard said. The captain looked at him with surprise. "Oh, have you not heard?" the wizard asked. "Lord Brambleberry's veteran and cultured warriors have had quite enough of this uncouth City of Sails and intend to head back to their own City of Splendors before the winter closes the boat lanes. I don't know when they'll go, but have heard some remark that the next favorable tide wouldn't be soon enough."

Deudermont sighed and dropped his head in his hand. "Offer them bonuses if they will remain through the winter," he said.

"Bonuses?"

"Large ones—as much as we can afford."

"I see. You will spend all our gold on your folly before you admit you were wrong."

Deudermont's head snapped up and around so he could glare at the wizard. *"Our* gold?"

"Yours, my captain," Robillard said with a deep bow.

"I was not wrong," said Deudermont. "Time is our ally."

"You will need more tangible allies than that."

"The Mirabarrans . . ." Deudermont said.

"They have closed their gates," Robillard replied. "Our merchant friends from Mirabar suffered greatly when the Hosttower exploded. Many dwarves went straight to Moradin's Halls. You'll not see them on the wall with Luskan's city guard anytime soon."

Deudermont felt and looked old indeed at that moment of great trial. He sighed again and muttered, "The high captains . . ."

"You will need them," Robillard agreed.

"We already have Suljack."

"The one least respected by the other four, of course."

"It's a start!" Deudermont insisted.

"And the others will surely come along to our side, since you know some of them so well already," Robillard said with mock enthusiasm.

Even Deudermont couldn't help but chuckle at that quip. Oh yes, he knew them. He had sunk the ships of at least two of the remaining four beneath them.

"My crew has never let me down," Deudermont said.

"Your crew fights pirates, not cities," came the reminder, stealing any comfort the already beleaguered governor might have garnered from his last remark.

Even Robillard recognized the man's despair and showed him some sympathy. "The remnants of the Hosttower. . . ."

Deudermont looked at him curiously.

"Arabeth and the others," Robillard explained. "I will put them in and around the crew in the market square, in their full Hosttower regalia."

"There is great bitterness against those insignias," Deudermont warned.

"A calculated risk," the wizard admitted. "Surely there are many in Luskan who would see any and all members of the Hosttower destroyed, but surely, too, there are many who recognize the role that Arabeth played in securing the victory we achieved, however great the cost. I wouldn't send her and her lessers out alone, to be sure, but among our crew, with your approval bolstering them, she and hers will serve us well."

"You trust her?"

"No, but I trust in her judgment, and now she knows that her existence here is predicated on the victory of Captain . . . of *Governor* Deudermont."

Deudermont considered the reasoning for a moment then nodded his agreement. "Send for her."

* * * * *

Arabeth Raurym left Deudermont's palace later that same day, pulling her cloak tight against the driving rain. She padded down the puddle-filled street, sweeping up attendants from every corner and alley until the full contingent of eleven former Hosttower wizards marched as a group. It wouldn't do for any of them to be out alone, with so many of Luskan's folk nursing fresh wounds at the hands of their previous comrades. Not a person in Luskan spoke of the Hosttower of the Arcane with anything but venom, it seemed.

She gave her orders as they walked, and as soon as they linked up with *Sea Sprite's* crew, just north of Illusk, Arabeth took her leave. She cast an enchantment upon herself, reducing her size, making her look like a small girl, and moved southeast into the city, heading straight for Ten Oaks.

To her relief, she was not recognized or bothered, and soon stood before the seated Kensidan, taking note that his newest—and reputedly strongest—bodyguard, that curious and annoying dwarf, was nowhere to be seen.

"Robillard understands the precarious perch upon which Deudermont stands," she reported. "They will not be caught unawares."

"How can they not understand when half the city is in conflict, or burning?"

"Blame Taerl and Baram," Arabeth reminded him.

"Blame them, or credit them?"

"You wanted Deudermont as a figurehead, to give credibility and bona fides to Luskan," the overwizard said.

"If Baram and Taerl decide to openly oppose Deudermont, all the better for those wise enough to pick up the pieces," Kensidan replied. "Whichever side proves victorious."

"You don't sound like you hold any doubts."

"I wouldn't bet against the captain of *Sea Sprite*. Of course, the battleground has changed quite dramatically."

"I wouldn't bet against whichever side Ships Kurth and Rethnor join."

"Join?" the son of Ship Rethnor asked.

Arabeth nodded, smiling as if she knew something Kensidan hadn't yet deduced.

"You wish to remain neutral in this fight, and savor the opportunities," Arabeth explained. "But one side—Deudermont's, I predict—will not grow weaker in the conflict. Nay, he will strengthen his hand, and dangerously so."

"I have considered that possibility."

"And if you allow it, will Deudermont's reign be any different than that of Arklem Greeth?"

"He isn't a lich. That's a start."

Arabeth folded her arms over her chest at the snide comment.

"We will see how it plays out," Kensidan said. "We will allow them—all three of them—their play, as long as it doesn't interfere with my own."

"Your shield guard is with Suljack?"

"I applaud your skill at deduction."

"Good," Arabeth said. "Taerl and Baram are not in good spirits toward Suljack, not after he sat behind Deudermont on the stage."

"I didn't think they would be, hence. . . ."

"You put him there? Surely you knew that Baram would go out of his mind with rage at the thought of Deuder—" She paused and a smile widened across her fair face as she sorted it all out. "Kurth could threaten you, but you don't think that likely—not, at least, until the rest of the city has sorted under the new hierarchy. With that confidence, the only threats to your gains would be Deudermont, who is now far too busy in simply trying to maintain some semblance of order, and an alliance of the lesser high captains, particularly Baram and Taerl, neither of whom have been fond of Ship Rethnor."

"I'm sure that Kurth is as pleased as I am that Baram and Taerl have revealed such anger at Suljack, poor Suljack," Kensidan remarked.

"You've been saying you intended to profit from the chaos," Arabeth replied with obvious admiration. "I didn't know that you meant to control that chaos."

"If I did control it, it wouldn't truly be chaos, now would it?"

"Herd it, then, if not control it."

"I would be a sorry high captain if I didn't work to ensure that the situation would lean in favor of my Ship."

Arabeth assumed a pose that was as much one of seduction as of petulance, with one hand on a hip thrust forward and a wicked little grin on her face. "But you are not a high captain," she said.

"Yes," Kensidan replied, seeming distant and unmoved. "Let us make sure that everyone understands the truth of that statement. I'm just the son of Ship Rethnor."

Arabeth stepped forward and knelt on the chair, straddling Kensidan's legs. She put a hand on each of his shoulders and drove him back under her weight as she pressed forward.

"You're going to rule Luskan even as you pretend that you don't," she whispered, and Kensidan didn't respond, though his expression certainly didn't disagree. "Kensidan the Pirate King."

"You find that alluring," he started to say, until Arabeth buried him in a passionate kiss.

CHAPTER

BECOMING ONE

H e stood against the snow.

It was not a gentle tumble of flakes, as with the previous storm, but a wind-whipped blizzard of stinging ice and bitter cold.

He didn't fight it. He accepted it. He took it into himself, into his very being, as if becoming one with the brutal surroundings. His muscles tensed and clenched, forcing blood into whitened limbs. He squinted, but refused to shut his eyes against the blow, refused to turn any of his senses off to the truth of Icewind Dale and the deadly elements—deadly to strangers, to foreigners, to weak southerners, to those who could not become one with the tundra, one with the frozen north wind.

He had defeated the spring, the muddy melt, when a man could disappear into a bog without a trace.

He had defeated the summer, the gentlest weather, but the time when the beasts of Icewind Dale came out in force, seeking food—and human flesh was a delicacy to most—to feed their young.

His defeat of autumn neared completion, with the first cold winds and first brutal blizzards. He had survived the brown bears, seeking to fatten their bellies before settling into their caves. He had survived the goblins, orcs, and orogs that challenged him for the meager pickings on the last hunt of the caribou.

And he would defeat the blizzard, the wind that could freeze a man's blood solid in his limbs.

But not this man. His heritage wouldn't allow it. His strength and determination wouldn't allow it. Like his father's father's father's father before him, he was of Icewind Dale.

He didn't fight the northwestern wind. He didn't deny the ice and the snow. He took them in as a part of himself, for he was greater than a man. He was a son of the tundra.

For hours he stood unmoving on a high rock, muscles braced against the wind, snow piling around his feet, then his ankles, then his long legs. The whole world became a dreamlike haze as ice covered his eyes. His hair and beard glistened with icicles, his heavy breath filled the air before him with fog, the cloud fast smashed apart by the driving pellets of ice and snow.

When he at last moved, even the howl of the wind could not muffle the sound of crunching and cracking. A deep, deep breath broke him free of the frozen natural shirt of ice, and he extended his arms out to his sides, hands clenching powerfully as if he were grasping and crushing the storm around him.

He threw his head back, staring up into the gray ceiling of heavy clouds, and let out a long, low roar, a primal grumble that came from his belly and denied Icewind Dale its prize.

He was alive. He had beaten the storm. He had beaten three seasons and knew that he was ready for the fourth and most trying.

Though piled to his thighs, the snow slowed him hardly at all as his powerful muscles drove him along. He stalked down the trails of the rocky hill, stepping sure-footed across patches bare of snow but thick with ice, and pounding right through the drifts, some taller than his nearly seven foot frame, as easily as a sword slashing a sheet of dried old parchment.

He came to the ledge above the entrance to a cave he had entered once, long, long ago. He knew it was inhabited again, for he had seen goblins, and the greater beast they named as their chieftain.

But still the cave was to be his winter home.

He dropped down lightly to a large stone that had been placed to partially cover the entrance. A dozen creatures with levers had moved it into place, but he alone, using nothing but his muscles—muscles made hard by the wind and the cold—braced himself and easily shoved the rock aside.

A pair of goblins began to whoop and holler at the intrusion, their cries of warning turning fast to terror as the icy giant stepped into their doorway, blocking the meager daylight.

Like a beast out of nightmares, he strode in, slapping aside their small and insignificant spears. He caught one goblin by the face and easily hoisted it from the ground with one arm. He shook it violently, all the while fending off the pathetic stabs of its companion, and when it at last stopped resisting, he smashed it hard into the wall of rock.

The second creature squealed and fled, but he threw the first into it, taking it down in a heap.

He stalked past, crushing the life out of the second goblin with a single heavy stomp to the back of its skinny neck.

Several of the creatures, females, too, presented themselves in the next room, some cowering, but they would find no mercy from the giant. A trio of small spears flew at him, only one connecting, striking him right in the chest, right in the thick of the curious gray fur cape he wore. The spear hit bone—the skull of the creature from which the cape had been fashioned, an unrecognizable thing under a layer of ice and snow. The spear had not the weight, nor the weight behind the throw, to penetrate, and it hung there, stuck in the folds and slowing the enraged giant not at all.

He caught a goblin in his huge hand, lifted it easily, and flung it across the chamber. It smashed into stone and fell still.

Others tried to run away, and he caught one and threw it. Then another went flying. With their backs to the wall, a pair of goblins found courage and turned to meet him, thrusting their spears to fend him off.

The giant tugged the spear from his cape, brought it up and bit it mid-shaft, tearing it in two, and advanced. With his batons, he slapped aside the spears, furiously, wildly, with speed and agility that seemed out of place in a man of his size and strength.

Again and again, he pushed the spears aside and closed, and he moved suddenly, swiftly, bashing the spears out wide and reversing his hands as he lurched forward, stabbing the batons into the chest of the respective goblins. He rolled his hands under and lifted the squealing creatures on the end of those batons, and slammed them together once and again, as one fell squirming and shrieking to the floor.

The other, stabbed by the sharp end of the spear, hung there in agony and the giant dropped it low and suddenly reversed, shoving it straight up as the spear slid deeper into its chest. He tossed the dying thing aside and stomped down on its fallen companion.

He stalked off in pursuit of the chieftain, the champion.

It was larger than he, a verbeeg, a true giant and not a man. It carried a heavy, spiked club and he held nothing in his hands.

But he didn't hesitate. He barreled right in, lowering his shoulder, accepting the hit of the club with the confidence that his charge would steal the energy from the swing.

His powerful legs drove on with fury, with the rage of the storm, the strength of Icewind Dale. He drove the verbeeg backward several strides and only the wall stopped his progress.

The spiked club fell aside and the verbeeg began slamming him with its mighty fists. One blew the air from his lungs, but he ignored the pain as he had ignored the bite of the cold wind.

The man leaped back and straightened, his balled fists exploding upward before him, slamming the verbeeg hard and breaking the grapple.

Giant and man reset immediately and crashed together like rutting caribou. The crack of bone against bone echoed through the cave and the few goblins who stayed around to watch, perplexed by the titanic battle, gasped to realize that had any of them been caught between those crashing behemoths, it would surely have been crushed to death.

Chins on shoulders, giant and man each clasped the other around the back and pressed with all his might. No punches or kicks mattered anymore. It was no contest of agility, but of sheer strength. And in that, the goblins took heart, and believed that their verbeeg leader could not be beaten.

Indeed, the giant, two feet taller, hundreds of pounds heavier, seemed to gain an advantage, and the man started to bend under the press, his legs began to tremble.

On the giant pushed, the timbre of its growl going from determination to victory as the mighty man bent.

But he was of the tundra, he was Icewind Dale. By birth and by heritage, he was Icewind Dale—indomitable, indefatigable, timeless, and unbending. His legs locked, as sturdy as young oaks, and the verbeeg could press no more.

"I . . . am . . . the . . . son . . . of . . ." he began, driving the giant back to even, and after a grunt and a renewed push that had him gaining more ground, he finished, ". . . Icewind . . . Dale!"

He roared and drove on. "I am the son of Icewind Dale!" he cried, and roared and roared and forced his arms downward, bending the stubborn verbeeg to a more upright, less powerful stance.

"I am the son of Icewind Dale!" he yelled again, and the goblins yelped and fled, and the verbeeg groaned.

He growled and pushed on with more fury and stunning strength. He bent the verbeeg awkwardly and it tried to twist away, but he had it and he pressed relentlessly. Bones started to crack.

"I am the son of Icewind Dale!" he cried, and his legs churned as he twisted and bent the giant. He had it down to its knees, bending it backward, shoulders leaning. A sudden and violent thrust and roar ended the resistance, shattering the verbeeg's spine.

Still the man drove on. "I am the son of Icewind Dale!" he proclaimed again.

He stepped back and grabbed the groaning, dying giant by the throat and the crotch and lifted it above him as he stood, as easily as if it weighed no more than one of its goblin minions.

"I am the son of Beornegar!" the victor cried, and he threw the verbeeg against the wall.

CHAPTER

24

"You're keeping Suljack alive?" old Rethnor asked Kensidan as they walked together along the decorated halls of the palace of Ship Rethnor.

"I gave him the dwarf," Kensidan replied. "I was beginning to find the little beast annoying anyway. He was starting to speak in rhymes—something his former master warned me about."

"Former master?" the old man said with a wry grin.

"Yes, father, I agree," the Crow replied with a self-deprecating chuckle. "I trust them only because I know that our best interests converge and lead us to the same place."

Rethnor nodded.

"But I cannot allow Baram and Taerl to kill Suljack—and I believe they want to do that very thing after seeing him on the dais with Deudermont."

"Sitting behind Deudermont has angered them so?"

"No, but it has presented the two with an opportunity they shan't pass up," Kensidan explained. "Kurth has bottled up his forces on Closeguard Island, riding out the storm. I've no doubt that he is instigating many of the fights on the mainland, but he wants the corpse of Luskan a bit more dead before he swoops upon her like a hungry vulture. Baram and Taerl believe that I'm wounded at present, because I was so strongly in Deudermont's court, and also, of course, because there has been no formal transition of power from you to me. To their thinking, the destruction of the Hosttower caused such devastation across the city that even my own followers are reeling and unsure, and so won't follow my commands into battle."

"Now why would Baram and Taerl think such a thing about the loyal foot-soldiers of Ship Rethnor?" the high captain asked.

"Why indeed?" replied the coy Kensidan, and Rethnor nodded again, smiling widely, the grin revealing that he thought his son played it perfectly.

"So you and Kurth have closed up," Rethnor said. "You didn't even appear at Deudermont's inauguration. Any gains to be made on the street by the other three lesser high captains have to be made now, and quickly, before either of you two, or Deudermont, comes out and crushes it all. Just to add a bit of fire to that smokepowder, you put Suljack on the stage with Deudermont, all the excuse that Taerl and Baram need."

"Something like that, yes."

"But don't let them get to him," Rethnor warned. "You'll be needing Suljack before this mess has ended. He's a fool, but a useful one."

"The dwarf will keep him safe. For now."

They came to the intersection of hallways leading to their respective rooms then, and parted ways, but not before Rethnor leaned over and kissed Kensidan on the forehead, a sign of great respect.

The old man shuffled down the corridor and through his bedroom door. "My son," he whispered, full of contentment.

He knew then, without doubt, that he had chosen right in turning Ship Rethnor over to Kensidan, instead of his other son, Bronwin, who was hardly ever in the city of late. Bronwin had been a disappointment to Rethnor, for he never seemed to be able to look beyond his most immediate needs, for treasure or for women, nor did he show any capacity for patience in satiating his many hungers. But Kensidan, the one they called the Crow, had more than made up for Bronwin's failings. Kensidan was every bit as cunning as his father, indeed, and probably even more so.

Rethnor lay down with that thought in mind, and it was a good last thought. For he never awakened.

* * * * *

He hustled her along the rain-soaked dark streets, taking great pains to keep the large cloak wrapped about her. He constantly glanced around—left, right, behind them—and more than once put a hand to the dagger at his belt.

Lightning split the sky and revealed many other people out in the torrent, huddled in alleyways and under awnings, or, pathetically, in the jamb of a doorway, as if trying to draw comfort out of mere proximity to a house.

The couple finally got to the dock section, leaving the houses behind, but that was even more dangerous terrain, Morik knew, for though fewer potential assailants watched their passage, so too did fewer potential witnesses.

"He went out—all the boats went out to moor so they wouldn't get cracked against the wharves," Bellany said to him, her voice muffled by the wet cloak. "Stupid plan."

"He didn't, and he wouldn't," Morik replied. "He's my coin and I've his word."

"A pirate's word."

"An honorable man's word," Morik corrected, and he felt vindicated indeed when he and Bellany turned a corner of a rather large storehouse to see one ship still in tight against the docks, bucking the breakers that rolled in on the front of the gathering storm. One after another, those storms assaulted Luskan, a sure sign that the wind had changed and winter was soon to jump the Spine of the World and bring her fury to the City of Sails.

The couple hustled down to the wharves, resisting the urge to sprint in the open across the boardwalk. Morik kept them to the shadows until they reached the nearest point to *Thrice Lucky*'s berth.

They waited in the deep shadows of the inner harbor storehouses until another lightning strike creased the sky and lit the area, and they looked left and right. Seeing no one, Morik grabbed Bellany's arm and sprinted straight for the ship, feeling vulnerable indeed as he and his beloved ran along the open pier.

When they got to the boarding plank, they found Captain Maimun himself, lantern in hand, waiting for them.

"Be quick, then," he said. "We're out now, or we're riding it out against the dock."

Morik let Bellany lead the way up the narrow wooden ramp, and went with her onto the deck and into Maimun's personal quarters.

"A drink?" the captain asked, but Morik held up his hand, begging off.

"I haven't the time."

"You're not coming out to mooring with us?"

"Kensidan won't have it," Morik explained. "I don't know what's going on, but he's pulling us all into Ten Oaks this night."

"You'd trust your beautiful lady to a rogue like me?" Maimun asked. "Should I be offended?" As he spoke of her, both he and Maimun turned to Bellany, and she fit that description indeed at that moment. Bathed in the light of many candles, her black hair soaked, her skin sparkling with raindrops, there was no other way to describe the woman as she pulled herself out of her heavy woolen weathercloak.

She tossed her wet hair out of her face casually, a movement that had both men fully entranced, and looked to them curiously, surprised to see them staring at her.

"Is there a problem?" she asked, and Maimun and Morik both laughed, which only confused the woman even more.

Maimun motioned toward her with the bottle and Bellany eagerly nodded.

"It must be very difficult out there if you're willing to sit aboard a ship in a storm," Maimun remarked as he handed her a glass of whiskey.

Bellany drained it in a single gulp and handed the glass back for a refill.

"I'm not with Deudermont and won't be," Bellany explained as Maimun poured. "Arabeth Raurym won the fight with Valindra, and Arabeth is no matron of mine."

"And if a former inhabitant of the Hosttower of the Arcane is not with Deudermont, then she's surely dead," Morik added. "Some have found refuge with Kurth on Closeguard Island."

"Mostly those who worked closely with him over the years, and I hardly know the man," Bellany said.

"I thought Deudermont had granted amnesty to all who fought with Arklem Greeth?" Maimun asked.

"For what it's worth, he did," said Morik.

"And it's worth a lot to the many attendants and non-practitioners who came out of the rubble of the Hosttower," said Bellany. "But for we who wove spells under the direction of Arklem Greeth, who are seen as members of the Arcane Brotherhood and not just the Hosttower, there is no amnesty—not with the common Luskar, at least."

Maimun handed her back her refilled glass, which she sipped instead of gulping. "Order has broken down across the city," the young captain said. "This was the fear of many when Deudermont and Brambleberry's intent became apparent. Arklem Greeth was a beast, and it was precisely that inhumanity and viciousness that kept the five high captains, and their men below them, in line. When the city rallied to Deudermont that day in the square, even I came to think that maybe, just maybe, the noble captain was strong enough of character and reputation to pull it off."

"He's running out of time," said Morik. "You'll find the murdered in every alley."

"What of Rethnor?" Maimun asked. "You work for him."

"Not by choice," said Bellany, and Morik's scowl at her was quite revealing to the perceptive young pirate captain.

"I'm not for knowing what Rethnor intends," Morik admitted. "I do as I'm told to do, and don't poke my nose into places it doesn't belong."

"That's not the Morik I know and love," said Maimun.

"Truth be told," Bellany agreed.

But Morik continued to shake his head. "I know what Rethnor's got behind him, and knowing that, I'm smart enough to just do as I'm told to do."

A call from the deck informed them that the last lines were about to be cast off.

"And you were told to return to Ship Rethnor this night," Maimun reminded Morik, leading him to the door. The rogue paused long enough to give Bellany a kiss and a hug.

"Maimun will keep you safe," he promised her, and he looked at his friend, who nodded and held up his glass in response.

"And you?" Bellany replied. "Why don't you just stay out here?"

"Because then Maimun couldn't keep any of us safe," Morik replied. "I'll be all right. If there's one thing I know as truth in all of this chaos, it's that Ship Rethnor will survive, however the fates weigh on Captain Deudermont."

He kissed her again, bundled up his cloak against the deepening storm, and rushed from *Thrice Lucky*. Morik waited at the docks just long enough to see the crew expertly push and row the ship far enough from the wharves to safely moor then he ran off into the rainy night. When he returned to Ship Rethnor Morik learned that the high captain had quietly passed away, and Kensidan the Crow was fully at the helm.

* * * * *

They entered from the continuing rain in a single and solemn line, moving through the entry rooms of Rethnor's palace to the large ballroom where the high captain lay in state.

All of the remaining four high captains attended, with Suljack the first to arrive, Kurth the last, and Baram and Taerl, tellingly, entering together.

Kensidan had assembled them, all four, in his private audience chamber when word arrived that the governor of Luskan had come to pay his respects.

"Bring him," Kensidan said to his attendant.

"He is not alone," the woman replied.

"Robillard?"

"And some others of *Sea Sprite*'s crew," the attendant explained.

Kensidan waved her away as if it didn't matter. "I tell you four now, before Deudermont joins us, that Ship Rethnor is mine. It was given to me before my father passed on, with all his blessings."

"Ye changing the name, are ye? Ship Crow?" Baram joked, but Kensidan stared at him hard and elicited a nervous cough.

"Any of you who think that perhaps Ship Rethnor is vulnerable now would be wise to think otherwise," Kensidan said, biting off the last word as the door opened and Governor Deudermont walked in, the ever-vigilant and ever-dangerous Robillard close behind. The others of *Sea Sprite* didn't enter, but were likely very close nearby.

"You have met Luskan's newest high captain?" Kurth asked him, motioning toward Kensidan.

"I didn't know it to be an inherited position," Deudermont said.

"It is," was Kensidan's curt response.

"So if the good Captain Deudermont passes on, I get Luskan then?" Robillard quipped, and he shrugged as Deudermont cast him an unappreciative look for the sentiment.

"Doubtin' that," said Baram.

"If you are to be the five high captains of Luskan, then so be it," said Deudermont. "I care not how you manage the titles as of now. What I care about is Luskan, and her people, and I expect the same from you all, as well."

The five men, unused to being spoken to in that manner and tone, all grew more attentive up, Baram and Taerl bristling openly.

"I ask for peace and calm, that the city can rebound from a trying struggle," said Deudermont.

"One yerself started, and who asked ye?" Baram replied.

"The people asked me," Deudermont retorted. "Your people among them—your people who marched with Lord Brambleberry and I to the gates of the Hosttower."

Baram had no answer.

But Suljack did, enthusiastically. "Aye, and Captain Deudermont's givin' us a chance to make Luskan the envy of the Sword Coast," he declared, surprising even Deudermont with his energy. But not surprising Kensidan, who had bid him to do that very thing, and not surprising Kurth, who offered a sly grin at Kensidan as the fool Suljack rambled on.

"My people are tiring and hurting bad," he said. "The war was tough on them, on us all, and now's the time for hoping for better and working together to get better. Know that Ship Suljack's with you, Governor, and we won't be fighting unless it's to save our own lives."

"My appreciation," Deudermont replied with a bow, his expression showing as much suspicion as gratitude, which was not lost on the perceptive Kensidan.

"If you will pardon me, Governor, I'm here to bury my father, not to discuss politics," said Kensidan, and he motioned to the door.

With a bow, Deudermont and Robillard departed, joining some others of their crew who had been stationed right outside the door. Suljack went next, then Baram and Taerl together, as they had entered, both grumbling unhappily.

"This passing changes nothing," Kurth paused to remark to the Crow as he moved to leave. "Except that you have lost a valuable advisor." He gave a little knowing laugh and left the room.

"I'm not much liking that one," the dwarf behind Kensidan's chair remarked a moment later.

Kensidan shrugged. "Be quick to Suljack," he ordered. "Baram and Taerl will be even more angry with him after he so openly pledged with Deudermont."

"What o' Kurth?"

"He won't move against me. He sees where this is leading, and he awaits the destination."

"Ye sure?"

"Sure enough to tell you again to get to Suljack's side."

The dwarf gave an exaggerated sigh and thumped past the chair. "Getting a little tired o' being told what to do," he mumbled under his breath, drawing a grin from Kensidan.

A few moments later, half the room where Kensidan sat alone darkened.

"You heard it all?" he stated as much as asked.

"Enough to know that you continue to put your friend in dire peril."

"And that displeases you?"

"It encourages us," said the voice of the unseen, the never-seen, speaker. "This is bigger than one alliance, of course."

"The dwarf will protect him," Kensidan replied, just to show that maybe it wasn't bigger than his alliance with Suljack.

"Don't doubt that," the voice assured him. "Half of Luskan's garrison would be killed trying to get past that one."

"And if more than that come, and Suljack is killed?" Kensidan asked.

"Then he will be dead. That is not the question. The question is what will Kensidan then do if his ally is lost?"

"I have many inroads to Suljack's followers," the head of Ship Rethnor replied. "None of them will form allegiance to Baram or Taerl, nor will I let them forgive those two for killing Suljack."

"The fighting will continue, then? Beware, for Kurth understands the depth of your trickery here."

The dwarf walked back into the room at that moment, his eyes widening at the darkness, at the unexpected visitation by his true masters.

Kensidan watched him just long enough to gauge his reaction then answered, "The chaos is Deudermont's worst enemy. My city guards don't report to their posts, nor do many, many others. Deudermont can give great speeches and make wonderful promises, but he cannot control the streets. He cannot keep the peasants safe. But I can keep mine safe, and Kurth his, and so on."

Beside him, the dwarf laughed, though he bit it off when Kensidan turned to regard him. "True enough," the head of Ship Rethnor admitted. " 'Tis the trap of competitive humanity, you see. Few men are content if others have more to be content about."

"How long will you let it proceed?" asked the voice in the darkness.

Kensidan shrugged. "That is up to Deudermont."

"He's stubborn to the end."

"Good enough," Kensidan said with a shrug.

The dwarf laughed again as he moved behind the chair to retrieve his forgotten weathercloak.

"I hope you live up to your reputation," Kensidan said to him as he passed by again.

"Been looking for something to hit for a long time," the dwarf replied. "Might even have a rhyme or two ready for me first battle."

Someone in the darkness groaned, and the dwarf laughed even louder and all but skipped from the room.

CHAPTER

VISION OF THE PAST

25

W e soon have to turn to Ten-Towns," Drizzt informed Regis one morning.
They were out on the tundra, and had been for a tenday since their
departure from Berkthgar and the Tribe of the Elk. They both knew they
should have gone back to one of the towns with winter coming in so fast and
hard. Prudence demanded such, for Icewind Dale winters were indeed deadly.

But they had stayed out, roaming from the Sea of Moving Ice to the south,
and the foothills of the Spine of the World. They had encountered two other
tribes, and had been greeted cordially, if not warmly, by both. Neither had any
word of Wulfgar, however, and indeed had counted him dead.

"He's not out here," Regis said after a while. "He must have gone south, out
of the dale."

Drizzt nodded, or tried to, but so unconvincing was he that his motion
seemed more a head shake of denial.

"Wulfgar was too upset at the revelation, embarrassed even, and so he went
right past Ten-Towns," Regis went on stubbornly. "When he lost his past, he
lost his home, and so he could not bear to remain here."

"And he traveled past Luskan?"

"We don't know that Wulfgar avoided Luskan. He might have gone in—
perhaps he signed on with a ship and is sailing the southern Sword Coast, out
by Memnon or even Calimport. Wouldn't he be amused to see us huddled in a
snowstorm looking for him?"

Drizzt shrugged. "It's possible," he admitted, but again, his tone and posture
conveyed no confidence.

249

"Whatever happened, we've seen no sign that he's out here, alone or with anyone else," said Regis. "He left Icewind Dale. He walked right past Ten-Towns last spring and moved south through the dale—or maybe he's back in that little fiefdom, Auckney was its name, with Colson! Yes, that's . . ."

Drizzt held up his hand to stop the rambling halfling. He, they, had no idea what had happened to Wulfgar, or to Colson for that matter, since she had left the Silver Marches with him but was not with him when he entered Ten-Towns those years ago. Perhaps Regis was correct, but more likely, Berkthgar, who understood Icewind Dale and who knew the turmoil within Wulfgar, had deduced it correctly.

So many men had ventured out alone on the tundra, to simply disappear—into a bog, under the snow, into the belly of a monster. . . . Wulfgar wouldn't have been the first, surely, nor would he be the last.

"We make for Ten-Towns today," Drizzt informed the halfling.

The dark elf stared up at the heavy gray sky, and knew that yet another snow was fast approaching, and one that would be colder and more driven by the winds—one that could kill them.

Regis started to argue, but just nodded and gave a sigh. Wulfgar was lost to them.

The pair set out forlornly, Regis following closely in Drizzt's trail—which wasn't much of a path in the snow, since the drow verily ran atop it—across the flat, white emptiness. Many times even Drizzt, who knew Icewind Dale so well, had to pause for a long while to regain his bearings.

By midday, the snow had begun to fall, lightly at first, but it steadily worsened, along with the howl of the northwestern gale. The pair bundled their cloaks tighter and leaned forward, pressing on.

"We should find a cave!" Regis shouted, his voice tiny against the wind.

Drizzt turned back and nodded, but before he turned forward again, Regis gave a yelp of alarm.

In the blink of an eye, Drizzt whirled, scimitars in hand, just in time to see a huge spear descend through the storm and drive into the ground just a few feet in front of him. He jumped back and tried to spot the thrower, but found his eyes drawn instead to the quivering weapon stuck into the ground before him.

The head of a verbeeg was tied to it, dangling at the end of a leather strap at the back of the spear.

Drizzt moved to it, glancing all around, and up, expecting a volley of similar missiles at any moment.

The giant head rolled over the spear shaft with the gusts of wind, lolling back and forth, staring at Drizzt with empty, dead eyes. Its forehead was curiously scarred. Drizzt used Twinkle to brush aside its thick shock of hair to get a better look.

"Wulfgar," Regis muttered, and Drizzt turned to regard him. The halfling stared at the verbeeg's scarred forehead.

"Wulfgar?" Drizzt replied. "This is a verb—"

"The pattern," Regis said, pointing to the scar.

Drizzt examined it more closely, and sucked in his breath with anticipation. The scar, a brand, really, was jumbled and imperfect, but Drizzt could make out the overlapping symbols of three dwarf gods—the same etching that Bruenor had carved into the head of Aegis-fang! Wulfgar, or someone else holding Aegis-fang, had used that warhammer's head to brand that verbeeg.

Drizzt stood up straight and looked all around. In the storm, the thrower could not have been too far away, particularly if he wanted to be sure he didn't skewer either Drizzt or Regis.

"Wulfgar!" he yelled, and it echoed off the nearby stones, but died quickly under the muffling blanket of falling snow and howling wind.

"It was him!" Regis cried, and he, too, began shouting for their lost friend.

But no voice came back to them, save the echoes of their own.

Regis continued to shout for a while, until Drizzt, grinning knowingly, finally halted him.

"What?" the halfling asked.

"I know this place—I should have thought of this before."

"Thought of what?"

"A cave, not so far away," Drizzt explained. "A place where Wulfgar and I first fought side-by-side."

"Against verbeegs," Regis said, catching on as he looked back to the spear.

"Against verbeegs," Drizzt confirmed.

"Looks like you didn't kill them all."

"Come along," Drizzt bade him.

The drow found his bearings then called in Guenhwyvar and sent her off and running in search of the cave. Her roars led them through the mounting storm, and though the distance was not far, no more than a few hundred yards, it took the pair some time to at last come to the opening of a deep, dark cave. Drizzt moved just inside and spent a long while standing there staring into the deeper darkness, letting his eyes adjust. He replayed that long ago battle as he did, trying to remember the twists and turns of the tunnels of Biggrin's Lair.

He took Regis by the hand and started in, for the halfling couldn't see nearly as well as the drow in unlit caverns. At the first intersection, a turn down to their left, they saw that not all the caverns were unlit.

Drizzt motioned for Guenhwyvar to lead and for Regis to stay put, and drew his blades. He moved cautiously and silently, one slow, short step at a time. Ahead of him, Guenhwyvar reached the lit chamber, the fire within silhouetting her so clearly he saw her ears go up and her muscles relax as she trotted in, out of his view.

He picked up his pace, replacing his blades in their sheaths. At the chamber entrance, he had to squint against the bright flames.

He hardly recognized the man sitting on the far side of that fire, hardly recognized that it was a man at all at first, for with all the layers of furs, he surely could have passed for a giant himself.

Of course, such had often been said of Wulfgar, son of Beornegar.

Drizzt started in, but Regis rushed past him, crying, "Wulfgar!" with great joy.

The man managed a smile back through his thick blond beard at the exuberant halfling.

"We thought you were dead," Regis gushed.

"I was," Wulfgar answered. "Perhaps I still am, but I'm nearly back to life." He pulled himself up straight but didn't stand as Drizzt and Regis neared. The barbarian motioned to two furs he had set out for them to sit upon.

Regis looked curiously to Drizzt for some answers, and the drow, more versed in the way of the barbarians, seconded Wulfgar's motion and took his own seat opposite the man.

"I have beaten three of the seasons," Wulfgar explained. "But the most difficult now steps before me in challenge."

Regis started to question the curious wording, but Drizzt stopped him with an upraised hand, and led by example as they waited for Wulfgar to tell his tale.

"Colson is back with her mother in Auckney," Wulfgar began. "As it should be."

"And her father, the foolish lord?" Drizzt asked.

"His foolishness has been tempered by the companionship of a fine woman, it seems," Wulfgar answered.

"It must have pained you," Regis remarked, and Wulfgar nodded slightly.

"When I traveled from Auckney to the main north-south trail, I didn't know which way I would turn. I fear I have abandoned Bruenor, and that is no small thing."

"He fares well," Drizzt assured his friend. "He misses you dearly, but his kingdom is at peace."

"At peace, with a host of orcs outside his northern door?" said Wulfgar, and it was Drizzt's turn to nod.

"The peace will not hold, and Bruenor will know war again," Wulfgar predicted.

"It's possible," the drow replied. "But because he showed patience and tolerance, any outbreak of war by the orcs will be met by Mithral Hall and a host of mighty allies. Had Bruenor continued the war against Obould, he would have fought it alone, but now, should it come to blows. . . ."

"May the gods keep him, and all of you, safe," Wulfgar said. "But what brought you here?"

"We journeyed to Mirabar as emissaries of Bruenor," the drow explained.

"Since we were in your neighborhood. . . ." Regis quipped, an assertion made funny by its ridiculousness—Mirabar was nowhere near Icewind Dale.

"We all wanted to know how you fared," Drizzt said.

"All?"

"We two, Bruenor, and Catti-brie." The drow paused to measure Wulfgar's expression, but to his relief saw no pain there. "She is well," he added, and Wulfgar smiled.

"Never did I doubt otherwise."

"Your father will return here soon to visit you," Regis assured the man. "Should he look for this cave?"

Wulfgar smiled at that. "Seek the banner of the elk," he replied.

"They think you dead," the halfling said.

"And so I was. But Tempus has been kind and has allowed me a rebirth in this place, his home."

He paused, and his crystal blue eyes, so much like the autumn sky of Icewind Dale, flashed. Regis started to say something, but Drizzt held him back.

"I made errors upon my return—too many," the barbarian said somberly a few heartbeats later. "Icewind Dale does not forgive, and does not often offer a second chance to correct a mistake. I had forgotten who I was and who my people were, and most of all, I had forgotten my home."

He paused and stared into the flames for what seemed like an hour. "Icewind Dale challenged me," he said quietly, as if speaking more to himself than to his friends. "Tempus dared me to remember who I was, and the price of failure would be—will be—my life.

"But I have won thus far," he said, looking up at the pair. "I survived the bears and hunters of the spring, the bottomless bogs of the summer, and the last frenzy of feeding in the autumn. I made this my home and painted it with the blood of the goblinkind and giantkin who lived here."

"We saw," Regis said dryly, but his smile was not infectious—not to Wulfgar at least.

"I will defeat the winter, my quest will be at an end, and I will return to the

Tribe of the Elk. I remember now. I am again the son of Icewind Dale, the son of Beornegar."

"They will have you back," Drizzt stated.

Wulfgar paused for a long while, and finally nodded his agreement, though slowly. "My people will forgive me."

"You will claim leadership again?" Regis asked.

Wulfgar shook his head. "I will take a wife and have as many children as we can. I will hunt the caribou and kill the goblins. I will live as my father lived, and his father before him, as my children will live and their children after them. There is peace in that, Drizzt, and comfort and joy and endlessness."

"There are many handsome women among your kin," Drizzt said. "Who wouldn't be proud to be the wife of Wulfgar, son of Beornegar?"

Regis scrunched up his face as he regarded the drow after that curious comment, but when he looked over at Wulfgar, he saw that Drizzt's words had apparently been well-spoken.

"I would have married more than a year ago," Wulfgar said. "There is one . . ." His voice trailed off with a little laugh. "I was not worthy."

"Perhaps she is still available," Drizzt offered, and Wulfgar smiled again, and nodded.

"But they think you dead," Regis blurted, and Drizzt scowled at him.

"I was dead," Wulfgar said. "On the day I left, I had never truly returned. Berkthgar knew it. They all knew it. Icewind Dale does not forgive."

"You had to earn your way back to this life," said Drizzt.

"I am again the son of Beornegar."

"Of the Tribe of the Elk—after the winter," said Drizzt, and he offered a sincere nod and smile of understanding.

"And you will not forget your friends?" Regis asked, breaking the silent communication between Drizzt and Wulfgar, both turning to regard him. "Well?" he said stubbornly. "Is there no place in the life of the son of Beornegar for those who once knew him and loved him? Will you forget your friends?"

The halfling's warmth melted the ice from Wulfgar's face, and he grinned widely. "How could I ever?" he asked. "How could anyone forget Drizzt Do'Urden, and the dwarf king of Mithral Hall, who was as my father for all those years? How could I forget the woman who taught me how to love, and who showed me such sincerity and honesty?"

Drizzt squirmed a bit at that reminder that it was his relationship with Catti-brie that had driven Wulfgar from them. But there was no malice, no regret, in Wulfgar's eyes. Just calm nostalgia and peace—peace as Drizzt hadn't seen in him in many, many years.

"And who could ever forget Regis of Lonelywood?" Wulfgar asked.

The halfling nodded appreciatively. "I wish you would come home," he whispered.

"I am home, at long last," said Wulfgar.

Regis shook his head and wanted to argue, but no words escaped the lump in his throat.

"You will one day challenge for the leadership of your tribe," Drizzt said. "It's the way of Icewind Dale."

"I am old among them now," Wulfgar replied. "There are many young and strong men."

"Stronger than the son of Beornegar?" Drizzt said. "I think not."

Wulfgar nodded in silent appreciation.

"You will one day challenge, and will again lead the Tribe of the Elk," Drizzt predicted. "Berkthgar will serve you loyally, as you will serve him until that day arrives, until you are again comfortable among the people and among the dale. He knows that."

Wulfgar shrugged. "I have yet to defeat the winter," he said. "But I will return to them in the spring, after the first draw of light and dark. And they will accept me, as they tried to accept me when first I returned. From there, I don't know, but I do know, with confidence, that ever will you be welcome among my people, and we will rejoice at your visits."

"They were gracious to us even without you there," Drizzt assured him.

Wulfgar again stared into the fire for a long, long while, deep in thought. Then he rose and moved to the back of the chamber, returning with a thick piece of meat. "I share my meal with you this night," he said. "And give you my ear. Icewind Dale will not be angry at me for hearing of that which I left behind."

"A meal for a tale," Regis remarked.

"We will leave at dawn's first light," Drizzt assured Wulfgar, and that drew a startled expression from Regis. Wulfgar, though, nodded in gratitude.

"Then tell me of Mithral Hall," he said. "Of Bruenor and Catti-brie. Of Obould—he is dead now, I hope."

"Not remotely," said Regis.

Wulfgar laughed, skewered the meat, and began to slow roast it.

They spent many hours catching up on the last four years, with Drizzt and Regis doing most of the talking, Drizzt running the litany of events and Regis adding color to every incident. They told him of Bruenor's grudging acceptance of the Treaty of Garumn's Gorge, for the good of the region, and of Obould's fledgling and tentative kingdom. Wulfgar just shook his head in obvious disapproval. They told him of Catti-brie's new endeavors alongside Lady Alustriel, turning to the Art, and surprisingly, the barbarian seemed quite pleased with the news, though he did quip, "She should bear your children."

With much prodding, Wulfgar finally related his own adventures, the road with Colson that led to Auckney and his decision that her mother should raise her—and his insistence and relief that the foolish lord of Auckney went along with the decision.

"She is better off by far," he said. "Her blood is not the blood of Icewind Dale, and here she would not have thrived."

Regis and Drizzt exchanged knowing looks, recognizing the open wound in Wulfgar's heart.

Regis was fast to change the subject at Wulfgar's next pause, telling of Deudermont's war in Luskan, of the fall of the Hosttower and the devastation that was general throughout the City of Sails.

"I fear that he moved too boldly, too swiftly," Drizzt remarked.

"But he is beloved," Regis argued, and a brief discussion and debate ensued about whether or not their friend had done the right thing. It was brief, because both quickly realized that Wulfgar cared little for the fate of Luskan. He sat there, his expression distant, rubbing his hands along the thick, sleek fur of Guenhwyvar, who lay beside him.

So Drizzt turned the discussion to times long past, to the first time he and Wulfgar had come to the verbeegs' lair, and to their walks up Bruenor's Climb on Kelvin's Cairn. They replayed their adventures, those long and trying roads they had walked and sailed, the many fights, the many pleasures. They were still talking, though the conversation slowed as the fire burned low, when Regis fell fast asleep, right there on a little fur rug on the stone floor.

He awoke to find Drizzt and Wulfgar already up, sharing breakfast.

"Eat quickly," Drizzt said to him. "The storm has subsided and we must be on our way."

Regis did so, silently, and a short while later, the three said their good-byes at the edge of Wulfgar's temporary home.

Wulfgar and Drizzt clasped hands firmly, eyes locking in deep and mutual respect. They fell into a tight hug, a bond that would last forever, then broke apart, Drizzt turning for the brightness outside. Wulfgar slapped Guenhwyvar on the rump as she trotted by.

"Here," Regis said to him, and held out a piece of scrimshaw he'd been working for some time.

Wulfgar took it carefully and lifted it up before his eyes, his smile widening as he recognized it as a carving of the Companions of the Hall: Wulfgar and Drizzt, Cattie-brie and Bruenor, Regis and Guenhwyvar, side-by-side, shoulder-to-shoulder. He chuckled at the likeness of Aegis-fang in his miniature's hand, at the sculpture of Bruenor's axe and Catti-brie's bow—a bow carried by Drizzt, he noted as he examined the scrimshaw.

"I will keep it against my heart and in my heart for the rest of my days," the barbarian promised.

Regis shrugged, embarrassed. "If you lose the piece," he offered, "well, if it's in your heart then you never can."

"Never," Wulfgar agreed, and he lifted Regis in a crushing hug.

"You will find your way back to Icewind Dale," he said in the halfling's ear. "I will surprise you on the banks of Maer Dualdon. Perhaps I will even take the moment to bait your hook."

The sun, meager though it was, seemed all the brighter to Regis and Drizzt that morning, as it reflected off the brilliant whiteness of new-fallen snow, glistening in their moist eyes.

PART

4

PRINCIPLES

AND PRAGMATISM

PRINCIPLES

AND PRAGMATISM

They are two men I love dearly, two men I truly respect, and as such, I'm amazed when I step back and consider the opposite directions of the roads of Wulfgar and Deudermont. Indeed, they are both true warriors, yet they have chosen different foes to battle.

Deudermont's road, I think, was wrought of frustration. He has spent more than two decades sailing the Sword Coast in pursuit of pirates, and no person in the memories of old elves has ever been so successful at such a dangerous trade. All honors were bestowed upon *Sea Sprite* when she put in to any of the major cities, particularly the all-important Waterdeep. Captain Deudermont dined with lords, and could have taken that title at his whim, bestowed by the grateful noblemen of Waterdeep for his tireless and effective service.

But for all that, it was upon learning the truth of the newest pirate advances, that the Hosttower of the Arcane supported them with magic and coin, that Captain Deudermont had to face the futility of his lifelong quest. The pirates would outlive him, or at least, they would not soon run out of successors.

Thus was Deudermont faced with an untenable situation and a lofty challenge indeed. He didn't shy, he didn't sway, but rather took his ship straight to the source to face this greater foe.

His reaction to a more terrible and wider world was to fight for control of that which seemed uncontrollable. And with such courage and allies, he may actually succeed, for the specter of the Hosttower of the Arcane is no more, Arklem Greeth is no more, and the people of Luskan have rallied to Deudermont's noble cause.

How different has been Wulfgar's path. Where Deudermont turned outward to seek greater allies and greater victories, Wulfgar turned inward, and returned his thoughts to a time and place more simple and straightforward. A time and place no less harsh or dangerous, to be sure, but one of clear definition, and one where a victory does not mean a stalemate with a horde of orcs, or a political concession for the sake of expediency. In Wulfgar's world, in Icewind Dale, there is no compromise. There is perfection of effort, of body, of soul, or there is death. Indeed, even absent mistakes, even if perfection is achieved, Icewind Dale can take a man, any man, at a whim. Living there, I know, is the most humbling of experiences.

Still, I have no doubt that Wulfgar will defeat Icewind Dale's winter season. I have no doubt that upon his return to the Tribe of the Elk at the spring equinox, he will be greeted as family and friend, to be trusted. I have no doubt that Wulfgar will one day again be crowned as chief of his tribe, and that, should a terrible enemy rise up in the dale, he will stand forward, with all the inspired tribes gratefully at his back, cheering for the son of Beornegar.

His legend is secured, but hardly fully written.

So one of my friends battles a lich and an army of pirates and sorcerers, while the other battles inner demons and seeks definition of a scattered and unique existence. And there, I think, rests the most profound difference in their respective roads. For Deudermont is secure in his time and place, and reaches from solid foundation to greater endeavors. He is confident and comfortable with, above all others, Deudermont. He knows his pleasures and comforts, and knows, too, his enemies within and without. Because he understands his limitations, so he can find the allies to help him step beyond them. He is, in spirit, that which Wulfgar will become, for only after one has understanding and acceptance of the self can one truly affect the external.

I have looked into the eyes of Wulfgar, into the eyes of the son of Beornegar, into the eyes of the son of Icewind Dale.

I fear for him no longer—not in body, not in soul.

And yet, even though Wulfgar seeks as a goal to be where Deudermont already resides, it's Deudermont for whom I now fear. He steps with confidence and so he steps boldly, but in Menzoberranzan we had a saying, "*Noet z'hin lil'avinsin.*"

"Boldly stride the doomed."

—Drizzt Do'Urden

CHAPTER

The man walked down the ally, glancing left and right. He knew he was right to be careful, for the cargo he would soon carry was among the most precious of commodities in Luskan that harsh winter.

He moved to a spot on the wall, one that seemed unremarkable, and knocked in a specific manner, three short raps, a pause, two short raps, a pause, and a final heavy thud.

The boards of the house parted, revealing a cleverly concealed window.

"Yeah?" asked the grumpy old man within. "Who ye for?"

"Seven," the man replied, and he handed over a note sealed with the mark of Ship Rethnor, cupping it around seven small chips, like those often used as substitutions for gold and silver in gambling games along the docks. Those too bore Ship Rethnor's mark.

"Seven, ye say?" replied the old man inside. "But I'm knowin' ye, Feercus Oduuna, and knowin' that ye got no wife and no brats, no brothers and naught but the one sister. That adds to two, if me brain's not gone too feeble."

"Seven chips," Feercus argued.

"Five bought, pocket-picked, or taken from a dead man?"

"If bought, then what's the harm?" Feercus argued. "I'm not stealing from my brothers of Ship Rethnor, nor killing them to take their chips!"

"So ye admit ye bought 'em?"

Feercus shook his head.

"Kensidan's not looking kindly on any black marketeering here, I'm telling ye for yer own sake."

"I offered to retrieve the goods for five others," Feercus explained. "Me sister and me, and Darvus's family, with no living man to come and no child old enough to trust to do it."

"Ah, and what might ye be getting from Missus Darvus in exchange for yer helpfulness?" the old codger asked.

Feercus flashed a lewd smile.

"More than that, if I'm knowin' Feercus— and I am," the old man said. "Ye're taking part o' the bargain in flesh, I'm not doubting, but ye're getting a fill for yer pocket, too. How much?"

"Has Kensidan outlawed that as well?"

"Nay."

"Then . . ."

"How much?" the old man insisted. "And I'll be asking Darvus's widow, and I'm knowin' her well, so ye best be tellin' me true."

Feercus glanced around again then sighed and admitted, "Four silver."

"Two for me," said the old man, holding out his hand. When Feercus didn't immediately hand over the coins, he wagged his fingers impatiently. "Two, or ye're not eating."

With a grumbled curse under his breath, Feercus handed over the coins. The old man retreated into the storehouse, and Feercus watched as he put seven small bags into a single sack, then returned and handed them out the window.

Again Feercus glanced around.

"Someone follow ye here?" the old man asked.

Feercus shrugged. "Lots of eyes. Baram or Taerl's men, I expect, as they're not eating so well."

"Kensidan's got guards all about the Ship," the old man assured him. "Baram and Taerl wouldn't dare to move against him, and Kurth's been paid off with food. Likely them eyes ye're seeing are the watching guards—and don't ye doubt that they'll not be friends o' Feercus, if Feercus is stealing or murdering them who're under the protection of Kensidan!"

Feercus held up the sack. "For widow Darvus," he said, and slung it over his shoulder as he started away. He hadn't gone more than a step when the window's shutter banged closed, showing no more than an unremarkable wall once more.

Gradually, Feercus managed to take his thoughts off the watching eyes he knew to be peering out from every alley and window, and from many of the rooftops, as well. He thought of his cargo, and liked the weight of it. Widow Darvus had promised him that she had some spices to take the tanginess out of the curious meat Kensidan handed out to all under his protection—and many more had come under his protection, swearing fealty to Ship Rethnor, throughout that cold and threadbare winter. Between that and the strange, thick mushrooms, Feercus Oduuna expected a wonderful meal that evening.

He promised himself that he wouldn't get too greedy and eat it all, and that his sister, all alone in her house since her husband and two children had died in the explosion of the Hosttower, would get more than her one-seventh share.

He glanced back once as he exited the alley, whispering his sincere thanks for the generosity of High Captain Kensidan.

* * * * *

In another part of Luskan, not far from the road Feercus traveled, several men stood on a street corner, a fire blazing between them over which they huddled for warmth. One man's stomach growled from emptiness and another punched him in the shoulder for the painful reminder.

"Ah, keep it quiet," he said.

"And how am I to stop it?" the man with the grumbling belly replied. "The rat I ate last night didn't go near to filling me, and I been throwin' up more of it than I put down!"

"All our bellies're grumbling," a third man said.

"Baram's got food coming out tonight, so he says," a fourth piped in hopefully.

"Won't be near enough," said the first, who punched the other's shoulder again. "Never near enough. I ain't been so hungry in all my days, not even when out on the water, days and days in a dead wind."

"A pity we're not for eating man flesh," the third said with a pathetic chuckle. "Lots o' fat bodies out on Cutlass Island, eh?"

"A pity we're not working for Rethnor, ye mean," said the first, and the others all snapped surprised glances his way. Such words could get a man killed in short order.

"Ain't even Rethnor—Rethnor's dead, so they're saying," said another.

"Aye, it's that boy o' his, the sneaky one they call the Crow," said the first. "He's gettin' food. Not knowing how, but he's gettin' it and feedin' his boys well this winter. I'm thinking that Baram'd be smart to stop arguing with him and start gettin' us some of that food!"

"And I'm thinking ye're talkin'll of us dead in an alley," one of the others said in a tone that offered no room for argument. As much a threat as a warning, the harsh comment ended the discussion abruptly and the group went back to rubbing their hands, saying nothing, but with their bellies doing enough complaining to aptly relay their foul sentiments.

* * * * *

The mood in the Cutlass was fine that night—a small gathering, but of men who had eaten well and who had fed their families properly, and all thanks to the generosity of the son of Rethnor.

Behind the bar, Arumn Gardpeck noticed a couple of new faces that night, as he was now seeing quite regularly. He nudged his friend and most reliable customer, Josi Puddles, and nodded his chin toward the new pair who sat in a corner.

"I'm not liking it," Josi slurred after glancing that way. "It's our tavern."

"More patrons, more coin," Arumn replied.

"More trouble, you mean," said Josi, and as if on cue, Kensidan's dwarf walked in and moved right up to Arumn.

The dwarf followed their gazes to the corner then said to Arumn, "From the avenue called Setting Sun," he said.

"Taerl's men, then," Josi replied.

"Or Kensidan's now, eh?" Arumn said to the dwarf, sliding the usual brew his way.

The dwarf nodded, his eyes never leaving the two men as he brought the flagon to his lips and drained it in a single draw, ale spilling out over his black, beaded beard. He stayed there for some time, staring and hardly listening to the continuing conversation between Josi and Arumn. Every so often, he motioned for another ale, which Arumn, who was eating quite well thanks to the generosity of Kensidan, was happy to supply.

Finally the two men departed and the dwarf drained one last flagon and followed them out into the street. He wasn't far behind when he exited, despite pausing for his last drink, because the pair had to pause as well to retrieve their weapons as they left. On Kensidan's command, weapons weren't allowed inside Arumn's establishment. That rule didn't apply to Kensidan's personal body-guard of course, and so the dwarf had not been similarly slowed.

He made no effort to conceal the fact that he was following the pair, one of whom stupidly glanced back several times. The dwarf thought they would confront him out in the street, with so many witnesses around, but to his surprise and delight, the pair slipped down a dark and narrow alleyway instead.

Grinning, he eagerly followed.

"Far enough," said a voice from the darkness beyond. Following the sound, the dwarf made out a single silhouette standing by a pile of refuse. "I'm not liking yer staring, black-beard, and liking yer following even less."

"Ye're for calling Captain Taerl's guards on me, I'm guessing," the dwarf replied, and he saw the man shift uncomfortably at the reminder that he was not on his home turf.

"H-here on—on Rethnor's invitation," the man stammered.

"Here to eat, ye mean."

"Aye, as invited."

"Nay, friend," the dwarf said. "Rethnor's welcoming them looking for a Ship to crew, not them looking to come in, eat, and go home to tell th' other high captains. Ye're a man o' Taerl, and good enough for ye."

"Switching," the man blurted.

"Bwahahaha," the dwarf taunted. "Ye been here five times now, yerself and yer hiding friend. And five times ye been on the road back home. A lot o' yer boys, too. Ye think we're for feeding ye, do ye?"

"I-I'm paying well," the man stammered.

"For what's not for sale," said the dwarf.

"If they're for selling, then it's for sale," said the man, but the dwarf crossed his burly arms over his chest and shook his head slowly.

From the roof to the dwarf's left came the man's companion, leaping down from on high, dagger thrust before him as if he thought himself a human spear. He apparently figured that he had the dwarf by surprise, an easy kill.

So did his friend, down the alley, who started a whoop of victory, one that ended abruptly as the dwarf exploded into motion, throwing his arms forward and over his head and springing a backward somersault. As he went over, he deftly pulled out his twin morningstars, and he landed solidly on the balls of his feet, leaning forward so that he easily reversed his momentum and plowed forward.

With surprising agility, the diving man managed to adjust to his complete miss and tuck into a fairly nimble roll that brought him right back to his feet. He spun, slashing with his dagger to keep the dwarf at bay.

The spiked head of a morningstar met that extended hand, and if the blow wasn't enough to shatter it, a coating on the ball exploded with magical power. The dagger, a misshapen and twisted thing, flew away, along with three fingers.

The man howled in agony and punched out with other hand as he brought the wounded one in close.

But again the dwarf was way ahead of him. As his first, right-hand morningstar swiped across to take the knife, his left arm went over his head, his second weapon spinning the same way as the first. Executing the block easily, the dwarf stepped forward and down. The punch went over his head as his second morningstar whipped around, the spiked head reaching out at the end of its black chain to take the man on the side of the knee.

The crack of bone drowned out the squeal of pain and the man's leg buckled and he flopped down to the ground.

His charging friend nearly tripped over him, but somehow held his balance, brandishing sword and dagger at the low-crouched dwarf. He thrust and slashed wildly, trying to overwhelm the dwarf with sheer ferocity.

And he almost got through the clever parries, but only because the dwarf was laughing too hard to more properly defend.

Frantic, trying hard to block out the pitiful crying of his broken friend, the man stabbed again, rushing forward.

He hit nothing, for the dwarf, in perfect balance, slipped out to the side.

"Ye're starting to try me patience," the dwarf warned. "Ye might be leaving with just a beating."

Too terrified to even comprehend that he had just been offered his life, the man spun and threw himself at the dwarf.

By the time the second morningstar ball smashed him on the side of his ribs, crunching them to dust, he realized his mistake. By the time that second ball smacked him again, in the head, he knew nothing at all.

His friend howled all the louder when the swordsman fell dead before him, his brains spilling out all over the cobblestones.

He was still howling when the dwarf grabbed him by the front of his shirt and with frightening strength stood him upright and smashed him against the wall.

"Ye're not listening to me, boy," the dwarf said several times, until the man finally shut up.

"Now ye get back to Setting Sun and ye tell Taerl's boys that this ain't yer place," said the dwarf. "If ye're with Taerl then ye ain't with Rethnor, and if ye ain't with Rethnor, then go and catch yerself some rats to eat."

The man gasped for breath.

"Ye hear me?" the dwarf asked, giving him a rough shake, and though it was with just one hand, the man couldn't have any more resisted it than he could the pull of a strong horse.

He nodded stupidly and the dwarf flung him down to the ground. "Crawl out o' here, boy. And if ye're meaning to crawl back, then do it with a pledge to Ship Rethnor."

The man replied, "Yes, yes, yes, yes . . ." over and over again as the dwarf calmly walked out of the alleyway, tucking his twin morningstars diagonally into their respective sheaths on his back as he went, and seeming as if nothing at all had just happened.

* * * * *

"You don't have to enjoy it so much," Kensidan said to the dwarf a short while later.

"Then pay me more."

Kensidan gave a little laugh. "I told you not to kill anyone."

"And I telled yerself that if they're drawing steel, I'm drawing blood," the dwarf replied.

Kensidan continued to chuckle and waved his hand in concession.

"They're getting' desperate," the dwarf said. "Not enough food in most quarters for Baram and Taerl."

"Good. I wonder how fondly they look upon Captain Deudermont now?"

"Governor, ye mean."

Kensidan rolled his eyes.

"Yer friend Suljack's getting more than them other two," said the dwarf. "If ye was to send him a bit o' ours on top o' what he's getting from Deudermont, he might be climbing up behind yerself and Kurth."

"Very astute," Kensidan congratulated.

"Been playing politics since afore yer daddy's daddy found his first breath," the dwarf replied.

"Then I would think you smart enough to understand that it's not in my interest to prop Suljack to new and greater heights."

The dwarf looked at Kensidan curiously for just a moment, then nodded. "Ye're making him Deudermont's stooge."

Kensidan nodded.

"But he's to take it to heart," the dwarf warned.

"My father has spent years protecting him, often from himself," said Kensidan. "It's past time for Suljack to prove he's worthy of our efforts. If he can't understand his true role beside Deudermont, then he's beyond my aid."

"Ye could tell him."

"And I would likely be telling Baram and Taerl. I don't think that's a good thing."

"How hard're ye meaning to press them?" the dwarf asked. "Deudermont's still formidable, and if they're throwing in with him . . ."

"Baram hates Deudermont to his soul," Kensidan assured the dwarf. "I count on you to gauge the level of discontent on the streets. We want to steal some of their men, but only enough to make sure that those two will understand their place when the arrows start flying. It's not in my interest to weaken them to anarchy, or to chase them to Deudermont's side for fear of their lives."

The dwarf nodded.

"And no more killing," Kensidan said. "Run the intruders out, show them a way to more and better food. Break a few noses. But no more killing."

The dwarf put his hands on his hips, thoroughly flustered by the painful command.

"You will have all the fighting you desire and more when Deudermont makes his move," Kensidan promised.

"Ain't no more fightin' than I'm desiring."

"The spring, early on," Kensidan replied. "We keep Luskan alive through the winter, but just barely. When the ships and the caravans don't arrive in the early spring, the city will disintegrate around the good capt—*governor*. His promises will ring as hollow as the bellies of his minions. He will be seen not as savior, but as a fraud, a flame without heat on a cold winter's eve."

And so it went through Luskan's long winter night. Supplies reached out from Ship Rethnor to Closeguard Island and Kurth, to Suljack and even a bit to Deudermont's new palace, fashioned from the former Red Dragon Inn, north of the river. From Deudermont, what little he had to spare, supplies went out to the two high captains in dire need, though never enough, of course, and to the Mirabarrans holed up in the Shield. And as the winter deepened, Suljack, prodded by Kensidan, came to spend more and more time by Deudermont's side.

The many ships riding out the winter in port got their food from Kurth, as Kensidan ceded to him control of the quay.

The coldest months passed, and were not kind to battered Luskan, and the people looked with weary eyes and grumbling bellies to the lengthening days, too weary and too hungry to truly hope for reprieve.

* * * * *

"I won't do it," Maimun said, and Kurth's eyes widened with surprise.

"A dozen ships, heavily laden and hardly guarded," the high captain argued. "Could a pirate ask for more?"

"Luskan needs them," said Maimun. "Your people fared well throughout the winter, but the folk on the mainland. . . ."

"Your crew ate well."

Maimun sighed, for indeed Kurth had been kind to the men and women of *Thrice Lucky*.

"You mean to drive Deudermont from power," the perceptive young pirate captain said. "Luskan looks to the sea and to the south, praying for food, and grain to replant the fields. There is not enough livestock in the city to support a tenth of the people living here, though only half of what Luskan once was remains."

"Luskan is not a farming community."

"What, then?" Maimun asked, but he knew the answer well enough.

Kurth and Kensidan wanted a free port, a place of trade where no questions would ever be asked, where pirates could put in and answer only to other pirates, where highwaymen could fence jewels and hide kidnap victims until the ransom arrived. Something had happened over the winter, Maimun knew, some subtle shift. Before the onset of the northern winds, the two plotting high captains had been far more cautious in their approach. In their apparent plan, Deudermont would rule Luskan and they would find ways around him.

Now they seemed to want the town for their own, in full.

"I won't do it," the young pirate captain said again. "I cannot so punish Luskan, whatever the expected outcome."

Kurth looked at him hard, and for a moment, Maimun expected that he would have to fight his way out of the tower.

"You are far too full of presumptions and assumptions," Kurth said to him. "Deudermont has his Luskan, and it serves us well to keep him here."

Maimun knew the lie for what it was, but he didn't let on, of course.

"The food will arrive from Waterdeep's fleet, but it will come through Closeguard and not through Deudermont's palace," Kurth explained. "And the ground caravans belong to Kensidan, again not to Deudermont. The people of Luskan will be grateful. Deudermont will be grateful, if we're clever. I had thought you to be clever."

Maimun had no answer to the high captain's scenario. Maimun knew Deudermont as well as any who were not currently crewing *Sea Sprite,* and he doubted the captain would ever be so foolish as to think Kurth and Kensidan the saviors of Luskan. Stealing for the reward was the oldest and simplest of pirate tricks, after all.

"I offered *Thrice Lucky* the flagship role as a tribute," Kurth said. "An offer, not an order."

"Then I politely refuse."

Kurth nodded slowly and Maimun's hand slid down to his belted sword, with all expectation that he was about to be killed.

But the blow never came, and the young pirate captain left Closeguard Island a short while later, making all haste back to his ship.

Back in Kurth's chamber, a globe of darkness appeared in a far corner, signaling that the high captain was not alone.

"He would have been a big help," Kurth explained. *"Thrice Lucky* is swift enough to get inside the firing line of Waterdeep's fleet."

"The defeat of the Waterdhavian flotilla is well in hand," the voice from the darkness assured him. "For the right price, of course."

Kurth gave a sigh and rubbed his hand over his sharp features, considering the cost against the potential gain. He considered many times in those moments that Kensidan would certainly handle the land caravan, that Kensidan was walking ever more boldly and more powerfully in no small part because of the food those strangers in the darkness were providing.

"See to it," he agreed.

CHAPTER

CIVILIZATION'S MELT

A tenday and a half," Regis complained as he and Drizzt made their way down the trail south of Bryn Shander.

"These storms can arrive anytime for the next two months," Drizzt replied. "Neither of us wants another two months in Ten-Towns." As he finished, he cast a sidelong glance at his companion to note the expected wistfulness in Regis's large eyes. It had not been a bad winter in Ten-Towns for the two of them, though the snow fell deep and the wind blew hard all those months. Still, strong too were the fires in the common rooms, and the many friendly conversations overwhelmed the wintry wind.

But as the winter waned, Drizzt had grown increasingly impatient. His business with Wulfgar was done, and he was satisfied that he would see his barbarian friend again, in better times.

He wanted to go home. His heart ached for Catti-brie, and though the situation had seemed stable, he couldn't help but fear for his friend Bruenor, living as he was under the shadow of twenty thousand orcs.

The drow ranger set a strong pace down the uneven trail, where mud had refrozen and melted many times over the past few days. Patches of snow had clung stubbornly to the ground, behind every rock and filling every crevice. It was indeed early to be making such a journey through the Spine of the World, but Drizzt knew that to wait was to walk through deeper and more stubborn mud.

Over the months, Icewind Dale had filled their sensibilities again, rekindling old memories and experiences, and bringing forth many of the lessons

275

their years there had taught them. They wouldn't lose their way among familiar landmarks. They wouldn't be caught unaware by tundra yetis or bands of goblins.

As Regis had feared, they awoke the next morning to find the air filled with snow, but Drizzt didn't lead the way to a cave.

"It will not be a strong storm," he assured the halfling repeatedly as they trudged along, and through good instinct or simply good fortune, his prediction proved correct.

Within a few days, they had made the trail through the Spine of the World, and soon after they entered the pass, the wind diminished considerably and not even the long shadows of the tall mountains to either side of them could cover the signs that spring fast approached.

"Do you think we'll meet the Luskar caravan?" Regis asked more than once, for his belt pouches bulged with scrimshaw and he was eager to get first pickings from the Luskar goods.

"Too early," Drizzt always answered, but as they crossed the miles through the mountain range, every step bringing them closer to the warming breezes of spring, his tone became more hopeful with each response. After all, in addition to the welcome sound of new voices and the luxuries such a caravan might offer, a strong and early showing by Luskan in Icewind Dale would go a long way toward calming Drizzt's anxieties about the depth and endurance of Deudermont's victory.

As they neared the southern end of the mountain pass, the trail widened and broke off in several directions.

"To Auckney, and Colson," Drizzt explained to Regis as they crossed one trail climbing up to the west. "Two days of marching," he answered in response to the halfling's questioning gaze. "Two days there and two days back."

"Straight to Luskan, then, for some sales and some food for the road east," Regis replied. "Or is it possible that we might find a former Hosttower associate—or Robillard, yes Robillard!—to fly us home on a magical chariot?"

Drizzt chuckled in reply, and wished it were so. "We will arrive back at Mithral Hall in good time," he said, "if you can stride longer with those short legs."

On they went, down out of the foothills, and soon after breaking camp one brilliant morning, they came over a rocky rise in sight of the City of Sails.

Their hearts didn't lift.

Smoke hung low and thick over Luskan, and even from a distance, the companions could see that large swaths of the city were still but blackened husks. It had not been a kind winter in Deudermont's city, if indeed it remained Deudermont's city.

Regis didn't complain as Drizzt picked up their pace, almost trotting down the winding road. They passed many farms north of the city but noted surprisingly little activity, though the melt had progressed enough south of the Spine of the World for the early preparations of spring planting to begin. When it became apparent that they wouldn't make the city that day, Drizzt veered off the road and led Regis to the door of one such farmhouse. He rapped loudly, and when the door swung open, the woman noted the black skin of her unexpected and hardly typical guest, and she jumped in surprise and gave a little yelp.

"Drizzt Do'Urden, at your service," Drizzt said with a polite bow. "Back from Ten-Towns in Icewind Dale to visit my good friend Captain Deudermont."

The woman seemed to ease considerably, for surely anyone that close to Luskan had heard of Drizzt Do'Urden even before his exploits beside Deudermont in throwing down Arklem Greeth.

"If it's shelter ye're seeking, then put up in the barn," she said.

"The barn would be most hospitable," said Drizzt, 'but truly it's more good conversation and news of Luskan that would do we weary travelers good."

"Bah, but what news? News o' yer friend the governor?"

Drizzt couldn't suppress a smile at hearing Deudermont still referred to as governor. He nodded his assent.

"What's to tell, then?" asked the woman. "He gets his cheers, but don't he? And oh, but that one can wag a pretty tongue. A great feeder o' the pig, none's doubting."

"But . . . ?" Drizzt prompted, catching the prissy sarcasm sharpening her voice.

"But not so much for feedin' them that's feedin' the pigs, eh?" she said. "And not so quick with the grain we're needin' for the fields."

Drizzt looked south toward Luskan.

"I'm sure the captain will see to it as soon as he is able," Regis offered.

"Which?" the woman asked, and Regis realized that his use of Deudermont's old title had been taken to mean one of Luskan's high captains, and that inadvertent misunderstanding, given the woman's suddenly hopeful tone, had hinted to both Regis and Drizzt that Deudermont had not yet established control over those five.

"So, are ye to be stayin'?" the woman asked after a lengthy silence.

"Aye, the barn," Drizzt replied, turning to face her again and putting on a supremely pleasant and cheery expression as he did.

The pair were out the next morning before the cock crowed, trotting fast down the road all the way to Luskan's North Gate—Luskan's *unguarded* North Gate, they realized to their surprise. The ironclad door was neither locked nor barred, and not a voice of protest came at them from either of the towers flanking it as they pushed it open and crossed into the city.

"To the Cutlass, or the Red Dragon?" Regis asked, moving to the wide stone stairway of the Upstream Span bridge, which opened up into the northern section of the city wherein lay Deudermont's makeshift palace. But Drizzt shook his head and marched straight down the span, crossing the Mirar with Regis skipping at his heels.

"The market," he explained. "The level of activity there will tell us much of Luskan's winter before we rendezvous with Deudermont."

"I think we've already seen too much of it," Regis muttered.

Glancing left and right, it was hard for Drizzt to argue the sentiment. The city was a battered place, with many buildings crumbling, many more burned out, and with haggard folk covered in dirty layers of rags milling about the streets. The unmistakable look of hunger played on their dark faces, the profound hopelessness that could only be stamped by months of misery.

"Have ye seen the caravan, then?" came the quickly familiar question soon after the pair stepped off the Upstream Span and into the city proper.

"Luskan's caravan north to Ten-Towns?" Regis asked.

The man looked at him incredulously, so much so that Regis's heart sank.

"Waterdeep's," he corrected the halfling. "A caravan's coming, don't ye know? And a great fleet of ships with food and warm clothes, and grain for the fields and pigs for the barn! Have ye seen it, boy?"

"Boy?" Regis echoed, but the man was too lost in his rambling to notice and pause for even a breath.

"Have ye seen the caravan? Oh, but she's to be a big one, they're saying! Enough food for to fill our bellies through the summer and the winter next. And all from Lord Brambleberry's people, they're saying."

All around the old man, people nodded and attempted, at least, to cheer a bit, though the sound was surely pathetic.

Barely three blocks into the city and still a long way from the market, Drizzt had seen enough. He turned Regis around and made for Dalath's Span, the remaining usable bridges across the Mirar, the closest to the harbor and the Red Dragon.

When at last they arrived at Deudermont's "palace," the companions found warm greetings and wide smiles. The guards ushered them right to the inner chambers, where Deudermont and Robillard met with a surly red-bearded dwarf Drizzt remembered from the Mirabarran contingent at the battle of the Hosttower.

"If we're interrupting . . ." Drizzt started to apologize, but Deudermont cut him short, leaping up from his seat and saying, "Nonsense! It's a good day in Luskan when Drizzt and Regis return."

"And Luskan's needing some good days," the dwarf remarked.

"And some meetings are better off interrupted," Robillard mumbled.

The dwarf turned on him sharply, drawing a smirk and a shrug from the cynical wizard.

"Aye," the dwarf said, "and some meetings go on longer than all what's needed saying's been said."

"Beautifully if confusedly expressed," said Robillard.

"Ah, but it might be a wizard's addled brain's what's needing unrattling," said the dwarf. "A good shake—"

"A flaming dwarf. . . ." Robillard added.

The dwarf growled and Deudermont sidled between the two. "Tell your fellows that their help through the winter was most appreciated," he said to the dwarf. "And when the first caravan arrives from the Silver Marches, we hope you will find your way to more generosity."

"Aye, soon as our own bellies ain't growling," the dwarf agreed, and with a final glare at Robillard and a tip of his wide-brimmed hat to Drizzt and Regis, he took his leave.

"It's good you have returned," Deudermont said, moving over to offer a handshake to his two friends. "I trust the Icewind Dale winter was no more harsh than what we suffered here."

"The city is battered," said Drizzt.

"And hungry," Regis added.

"Every priest in Luskan toils away throughout every day in prayers to their gods, creating food and drink," Deudermont said. "But their efforts are not nearly enough. Over at the Shield, the Mirabarrans tightened their belts considerably through the months, rationing their supplies, for they alone in Luskan had storehouses properly prepared for the winter."

"Not alone," Robillard corrected, and there was no missing the edge in his tone.

Deudermont conceded the point with a nod. "Some of the high captains seem to have avenues of securing food. All praise to Suljack, who has funneled good meat through this palace to the citizens, even to those who were not of his Ship."

"He's an idiot," said Robillard.

"He is a fine example to the other four," Deudermont quickly argued. "He puts Luskan above Ship, and alone among them, it seems, is wise enough to understand that the fate of Luskan will ultimately determine the fate of their private little empires."

"You have to act, and quickly," said Drizzt. "Or Luskan will not survive."

Deudermont nodded his agreement with every word. "A flotilla has left Waterdeep, and a great caravan winds its way up from the south, both laden with food and grain, and with soldiers to aid in calming the city. The lords of Waterdeep have rallied around the work of the late Lord Brambleberry, that his efforts will not be in vain."

"They don't want one of their own to look as stupid as the whispers make him out to be," Robillard clarified, and even Drizzt couldn't help but chuckle at that. "Expect too much from the flotilla and caravan at your peril," the wizard warned Deudermont. "They're laden well with food, no doubt, but a few dozen sellswords would be a dozen or two more than I'll be willing to wager they've offered. They have a way of looking more generous than they actually are, these lords."

Deudermont didn't bother to argue the point. "They will both arrive within the next couple of tendays, say the scouts. I secured a promise of extra food from our dwarf friend Argithas of Mirabar. The Mirabarrans agreed to accelerate their tithing to the city in anticipation of the re-supply, though their storehouses are near empty. Mirabar has stood strong with me through the winter—I would bid you to relay our gratitude to Marchion Elastul when you return to the Silver Marches."

Drizzt nodded.

"What choice did they have?" Robillard asked. "We're the only acre of sanity left in Luskan!"

"The caravans—" said Deudermont.

"Are a temporary reprieve."

Deudermont shook his head. "We will use the example of Suljack to enlist the other four," he reasoned. "They will end their foolish warring and support the city or their people will turn against them, as the whole of the city turned against Arklem Greeth."

"The people on the streets appear desperate," said Regis, and Deudermont nodded.

"The times are hard," he replied. "The relief of summer will allow them to look beyond their misery and seek long-term solutions to the ills of the city. Those solutions lie with me and not with the high captains, unless those old seadogs are smart enough to understand the needs of the city beyond their own narrow streets."

"They're not," Robillard assured him. "And we'd do well to climb on *Sea Sprite* and sail back to Waterdeep."

"I would go without food for a winter and more if only I heard a word of encouragement from Robillard," Deudermont remarked with a heavy sigh.

The wizard snickered, threw his arm across the back of his chair, and turned away.

"Enough of our misery," Deudermont said. "Tell me of Icewind Dale, and of Wulfgar. Did you find him?"

Drizzt's smile surely answered before the drow began to recant his tale of the journey.

CHAPTER

P R E S S U R E

The small bit of water they had put in the pot bubbled and steamed away, its aroma eliciting many licks of anticipation. The dark meat, twenty pounds of basted perfection, glistened from the surface burns of fast cooking, for not a one of the band of highwaymen was willing to wait the hours to properly prepare the unexpected feast.

The moment the cook announced it was done, the group began tearing at it eagerly, ripping off large chunks and shoving them into hungry mouths so that their cheeks bulged like rodents storing food for the winter. Every now and then one or another paused just long enough to lift a toast to Ship Rethnor, who had supplied them so well. And all that the generous son of the recently-deceased high captain had asked for in return was that the band waylay a caravan, and with all proceeds of the theft going to the highwaymen.

"They give us food for taking food," one rogue observed with a chuckle.

"And give us help in taking it," another agreed, indicating a small keg of particularly effective poison.

So they cheered and they ate, and they laughed and cheered some more for the son of Ship Rethnor.

The next morning, they watched from a series of low forested hills as the expected caravan, more than two dozen wagons, wound its way up the road from the south. Many guards accompanied the train—proud Waterdhavian soldiers—and even several wizards.

"Remember that we've a whole tenday," Sotinthal Magree, the leader of the

Luskar band, told his fellows. "Sting and run, sting and run—wear them down day after day."

The others nodded as one. They didn't have to kill all of the guards. They didn't have to stop all of the wagons. If less than half of the wagons and less than half of the supplies got through to Luskan, Ship Rethnor would be satisfied and the highwaymen would share in the bounty.

That morning, a volley of crossbow quarrels flew out at the teams of the last two wagons in line, horses and guards alike. From a safe distance and with light crossbows, such an attack would hardly have bothered the seasoned travelers, but even the slightest scratch from a poisoned quarrel brought down even the largest of the draft horses.

The group of guards that charged out at the attackers similarly found their numbers halved with a second, more concentrated volley. Minor wounds proved devastating. Strong men crumbled to the ground in a deep and uncompromising sleep.

The crossbowmen melted into the woods before any close engagement could begin and from the other side of the road, a small group of grenadiers found their openings and charged the weakest spans of the caravan, hurling their fiery missiles of volatile oil and running off in fast retreat.

When some guards gave chase they found themselves caught in a series of spring traps, swinging logs and deviously buried spikes, all tipped, once again, with that devious poison.

By the end of the encounter, two wagons and their contents were fully engulfed in flames and two others damaged so badly that the Waterdhavians had to strip one to salvage the other. The caravan had lost several horses to flames or to injuries caused when the sleeping poison had sent them falling to the ground. A trio of guards had been murdered in the woods.

"They've no plan for the likes of us," Sotinthal told his men that night as they shadowed the caravan. "Like the dwarf told us they wouldn't. They're thinking that all the folk north of Waterdeep would welcome their passing and the food and grain they're bringing. A straight-on attack by monsters? Aye. A hungry band o' highwaymen? Aye. But not the likes of us—well fed and not needing their goods, well rewarded and not needing to fight them straight up."

He ended with a laugh that proved infectious around the campfire, and he wondered what tricks he and his fellows might use on the caravan the following day.

The next night, Sotinthal congratulated himself again, for the heavy boulder his men had rolled down the hill had taken out another wagon, destroying two of its wheels and spilling sacks of grain across the ground.

Their biggest cheer of all came three nights later, when a well-placed fiery arrow had lit up the oil-soaked understructure of a small bridge across a fast-moving stream, taking two wagons in the ensuing blaze and leaving five stranded on one side of the water, the men of the dozen-and-four on the other side staring helplessly.

Over the next two days, Sotinthal's men picked away at the Waterdhavians as they tried to find a ford or rebuild some measure of a bridge that could get the rest of their wagons across the stream.

The leader of the highwaymen knew the battered Waterdhavians were approaching their breaking point, and he was not surprised, though surely elated, when they simply ferried the supplies back over the stream to the south, overloaded the remaining wagons, and set off to the south, back to Waterdeep.

Kensidan would pay him well indeed.

* * * * *

"He is in her mind," the voice in the shadows said to Arklem Greeth. "Calming her, reminding her that her life remains and that eternity allows her to pursue that which she longs."

The lich resisted the urge to dispel the darkness and view the speaker, if only to confirm his guess about his identity. He looked over at poor Valindra Shadowmantle, who seemed at peace for the first time since he'd resurrected her consciousness inside her dead body. Arklem Greeth knew well the shock of death, and of undeath. After his own transformation to lichdom, he had battled many of the same anxieties and losses that had so unsettled Valindra, and of course he had spent many years in preparation for that still-shocking moment.

Valindra's experience had been far more devastating to the poor elf. Her heritage alone meant that she had expected several more centuries of life; with elves, the craving for immortality was not nearly as profound a thing as the desperation of short-lived humans. Thus, Valindra's transformation had nearly broken the poor soul, and would likely have turned her into a thing of utter and unrelenting hatred had not the voice in the shadows and his associate unexpectedly intervened.

"He tells me that the effort to keep her calm will be great indeed," the voice said.

"As will the price, no doubt," Arklem Greeth said.

Soft laughter came back at him. "What is your intent, Archmage?"

"With?"

"Luskan."

"What remains of Luskan, you mean," Arklem Greeth replied, in a tone that indicated he hardly cared.

"You remain within the city walls," said the voice. "Your heart is here."

"It was a profitable location, well-situated for the Arcane Brotherhood," the lich admitted.

"It can be again."

Despite not wanting to play his hand, Arklem Greeth couldn't help but lean forward.

"Not as it was, to be sure, but in other ways," said the voice.

"All we have to do is kill Deudermont. Is that what you are asking of me?"

"I'm asking nothing, except that your plans remain known to me."

"That is not nothing," said Arklem Greeth. "In many circles, such a price would be considered extravagant."

"In some circles, Valindra Shadowmantle would lose her mind."

Arklem Greeth had no answer to that. He glanced again at his beloved.

"Deudermont is well-guarded," said the voice. "He is not vulnerable while still in Luskan. The city is under considerable stress, as you might expect, and Deudermont's future as governor will depend upon his ability to feed and care for the people. So he has turned to his friends in Waterdeep, by land and by sea."

"You ask me to be a highwayman?"

"I told you that I asked nothing other than to know your plans as you evolve them," said the voice. "I had thought that one such as you, who need not draw air, who feels not the cold of the sea, would be interested to know that your hated enemy Deudermont is desperately awaiting the arrival of a flotilla from Waterdeep. It is presently sailing up the coast and the soft belly of supply ships is too well guarded for any pirates to even think of attacking."

Arklem Greeth sat perfectly still, digesting the information. He looked again at Valindra.

"My friend is not in her mind any longer," said the voice, and Arklem Greeth sharpened his focus on the undead woman, and was greatly encouraged as she didn't melt into a well of despair.

"He has shown her possibilities," said the voice. "He will return to her to reinforce the message and help her through this difficult time."

Arklem Greeth turned to the magical darkness. "I'm grateful," he said, and sincerely.

"You will have many years to repay us," said the voice, and it melted away as the darkness dissipated.

Arklem Greeth went to his beloved Valindra, and when she didn't respond to him, he sat and draped an arm around her.

His thoughts, though, sailed out to sea.

* * * * *

"It has not been a good winter," Deudermont admitted to Drizzt and Regis in the palace that day. "Too many dead men, too many shattered families."

"And during it all, the idiots fought each other," Robillard interjected. "They should have been out fishing and hunting, preparing the harvested crops and pooling their supplies. But would they?" He scoffed and waved his hand at the city beyond the window. "They fought amongst themselves—high captains posturing, guildless rogues murdering. . . ."

Drizzt listened to every word, but never took his eyes off Deudermont, who stared out the window and winced at every one of Robillard's points. There was no disagreement—how could there be, with smoke rising from every quarter of Luskan and with bodies practically lining the streets? There was something else in Deudermont's posture that, even more than the words, revealed to Drizzt how brutal the winter had been. The weight of responsibility bowed the captain's shoulders, and worse, Drizzt realized, was breaking his heart.

"The winter has passed," the drow said. "Spring brings new hope, and new opportunities."

Deudermont finally turned, and brightened just a bit. "There are promising signs," he said, but Robillard scoffed again. "It's true! High Captain Suljack sat behind me on that day when I was appointed as governor, and he has stood behind me since. And Baram and Taerl have hinted at coming around to a truce."

"Only because they have some grudge with Ship Rethnor and fear the new leader of that crew, this creature Kensidan, whom they call the Crow," said Robillard. "And only because Ship Rethnor ate well through the winter, but the only food Baram and Taerl could find came from the rats or came through us."

"Whatever the reason," Deudermont replied. "The Mirabarrans suffered greatly in the explosion of the Hosttower and have not opened the gates of the Shield District to the new Luskan, but with the spring, they may be persuaded to look toward the opportunities before us instead of the problems behind us. And we will need them this trading season. I expect Marchion Elastul will let the food flow generously, and on credit."

Drizzt and Regis exchanged concerned looks at that, neither overly impressed by the goodness of Elastul's heart. They had dealt with the man several times in the past, after all, and more often than not, had left the table shaking their heads in dismay.

"Elastul's daughter, Arabeth, survived the war and may help us in that,"

Deudermont said, obviously noting their frowns.

"It's all about food," Robillard said. "Who has it and who will share it, whatever the price. You speak of Baram and Taerl, but they're our friends only because we have the dark meat and the fungus."

"Curiously put," said Drizzt.

"From Suljack," Robillard explained, "who gets it from his friend in Ship Rethnor. Suljack has been most generous, while that young high captain of Rethnor ignores us as if we don't exist."

"He is unsure, like the Mirabarrans, perhaps," Regis offered.

"Or he is too sure of his position," Robillard said in a grim tone that Kensidan, had he heard, would have certainly taken as a warning.

"The spring will be our friend," Deudermont said as the door opened and his attendant indicated that dinner was served. "Caravans will arrive by land and by sea, laden with goods from the grateful lords of Waterdeep. With that bargaining power in my hands, I will align the city behind me and drag the high captains along, or I will rouse the city behind me and be rid of them."

"I hope for the latter," Robillard said, and Drizzt and Regis were not surprised.

They moved into the adjacent room and sat at Deudermont's finely appointed table, while attendants brought out trays of the winter's unexpected staple.

"Eat well, and may Luskan never be hungry again!" Deudermont toasted with his feywine, and all the others cheered that thought.

Drizzt gathered up knife and fork and went to work on the large chunk of meat on his plate, and even as that first morsel neared his lips, a familiar sensation came over him. The consistency of the meat, the smell, the taste. . . .

He looked at the side dish that ringed his main course, light brown mushrooms speckled with dots of purple.

He knew them. He knew the meat—deep rothé.

The drow fell back in his chair, mouth hanging open, eyes unblinking. "Where did you get this?"

"Suljack," Deudermont replied.

"Where did he get it?"

"Kensidan, likely," said Robillard as both he, Deudermont, and Regis stared at Drizzt curiously.

"And he?"

Robillard shrugged and Deudermont admitted, "I know not."

But Drizzt was afraid that he did.

* * * * *

If Valindra Shadowmantle's corpse had indeed been animated, she didn't show it those hours subsequent to the strangers' visit in Arklem Greeth's subterranean palace. She didn't sway, didn't moan, didn't blink her dead eyes, and any attempts to reach the woman were met with utter emptiness.

"But it will pass," Arklem Greeth told himself repeatedly as he moved through the sewers beneath Illusk and Closeguard Island, collecting allies for his journey.

All the while, he considered the intruders to his subterranean palace. How had they so easily gotten past his many wards and glyphs? How had they even known that his extradimensional room had been anchored down there in the sewers? What magic did they possess? Psionics, he knew, from the one who had entered Valindra's consciousness to calm her, but were they truly powerful enough in those strange arts to utilize them to neuter his own skilled magical wards? An involuntary shudder coursed Greeth's spine—the first time anything like that had happened in his decades of lichdom—but it was true. Arklem Greeth feared the visitors who had come unbidden, and Arklem Greeth rarely feared anything.

That fear, as much as his hatred for Captain Deudermont, drove the lich along his course.

With an army of unbreathing, undead monsters behind him, Arklem Greeth went out into the harbor then out to sea, steadily, tirelessly moving south. He found more of his unbreathing soldiers in the deeper waters—ugly lacedon ghouls—and easily brought them under his sway. The undead were his to control. Skeletons and zombies, ghouls and ghasts, wights and wraiths proved no match for his superior and dominating willpower.

Arklem Greeth swept them up in his wake, continuing south all the while, paralleling the shore as he knew the Waterdhavian ships would do. His army needed no rest in the depths, where day and night were not so different. With their webbed, clawing hands, the lacedons moved with great speed, weaving through the watery depths with the grace of dolphins and the impunity of a great shark or whale. They stayed low, far from the surface, sliding past the reeds and weeds, crossing low over reefs, where even the mighty and fierce eels stayed deep in their holes to avoid the undead things. Only through a great expenditure of magic could Arklem Greeth hope to pace the aquatic ghouls, and so he commanded a pair to tow him along with them. Every so often, the powerful lich opened dimensional doors, transporting himself and his ghoulish coachmen far ahead of the undead army, that he would note the ships long before engaging them.

Well-versed in the ways of the ocean, Greeth suspected that the ships might be near when he first spotted the inevitable companions of any such flotilla: a lazily-swimming and circling school of hammerhead sharks, common as vultures along the perilous Sword Coast.

Greeth could have led his lacedon army wide of the small group, but the lich had grown bored of the long journey. He willed his escorts in a straight-line ascent toward the school, and he started the festivities by rolling forth a ball of lightning at the nearest sharks. They popped and jerked at the sparking intrusion, a pair hung stunned in the water and several others darted fast out of sight in the murky water.

The lacedons swam furiously past Greeth, their hunger incited. They tore into the closest sharks, and the stunned pair thrashed and rolled. A ghoulish arm was torn free, and floated down past the amused Arklem Greeth. He watched as another lacedon, clamped firmly in the jaws of a hammerhead, was shaken to pieces.

But the undead could not be intimidated, and they swarmed the shark with impunity, their claws slashing through its tough skin, filling the dark water with blood.

The school came on in full, a frenzy of biting and tearing, a bloodlust that made ghoul and shark alike a target for those razor teeth.

Greeth stayed safely to the side, reveling in the fury, the primal orgy, the ecstasy and agony of life and pain, death and undeath. He measured his losses, the ghouls bitten in half, the limbs torn asunder, and when he finally reached the point of balance between voyeuristic pleasure and practical consideration, he intervened in a most definitive way, conjuring a cloud of poison around the entirety of the battlefield.

The lacedons were immune, of course. The sharks fled or died, violently and painfully.

It took great concentration for Greeth to control the bloodthirsty ghouls, to keep them from pursuing, to put them back in line and on course, but soon enough the undead army moved along as if nothing had transpired.

But Greeth knew that they were even more anxious and eager than normal, that their hunger consumed them.

Thus, when at last those ships floated over Arklem Greeth's army, Greeth was well-prepared and his beastly army was more than ready to strike.

In the dark of night, the ships at half-sail and barely moving in still air and calm waters, Arklem Greeth turned his forces loose. Three score lacedons swam up beneath one boat like a volley of swaying arrows. One by one, they disappeared out of the water, and the archmage arcane could only imagine them scaling the side of the low, cargo-laden ship, padding softly onto the deck where half-asleep lookouts yawned with boredom.

The lich lamented that he wouldn't hear their dying screams.

He knew soon after that his ghoulish soldiers were tearing apart the crew and rigging, for the ship above him turned awkwardly and without apparent purpose.

A second ship came in fast, as Arklem Greeth had expected, and it was his to intercept. Many ships of the great ports were well-guarded from magical attacks, of course, with wards all along their decks and hull.

But those defenses were almost always exclusively above or just below the waterline.

The lich led the way in to the bottom of the ship with a series of small magical arrows. He concentrated his firing and soon the water near his target points hissed and fizzed as the arrows pumped acid into the old wood of the hull. By the time Arklem Greeth arrived at the spot, he could easily punch his hand through the compromised planks.

From that hand flew a small fiery pea, arcing up into the hull before exploding into a raging fireball.

Again the lich could only imagine the carnage, the screams and confusion!

In moments, men began diving into the water, and his lacedons, their job complete on the first ship, plunged in behind. What beauty those creatures showed in their simple and effective technique, swimming up gracefully below the splashing sailors, tearing at their ankles, and dragging them down to watery deaths.

The ship he had fireballed continued on its course, not slowing in the least as it reached the first target. Arklem Greeth couldn't resist. He swam up and poked his head out of the water, and nearly cackled with glee in watching the tangled ships share the hungry fire.

More ships approached from every direction. More desperate men jumped into the water and the lacedons dragged them down.

All the darkness echoed with horrified screams. Arklem Greeth picked a second target and turned it, too, into a great fiery disaster. Calls for calm and composure could not match the terror of that night. Some ships dropped sail and clustered together, while others tried to run off under full sail, committing the fatal error of separating from their companion vessels.

For they couldn't outrun the lacedons.

The ghouls fed well that night.

CHAPTER
W R O N G   C H O I C E

"There's not enough," Suljack complained to Kensidan after the most recent shipment of food had arrived. "Barely half of the last load."

"Two-thirds," Kensidan corrected.

"Ah, we're running low, then?"

"No."

The flat answer hung in the air for a long while. Suljack studied his young friend, but Kensidan didn't blink, didn't smirk, gave no expression at all.

"We're not running low?" Suljack asked.

Kensidan didn't blink and didn't answer.

"Then why two-thirds, if that's what it was?"

"It's all you need," Kensidan replied. "More than you need, judging from the load you dropped at the Red Dragon Inn. I trust that Deudermont paid you well for the effort."

Suljack licked his lips nervously. "It's for the better."

"For whose better? Mine? Yours?"

"Luskan's," said Suljack.

"What does that even mean?" asked Kensidan. "Luskan's? For the betterment of Luskan? What is Luskan? Is it Taerl's Luskan, or Baram's? Kurth's or Rethnor's?"

"It's no time to be thinking of it like that," Suljack insisted. "We're one now, for the sake of all."

"One, behind Deudermont."

"Aye, and it was you that put me behind him that day when he became governor—and you should've been there! Then you'd know. The people ain't caring about which high captain's which, or about which streets're whose. They're needing food, and Deudermont's helping."

"Because you're giving my supplies to Deudermont."

"I'm giving them to Luskan. We've got to stand as one."

"We knew the winter would be difficult when we goaded Deudermont to attack the Hosttower," said Kensidan. "You do remember we did that, yes? You do understand the purpose of it all, yes?"

"Aye, I know it all full well, but things've changed now. The city's desperate."

"We knew it would be."

"But not like this!" Suljack insisted. "Little kids starving dead in their mother's arms . . . I could sink a ship and watch her crew drown and not think a bit about it—you know it—but I can't be watching that!"

Kensidan shifted in his chair and brought one hand up to cup his chin. "So Deudermont is the savior of Luskan? This is your plan?"

"He's the governor, and through it all, the people are with him."

"With him all the more if he's doling out food to them, I would expect," said Kensidan. "Am I to expect him to be a friend to Ship Rethnor when Baram and Taerl unite against me? Am I to expect those now growing more loyal to Deudermont to turn from him to support my work?"

"He's feeding them."

"So am I!" Kensidan shouted, and all the guards in the room turned sharply, unused to hearing such volatility from the always-composed son of Rethnor. "As suits me, as suits us."

"You want me to stop supplying him."

"Brilliant deduction—you should apply to the Hosttower, if we ever revive it. What I want more is for you to remember who you are, who we are, and the point of all of this trouble and planning."

Suljack couldn't help himself as he slowly shook his head. "Too many fallen," he said quietly, talking to himself more than to Kensidan. "Too high a price. Luskan stands as one, or falls."

He looked up, into the eyes of an obviously unimpressed Crow.

"If you've not the stomach for this," Kensidan began, but Suljack held up his hand to defeat the notion before it could be fully expressed.

"I will give him less," he said.

Kensidan started to respond, sharply, but bit it off. He turned to one of his attendants instead, and said, "Get the other third of Suljack's supplies packed on a wagon."

"Good man!" Suljack congratulated. "Luskan stands as one, and she'll get through this time of pain."

"I'm giving them to you," Kensidan said, his tone biting. "To you. They are yours to do with as you see fit, but remember our purpose in all of this. Remember why we put Deudermont together with Brambleberry, why we let the good captain know of the Hosttower's involvement with the pirates, why we tipped the Silver Marches to the advances of the Arcane Brotherhood. Those events were planned with purpose—you alone among my peers know that. So I give to you your rations, in full, and you are to do with them as you judge best."

Suljack started to respond, but bit it off and stood taking a long measure of Kensidan. But again, of course, the Crow assumed an unreadable posture and expression. With a nod and a smile of gratitude, Suljack left the room.

The dwarf slowly followed, letting the high captain get long out of earshot before he whispered to Kensidan, "He's to choose Deudermont."

"Wrong choice," Kensidan replied.

The dwarf nodded and continued out behind Suljack.

* * * * *

Amid the cries and the men rushing around, Suljack ran to the window overlooking the dark street, the dwarf close behind.

"Baram or Taerl?" the high captain asked Phillus, one of his most trusted guards, who knelt beside a second window, bow in hand.

"Might be both," the man replied.

"Too many," said another of the guards in the room.

"Both, then," said another.

Suljack rubbed his hands across his face, trying to comprehend the meaning of it all. The second shipment had arrived from Ship Rethnor earlier that same day, but it had come with a warning that High Captains Baram and Taerl were growing increasingly angry with the arrangements.

Suljack had decided to send the excess food to Deudermont anyway.

Directly below him in the street, the fighting had all but ended, with the combatants moving off to the alleyways, Suljack's men in pursuit, and the stripped and shattered wagons lay in ruins.

"Why would they do this?" the high captain asked.

"Might be that they're not liking yerself climbing over them in Deudermont's favor," said the dwarf. "Or might be that both o' them're still hating Deudermont o' *Sea Sprite* too much to agree with yer choices."

Suljack waved him to silence. Of course he knew all of that reasoning, but still it shocked him to think that his peers would strike out so boldly at a time of such desperation, even with relief reportedly well on its way.

He came out of his contemplation at the sound of renewed fighting across the street below him, and just down an alleyway. When one man came into view, looking back and down the alley, Phillus put up his bow and took deadly aim.

"Baram, or Taerl?" Suljack asked as Phillus let fly.

The arrow struck true. The man let out a howl and staggered back under cover, just as another man, one of Suljack's, came screaming out of the alley, blood streaming from a dozen wounds.

"That's M'Nack!" Phillus cried, referring to a favored young soldier of the Ship.

"Go! Go! Go!" Suljack yelled to his guards, and they all ran from the room, except for the dwarf and Phillus. "Kill any who come out in pursuit," Suljack instructed his deadly archer, who nodded and held his bow steady.

As the room all but cleared, Suljack went closer to the window, pulling it open and peering out intently. "Baram, Taerl, or both?" he asked quietly, his gaze roving the street, looking for some hint.

Across the way, the man Phillus had pegged stumbled out and away. A second arrow shot off, but missed the staggering thief, though it came close enough to make the man turn and look up at the source.

Suljack's jaw dropped open when he recognized the minor street thug. "Reth—?" he started to ask when he heard a thump to the side.

He turned to see Phillus lying on the floor, his head split open, a familiar spiked morningstar lying beside him.

He turned farther to see the dwarf, holding Phillus's bow, drawn and set.

"Wh—?" he started to ask as the dwarf let fly, the arrow driving into Suljack's gut and taking his breath. He staggered and fought to stand as the dwarf calmly reloaded and shot him again.

On the ground and crying, Suljack started to crawl away. He managed to gasp, "Why?"

"Ye forgot who ye were," the dwarf said, and put a third arrow into him, right in the shoulder blade.

Suljack continued to crawl, gasping and crying loudly,

A fourth arrow nicked his spine and stabbed into his kidney.

"Ye're just making it hurt more," the dwarf calmly explained, his voice distant, as if coming from far, far away.

Suljack hardly felt the next arrow, or the one after that, but he somehow knew that he wasn't moving anymore. He tried futilely to cry out, but found one last fleeting hope when he heard the dwarf cry out, "Murder!"

He managed to shift his head far enough to see the dwarf holding Phillus up in the air, and with three short running strides, he launched the already-dead guard crashing through the window to plummet to the hard street below. Phillus's broken bow, the dwarf having snapped it in half, followed in short order.

The last thing Suljack saw before darkness closed was the dwarf sliding down beside him. The last thing he heard was the dwarf crying out, "Murder! He shot the boss! Phillus the dog shot the boss! Oh, murder!"

CHAPTER

DEUDERMONT'S GAUNTLET

Three spears flew down the alley almost simultaneously, all thrown with great anger and strength. Desperate defenders angled bucklers to deflect or at least minimize the impact. But the spears never made it to the opposing lines, for a lithe figure sprang from an open window, tumbled to the street, and a pair of curved blades worked fast to chop at the missiles as they passed, driving them harmlessly aside.

The defenders cheered, thinking a new and mighty ally had come, and the spearmen cursed, seeing their impending doom in the fiery eyes and spinning blades of the deadly dark elf.

"What madness is this?" Drizzt demanded, turning repeatedly to encompass all the combatants with his accusation.

"Be asking *them!*" cried one of the spearmen. "Them who killed Suljack!"

"Be asking *them!*" the leader of the defenders retorted. "Them who came to wage war!"

"Murderers!" cried a spearman.

"By your lies!" came the response.

"The city is dying around you!" Drizzt cried. "Your disputes can be resolved, but not until . . ." He ended there since, with another cry of, "Murderers!" the spearmen flooded into the alleyway and charged. On the opposite side, the defenders responded with, "Lying thieves!" and similarly rushed.

Leaving Drizzt caught in the middle.

Suljack, or Taerl? The question swirled in Drizzt's thoughts as the choice became urgent. With which Ship would he side? Whose claim was stronger?

How could he assume the role of judge with so little information? All of those thoughts and troubling questions played through his mind in the few heart-beats he had before being crushed between the opposing forces, and the only answer he could fathom was that he could not choose.

He belted his scimitars and ran to the side of the alleyway, springing upon the wall and pulling himself up out of harm's way. He found a perch on a win-dowsill and turned to watch helplessly, shaking his head.

Fury drove the Suljack crew. Those behind the leading wall of flesh who couldn't punish their enemies in melee threw any missiles they could find: spears, daggers, even pieces of wood or stone they managed to tear from neigh-boring buildings.

Taerl's defenders seemed no less resolute, if more controlled, forming a proper shield wall to defend the initial collision, showing patience as the rage of the attackers played out.

Drizzt didn't have the detachment necessary to admire or criticize either side's tactics, and didn't have the heart to even begin to predict which side would win. He knew in his gut that the outcome was assured, that all of Luskan would surely lose.

Only his quick instincts and reflexes saved his life as one of Suljack's men, unable to get a clear shot at Taerl's defenders, instead lifted his crossbow at Drizzt and let fly. The drow dodged at the last instant, but still got slashed across the back of his shoulder before his mithral shirt turned the bolt. The effort nearly sent him tumbling from his perch.

His hand went to his scimitar, and his eyes discerned a path down the wall and to the alleyway near the archer.

But pity overruled his anger, and he responded instead by calling upon his hereditary power to create a globe of darkness around the fool with the crossbow. Drizzt understood that he had no place in that fight, that he could accomplish nothing positive with combatants who were beyond reason. The weight of that tugged at him as he scaled the building to the roof and made off from the alley, trying to leave the screams of rage and pain behind him.

They were before him as well, however, just two streets down, where two mobs had engaged in a vicious, confused battle along the avenue separating the Ships of Baram and Taerl. As he ran along the rooftops above them, the drow tried to make out the allegiance of the fighters, but whether it was Ship Baram against Ship Taerl, or Suljack against Baram, or a continuation of Suljack and Taerl's fight, or perhaps even another faction all together, he couldn't tell.

Off in the distance, halfway across the city, near the eastern wall, flames lit up the night.

* * * * *

"Triple the guard at the mainland bridge," High Captain Kurth instructed one of his sergeants. "And set patrols to walk the length and breadth of the shoreline."

"Aye!" replied the warrior, clearly understanding the urgency as the sounds of battle drifted to Closeguard Island, along with the smell of smoke. He ran from the room, taking a pair of soldiers with him.

"It's mostly Taerl and Suljack's crews, I'm told," another of the Kurth sergeants informed the high captain.

"Baram's in it thick," another added.

"It's mostly the kid o' Rethnor, from my guess," said another of the men, moving to stand beside Kurth as he looked out to the mainland, where several fires blazed brightly.

That prompted a disagreement among the warriors, for though rumors abounded about Kensidan's influence in the fighting, the idea that Taerl and Baram had gone against Suljack without prompting was not so far-fetched, particularly given the common knowledge that Suljack had thrown in with Deudermont.

Kurth ignored the bickering. He knew full well what was going on in Luskan, who was pulling the strings and inciting the riots. "Will there be anything left when that fool Crow is through?" he mumbled under his breath.

"Closeguard," answered the sergeant standing beside him, and after a moment's thought, Kurth nodded appreciatively at the man.

A stark cry, a shriek, from outside the room ended the bickering and interrupted Kurth's contemplation. He turned, his eyes and the eyes of every man and woman in the room widening with shock as an uninvited guest entered.

"You live!" one man cried, and Kurth snickered at the irony of that notion. Arklem Greeth had not "lived" in decades.

"Be at ease," the lich said to all around, holding up his hands in an unthreatening manner. "I come as a friend."

"The Hosttower was blasted apart!" the man beside Kurth shouted.

"'Twas beautiful, yes?" the lich responded, smiling with his yellow teeth. He tightened up almost immediately, though, and turned directly to High Captain Kurth. "I would speak with you."

A dozen swords leveled on Arklem Greeth.

"I understand and accept that you had no real choice but to open the bridges," said Arklem Greeth, but not a sword lowered at the assurance.

"How are you alive, and why are you here?" Kurth asked, and he had to work very hard to keep the tremor from his voice.

301

"As no enemy, surely," the lich replied. He looked around at the stubborn warriors and gave a profound, but breathless, sigh. "If I came to do ill, I would have engulfed the lowest floor of this tower in flames and would have assailed you with a magical barrage that would have killed half of your Ship before you ever realized the source," he said. "Please, my old friend. You know me better than to think I would need to get you alone to be rid of you."

Kurth spent a long while staring at the lich. "Leave us," he instructed his guards, who bristled and muttered complaints, but eventually did as they were told.

"Kensidan sent you?" Kurth asked when he was alone with the lich.

"Who?" Arklem Greeth replied, and he laughed. "No. I doubt the son of Rethnor knows I survived the catastrophe on Cutlass Island. Nor do I believe he would be glad to hear the news."

Kurth cocked his head just a bit, showing his intrigue and a bit of confusion.

"There are others watching the events in Luskan, of course," said Arklem Greeth.

"The Arcane Brotherhood," reasoned Kurth.

"Nay, not yet. Other than myself, of course, for once more, and sooner than I expected by many years, I find myself intrigued by this curious collection of rogues we call a city. No, my friend, I speak of the voices in the shadows. 'Twere they who guided me to you now."

Kurth's eyes flashed.

"It will end badly for Captain Deudermont, I fear," said Arklem Greeth.

"And well for Kensidan and Ship Rethnor."

"And for you," Arklem Greeth assured him.

"And for you?" Kurth asked.

"It will end well," said the lich. "It already has, though I seek one more thing."

"The throne of Luskan?" Kurth asked.

Arklem Greeth again broke out in that wheezing laugh. "My day in public here is done," he admitted. "I accepted that before Lord Brambleberry sailed into the Mirar. It's the way of things, of course. Expected, accepted, and well planned for, I assure you. I could have defeated Brambleberry, likely, but in doing so, I would have invoked the wrath of the Waterdhavian lords, and thus caused more trouble for the Arcane Brotherhood than the minor setback we received here."

"Minor setback?" Kurth indignantly replied. "You have lost Luskan!"

Greeth shrugged, and Kurth's jaw clenched in anger. "Luskan," said again, giving the name great weight.

"It is but one city, rather unremarkable," said Greeth.

"Not so," Kurth replied, calling him on his now-obvious bluff. "It is a hub of a great wheel, a center of weight for regions of riches, north, east and south, and with the waterways to move those riches."

"Be at ease, friend," said Greeth, patting his hands in the air. "I do not diminish the value of your beloved Luskan."

Kurth's expression aptly reflected his disagreement with that assessment.

"Only because I know our loss here to be a temporary thing," Greeth explained. "And because I expect that the city will remain in hands competent and reasonable," he added with a deferential and thoroughly disarming bow toward Kurth.

"And so you plan to leave?" Kurth asked, not quite sorting it all out. He could hardly believe, after all, that Arklem Greeth—the fearsome and ultimately deadly archmage arcane—would willingly surrender the city.

The lich shrugged, a collection of mucus and seawater in its lungs crackling with the movement. "Perhaps. But before I go away, I wish to repay a certain traitorous wizard. Two, actually."

"Arabeth Raurym," Kurth reasoned. "She plays both sides of the conflict, moving between Deudermont and Ship Rethnor."

"Until she is dead," said the lich. "Which I very much intend."

"And the other?"

"Robillard of *Sea Sprite*," the lich said in a tone as close to a sneer as the breathless creature could imitate. "Too long have I suffered the righteous indignation of that fool."

"Neither death would sadden me," Kurth agreed.

"I wish you to facilitate that," said Arklem Greeth, and Kurth lifted an eyebrow. "The city unravels. Deudermont's dream will falter, and very soon."

"Unless he can find food and—"

"Relief will not come," the lich insisted. "Not soon enough, at least."

"You seem to know much for one who has not shown himself in Luskan for many months. And you seem to be quite certain in your assurances."

"Voices in the shadows. . . ." Arklem Greeth replied with a sly smile. "Let me tell you of our observant and little-seen allies."

Kurth nodded and the lich spoke openly, only confirming that which Morik the Rogue, at Kensidan's bidding, had already explained. The high captain did well to hide his consternation at the further unwelcome evidence of yet another powerful player in the tug-of-war that was Luskan, particularly a player with a reputation so vile and unpredictable. Not for the first time did High Captain Kurth question Kensidan's judgment in helping to facilitate the Luskan disaster.

And not for the last time, either, he thought as Arklem Greeth told his dark tale of lacedon ghouls and murdered sailors.

* * * * *

"We act now or we lose Luskan," Governor Deudermont announced to Robillard, Drizzt, Regis, and some of his other commanders almost as soon as Drizzt delivered the news of the melee in the streets. "We must calm them until the caravans arrive."

"They will hear no reason," said Drizzt.

"Simpletons," Robillard muttered.

"They seek a focus for their frustrations," said Deudermont. "They are hungry and frightened, and grieving. Every family has suffered great losses."

"You overestimate the spontaneity of the moment," Robillard warned. "They are being goaded . . . and supplied."

"The high captains," Deudermont replied, and the wizard shrugged at the obvious answer.

"Indeed," the governor continued. "The four fools construct small empires within the city and posture now with swords."

Drizzt glanced at the luncheon platters still set on the table, and the scraps of meat—of deep rothé meat—and he wondered if there was even more posturing going on than the infighting of the high captains. He kept his fears silent, though, as he had when they'd first surfaced at dinner the previous night. He had no idea who had opened the trade channels necessary to get deep rothé and Underdark mushrooms, or with whom that enterprising high captain might be trading, but there was chaos in Luskan, and Drizzt's life experiences associated that state with one race in particular.

"We must act immediately," Deudermont announced. He turned to Robillard. "Go to the Mirabarrans and bid them to reinforce and keep safe the Red Dragon Inn."

"We're leaving?" Regis asked.

"To *Sea Sprite*, I pray," said Robillard.

"We need to cross the bridge," Deudermont answered. "Our place now is in Luskan proper. The Mirabarrans can control the north bank. Our duty is to step into the middle of the fighting and force the competing high captains back to their respective domains."

"One Ship is without her captain," Drizzt reminded him.

"And there we will go," Deudermont decided. "To Suljack's palace, which I will declare as the temporary Governor's Residence, and we will ally with his people in their time of need."

"Before the vultures can tear the carcass of Ship Suljack to bits?" Regis asked.

"Precisely."

"*Sea Sprite* would be a better choice," said the wizard.

"Enough, Robillard! You weary me."

"Luskan is already dead, Captain," the wizard added. "You haven't the courage to see it clearly."

"The Mirabarrans?" Deudermont asked in a sharper tone, and Robillard bowed and said no more, leaving the room immediately and the Red Dragon soon after to enlist the men and dwarves of the Shield District.

"We will announce our presence in no uncertain terms," Deudermont explained when the wizard was gone. "And will fight to protect any and all who need us. Through strength of resolve and sword we will hold Luskan together until the supplies arrive, and we will demand fealty to the city and not the Ship."

It was obvious that he was thinking on his feet. "Call in the magistrates and all of the city guard," he said, speaking as much to himself as to anyone else. "We will show them stakes. Now is the time for us to stand strong and resolute, the time to rally the city around us and force the high captains to acquiesce to the greater good." He paused and looked directly at Drizzt, showing the drow his strength before squarely laying down the gauntlet.

"Or they will lose their standing," he said. "We will dissolve the ship of any who will not swear fealty to the office of governor."

"To you, you mean," said Regis.

"No, to the office and to the city. They are bigger than any man who occupies the seat."

"A bold statement," said Drizzt. "Lose their standing?"

"They had their chance to show their value to Luskan throughout the long winter night," Deudermont steadfastly replied. "Other than Suljack, to a one, they failed."

The meeting adjourned on that grim note.

* * * * *

" 'E's on our side, what?" one of the soldiers formerly of Ship Suljack who had just signed on with Deudermont asked his companion when they exited the palace to join the fighting, only to spot Drizzt Do'Urden at work on a couple of Baram's ruffians.

"Aye, and that's why meself's noddin' yes to Deudermont," said the other.

The first nodded back as they watched the drow in action. One of Baram's boys took an awkward swing, apparently trying to cut the drow's legs out from under him, but Drizzt nimbly jumped, snapping a kick in the man's face as he came over.

The second thug came in hard with a straight thrust from the side, but the drow's scimitars beat him to the mark. One blade crossed to easily drive the thug's sword out wide, the other stabbed straight out, driving right against the man's throat. Drizzt then swept his free blade back across in time to loop it over the other ruffian's blade as it came up from its low position. A twist and flick of the drow's wrist had that one flying free and the suddenly unarmed ruffian, like his friend who stood immobilized with a sharp tip against his throat, was caught.

"The fight is done for you," Drizzt announced to the pair, and neither was in a position to disagree.

The two men rushed down the alley to join the drow, skidding to an abrupt stop as Drizzt turned a wary eye on them.

"We're with Deudermont!" they yelled together.

"Just signed up," one clarified.

"These two are fairly caught," Drizzt explained, and turned to his prisoners. "I will have your words of honor that you are out of the fight, or I will spill your lifeblood here and now."

Baram's boys looked at each other helplessly, then offered undying oaths as Drizzt prodded with his blades.

"Take them to the eastern wing of the first floor," Drizzt instructed the new Deudermont recruits. "No harm is to come to them."

"But they're with Baram!" one protested.

"Was them what killed Suljack!" said the other.

Drizzt silenced them with an even stare. "They're caught. Their fight is ended. And when this foolishness is done, they will again become a part of Luskan, a city that has seen far too much death."

"Oh yes, yes, Mister Regis, sir," a voice interrupted, and all five at Drizzt's encounter glanced to see Regis entering the far end of the alleyway. A pair of thugs—Taerl's boys—trailed him stupidly, their eyes locked on a particularly fascinating ruby that Regis spun at the end of a chain.

"No more fightin' for me," said the other hypnotized fool.

Regis walked right by Drizzt and the others, offering a profound sigh at the inanity of it all.

"We win by preserving the heart and soul of Luskan," Drizzt explained to the thoroughly confused new recruits. "Not by killing everyone who's not now with our cause." Drizzt nodded to the still-armed ruffian to drop his blade, and when he didn't immediately respond, the drow prodded him again in the throat.

His blade fell to the cobblestones. With his scimitars, Drizzt then guided the pair to the new recruits. "Take them to the eastern wing."

"Prisoners," one of the new recruits said, nodding.

"Aye," said the other, and they started off, the captured thugs before them and following the same line as Regis and his two captives.

Despite the enormity of the calamity around them—the streets around Deudermont's new palace were thick with fighting, as both Baram and Taerl, at least, had come against the governor fully—Drizzt couldn't help but chuckle, particularly at Regis and his effective tactics.

That grin was blown away a few moments later, however, when Drizzt ran to the far end of the alleyway, arriving just in time to see the less subtle Robillard engulf an entire building in a massive fireball. Screams emanated from inside the burning structure and one man leaped out of a second story window, his clothing fully aflame.

Despite his and Deudermont's hopes to keep the battle as bloodless as possible, Drizzt understood that before the fight was over, many more Luskar would lie dead.

The drow rubbed his weary eyes and blew a long and resigned sigh. Not for the first time and not for the last, he wished he could rewind time to when he and Regis had first arrived in the city, before Deudermont and Lord Brambleberry had begun their fateful journey.

CHAPTER

THE PROVERBIAL STRAW

Deudermont, Robillard, Drizzt, Regis, and the others gathered in the governor's war room shared a profound sense of dread from the look on Waillan Micanty's face as he entered the room.

"Waterdhavian flotilla came in," the man said.

"And . . . ?" Deudermont prompted.

"One boat," Micanty replied.

"One?" Robillard growled.

"Battered, and with her crew half dead," Micanty reported. "All that's left of the flotilla. Some turned back, most are floating empty or have been sent to the bottom."

He paused, but no one in the room had the strength to ask a question or offer a response, or even, it seemed, to draw breath.

"Was lacedons, they said," Micanty went on. "Sea ghouls. Scores of 'em. And something bigger and stronger, burning ships with fire that came up from the deep."

"Those ships were supposed to be *guarded!*" Robillard fumed.

"Aye, and so they were," Waillan Micanty replied, "but not from below. Hundreds of men dead and most all of the supplies lost to the waves."

Deudermont slipped into his chair, and it seemed to Drizzt that if he had not, he might have just fallen over.

"The folk of Luskan won't like this," Regis remarked.

"The supplies were our bartering card," Deudermont agreed.

"Perhaps we can use the sea ghouls as a new, common enemy," Regis offered. "Tell the high captains that we have to join together to win back the shipping lanes."

Robillard scoffed loudly.

"It's something!" the halfling protested.

"It's everything, perhaps," Deudermont agreed, to Regis's surprise most of all.

"We have to stop this warring," the governor went on, addressing Robillard most of all. "Declare a truce and sail side-by-side against these monstrosities. We can sail all the way to Waterdeep and fill our holds with—"

"You've lost your mind," Robillard interrupted. "You think the four high captains will join an expedition that will only secure *your* power?"

"For their own good as well," the governor argued. "To save Luskan."

"Luskan is already dead," said Robillard.

Drizzt wanted to argue with the wizard, but found no words to suffice.

"Send word to the high captains for parlay," Deudermont ordered. "They will see the wisdom in this."

"They will not!" Robillard insisted.

"We have to try!" Deudermont shouted back and the wizard scoffed again and turned away.

Regis sent a concerned look Drizzt's way, but the drow had little comfort to offer him. They both had spent the previous day battling in the streets around Suljack's palace, and both knew that Luskan teetered on the brink of disaster, if indeed she wasn't already there. The only mitigating factor seemed to be the wealth of supplies streaming up from Waterdeep, and if most of those were not to arrive. . . .

"We have to try," Deudermont said again, his tone and timbre more quiet, even, and controlled.

But there was no mistaking the desperation and fear embedded in that voice.

* * * * *

Baram and Taerl wouldn't come to him personally, but sent a single emissary to deliver their message. Kurth and Kensidan didn't even answer his request for a parlay.

Deudermont tried to put a good face on the rejection, but whenever he thought that Robillard or Drizzt weren't looking his way, he sighed.

"Twenty-seven?" Robillard asked in a mocking tone. "A whole day of fighting, a dozen men dead or near it on our side, and all we've got to show for our work are twenty-seven prisoners, and not a one of them pledging to our cause?"

"But all agreeing that they're out of the fight, so if we win . . ." Drizzt started to reply.

Robillard cut him off with a smirk and said, "If?"

Drizzt cleared his throat and glanced at Deudermont, then went on, "When we win, these men will join with us. Luskan need not be burned to the ground. Of that much, I'm sure."

"That isn't much, Drizzt," Robillard said, and the drow could only shrug, having little evidence to prove the wizard wrong. They had held Suljack's palace that first day, but the enemy seemed all around them, and several of the adjoining streets were fully under the control of Baram and Taerl. They had indeed lost at least twelve fighters, and who knew how many more had been killed out in the streets near the palace?

Deudermont couldn't win a war of attrition. He didn't have thousands behind him, unlike when he'd gone against Arklem Greeth. The supplies might have renewed that faith in him, but the main source had been destroyed at sea and nothing else had arrived.

Regis entered the war room then to announce the arrival of Baram and Taerl's ambassador. Deudermont sprang out of his seat and rushed past the other two, urging Regis along to the audience chamber.

The man, a scruffy-looking sea dog with a hairline that had receded to the back of his scalp, wild gray strands hanging all about him, waited for them, picking his nose as Deudermont entered the room.

"Don't waste me time," he said, flicking something off to the floor and staring at Deudermont the way a big dog might look upon a cornered rodent—hardly the usual look Captain Deudermont of *Sea Sprite* was used to seeing from such a bilge rat.

"Baram and Taerl should have come and saved you the trouble then," Deudermont replied, taking a seat before the man. "They had my word that no harm would befall them."

The man snickered. "Same word ye gived to Suljack, not a doubt."

"You believe I was involved in the death of Suljack?" Deudermont asked.

The man shrugged as if it hardly mattered. "Baram and Taerl ain't no fools, like Suljack," he said. "They'd be needing more than yer word to believe the likes of Captain Deudermont."

"They project their own sense of honor upon me, it would seem. I'm a man of my word," he paused and motioned for the man to properly introduce himself.

"Me own name ain't important, and I ain't for tellin' it to the likes o' yerself."

Behind Deudermont, Robillard laughed and offered, "I can discover it for you, Cap—Governor."

"Bah, no one'd tell ye!" the ambassador said with a growl.

"Oh, you would tell me, and do not doubt it," the wizard replied. "Perhaps I would even etch it on your gravestone, if we bothered to get you a gravesto—"

"So much for yer word, eh Captain?" the sea dog said with a broken-toothed grin, just as Deudermont held up his hand to silence the troublesome Robillard.

"Baram and Taerl sent you here to hear my offer," said Deudermont. "Tell them . . ."

The filthy ambassador started laughing and shaking his head. "Nothing they want to hear," he interrupted. "They sent me here with *their* offer. Their only offer." He stared at Deudermont intensely. "Captain, get on yer *Sea Sprite* and sail away. We're givin' ye that, and it's more than ye deserve, ye fool. But be knowing that we're givin' ye it on yer word that ye'll not e'er again sink any ship what's carrying the colors o' Luskan,"

Deudermont's eyes widened then narrowed dangerously.

"That's yer deal," the sea dog said.

"I'm going to burn this city to rubble," Robillard growled under his breath, but then he shook his head and added, "Take the offer, Captain. To the Nine Hells with Luskan."

Beside Robillard, Drizzt and Regis exchanged concerned glances, and both of them were thinking the same thing, that maybe it was time for Deudermont to admit that he could not succeed in the City of Sails, as he'd hoped. They had been out on the streets the previous day, after all, and had seen the scale of the opposition.

For a long while, the room lay silent. Deudermont put his chin in his hand and seemed deep in thought. He didn't look back to his three friends, nor did he pay any heed at all to the ambassador, who stood tapping his foot impatiently.

Finally, the governor of Luskan sat up straight. "Baram and Taerl err," he said.

"Only deal ye're gettin'," said the pirate.

"Go and tell your bosses that Luskan will not go to the Nine Hells, but that they surely shall," said Deudermont. "The people of Luskan have entrusted me to lead them to a better place, and to that place we will go."

"And where might all these people be?" the pirate asked with dripping sarcasm. "Might they be shooting arrows at ye're boys even as we're talkin'?"

"Be gone to your masters," said Deudermont. "And know that if I see your ugly face again, I will surely kill you."

The threat, delivered so calmly, seemed to unsettle the man, and he staggered backward a few steps, then turned and rushed from the room.

"Secure a route from here to the wharves," Deudermont instructed his friends. "If we're forced into retreat, it will be to *Sea Sprite*."

"We could just walk there, openly," said Robillard, and he pointed at the door through which the ambassador had just exited.

"If we leave, it will be a temporary departure," Deudermont promised. "And woe to any ship we see flying Luskan's colors. And woe to the high captains when we return, Waterdhavian lords at our side."

* * * * *

"The reports from the street are unequivocal," Kensidan announced. "This is it. There will be no pause. Deudermont wins or he loses this day."

"He loses," came the voice from the shadows. "There is no relief on the way from Waterdeep."

"I don't underestimate that one, or his powerful friends," said the Crow.

"Don't underestimate his powerful enemies," the voice replied. "Kurth succeeded in defeating the flotilla, though no ships from Luskan got near to it."

That turned Kensidan away from the window, to peer at the globe of darkness.

"Kurth has an ally," the voice explained. "One Deudermont believes destroyed. One who does not draw breath, save to find his voice for powerful magical dweomers."

The Crow considered the cryptic clues for a moment then his eyes widened and he seemed as near to panic as anyone had ever seen him. "Greeth," he mumbled.

"Arklem Greeth himself," said the voice. "Seeking revenge on Deudermont."

The Crow began to stalk the room, eyes darting all around.

"Arklem Greeth will not challenge you," the voice in the darkness promised. "His days of ruling Luskan are at an end. He accepted this before Deudermont moved on the Hosttower."

"But he aligns with Kurth. Whatever your assurances regarding the archmage arcane, you cannot make the same with regard to Kurth!"

"The lich will not go against us, whatever High Captain Kurth might ask of him," the unseen speaker said with confidence.

"You cannot know that!"

A soft chuckle came from the darkness, one that ended any further debate on the subject, and one that sent a shiver coursing Kensidan's spine, a reminder of who it was he was dealing with, of who he had trusted—trusted!—throughout his entire ordeal.

"Move decisively," the voice prompted. "You are correct in your assessment that this day determines Luskan's future. There is nothing but the angled wall of a corner behind you now."

CHAPTER

THE ONE I WOULD KILL

W e should be on the shore with the captain!" one woman cried.

"Aye, we can't be letting him fight that mob alone!" said another of *Sea Sprite*'s increasingly impatient and upset crew. "Half the city's come against him."

"We were told to guard *Sea Sprite*," Waillan Micanty shouted above them all. "Captain Deudermont put no 'unless' in our orders! He said stay with *Sea Sprite* and keep her safe, and that's what we're to do—all of us!"

"While he gets himself killed?"

"He's got Robillard with him, and Drizzt Do'Urden," Waillan argued back, and the mention of those two names did seem to have a calming effect on the crew. "He'll get to us if he needs to get to us—and what a sorry bunch of sailors we'd be to lose the ship and his one chance at escaping!"

"Now, to your stations, one and all," he ordered. "Turn your eyes to the sea and the many pirates moored just outside the harbor."

"They all fought *with* us," a crewman remarked.

"Aye, against Arklem Greeth," said Waillan. "And most of those coming against Captain Deudermont now marched with him to the Hosttower. The game's changed, so be on your guard."

There was a bit of grumbling, but *Sea Sprite*'s veteran crew scurried back to their respective watch and gunnery posts and most managed to tear their eyes from the signs of fighting in the city proper to focus again on any possible threats to their own position.

And not a moment too soon, for Waillan Micanty had barely finished speaking when the crewman in the crow's nest shouted down, "Starboard!" Then clarified, "The water line!" as Micanty and others rushed to the rail.

As chance would have it, the first lacedon scaling *Sea Sprite*'s hull pulled over the rail right in front of Micanty himself, who met it with a heavy slash of his saber.

"Ghouls!" he cried. "Ghouls aboard *Sea Sprite!*"

And so came Arklem Greeth's horrid minions, splashing out of the water all around the pirate hunter. Crewmen rushed to and fro, weapons drawn, determined to cut the beasts down before they could get a foothold, for if the lacedons managed to get onto the deck, they all knew that their own ranks would quickly thin. Waillan Micanty led the way, bludgeoning and cutting ghoul after ghoul, rushing from starboard to port just in time to drive back over the rail the first of the lacedons attacking that side of the vessel.

"Too many!" came a cry from aft, near the catapult, and Waillan turned to see ghouls standing up straight on the deck, and to see a pair of the catapult crew fall paralyzed to the deck. His gaze immediately went out to the deeper waters and the many ships anchored there. The catapult was down. *Sea Sprite* was vulnerable.

He charged the breach, calling for crewmen to join him, but when one rushed into his wake, Waillan, recognizing the terrible danger, stopped the woman. "Contact Robillard," he bade her. "Tell him of our situation."

"We can win," the woman, an apprentice of Robillard's, replied.

But Waillan was hearing none of it. "Now! Tell him!"

The mage nodded reluctantly, her gaze still locked on the fight on the aft deck. She did turn, though, and scrambled down the bulkhead.

Sitting invisibly in *Sea Sprite*'s hold, Arklem Greeth watched her move to the crystal ball with great anticipation and amusement.

* * * * *

"The same force that destroyed the Waterdhavian flotilla," Deudermont remarked when Robillard relayed the predicament of *Sea Sprite*. "Perhaps they followed the one surviving ship to us."

The wizard considered the reasoning for a moment then nodded, but he was thinking of much more sinister possibilities given the nature and coordination of the lacedon attack, and the fact that it was occurring right in Luskan Harbor, where such attacks were unprecedented.

"Go to them and clear *Sea Sprite,*" Deudermont bade his friend.

"We have our own problems here, Captain," Robillard reminded him, but it was clear from his tone that he didn't really disagree with Deudermont's command.

"Be quick then," said the captain. "Above all else, that ship must remain secure!"

Robillard glanced at the door leading to the stairs and the palace's front exit. "I will go, and hopefully return at once," the wizard announced. "But only on your promise that you will find Drizzt Do'Urden and stay tight to his side."

Deudermont couldn't suppress a grin. "I survived for many years without him, and without you," he said.

"True, and your old arms aren't nearly as swift with your sword anymore," the wizard replied without hesitation. He threw the captain a wink and collected his gear then began casting a spell to transport him to *Sea Sprite*'s deck.

* * * * *

High Captain Baram slapped aside the frantic scout and took a clearer look at the influx swarming through the square just three blocks from Suljack's palace and Deudermont.

Taerl rushed up beside him, similarly holding his breath, for they both knew at once the identity of the new and overpowering force that had come on the scene. Ship Rethnor was about to join the fight in full.

"For us, or for Deudermont?" Taerl asked. Even as he finished, one small group of Baram's boys inadvertently charged out in front of Rethnor's swarm. Baram's eyes widened, and Taerl let out a gasp.

But the dwarf leading the way for Rethnor engaged those men with words, not morningstars, and as the forces parted, Ship Rethnor's contingent angling off to the side, the two high captains found their hoped-for answer.

Ship Rethnor had come out in full against Deudermont.

* * * * *

"Oh oh," Regis said from his perch on a low roof overlooking an alley from which Drizzt had just chased a trio of Taerl's ruffians.

Drizzt started to ask the halfling for a clarification, but when he saw the look on Regis's face, he just ran to the spot, leaped and spun to catch the trim of the roof in a double backhanded grasp then curled and tucked his legs, rolling them right up over him to the roof. As soon as he set himself up there, he understood the halfling's sentiments.

Like a swarm of ants, Ship Rethnor's warriors streamed along several of the streets, chasing Deudermont's forces before them with ease.

"And out there," Regis remarked pointing to the northwest.

Drizzt's heart sank lower when he followed that motion, for the gates on

Closeguard Island were open once more, High Captain Kurth's forces streaming onto and across the bridge. Looking back to Kensidan's fighters, it wasn't hard to figure out which side Kurth favored.

"It's over," said Drizzt.

"Luskan's dead," Regis agreed. "And we've got to get Deudermont out of here."

Drizzt gave a shrill whistle and a moment later Guenhwyvar leaped from rooftop to rooftop to join him.

"Go to the docks, Guen," the drow bade the panther. "Find a route for me."

Guenhwyvar gave a short growl and leaped away.

"Let us hope that Robillard has a spell of transportation available and ready," Drizzt explained to Regis. "If not, Guen will lead us." He jumped down to the alleyway and helped slow Regis's descent as the halfling came down behind him. They turned back the way they had come, picking the fastest route to the palace, toward a service door for the kitchen.

They had barely gone a few steps, though, when they found the way blocked by a most strange-looking dwarf.

"I once met me Drizzit the drow," he chanted. "The two of us suren did have a good row. He did dart and did sting, how his blades they did sing, till me morningstars landed a blow!"

Drizzt and Regis stared at him open-mouthed.

"Bwahahahaha!" the dwarf bellowed.

"What a curious little beast," Regis remarked.

* * * * *

Robillard landed on the deck of *Sea Sprite* holding up a gem that spread forth a most profound and powerful light, as if he had brought a piece of the sun with him. All around him, lacedons cowered and shrieked, their greenish-gray skin curling and shriveling under the daunting power of that sunlike beacon.

"Kill them while they cower!" Waillan Micanty shouted out, seeing so many of the crew stunned by the sudden and dominating appearance of their heroic wizard.

"Drive them off!" another man shouted, and his gaff hook tore into a ghoul as it shielded its burning eyes from the awful power of the gemstone.

All over the deck, the veteran crew turned the tide of the battle, with many lacedons simply leaping overboard to get away from the awful brightness and many more falling to deadly blows of sword and club and gaff hook.

Robillard sought out Micanty and handed him the brilliant gem. "Clear the ship," he told the dependable sailor. "And prepare to get us out of the harbor and to open waters. I'm off for Deudermont."

He started casting a teleport spell to return him to the palace then, but nearly got knocked off his feet as *Sea Sprite* shuddered under the weight of a tremendous blast. Licks of flame poked up from the deck planks, and Robillard understood then the blast to be magical, and to have come from *Sea Sprite's* own hold!

Without a word to Micanty, the wizard rushed to the bulkhead and threw it wide. He leaped down the stairs and saw his apprentice at once, lying charred and quite dead beside the burning table upon which still sat the crystal ball. Robillard's gaze darted all about—and stopped cold when he saw Arklem Greeth, sitting comfortably on a stack of grain sacks.

"Oh, do tell me that you expected me," the lich said. "Certainly you were smart enough to realize that I hadn't destroyed myself in the tower."

Robillard, his mouth suddenly very dry, started to answer, but just shook his head.

* * * * *

With great reluctance, Captain Deudermont headed out of his audience chamber toward the kitchen and the service door, where he knew Drizzt to be. For the first time in a long time, the captain's thoughts were out to sea, to *Sea Sprite* and his many crewmen still aboard her. He couldn't begin to guess what had precipitated the attack of undead monsters, but surely it seemed too detrimental and coordinated with the fighting in the streets to have been a coincidence.

A shout from a corridor on his left stopped Deudermont and brought him back to the moment.

"Intruders in the palace!" came the cry.

Deudermont drew out his sword and started down that corridor, but only a couple of steps. He had promised Robillard, and not out of any thought for his own safety. It was not his place, it could not be his place, to engage in street fights unless there was some hope of winning out.

Somewhere in the vast array of rooms behind him, a window shattered, then another.

Enemies were entering Suljack's palace, and Deudermont had not the force to repel them.

He turned fast again, cursing under his breath and speeding for the kitchen.

The form came at him from the side, from a shadow, and the captain only noticed it out of the corner of his eye. He spun with catlike grace, swiping his sword across in a gradual arc that perfectly parried the thrusting spear. A sudden reversal sent the sword slashing back down across the chest of his attacker, opening a wide gash and sending the man crashing back into the shadows, gurgling with pain.

Deudermont rushed away. He needed to link up with Drizzt and Regis, and with them pave an escape route for those loyal to his cause.

He heard a commotion in the kitchen and kicked open the door, sword at the ready.

Too late, Deudermont knew, as he watched a cook slide to the floor off the end of a sword, clutching at the mortal wound in his chest. Deudermont followed that deadly line to the swordsman, and couldn't hide his surprise at the garish outfit of the flamboyant man. He wore a puffy and huge red-and-white striped shirt, tied by a green sash that seemed almost a wall between the bright colors of the shirt and the even brighter blue of the man's pants. His hat was huge and plumed, and Deudermont could only imagine the wild nest of hair crimped beneath it, for the man's beard nearly doubled the size of his head, all black and wild and sticking out in every direction.

"We're knowin' yer every move then, ain't we Captain Deudermont?" the pirate asked, licking his yellow teeth eagerly.

"Argus Retch," Deudermont replied. "So, the reports of your insult to good taste weren't exaggerated after all."

The pirate cackled with laughter. "Paid good gold for these," he said, and wiped his bloody sword across his pants—and though the blade did wipe clean, his obviously magical pants showed not a spot of the blood.

Deudermont resisted the urge to reply with a snide comment regarding the value of such an outfit and the possible fashion benefits of soiling the damned ugly thing, but he held his tongue. There would be no bargaining with the pirate, obviously, nor did the captain want to—particularly since a man loyal to Deudermont, an innocent man, lay dead at Retch's feet.

In reply, then, Deudermont presented his sword.

"Ye got no crew to command here, Captain," Argus Retch answered in response, lifting his own blade and drawing out a long dirk in his other hand. "Oh, but ye're the best at maneuverin' ships, ain't ye? Let's see how you turn a blade!" With that, he leaped forward, stabbing with his sword, and when that got deflected aside, he turned with the momentum and slashed his dirk across wildly.

Deudermont leaned back out of range of that swipe and quickly brought his sword before him, managing a thrust of his own that didn't get near to hitting the pirate, but managed to steal Retch's offensive initiative and force him back on his heels. The pirate went down low then, legs wide, blades presented forward, but wide apart, as well.

He began to circle in measured steps.

Deudermont turned with him, watching for some tell, some sign that the man would explode into an aggressive attack once more, and also take in the room, the battlefield. He noted the island counter, all full of cooking pots and bowls, and the narrow cabinets lined side-to-side along the side wall.

Retch's jaw clenched and Deudermont noted it clearly, and so he was hardly surprised as the pirate leaped forward, sword stabbing.

Deudermont easily slipped beside the cooking island, and Retch's succeeding dagger swipe missed by several feet.

"Stand still and fight me, ye dog!" Retch bellowed in protest, giving chase around the island.

Deudermont grinned at him, egging him on. The captain continued his retreat down the backside of the island, then around to the front, putting himself between the island and the row of cabinets.

Retch pursued, growling and slashing.

Deudermont stopped and let him close, but only so that he could grab the nearest cabinet with his free left hand and topple it forward, to fall right in front of the pirate. Retch leaped it, only to bang against the second cabinet as it similarly toppled, then the fourth, Deudermont having safely retreated past the third without pulling it down.

"I knew ye was a coward!" Retch cried, ending in a sputter as Deudermont used the moment while the pirate dodged the falling cabinet to swing his sword low and hard across the top of the island, smashing bowls and sending liquid and powdery flour flying at Argus Retch. The pirate waved his hands, futilely trying to block, and wound up with his face powdered in white, with several wet streaks along one cheek. His beard, too, lost its black hue in the flour storm.

Sputtering and spitting, he came forward, and turned his shoulder to rush sidelong past as Deudermont reached out for yet another cabinet to topple.

But Deudermont didn't pull down the cabinet. Instead he used Retch's defensive turn and the line of his free hand to step forward. He executed a quick double parry, sword and dirk, then stepped inside Retch's sword reach and slugged the pirate hard in the face.

Retch's nose cracked and blood poured forth to cake with the flour on his lip.

Deudermont started back, or seemed to, but in truth, he was merely rotating his shoulders, having reached back and turned his own sword expertly.

Retch came forward in outraged pursuit, thinking to stab the captain with his dagger, and shouting, "Curse ye, cheatin' dog!"

At least, that's what he meant to say, but he found his dagger going right by the captain and his words choked short as Deudermont's fine sword drove up under his jaw, through his mouth and into his brain, and right through that with such force as to lift the hat right from Argus Retch's head.

Deudermont did get stuck by the dagger for his daring move, but there was no strength behind the strike, for the pirate was already dead.

Still, Retch kept that surprised and outraged, wide-eyed expression for a long few heartbeats before falling forward, past the dodging captain, to land face-down on the floor.

"I wish I had the time to extend our battle, Argus Retch," Deudermont said to the corpse, "but I've business to attend to more important than satisfying the sense of fair play from the likes of you."

* * * * *

"Good that ye're slowin'! Ye'd be smarter to be rowin', cause this way ye ain't goin', ye know?" the dwarf bellowed, apparently amusing himself beyond all reason as he ended with a howling, "Bwahahahaha!"

"Oh, do kill him," Regis said to Drizzt.

"The fight is over, good dwarf," Drizzt said.

"I ain't thinking that," replied the dwarf.

"I'm going to get my captain, to usher him away," Drizzt explained. "Luskan is not for Deudermont, so it has been decided by the Luskar themselves. Thus, we go. There is no reason to continue this madness."

"Nah," the dwarf spouted, unconvinced. "I been wantin' to test me morningstars against the likes o' Drizzt Do'Urden since I heared yer name, elf. And I been hearin' yer name too many times." He drew his morningstars from over his shoulders.

Drizzt scimitars appeared in his hands as if they had been there all along.

"Bwahahahaha!" the dwarf roared in laughing applause. "As quick as they're saying, are ye?"

"Quicker," Drizzt promised. "And again I offer you this chance to be gone. I've no fight with you."

"Now there's a wager I'm willin' to take," said the dwarf, and he came forward, laughing maniacally.

CHAPTER

There could be no mistaking the Crow's forward leaning posture as he approached Arabeth Raurym, who had been summoned to his audience chamber at Ten Oaks.

Where lie your loyalties?" he asked.

Arabeth tried to keep her own posture firm and aggressive, but failed miserably as the small but strangely intimidating young man strode toward her. "Are you threatening me, an Overwizard of the Hosttower of the Arcane?"

"The what?"

"The achievement still merits respect!" said Arabeth, but her voice faltered just a bit when she noted that the Crow had drawn a long, wicked dagger. "Back, I warn you . . ."

She retreated a few quick steps and began waving her arms and chanting. Kensidan kept the measure of his approach and seemed in no hurry to interrupt her spellcasting. Arabeth blasted him full force with a lightning bolt, one that should have lifted him out of his high boots, however tight the lacing, and sent him flying across the room to slam into the back wall, a blast that should have burned a hole into him and sent his black hair to dancing, a blast that should have sent his heart to trembling before stopping all together.

Nothing happened.

The lightning burst out from Arabeth's fingers, then just . . . stopped.

* * * * *

Arabeth's face crinkled in a most unflattering expression and she gave a little cry and stumbled to her right, toward the door.

At that moment, Kensidan, tingling with power, knew he'd been right to trust the voices in the darkness all along. He rushed forward just enough to tap Arabeth on the shoulder as she rushed past, and in that touch, he released all of the energy of her lightning bolt, energy that had been caught and held.

The woman flew through the air, but not so far, for she had enacted many wards before entering the room and much of the magic was absorbed. Of more concern, a globe of blackness appeared at the door, blocking her way. She gave a little yelp and staggered off to the side again, the Crow laughing behind her.

Three figures stepped out from the globe of darkness.

Kensidan watched Arabeth all the while, grinning as her eyes opened, as she tried to scream, and stumbled again, falling to the floor on her behind.

The second of the dark elves thrust his hands out toward her, and the woman's screams became an indecipherable babble as a wave of mental energy rushed through her, jumbling her thoughts and sensibilities. She continued her downward spiral to lay on the floor, babbling and curling up like a frightened child.

"What is your plan?" said the leader of the drow, the one with the gigantic plumed hat and the foppish garb. "Or do you intend to have others fight all of your battles this day?"

Kensidan nodded, an admission that it did indeed seem that way. "I must make my mark for the greater purpose we intend," he agreed.

"Well said," the drow replied.

"Deudermont is mine," the high captain promised.

"A formidable foe," said the drow. "And one we might be better off allowing to run away."

Kensidan didn't miss that the psionicist gave his master a curious, almost incredulous look at that. A free Deudermont wouldn't give up the fight, and would surely return with many powerful allies.

"We shall see," was all the Crow could promise. He looked to Arabeth. "Don't kill her. She will be loyal . . . and pleasurable enough."

The drow with the big hat tipped it at that, and Kensidan nodded his gratitude. Then he flipped his cloak up high to the sides and as it descended, Kensidan seemed to melt beneath its dropping black wings. Then he was a bird, a large crow. He flew to the sill of his open window and leaped off for Suljack's palace, a place he knew quite well.

"He will be a good ally," Kimmuriel said to Jarlaxle, who had resumed the helm of Bregan D'aerthe. "As long as we never trust him."

A wistful and nostalgic sigh escaped Jarlaxle's lips as he replied, "Just like home."

* * * * *

Any thoughts Regis had of rushing in to help his friend disappeared when Drizzt and this curious dwarf joined in battle, a start so furious and brutal that the halfling figured it to be over before he could even draw his—in light of the titanic struggle suddenly exploding before him—pitiful little mace.

Morningstar and scimitar crossed in a dizzying series of vicious swings, more a matter of the combatants trying to get a feel for each other than either trying to land a killing blow. What stunned Regis the most was the way the dwarf kept up with Drizzt. He had seen the dark elf in battle many times, but the idea that the short, stout, thick-limbed creature swinging unwieldy morningstars could pace him swing for swing had the halfling gaping in astonishment.

But there it was. The dwarf's weapon hummed across and Drizzt angled his blade, swinging opposite, just enough to force a miss. He didn't want to connect a thin scimitar to one of those spiked balls.

The morningstar head flew past and the dwarf didn't pull it up short, but let it swing far out to his left to connect on the wall of the alleyway, and when it did, the ensuing explosion revealed that there was more than a little magic in that weapon. A huge chunk of the building blasted away, leaving a gaping hole.

Pulling his own swing short, his feet sped by his magical anklets, Drizzt saw the opening and charged ahead, only wincing slightly at the crashing blast when the morningstar hit the wooden wall.

But the slight wince was too much; the momentary distraction too long. Regis saw it and gasped. The dwarf was already into his duck and turn as the spiked ball took out the wall, coming fast around, his left arm at full extension, his second morningstar head whistling out as wide as it could go.

If his opponent hadn't been a dwarf, but a taller human, Drizzt likely would have had his left leg caved in underneath him, but as the morningstar head came around a bit lower, the drow stole his own forward progress in the blink of a surprised eye and threw himself into a leap and back flip.

The morningstar hit nothing but air, the drow landing lightly on his feet some three strides back from the dwarf.

Again, against a lesser opponent, there would have been a clear opening then. The great twirling swing had brought the dwarf to an overbalanced and nearly defenseless state. But so strong was he that he growled himself right out of it. He ran a couple of steps straight away from Drizzt, diving into a forward roll and turning as he did so that when he came up, over, and around, he was again directly squared to the drow.

More impressively, even as he came up straight, his arms already worked the morningstars, creating a smooth rhythm once again. The balls spun at the ends of their respective chains, ready to block or strike.

"How do you hurt him?" Regis asked incredulously, not meaning for Drizzt to hear.

The drow did hear, though, as was evidenced by his responding shrug as he and the dwarf engaged yet again. They began to circle, Drizzt sliding to put his back along the wall the morningstar had just demolished, the dwarf staying opposite.

It was the look on Drizzt's face as he turned the back side of that circle that alerted Regis to trouble, for the drow suddenly broke concentration on his primary target, his eyes going wide as he looked Regis's way.

Purely on instinct, Regis snapped out his mace and spun, swinging wildly.

He hit the thrusting sword right before it would have entered his back. Regis gave a yelp of surprise, and still got cut across his left arm as he turned. He fell back against the wall, his desperate gaze going to Drizzt, and he found himself trying to yell out, "No!" as if all the world had suddenly turned upside down.

For Drizzt had started to sprint Regis's way, and so quick was he that against almost any enemy, he would have been able to cleanly disengage.

But that dwarf wasn't any enemy, and Regis could only stare in horror as the dwarf's primary hand weapon, the one that had blown so gaping a hole in the building, came on a backhand at the passing drow.

Drizzt sensed it, or anticipated it, and he dived into a forward roll.

He couldn't avoid the morningstar, and his roll went all the faster for the added momentum.

Amazingly, the blow didn't prove lethal, though, and the drow came right around in a full run at Regis's attacker—who, spying his certain doom, tried to run away.

He didn't even begin his turn, backstepping still, when Drizzt caught him, scimitars working in a blur. The man's sword went flying in moments, and he fell back and to the ground, his chest stabbed three separate times.

He stared at the drow and at Regis for just a moment before falling flat.

Drizzt spun as if expecting pursuit, but the dwarf was still far back in the alleyway, casually spinning his morningstars.

"Get to Deudermont," Drizzt whispered to Regis, and he tucked one scimitar under his other arm and put his open hand out and low. As soon as Regis stepped into it, Drizzt hoisted him up to grab onto the low roof of the shed and pull himself over as Drizzt hoisted him to his full outstretched height.

The drow turned the moment Regis was out of sight, scimitars in hand, but still the dwarf had not approached.

"Could've killed ye to death, darkskin," the dwarf said. "Could've put me magic on the ball that clipped ye, and oh, but ye'd still be rollin'! Clear out o' the streets and into the bay, ye'd still be rollin'! Bwahahahaha!"

Regis looked to Drizzt, and was shocked to see that his friend was not disagreeing.

"Or I could've just chased ye down the hall," the dwarf went on. "Quick as ye were rid o' that fool wouldn't've been quick enough to set yerself against the catastrophe coming yer way from behind!"

Again, the drow didn't disagree. "But you didn't," Drizzt said, walking slowly back toward his adversary. "You didn't enact the morningstar's magic and you didn't pursue me. Twice you had the win, by your own boast, and twice you didn't take it."

"Bah, wasn't fair!" bellowed the dwarf. "What's the fun in that?"

"Then you have honor," said Drizzt.

"Got nothin' else, elf."

"Then why waste it?" Drizzt cried. "You are a fine warrior, to be sure. Join with me and with Deudermont. Put your skills—

"What?" the dwarf interrupted. "To the cause of good? There ain't no cause of good, ye fool elf. Not in the fightin'. There's only them wantin' more power, and the killers like yerself and meself helpin' one side or the other side—they're both the same side, ye see—climb to the top o' the hill."

"No," said Drizzt. "There is more."

"Bwahahahaha!" roared the dwarf. "Still a young one, I'm guessin'!"

"I can offer you amnesty, here and now," said Drizzt. "All past crimes will be forgiven, or at least . . . not asked about."

"Bwahahahaha!" the dwarf roared again. "If ye only knowed the half of it, elf, ye wouldn't be so quick to put Athrogate by yer side!" And with that, he charged, yelling, "Have at it!"

Drizzt paused only long enough to look up at Regis and snap, "Go!"

Regis had barely clambered two crawling steps up the steep roof when he heard the pair below come crashing together.

* * * * *

"Scream louder," the Crow ordered, and he twisted his dagger deeper into the belly of the woman, who readily complied.

A moment later, Kensidan, giggling at his own cleverness, tossed the pained woman aside, as the door to the room crashed open and Captain Deudermont, diverted by the screams from his rush to the kitchen service door of Suljack's palace, charged in.

"Noble to a fault," said Kensidan. "And with the road of retreat clear before you. I suppose I should salute you, but alas, I simply don't feel like it."

Deudermont's gaze went from the injured woman to the son of Rethnor, who reclined casually against a window sill.

"Have you taken in the view, Captain?" Kensidan asked. "The fall of the City of Sails . . . It's a marvelous thing, don't you think?"

"Why would you do this?" Deudermont asked, coming forward in cautious and measured steps.

"I?" Kensidan replied. "It was not Ship Rethnor that went against the Hosttower."

"That fight is ended, and won."

"This fight is that fight, you fool," said Kensidan. "When you decapitated Luskan, you set into motion this very struggle for power."

"We could have joined forces and ruled from a position of justice."

"Justice for the poor—ah, yes, that is the beauty of your rhetoric," Kensidan replied in a mocking tone, and he hopped up from the window sill and drew his sword to compliment the long dagger. "And has it not occurred to the captain of a pirate hunter that not all the poor of Luskan are so deserving of justice? Or that there are afoot in the city many who wouldn't prosper as well under such an idyllic design?"

"That is why I needed the high captains, fool," Deudermont countered, spitting every word.

"Can you be so innocent, Deudermont, as to believe that men like us would willingly surrender power?"

"Can you be so cynical, Kensidan, son of Rethnor, as to be blind to the possibilities of the common good?"

"I live among pirates, so I fought them with piracy," Kensidan replied.

"You had a choice. You could have changed things."

"And you had a choice. You could have minded your own business. You could have left Luskan alone, and now, more recently, you could have simply gone home. You accuse me of pride and greed for not following you, but in truth, it's your own pride that blinded you to the realities of this place you would remake in your likeness, and your own greed that has kept you here. A tragedy, indeed, for here you will die, and Luskan will steer onto a course even farther from your hopes and dreams."

On the floor, the woman groaned.

"Let me take her out of here," Deudermont said.

"Of course," Kensidan replied. "All you have to do is kill me, and she's yours."

Without any further hesitation, Captain Deudermont launched himself forward at the son of Rethnor, his fine sword cutting a trail before him.

328

Kensidan tried to execute a parry with his dagger, thinking to bring his sword to bear for a quick kill, but Deudermont was far too fast and practiced. Kensidan wound up only barely tapping the thrusting sword with his dagger before flailing wildly with his own sword to hardly move Deudermont's aside.

The captain retracted quickly and thrust again, pulled up short before another series of wild parry attempts, then thrust forth again.

"Oh, but you are good!" said Kensidan.

Deudermont didn't let up through the compliment, but launched another thrust then retracted and brought his sword up high for a following downward strike.

Kensidan barely got his sword up horizontally above him to block, and as he did, he turned, for his back was nearing a wall. The weight of the blow had him scrambling to keep his feet.

Deudermont methodically pursued, unimpressed by the son of Rethnor's swordsmanship. In the back of his mind, he wondered why the young fool would dare to come against him so. Was his hubris so great that he fancied himself a swordsman? Or was he faking incompetence to move Deudermont off his guard?

With that warning ringing in his thoughts, Deudermont moved at his foe with a flurry, but measured every strike so he could quickly revert to a fully defensive posture.

But no counterattack came, not even when it seemed as if he had obviously overplayed his attacks.

The captain didn't show his smile, but the conclusion seemed inescapable: Kensidan was no match for him.

The woman groaned again, bringing rage to Deudermont, and he assured himself that his victory would strike an important blow for the retribution he would surely bring with him on his return to the City of Sails.

So he went for the kill, skipping in fast, smashing Kensidan's sword out wide and rolling his blade so as to avoid the awkward parry of the dagger.

Kensidan leaped straight up in the air, but Deudermont knew he would have him fast on his descent.

Except that Kensidan didn't come down.

Deudermont's confusion only multiplied as he heard the thrum of large wings above him and as one of those large black-feathered appendages batted him about the head, sending him staggering aside. He turned and waved his sword to fend him off, but Kensidan the Crow wasn't following.

He set down with a hop on three-toed feet, a gigantic, man-sized crow. His bird eyes regarded Deudermont from several angles, head twitching left and right to take in the scene.

"A nickname well-earned," Deudermont managed to say, trying hard to parse his words correctly and coherently, trying hard not to let on how off balance the man's sudden transformation into the outrageous creature had left him.

The Crow skipped his way and Deudermont presented his sword defensively. Wings going wide, the Crow leaped up, clawed feet coming forward, black wings assaulting Deudermont from either side. He slashed at one, trying to fall back, and did manage to dislodge a few black feathers.

But the Crow came on with squawking fury, throwing forward his torso and feet as he beat his wings back. Deudermont tried to bring his sword in to properly fend the creature off. Six toes, widespread, all ending with lethal talons clawed at him.

He managed to nick one of the feet, but the Crow dropped it fast out of harm's way, while the other foot slipped past the captain's defenses and caught hold of his shoulder.

The wings beat furiously, the Crow changing his angle as he raked that foot down, tearing the captain from left shoulder to right hip.

Deudermont brought his sword slashing across, but the creature was too fast and too nimble, and the taloned foot slipped out of his reach. The bird came forward and pecked the captain hard in the right shoulder, sending him flying to the ground, stealing all sensation and strength from his sword arm.

A wing beat and a leap had the Crow straddling the fallen man. Deudermont tried to roll upright, but the next peck hit him on the head, slamming him back to the floor.

Blood poured down from his brow across his left eye and cheek, but more than that, opaque liquid blurred the captain's sight as, thoroughly dazed, he faded in and out of consciousness.

* * * * *

Regis kept his head down, focusing solely on the task before him. Crawling on hands and knees, picking each handhold cautiously but expediently, the halfling made his way up the steep roof.

"Have to get to Deudermont," he told himself, pulling himself along, increasing his pace as he gained confidence with the climb. He finally hit his stride and was just about to look up when he bumped into something hard. High, black boots filled his vision.

Regis froze and slowly lifted his gaze, up past the fine fabric of well-tailored trousers, up past a fabulously crafted belt buckle, a fine gray vest and white shirt, to a face he never expected.

"You!" he cried in dismay and horror, desperately throwing his arms up before his face as a small crossbow leveled his way.

The exaggerated movement cost the halfling his balance, but even the unexpected tumble didn't save him from being stuck in the neck by the quarrel. Down the roof Regis tumbled, darkness rushing up all around him, stealing the strength from his limbs, stealing the light from his eyes, stealing even his voice as he tried to cry out.

* * * * *

The dwarf's swings didn't come any slower as he rejoined battle against Drizzt. And Drizzt quickly realized that the dwarf wasn't even breathing hard. Using his anklets to speed his steps, Drizzt pushed the issue, scampering to the left, then right back around the dwarf, and out and back suddenly as the furious little creature spun to keep up.

The drow worked a blur of measured strikes, and exaggerated steps, forcing the stubby-limbed dwarf to rush every which way.

The flurry went on and on, scimitars rolling one over the other, morningstars spinning to keep pace, and even, once in a while, to offer a devious counterstroke. And still Drizzt pressed, rushing left and back to center, right and all the way around, forcing the dwarf to continually reverse momentum on his heavier weapons.

But Athrogate did so with ease, and showed no labored breath, and whenever a thrust or parry connected, weapon to weapon, Drizzt was reminded of the dwarf's preternatural strength.

Indeed, Athrogate possessed it all: speed, stamina, strength, and technique. He was as complete a fighter as Drizzt had ever battled, and with weapons to equal Drizzt's own. The first morningstar kept coating over with some explosive liquid, and the second head leaked a brownish fluid. The first time that connected in a parry against Icingdeath, Drizzt was sure he felt the scimitar's fear. He brought the blade back for a quick inspection as he broke away, angling for a new attack, and noted dots of brown on is shining metal. It was rust, he realized, and realized, too, that only the mighty magic of Icingdeath had saved the blade from rotting away in his hand!

And Athrogate just kept howling, "Bwahahahaha!" and charging on with abandon.

Seeming abandon, because never, ever, did the dwarf abandon his defensive technique.

He was good. Very good.

But so was Drizzt Do'Urden.

The dark elf slowed his attacks and let Athrogate gain momentum, until it was the dwarf, not the drow, pressing the advantage.

"Bwahahahaha!" Athrogate roared, and sent both his morningstars into aggressive spins, low and high, working one down, the other up in a dizzying barrage that nearly caught up to the dodging, parrying drow.

Drizzt measured every movement, his eyes moving three steps ahead. He thrust into the left, forcing a parry, then went with that block to send his scimitar out wide but in an arcing movement that brought it back in again, sweeping down at his shorter opponent's shoulder.

Athrogate was up to the task of parrying, as Drizzt knew he would be, bringing his left-hand morningstar flying up across his right shoulder to defeat the attack.

But it wasn't really an attack, and Icingdeath snuck in for a stab at Athrogate's side. The dwarf yelped and leaped back, clearing three long strides. He laughed again, but winced, and brought his hand down against his rib. When he brought that hand back up, both Drizzt and he understood that the drow had drawn first blood.

"Well done!" he said, or started to, for Drizzt leaped at him, scimitars working wildly.

Drizzt rolled them over each other in a punishing alternating downward and straightforward slash, keeping them timed perfectly so that one morningstar could not defeat them both, and keeping them angled perfectly so that Athrogate had to keep his own weapons at a more awkward and draining angle, up high in front of his face.

The dwarf's grimace told Drizzt that his stab in the ribs had been more effective than Athrogate pretended, and holding his arms up in such a manner was not comfortable at all.

The drow kept up the roll and pressed the advantage, driving Athrogate ever backward, both combatants knowing that one slip by Drizzt would do no more than put them back at an even posture, but one slip by Athrogate would likely end the fight in short order.

The dwarf wasn't laughing anymore.

Drizzt pressed him even harder, growling with every rolling swing, backing Athrogate back down the alley the way Drizzt had come, away from the palace.

Drizzt caught the movement out of the corner of his eye, a small form rolling limply off the roof. Without a whimper, without a cry of alarm, Regis, tumbled to the ground and lay still.

Athrogate seized the distraction for his advantage, and cut back and to his right, then smashed his morningstar across to bat the drow's chopping scimitar out far to the side with such force—and an added magical explosion—that Drizzt had to disengage fully and scamper to the opposite wall to simply hold onto the blade.

Drizzt got a look at Regis, lying awkwardly twisted in the alleyway's gutter. Not a sound, not a squirm, not a whimper of pain. . . .

He was somewhere past pain; it seemed to Drizzt as if his spirit had already left his battered body.

And Drizzt couldn't go to him. Drizzt, who had chosen to return to Luskan, to stand with Deudermont, couldn't do anything but look at his dear friend.

* * * * *

At sea, it's said that danger can be measured by the scurry of the rats, and if that model held true, then the battle between Robillard and Arklem Greeth in the hold of *Sea Sprite* ranked right up alongside beaching the boat on the back of a dragon turtle.

All manner of evocations flew out between the dueling wizards, fire and ice, magical energy of different colors and inventive shapes. Robillard tried to keep his spells more narrow in scope, aiming *just* for Arklem Greeth, but the lich was as full of hatred for *Sea Sprite* herself as he was for his old peer in the Hosttower. Robillard threw missiles of solid magic and acidic darts. Greeth responded with forked lightning bolts and fireballs, filling the hold with flame.

Robillard's work on the hull with magical protections and wards, and all manner of alchemical mixtures, had been as complete and as brilliant as the work of any wizard or team of wizards had ever put on any ship, but he knew with every mighty explosion that Arklem Greeth tested those wards to their fullest and beyond.

With every fireball, a few more residual flames burned for just a few heartbeats longer. Every successive lightning bolt thumped the planking out a bit wider, and a little more water managed to seep in.

Soon enough, the wizards stood among a maelstrom of destruction, water up to their ankles, *Sea Sprite* rocking hard with every blast.

Robillard knew he had to get Arklem Greeth out of his ship. Whatever the cost, whatever else might happen, he had to move the spell duel to another place. He launched into a mighty spell, and as he cast it, he threw himself at Greeth, thinking that both he and his adversary would be projected into the Astral Plane to finish the insanity.

Nothing happened, for the archmage arcane had already applied a dimensional lock to the hold.

Robillard staggered as he realized that he was not flying on another plane of existence, as he had anticipated. He threw his arms up defensively as he righted himself, for Arklem Greeth brought in a gigantic disembodied fist that punched at him with the force of a titan.

The blow didn't break through the stoneskin dweomer of mighty Robillard, but it did send him flying back to the other end of the hold. He hit the wall hard, but felt not a thing, landing lightly on his feet and launching immediately into another lightning bolt.

Arklem Greeth, too, was already into a new casting, and his spell went off right before Robillard's, creating a summoned wall of stone halfway between the combatants.

Robillard's lightning bolt hit that stone with such tremendous force that huge chunks flew, but the bolt also rebounded into the wizard's face, throwing him again into the wall behind him.

And he had exhausted his wards. He felt that impact, and felt, too, the sizzle of his own lightning bolt. His heart palpitated, his hair stood on end. He kept his awareness just enough to realize that *Sea Sprite* was listing badly as a result of the tremendous weight of Arklem Greeth's summoned wall. From up above he heard screaming, and he knew that more than one of *Sea Sprite*'s crew had fallen overboard as a result.

Across the way, beyond the wall, Arklem Greeth cackled with delight, and in looking at the wall, Robillard understood that the worst was yet to come. For Greeth had offset it on the floor and had lined it along with the length and not the breadth of the ship, but he had not anchored it!

So as *Sea Sprite* listed under the great weight, so too leaned the wall, and it was beginning to tip.

Robillard realized that he couldn't stop it, so he found a moment of intense concentration instead and focused on his most-hated enemy. The wall fell, clearing the ground between the wizards, and Robillard let fly another devastating lightning blast.

So intent was he on his stone wall tumbling into *Sea Sprite*'s side planking, crashing through the wood, that Arklem Greeth never saw the bolt coming. He flew backward under the power of the stroke and hit the wall even as the side of the hull broke open and Luskan Harbor rushed in.

Robillard beat the rush of water, launching himself upon Arklem Greeth. Energy crackled through his hands, one electrical discharge after another.

Arklem Greeth fought back physically, tearing at Robillard with undead hands.

They held their death grip on each other as the sea turned *Sea Sprite* farther on her side, taking her down into the harbor. Spell after spell leaped from Robillard's fingers into the lich, blasting away at his magical defenses, and when those were finally beaten, as was his very life-force, still Arklem Greeth merely held on.

The lich didn't need to breathe, but Robillard surely did.

The pitch of the sinking ship sent them out through the hole in the hull, tumbling amidst the debris, rocks, and weeds of Luskan Harbor.

Robillard felt his ears pop under the pressure and knew his lungs wouldn't be far behind. But he held on, determined to end the struggle at whatever cost. The sight of *Sea Sprite,* the wreckage of his beloved *Sea Sprite,* spurred him on and he resisted the urge to break free of Arklem Greeth and focused instead on continuing his electrical barrage on the lich—even though every powerful discharge stung him as well in the conducting water.

It seemed like a dozen, dozen spells. It seemed like his lungs would surely burst. It seemed like Arklem Greeth was mocking him.

But the lich simply let go, and the face the surprised Robillard looked into was dead, not undead.

Robillard shoved away and kicked off the bottom, determined not to die in the arms of the hideous Arklem Greeth. Instinctively he clawed for the surface, and saw the water growing lighter above him.

But he knew he wouldn't make it.

* * * * *

"Sea Sprite!" more than one sailor of *Thrice Lucky,* and of every other ship moored in the area, cried out in astonishment. To those men and women, friend and enemy of Deudermont's ship alike, the sight before them seemed impossible.

The waves took *Sea Sprite* and smashed her up on a line of rocks, just one rail of her glorious hull and her three distinctive masts protruding from the dark waters of Luskan Harbor.

It could not be. In the minds of those who knew the ship as friend or foe, the loss of *Sea Sprite* proved no less traumatic than the disintegration of the Hosttower of the Arcane, a sudden and unimaginable change in the landscape that had shaped their lives.

"Sea Sprite!" they cried as one, pointing and jumping.

Morik the Rogue and Bellany rushed to *Thrice Lucky*'s rail to take in the awful scene.

"What are we to do?" Morik asked incredulously. "Where is Maimun?" He knew the answer, and so did many others echoing that very sentiment, for their captain had gone ashore less than an hour earlier.

Some crewmen called for lifelines, to weigh anchor to rush to the aid of the crew in the water. Bellany did likewise and started for a lifeboat, but Morik grabbed her by the shoulder and spun her to face him.

"Make me fly!" he bade her, and she looked at him curiously.

"Give me flight!" he screamed. "You've done it before!"

"Flight?"

"Do it!"

Bellany rubbed her hands together and tried to focus, tried to remember the words as the insanity around her only multiplied. She reached out and touched Morik on the shoulder and the man leaped up to the rail and out from the ship.

He didn't fall into the water, though, but flew out across the bay. He scanned, trying to figure out where he was most needed, then cut across for the downed vessel herself, fearing that some of the crew might be trapped aboard her.

Then he crossed over a form in the water, just under the surface but sinking fast, and willed himself to stop. He slapped his hand down, plunging it through the waves, and grabbed hard on the fine fabric of a wizard's robes.

* * * * *

"Ah, the glorious pain," Kensidan taunted. Deudermont again tried to pull himself up and the Crow pecked him hard on the forehead, slamming him back to the floor.

The room's door banged open. "No!" cried a voice familiar to both men. "Let him go!"

"Are you mad, young pirate?" the Crow cackled as he turned to regard Maimun. He spun back and slammed Deudermont hard again, smashing him flat to the floor.

Maimun responded with a sudden and brutal charge, flashing sword leading the way. Kensidan beat his wings and tried to extricate himself from the close quarters, but Maimun's fury was too great and his advantage too sudden and complete. The wings battered around the perimeter of the fight, but Maimun's sword cut a narrower and more direct line.

In the span of a few heartbeats, Maimun had Kensidan pinned at the end of his blade, and when Kensidan tried to turn the sword with his beak, Maimun got the blade inside the Crow's mouth.

Given that awkward and devastating clutch, Kensidan could offer no further resistance.

Maimun, breathing hard, clearly outraged, held the pose and the pin for a long breath. "I give you your life," he said finally, easing the blade just a bit. "You have the city—there will be no challenge. I will go, and I'm taking Captain Deudermont with me."

Kensidan looked over at the battered and bloody form of Deudermont and started to cackle, but Maimun stopped that with a prod of his well-placed blade.

"You will allow us clear passage to our ships, and for our ships out of Luskan Harbor."

"He is already dead, fool, or soon enough to be!" the Crow argued, slurring every word, as he spouted them around the hard steel of a fine blade.

The words nearly buckled Maimun's knees. His thoughts swirled back in time to his first meeting with the captain. He had stowed away on *Sea Sprite*, fleeing a demon intent on his destruction. Deudermont had allowed him to stay. *Sea Sprite*'s crew, generous to a fault, had not abandoned him when they'd learned the truth of his ordeal, even when they discerned that having Maimun aboard made them targets of the powerful demon and its many deadly allies.

Captain Deudermont had saved young Maimun, without a doubt, and had taken him under his wing and trained him in the ways of the sea.

And Maimun had betrayed him. Though he had never expected it to come to so tragic an end, the young pirate captain could not deny the truth. Paid by Kensidan, Maimun had sailed Arabeth to *Quelch's Folly*. Maimun had played a role in the catastrophe that had befallen Luskan, and in the catastrophe that had lain Captain Deudermont low before him.

Maimun turned back sharply on Kensidan and pressed the sword in tighter. "I will have your word, Crow, that I will be allowed free passage, with Deudermont and *Sea Sprite* beside me."

Kensidan stared at him hatefully with those black crow eyes. "Do you understand who I am now, young pirate?" he replied slowly, and as evenly as the prodding blade allowed. "Luskan is mine. I am the Pirate King."

"And you're to be the dead Pirate King if I don't get your word!" Maimun assured him.

But even as Maimun spoke, Kensidan all but disappeared beneath him, almost instantly reverting to the form of a small crow. He rushed out from under the overbalanced Maimun and with a flap of his wings, fluttered up to light on the windowsill across the room.

Maimun wrung his hands on his sword hilt, grimacing in frustration as he turned to regard the Crow, expecting that his world had just ended.

"You have my word," Kensidan said, surprising him.

"I have nothing with which to barter," Maimun stated.

The Crow shrugged, a curious movement from the bird, but one that conveyed the precise sentiment clearly enough. "I owe Maimun of *Thrice Lucky* that much, at least," said Kensidan. "So we will forget this incident, eh?"

Maimun could only stare at the bird.

"And I look forward to seeing your sails in my harbor again," Kensidan finished, and he flew away out the window.

Maimun stood there stunned for a few moments then rushed to Deudermont, falling to his knees beside the broken man.

* * * * *

His first attacks after seeing Regis fall were measured, his first defenses almost half-hearted. Drizzt could hardly find his focus, with his friend lying there in the gutter, could hardly muster the energy necessary to stand his ground against the dwarf warrior.

Perhaps sensing that very thing, or perhaps thinking it all a ploy, Athrogate didn't press in those first few moments of rejoined battle, measuring his own strikes to gain strategic advantage rather than going for the sudden kill.

His mistake.

For Drizzt internalized the shock and the pain, and as he always had before, took it and turned the tumult into a narrowly-focused burst of outrage. His scimitars picked up their pace, the strength of his strikes increasing proportionately. He began to work Athrogate as he had before the fall of Regis, moving side to side and forcing the dwarf to keep up.

But the dwarf did match his pace, fighting Drizzt to a solid draw strike after thrust after slash.

And what a glorious draw it was to any who might have chanced to look on. The combatants spun with abandon, scimitars and morningstars humming through the air. Athrogate hit a wall again, the spiked ball smashing the wood to splinters. He hit the cobblestones before the backward-leaping drow and crushed them to dust.

And there Drizzt scored his second hit, Twinkle nicking Athrogate's cheek and taking away one of his great beard's braids.

"Ah, but ye'll pay for that, elf!" the dwarf roared, and on he came.

To the side, Regis groaned.

He was alive.

He needed help.

Drizzt turned away from Athrogate and fled across the alleyway, the dwarf in close pursuit. The drow leaped to the wall, throwing his shoulders back and planting one foot solidly as if he meant to run right up the side of the structure.

Or, to Athrogate's discerning and seasoned battle sensibilities, to flip a backward somersault right over him.

The dwarf pulled up short and whirled, shouting "Bwaha! I'm knowin' that move!"

But Drizzt didn't fly over him and come down in front of him, and the drow, who had not used his planted foot to push off, and who had not brought his second foot up to further climb, replied, "I know you know."

From behind the turned dwarf, down the alley, Guenhwyvar roared, like an exclamation point to Drizzt's victory.

For indeed the win was his; he could only pray that Regis was not beyond his help. Icingdeath slashed down at Athrogate's defenseless head, surely a blow that would split the dwarf's head apart. He took little satisfaction in that win as his blade connected against Athrogate's skull, as he felt the transfer of deadly energy.

But the dwarf didn't seem to even feel it, no blood erupted, and Drizzt's blade didn't bounce aside.

Drizzt had felt that curious sensation before, as if he had landed a blow without consequence.

Still, he didn't sort it out quickly enough, didn't understand the source.

Athrogate spun, morningstars flying desperately. One barely clipped Drizzt's blade, but in that slightest of touches, a great surge of energy exploded out of the dwarf and hurled Drizzt back against the wall with such force that his blades flew from his hands.

Athrogate closed, weapons flying with fury.

Drizzt had no defense. Out of the corner of one eye, he noted the rise of a spiked metal ball, glistening with explosive liquid.

It rushed at his head, the last thing he saw.

EPILOGUE

Don't you die! Don't you die on me!" Maimun cried, cradling Deudermont's head. "Damn you! You can't die on me!"

Deudermont opened his eyes—or one, at least, for the other was crusted closed by dried blood.

"I failed," he said.

Maimun hugged him close, shaking his head, choking up.

"I have been . . . a fool," Deudermont gasped, no strength left in him.

"No!" Maimun insisted. "No. You tried. For the good of the people, you tried."

And something strange came over young Maimun in that moment, a revelation, an epiphany. He was speaking on Deudermont's behalf at that moment, trying to bring some comfort in a devastating moment of ultimate defeat, but as he spoke the words, they resonated within Maimun himself.

For Deudermont had indeed tried, had struck out for the good of those who had for years, in some cases for all their lives, suffered under the horror of Arklem Greeth and the five corrupt high captains. He had tried to be rid of the awful Prisoner's Carnival, to be rid of the pirates and the lawlessness that had left so many corpses in its bloody wake.

Maimun's own accusations against Deudermont, his claims that Deudermont's authoritarian nature was no better for the people he claimed to serve than were the methods of the enemies he tried to defeat, rang hollow to the young pirate in that moment of great pain. He felt unsure of himself, as if the axioms upon which he had built his adult life were neither as resolute nor as

morally pure, and as if Deudermont's imposition of order might not be so abso-
lutely bad, as he had believed.

"You tried, Captain," he said. "That is all any of us can ever do."

He ended with a wail, for he realized that the captain had not heard him, that
Captain Deudermont, who had been as a father to him in years past, was dead.

Sobbing, Maimun gently stroked the captain's bloody face. Again he thought
of their first meeting, of those early, good years together aboard *Sea Sprite.*

With a growl of defiance, Maimun cradled Deudermont, shoulders and
knees, and gently lifted the man into his arms as he stood straight.

He walked out of Suljack's palace, onto Luskan's streets, where the fighting
had strangely quieted as news of the captain's demise began to spread.

Head up, eyes straight ahead, Maimun walked to the dock, and he waited
patiently, holding Deudermont all the while, as a small boat from *Thrice Lucky*
was rowed furiously to retrieve him.

* * * * *

"Oh, but what a shot ye took on yer crown, and if yer head's hurting as
much as me own, then suren yer head's hurtin' more'n ever ye've known!
Bwahahaha!"

The dwarf's rhyming words drew Drizzt out of the darkness, however much
he wanted to avoid them. He opened his groggy eyes, to find himself sitting in
a comfortably-adorned room—a room in the Red Dragon Inn, he realized, a
room in which he and Deudermont had shared several meals and exchanged
many words.

And there was the dwarf, Athrogate, his adversary, sitting calmly across from
him, weapons tucked into their sheaths across his back.

Drizzt couldn't sort it out, but then he remembered Regis. He bolted upright,
eyes scanning the room, hands going to his belt.

His blades were not there. He didn't know what to think.

And his confusion only heightened when Jarlaxle Baenre and Kimmuriel
Oblodra walked into the room.

It made sense, of course, given Drizzt's failed—psionically blocked—strike
against Athrogate, and he placed then the moment when he had felt that strange
sensation of his energy being absorbed before, in a fight with Artemis Entreri, a
fight overseen by this very pair of drow.

Drizzt fell back, a bitter expression clouding his face. "I should have guessed
your handiwork," he grumbled.

"Luskan's fall?" Jarlaxle asked. "But you give me too much credit—or blame,
my friend. What you see around you was not my doing."

Drizzt eyed the mercenary with clear skepticism.

"Oh, but you wound me with your doubts!" Jarlaxle added, heaving a great sigh. He calmed quickly and moved to Drizzt, taking a chair with him. He flipped it around and sat on it backward, propping his elbows on the high back and staring Drizzt in the eye.

"We didn't do this," Jarlaxle insisted.

"My fight with the dwarf?"

"We did intervene in that, of course," the drow mercenary admitted. "I couldn't have you destroying so valuable an asset as that one."

"And yes, you surely could have," Kimmuriel muttered, speaking in the language of the drow.

"All of it, I mean," Jarlaxle went on without missing a beat. "This was not our doing, but rather the work of ambitious men."

"The high captains," Drizzt reasoned, though he still didn't believe it.

"And Deudermont," Jarlaxle added. "Had he not surrendered to his own foolish ambition. . . ."

"Where is he?" Drizzt demanded, sitting up tall once more.

Jarlaxle's expression grew grim and Drizzt held his breath.

"Alas, he has fallen," Jarlaxle explained. "And *Sea Sprite* lays wrecked on rocks in the harbor, though most of her crew have escaped the city aboard another ship."

Drizzt tried not to sink back, but the weight of Deudermont's death fell heavily on his shoulders. He had known the man for so many years, had considered him a dear friend, a good man, a great leader.

"This was not my work," Jarlaxle insisted, forcing Drizzt to look him in the eye. "Nor the work of any of my band. On my word."

"You lurked around its edges," Drizzt accused, and Jarlaxle offered a conciliatory shrug.

"We meant to . . . indeed, we *mean* to, make the most of the chaos," Jarlaxle said. "I'll not deny my attempt to profit, as I would have tried had Deudermont triumphed."

"He would have rejected you," Drizzt spat, and again, Jarlaxle shrugged.

"Likely," he conceded. "Then perhaps it's best for me that he didn't win. I didn't create the end, but I will certainly exploit it."

Drizzt glared at him.

"But I'm not without some redeeming qualities," Jarlaxle reminded. "You are alive, after all."

"I would have won the fight outright, had you not intervened," Drizzt reminded him.

"That fight, perhaps, but what of the hundred following?"

Drizzt just continued to glare, unrelenting—until the door opened and Regis, battered, but very much alive, and seeming quite well considering his ordeal, stepped into the room.

* * * * *

Robillard stood at the rail of *Thrice Lucky,* staring back at the distant skyline of Luskan.

"Was Morik the Rogue who plucked you from the waves," Maimun said to him, walking over to join him.

"Tell him I won't kill him, then," Robillard replied. "Today."

Maimun chuckled, though there remained profound sadness behind his laugh, at the unrelenting sarcasm of the dour wizard. "Do you think *Sea Sprite* might be salvaged?" he asked

"Do I care?"

Maimun found himself at a loss to reply to the blunt answer, though he suspected it to be more an expression of anger and grief than anything else.

"Well, if you manage it, I can only hope that you and your crew will be too busy exacting revenge upon Luskan to chase the likes of me across the waves," the young pirate remarked.

Robillard looked at him, finally, and managed a smirk. "Neither fight seems worth a pile of rotting fish," he said, and he and Maimun looked at each other deeply then, sharing the moment of painful reality.

"I miss him, too," Maimun said.

"I know you do, boy," said Robillard.

Maimun put a hand on Robillard's shoulder, then walked away, leaving the wizard to his grief. Robillard had guaranteed him safe passage for *Thrice Lucky* through Waterdeep, and he trusted the wizard's words.

What the young pirate didn't trust at that moment were his own instincts. Deudermont's fall had hit him profoundly, had made him think, for the first time in many years, that the world might be more complicated than his idealistic sensibilities had allowed.

* * * * *

"We could not have asked for a better outcome," Kensidan insisted to the gathering at Ten Oaks. Baram and Taerl exchanged doubtful looks, but Kurth nodded his agreement with the Crow's assessment.

The streets of Luskan were quiet again, for the first time since Deudermont and Lord Brambleberry had put into the docks. The high captains had retreated to their respective corners; only Suljack's former domain remained in disarray.

"The city is ours" Kensidan said.

"Aye, and half of it's dead, and many others have run off," Baram replied.

"Unwanted and unnecessary fodder," said Kensidan. "We who remain, control. None who don't trade for us or fight for us or otherwise work for us belong here. This is no city for families and mundane issues. Nay, my comrades, Luskan is a free port now. A true free port. The only true free port in all the world."

"Can we survive without the institutions of a real city?" Kurth asked. "What foes might come against us, I wonder?"

"Waterdeep? Mirabar?" Taerl asked.

Kensidan grinned. "They will not. I have already spoken to the dwarves and men of Mirabar who live in the Shield District. I explained to them the benefits of our new arrangement, where exotic goods shall pass through Luskan's gates, in and out, without restriction, without question. They expressed confidence that Marchion Elastul would go along, as has his daughter, Arabeth. The other kingdoms of the Silver Marches will not pass over Mirabar to get to us." He looked slyly to Kurth as he added, "They will accept the profits with feigned outrage, if any at all."

Kurth offered an agreeing grin in return.

"And Waterdeep will muster no energy to attack us," Kensidan assured them. "To what end would they? What would be their gain?"

"Revenge for Brambleberry and Deudermont," said Baram.

"The rich lords, who will get richer by trading with us, will not wage war over that," Kensidan replied. "It is over. Arklem Greeth and the Arcane Brotherhood have lost. Lord Brambleberry and Captain Deudermont have lost. Some would say that Luskan herself has lost, and by the old definition of the City of Sails, I could not disagree.

"But the new Luskan is ours, my friends, my comrades," he went on, his ultimately calm demeanor, his absolute composure, lending power to his claims. "Outsiders will call us lawless because we care not for the minor matters of governance. Those who know us well will call us clever because we four will profit beyond anything we ever imagined possible."

Kurth stood up, then, staring at Kensidan hard. But only for a moment, before his face cracked into a wide smile, and he lifted his glass of rum in toast, "To the City of Sails," he said.

The other three joined in the toast.

* * * * *

Beneath the City of Sails, Valindra Shadowmantle sat unblinking, but hardly unthinking. She had felt it, the demise of Arklem Greeth, stabbing at her as profoundly as any dagger ever could. The two were linked, inexorably, in undeath, she as the unbreathing child of the master lich, and so his fall had stung her.

She at last turned her head to the side, the first movement she'd made in many days. There on a shelf, from within the depths of a hollowed skull, it sparkled—and with more than simple reflection of the enchanted light set in the corners of the decorated chamber.

Nay, that light came from inside the gem, the phylactery. That sparkle was the spark of life, of undeath existence, of Arklem Greeth.

With great effort, her skin and bones crackling at the first real movement in so many days, Valindra stood and walked stiff-legged over to the skull. She rolled it onto its side and reached in to retrieve the phylactery. Lifting it to her eyes, Valindra stared intently, as if trying to discern the tiny form of the lich.

But it appeared as just a gem with an inner sparkle, a magical light.

Valindra knew better. She knew that she held the spirit, the life energy, of Arklem Greeth in her hand.

To be resurrected into undeath, a lich once more, or to be destroyed, utterly and irrevocably?

Valindra Shadowmantle smiled and for just a brief moment, forgot her calamity and considered the possibilities.

He had promised her immortality, and more importantly, he had promised her power.

Perhaps that was all she had left.

She stared at the phylactery, the gemstone prison of her helpless master, feeling and basking in her power.

* * * * *

"It's all there," Jarlaxle insisted to Drizzt on the outskirts of Luskan as evening fell.

Drizzt eyed him for just a moment before slinging the pack over his shoulder.

"If I meant to keep anything, it would have been the cat, certainly," Jarlaxle said, looking over, and leading Drizzt's gaze to Guenhwyvar, who sat contentedly licking her paws. "Perhaps someday you'll realize that I'm not your enemy."

Regis, his face all bruised and bandaged from his fall, snorted at that.

"Well, I didn't mean for you to roll off the roof!" Jarlaxle answered. "But of course, I had to put you to sleep, for your own sake."

"You didn't give me everything back," Regis snarled at him.

Jarlaxle conceded the point with a shrug and a sigh. "Almost everything," he replied. "Enough for you to forgive me my one indulgence—and rest assured that I have replaced it with gems more valuable than anything it would have garnered on the open market."

Regis had no answer.

"Go home," Jarlaxle bade them both. "Go home to King Bruenor and your beloved friends. There is nothing left for you to do here."

"Luskan is dead," Drizzt said.

"To your sensibilities, surely so," Jarlaxle agreed. "Beyond resurrection."

Drizzt stared at the City of Sails for a few moments longer, digesting all that had transpired. Then he turned, draped an arm over his halfling friend, and led Regis away, not looking back.

"We can still save Longsaddle, perhaps," Regis offered, and Drizzt laughed and gave him an appreciative shake.

Jarlaxle watched them go until they were out of sight. Then he reached into his belt pouch to retrieve the one item he had taken from Regis: a small scrimshaw statue the halfling had sculpted into the likeness of Drizzt and Guenhwyvar.

Jarlaxle smiled warmly and tipped his great cap to the east, to Drizzt Do'Urden.